THE DIPLOMAT'S DAUGHTER

THE DIPLOMAT'S DAUGHTER

KARIN TANABE

THORNDIKE PRESS
A part of Gale, a Cengage Company

GALE
A Cengage Company

Farmington Hills, Mich • San Francisco • New York • Waterville, Maine
Meriden, Conn • Mason, Ohio • Chicago

Thorndike Press® Large Print Basic.
The text of this Large Print edition is unabridged.
Other aspects of the book may vary from the original edition.
Set in 16 pt. Plantin.

LIBRARY OF CONGRESS CATALOGING-IN-PUBLICATION DATA

Names: Tanabe, Karin, author.
Title: The diplomat's daughter / by Karin Tanabe.
Description: Large print edition. | Waterville, Maine : Thorndike Press, a part of Gale, a Cengage Company, 2017. | Series: Thorndike Press large print basic
Identifiers: LCCN 2017027108 | ISBN 9781432841126 (hardcover) | ISBN 1432841122 (hardcover)
Subjects: LCSH: World War, 1939-1945—Fiction. | Man-woman relationships—Fiction. | Large type books. | BISAC: FICTION / Historical. | FICTION / Romance / Historical. | FICTION / Literary. | GSAFD: Romantic suspense fiction. | Love stories.
Classification: LCC PS3620.A6837 D57 2017b | DDC 813/.6—dc23
LC record available at https://lccn.loc.gov/2017027108

Published in 2017 by arrangement with Atria Books, an imprint of Simon & Schuster, Inc.

Printed in the United States of America
1 2 3 4 5 6 7 21 20 19 18 17

For those seeking refuge today.
May you find open doors and
open arms.

PART ONE

Prologue

Emi Kato
October 1943

Emi Kato had always liked boats. She'd been sailing on them since she could hold her head up, and had grown to feel like they were the most authentic place for her to be — floating on water between countries.

At twenty-one, she'd embraced her status as a wanderer, though her parents encouraged her to call it journeying. They often reminded Emi that the family was perpetually heading abroad not for curiosity's sake, but for her father's important career. Norio Kato was a Japanese diplomat, and Emi, his beloved only child. Her circumstance, always wedged right between her elegant parents, meant she'd been packed up like a suitcase since she was small, transported to countries so different from hers that they felt inverted. Over time, she learned that they'd slowly rotate, eventually becoming an extension of her home.

But in the fall of 1943, Emi's world had rotated the wrong way. After four years in America, she found herself standing on a boat quite unlike the luxury ocean liners of her childhood. Crowded in like a matchstick, she was being forced to sail back to Japan and into the uncertainty of war.

For two hours, Emi had been moving restlessly around the massive Swedish ocean liner, bracing herself in the cold as she tried to get as close to the bow as possible. Finally, unable to remain polite any longer, she jostled a young couple that had stood as firm as figureheads for the last thirty minutes, and thrust her thin frame past them and into the railing, ignoring their protests. She hoped that if she stared straight ahead, she might experience even a fleeting sense of freedom, a feeling she'd been desperate for since 1941, when she was corralled away from her home in Washington, D.C.

Emi looked out at the line where the ocean met the sky and was mesmerized by the perfect, threadlike offing. In a few moments, just past dusk, as the massive white boat floated through the warm waters of the Southern Hemisphere, the water and the evening sky would blur the line and blend into a pigmented squid-ink blue. She watched the world in front of her, the horizon line now impossible to discern, and thought that even when men were trying their best to become monsters, nature refused to give in. What was beyond her couldn't be easily altered by human stupidity.

Emi turned around on the illuminated boat deck and looked down at her dirty black loafers, the toes almost worn through. Before she left America, her father had written and said that all the women in Japan, even the ones of a certain ilk, were wearing monpe, the baggy cotton pants donned by farmers, and not to bother with anything but her shabbiest clothes. Practicality and warmth was all she need be concerned about in Japan. Since the boat was so dirty, Emi had started dressing for war already, though she would have to wait until she was home to buy what he'd recommended. She frowned at the thought of herself in the shapeless baggy trousers. What a long way it was from her old life of tailored dresses and starched school uniforms.

"Where are we?" her mother asked quietly. She'd come up behind her daughter and placed her hands on Emi's slight shoulders, interrupting her worries. Where Emi was tall and confident, her mother, Keiko, was delicate and quiet, with a ghostly pale face and nearly black eyes. An expert at floating through life effortlessly, she always seemed to materialize out of nowhere. "We've been on this boat for so long it's starting to feel like they're taking us the wrong way around the world."

Emi turned around and watched her mother rub her temples with her thin, papery hands. They looked dry and tight — surely from all the time they'd spent in the sun — as if they might creak like a door hinge when she folded them. Her fragile fingers reminded Emi of the part of the world they just left. She hoped to never see it again. "We are enclosed in barbed wire," Keiko had written to her best friend when they'd arrived in the American Southwest. Emi had leaned over her shoulder and told her not to bother complaining. That the censors would black out all the important words anyway, especially the grievances.

"I think we're near Africa," said Emi, turning back around and leaning closer against the railing. They weren't supposed to get so close to the edges of the ship, her mother reminded her. The crew was afraid a wave might bump the thin Japanese women right off the boat. Or that they'd pitch themselves overboard in a fit of anxiety.

"Africa?" said Keiko, trying to move her daughter back a few inches. She grabbed the sleeve of her gabardine coat, which had been in the bottom of a suitcase since the spring of 1942. "You know better than to say something so ill-informed. Where in Africa?"

"South Africa," said Emi, squinting in the darkness and taking a tiny step back to appease her mother. "Port Elizabeth. On the coast between Cape Town and Durban. I don't know a thing about the town past its geography so we shall see what it brings."

"I doubt that," said her mother, reaching up and resting her hand on her daughter's head. "Despite your charm, they're not going to let you sightsee on this stop."

Emi moved her forehead back so that Keiko's hand slipped off. She was in the mood to shut out the world as best she could, even her mother's comforting touch. "I'm sorry, Mama," she said. "I'm desperate to be alone."

"Come back down soon," said Keiko, giving her daughter some space. "If you haven't noticed, it's about to storm." She pointed to the choppy water and said, "You're only feet from plunging into the ocean and I'm not dressed for mourning, so please don't sink to the bottom. Not tonight." Emi nodded and went to move her long black hair out of her face, the strands, hard with salt water, clinging to her skin like octopus tentacles.

"Be careful," said Keiko, pulling Emi back a few more inches before leaving her to herself.

Despite years of her mother pecking over her appearance, Emi cared very little about how she looked, a privilege granted to the beautiful. She let Keiko and her amah choose her clothes until she turned sixteen and, surprisingly, had never adopted the vanity they thought she would. But recently, she'd grown aware of how weeks on a crowded ship could make a person unsightly. She saw plainly how gaunt her body had become, how her cheekbones looked jagged and hollow, her breasts flat, her stomach concave. And she knew that she smelled like the boat, too, giving off the sharp scent of salt water and sweat with every step she took.

At the sound of thunder close by, Emi and the other passengers on deck craned their necks, imagining the storm clouds starting to collect overhead like a swarm of hungry birds. Emi looked at the other tired Japanese passengers around her, as pale and gaunt as she, and was glad that the whistling wind and increasingly choppy water drowned out their sounds. She didn't want to focus on where she was at present, but where boats had taken her before — to London, Vienna, Berlin — the cities she had multiplied in.

It wasn't just her cells that had expanded over the years; it was her spirit. In Europe, she'd shed the skin of a girl with finite possibilities and become one who spoke three languages, who was as happy out of her country as in, who could discover the world and fall in love with it, without the boundaries of her nation, or gender, getting in the way. She had managed to remain that girl until the war broke out and suddenly her future became uncertain, riddled with fear and anxiety.

"Wien," she said out loud in German as the water started to splash onto the deck. She'd been speaking English for the last four years and the word sounded strange on her tongue.

Vienna. It was the place she missed the most.

The wind was starting to get too strong for her to stay on deck. A moment more, Emi thought, and laid her head down on her prime spot of railing, her left cheek cold against her intertwined hands. She was well aware that Vienna might not exist in a few

15

years. And if it did, it certainly wouldn't be her Vienna.

"But I lived there once," she whispered, remembering the sweeping view of several ornate Gothic buildings from her family's apartment windows. The St. Stephan's Cathedral spires, the tarnished brass dome, the tower with its swinging bell cast from cannons — these were as familiar to her as her childhood home.

And Leo. The best part of Vienna was of course Leo Hartmann.

For two years, he was the fuel that fizzed inside her, racing through her electric blue veins like the most perfect disease. He had defined her adolescence in Vienna and helped keep the realities of what was happening in the city away. But even a love as new and rope-strong as Emi and Leo's couldn't push war away forever. In 1938, hate took over the gray city like a fire bathed in oxygen.

It was the year that the world started melting at the edges, tolerance receding through the cracks, unable to be saved.

Emi thought it couldn't get worse than 1938, but two years later, her own Japan aligned themselves with the Third Reich, and with that decision came the culpability of Emi Kato.

It had nothing to do with her, Keiko had said countless times, helping her daughter into bed the night the news broke that Japan signed the Tripartite Pact with Germany and fascist Italy. They had done all they could to help the Hartmanns, and Leo's fate was anything but her fault.

"But we are contributing to it!" she had yelled. "Father is! He works for the government. Our family — we are all complicit now!" Tears had swallowed her words as her mother had tried repeatedly to assure her that Leo would be safe.

"He won't be," Emi had moaned. "It's 1940. No one is safe, especially not him."

But despite the feverish guilt that Emi felt about Japan's alliance with Germany, Leo didn't blame her. He assured her in his letters that of course he was able to separate her from the machinery of the Japanese government. They were both victims of circumstance.

It had been four years since she'd lived in Vienna, since she'd seen Leo, but before she was forced to move from the East Coast, they had written to each other weekly. Now that was all she wanted. To be able to talk to him again, if only through ink stains.

But did she deserve to? The thought nagged at her as she shifted her feet on the

17

slippery deck, bracing herself against the weather. Would her new shame be painfully apparent in her letters?

She shut her eyes, wincing with guilt.

Why had she done it? It was just the situation she'd been forced into, she told herself. Locked in like a prisoner, desperate for company, for some sort of happiness. And Christian was so much like her. He was American, not Japanese, but he was a German-American. Almost as hated as she was. Besides, he was just a child. Not even eighteen. It wasn't serious, not like Leo.

Christian Lange was a fling that should have been avoided. She could have avoided it, she scolded herself. But she didn't. Because, if she was honest, there was something about him that she was feverishly drawn to, something she needed in those painful months, locked inside their peculiar desert prison, that only he could give.

Emi looked out at the water, and despite the darkness engulfing the boat, felt certain that they were approaching South Africa. It had been days since they'd seen land. How far behind her Christian and Leo both were now. She was no longer buoyed by love or lust, the dual forces that had carried her through the uncertainty of the last four years. All she had were the wood and steel of the boat keeping her alive and the deep black water she hoped would deliver them safely back to Japan.

"And then what?" she asked her mother, finally inside the boat, safe from the carrying wind. "What happens once we're home?"

"What else?" Keiko said, smiling sadly. "Survival."

CHAPTER 1

Christian Lange
January 1943

River Hills, Wisconsin, boasted nights marked by silence, as if everyone inhabiting the curling streets was lying peacefully asleep, pink mouths slightly agape, breathing one collective breath. Villages and towns had sprung up all along Lake Michigan over the years, but only River Hills began with the promise that residents' palatial homes would be concealed by the area's wild verdancy. Houses were built on lots no smaller than five acres, hidden down winding driveways, behind a camouflage of trees. The village's founders had reasoned that wealth and nature should exist in perfect tranquility, and the 560 inhabitants who had sunk their roots there agreed.

So when a sharp knock on the double front door jolted awake the three residents of 9000 River Road on a still January night, they never would have guessed that it wasn't the pounding of dreams arousing them but rather something more: a tiny fracture in their reality.

Just one week before, the Lange family had ushered in 1943 with champagne and the pleasant tinkling of laughter. In the company of the esteemed congressman from Wisconsin's fourth district with the long Polish name — who said he could only stay for an hour and one drink, but stayed for five and a few bottles — the family had moved excitedly through the house, greeting their guests, buzzing with anticipation for the new year.

But it wasn't just the congressman who gave their soiree its clout. River Hills' most glamorous young wives, and the men who made Milwaukee run, had also walked through the Langes' front door, greeted by the family with the warmth reserved for old friends. They were somebodies who would always remain somebodies, Franz and Helene Lange thought to themselves, just like they did every year when they opened the door for the first guest. Hadn't the war proven that? Even the owner of the city's baseball club and his glamorous horsewoman of a wife, who still wore her mink sable, had stopped by for nearly thirty minutes. And when they left, light as champagne corks, they'd said they were reluctant to go, as the Langes' would surely be the best party of the night. Helene had blushed and said, "Of course it won't be. With your circle of friends?" But she knew they were right. She and her husband did throw a wonderful party. Helene was sure of that.

She wasn't skilled at everything, but Helene Lange was an accomplished hostess. She knew to always have double the amount of food per guest, as even those who declined would end up coming, and to have the waiters refill the drinks before they were half-consumed. "A party feels wrong in these uncertain times," a few guests had said when they arrived, but that sentiment was forgotten when they saw the sizzling suckling pig with rosemary and garlic potatoes and caviar garnish being served in enormous quantities. Helene knew that during war, delicacies were appreciated even more.

It was true that all over the country, celebrations had been muted out of respect for the conflict raging abroad, but Helene and Franz were sure they were exempt from such behavior. Their annual New Year's Eve party was buoyed by a decadence and happiness that floated above life's annoyances and it shouldn't be canceled because of what was happening thousands of miles away. More important, everyone associated the evening with Lange Steel, and that helped the family's bank accounts swell.

Franz Lange, an engineer by trade, had founded Lange Steel only seven years after immigrating to the United States in 1921 and molded it into one of the Midwest's largest producers of steel wire. For a company like Lange, war had been a boon, turning its profits ever upward. With peace nowhere in sight, forty-seven-year-old, perpetually power-hungry Franz was even thinking of expansion. On that New Year's Eve, he and his graceful wife, Helene, had of course shared sympathetic thoughts for those fighting and prayers for families dealing with loss, but imagined the best was yet to come for them and their only child, Christian.

As the sound of a tree branch grazing a window echoed through the room, there was another knock on the door.

"Is your father in here?" the anxious voice of Helene Lange whispered from just outside Christian's open bedroom door.

"He's not with you?" Christian asked, his pitch newly baritone. He was already sitting up in bed, his goose feather pillows strewn across the floor next to him.

"He must have fallen asleep listening to the radio," said Helene, looking around her son's room as if she didn't quite believe that her husband was not there.

"The news of the Russian troop movements in Stalingrad," Christian reminded his mother. "He was listening to the report after supper."

When the fist hit the door a third time, Christian pushed his blankets back, let them slide onto the carpeted floor, and stood up next to his mother. "Dad must be awake now —" he said. He stopped midsentence as they heard the distinct creak of their front door. Then a voice unmarked by a midwestern twang rang through the still house.

"You are Franz Lange?"

In River Hills, it was always a good thing to be Franz Lange. Franz Lange had a glamorous wife, a big house, and a son who grew more handsome with every sunrise. But from the sound of his voice, this night crawler did not care for Franz Lange.

For Christian, it was the note of callousness that snapped him wide awake. Suddenly, he knew who these men were. He had thought of them often in the past year, but they had seemed more like fictional characters, laughable villains in a police novel, not brusque men who could push into his home. His mother retied the belt of her thin pink robe, higher than usual since her stomach had grown noticeably larger over the holidays, and motioned to her son to follow her down the stairs.

There were many kinds of people in Milwaukee, but there was only one kind of person in River Hills — rich. And the two strangers standing in the Langes' foyer did not look rich. One was tall and fair like the Lange men, the other dark-haired and stout, with a hairline that stopped just an inch above his shaggy eyebrows. Once inside, they had pulled out identification cards, showing they were who Christian had guessed: FBI agents. The shorter one was Smith, the taller Jakobsson. A Swedish name to match his yellow Viking hair, thought Christian, though his cheap suit undercut his good looks.

Christian felt himself grab on to his mother's robe, a childish instinct that surprised them both. She reached for his hand.

"You all deaf? Family of mutes?" asked the shorter one. "We've been standing there knocking for damn near ten minutes. I was about to bust down the door. It's snowing, you know?"

"I'm sorry," Franz said, offering to take

26

their coats, an offer that was rudely waved off. "It's rather late. I'm afraid we were all sound asleep."

"Sure you were." Smith removed his hat and looked up at Franz. "We have permission to search your home, Mr. Lange. I'm sure you know why."

"Because I am German and we are at war," said Franz. "I am not ignorant of what is happening in the world." He turned around and looked at his wife. "Helene, please, fetch our papers," he said, a touch too haughtily given the circumstances. "He, Christian, is American," he said of his son, who had remained a step behind his mother. Helene reluctantly let go of her son's hand and rushed back up the carpeted hallway without a word, nodding for Christian to follow her. The two men walked farther inside.

While the family was prepared to watch the agents start turning the house upside down, searching every corner, every drawer — as they'd been told was their practice — all the men did at first was stroll through the rooms as if they were guests, examining the expensive furniture and peering out the window at the faint outline of the nearby Milwaukee River, only visible because of the night's blue-tinted full moon.

Helene and Christian were allowed to change into day clothes, though when Christian emerged from his room without socks, it was clear his nerves had gotten the better of his dress sense. Helene, her red hair hastily pinned up, handed the taller man their alien registration cards, their German passports, and Christian's American one.

"He is an American," she said of her son, echoing her husband. "And we are legal residents." She pointed at their photos and the round stamps embossed years ago in a bland government building in Milwaukee. "My husband is a pillar of this community," she declared. "Franz Lange. Everyone here knows Franz Lange."

Christian put his hand on her shoulder and gave it a slight squeeze, sure that trying to defend themselves was not the right course of action with such men. But Helene continued. "We are members of the country club," she said, waving in its general direction. "The one on Range Line Road. The best in Milwaukee."

Christian wished his mother would stop. She sounded desperate, and desperation made her sound guilty.

Jakobsson took the documents from her and flipped roughly through the small

28

stamped pages, his fingers playing with the edges, then turned to study the expensive Karl Caspar drawing on the wall. The black-and-white depiction of Christ's crucifixion, expertly framed in gold-painted wood, had been given by the artist to Franz's wealthy parents years ago. "Your golfing habits," Jakobsson said to Helene coldly, "are of no interest to me."

To Helene, who had never succeeded in diluting her thick German accent, being a member of the Milwaukee Country Club was the ultimate badge of Americanness. The club was where she and her family celebrated the Fourth of July, where she and other housewives browned themselves — or reddened themselves, as in her case — by the large swimming pool. It was one of two at the club, she had written to her mother when they were first accepted as members. Her husband went as often as she did, playing golf and making important connections to build up Lange steel.

Franz had lost his accent much faster than Helene, had assimilated more rapidly, too, and she admired him almost too much for it. He had grown up in cosmopolitan Berlin and had started studying English much younger than she had, and in the right schools. He spoke German like an aristocrat, English first like an Englishman and now like an upper-crust American, and was even proficient in French. She was the daughter of a baker and had spent her childhood and adolescence in a rural town with chickens and a donkey named Aldo. She would never lose her accent.

Franz's easy command of English was something he'd liked to show off when the two had started dating in Berlin. He was a young engineer, and she was a violin student at the Stern Conservatory.

Because of her reserve, Franz didn't seduce her in the forthright way he had used — many times successfully — with other women. Instead, he went the playground route and teased her about the color of her hair, calling her Mrs. Tomato Soup in his proper English. The nickname stuck, and even years later he would use it when he had had too much wine and they were rediscovering each other in bed at night.

Their son had picked up on it, too, even though it was supposed to be reserved for private moments, and for some reason that silly name came to him now as he watched his mother standing rigidly under the light of the dining room chandelier. Tomato soup — that was as American as it got, wasn't it? So why were the agents there?

The Lange family didn't live in the pre-dominantly German area of Milwaukee, Franz didn't belong to the German Club, and he didn't frequent beer halls full of im-migrants. And while the three spoke the language to each other when alone, they always spoke English outside the house. Still, here were two brusque men walking around their home as if they were planning to measure the walls and move in.

Christian and his parents had talked about such visitations in whispers since the bomb-ing of Pearl Harbor at the end of 1941. Since then, they had heard of some Ger-man nationals being arrested in Milwaukee, had been told how their houses were scoured by agents, but they weren't *their* kind of people. And so few of them were being arrested in proportion to their num-bers. There were millions of German-Americans in the United States. Surely, the Langes thought, the odds would protect them.

The Japanese were the ones being tar-geted, everyone said. Christian had heard the news reports, had seen pictures of white children in magazines holding up placards that read "Jap-hunting season" and "yellow peril." Signs like that were all over Califor-nia. Those people were at risk, not his parents. Not him. The images had made him feel sick, but part of him had been relieved it was them, thinking that it meant he had been spared. The Germans, the Italians, and the Japanese were all the enemies of the United States. The Axis, all allies.

Franz and Helene were so confident of their safety that they never shielded their son from their conversations. He should know what was happening in their country, in their state, and in the world at war, they thought, and he should trust that it would have almost no effect on him. No one would come for Franz, since he employed more than one hundred people, almost all American citizens. So by the time 1942 had wound down, the three Langes were sure they would safely ride out the war.

But here they were, and Christian was having trouble not thinking the worst. The draft age had been changed to eighteen the year before, but just a few months shy of his eighteenth birthday, he hadn't been concerned. He had college ahead of him, not war. His parents had assured him that he would not be drafted, just as they assured him that the FBI would not knock on their door. Perhaps, thought Christian, they were wrong about both.

Christian watched the two men open the

drawers in his father's office, knocking about the wooden desk that he'd loved sitting at as a boy. They riffled through Franz's papers as he stood there, looking foolish.

"What is it you are searching for?" Franz finally asked. "Surely the fact that we are German citizens is not enough reason for you to tear apart our home in the middle of the night."

Christian looked away from the men, relieved that his father was finally standing up for his family.

"That's more than enough, Mr. Lange," said Jakobsson, the blue veins in his neck protruding with excitement. "We are at war with your country. Your rights, or these rights you assume incorrectly that you have, no longer exist. We can search whomever we please, whenever we please, if they are citizens of a country we are fighting against. If you've got a problem with that, take it up with J. Edgar Hoover."

Smith, busy thumbing through Franz's bank ledgers, raised his eyebrows at the sight of the high-six-figure balances.

"We're looking for dangerous enemy aliens, and we are authorized to do all we need to find them," Jakobsson went on, looking a little too long at a picture of Helene in a low-cut evening dress on Franz's desk, her pale chest filling half the frame. "But to be frank with you, Mr. Lange," he said, waving his arms around to indicate the house, "all this is ancillary. I don't need to search this house. I don't need these letters." He flipped a few onto the floor. "Though I will be taking some of them with me."

He folded a pile of documents and handed them to his colleague. Pausing a moment, he took the framed picture of young Helene. He ran his finger lewdly over the image before saying, "My real questions lie here." He patted his worn briefcase and pulled it onto the desk, where he opened it slowly.

"This, Mr. Lange," he said, pointing to the top of the pile of papers, "is a letter written by you to Fritz Kuhn, the head of the German American Bund. In it, you write all about your support of the Nazi Party and how you intended to help spread its message in America, particularly the Midwest, where President Franklin D. *Rosenfeld* has less influence. You even say proudly that you've funded programs for Nazi youth in Grafton, Wisconsin, for several years. Makes for a disturbing read."

"You must be joking," Franz said, reaching for the paper. Jakobsson pulled it away before he could touch it.

"I didn't write any such letter," Franz said firmly. "I would never say, or write, such things. And I have never had any interaction with Fritz Kuhn or the Bund."

"Is this not your writing, Mr. Lange?" asked Jakobsson.

"No!" said Franz, trying to grab the paper again. Jakobsson pulled it out of his reach, obviously amused by his game.

"So you are not a member of the Bund? And you did not give money to the camp in Grafton in the thirties? What was it called?" he asked his colleague.

"Camp Hindenburg," said Smith. "It was full of Nazi youth running around raising swastikas and hating Jews."

"Right," said Jakobsson. "That's the place."

"Of course not," Franz said, struggling to remain polite, his body tense with restraint. "I have nothing to do with that camp or that Nazi group. I take great issue with its presence in America."

Christian looked at his father, his square jaw tight, his light eyes starting to water from frustration. There had to be an explanation. He had never heard Franz say a positive word about the Nazis, but he had never been a rallying force against them, either.

"But you knew it was an American Nazi group. You just said so," said Jakobsson, smiling.

"No, *you* said so," Franz replied. "I'm repeating your words."

"Yet there is this letter," said Jakobsson, flicking the paper. "It looks quite a bit like your writing. I would call it identical." He finally put it down on the desk next to a condolence letter that Franz had been composing to a colleague. The handwriting on the two documents — slanted to the left, big capitals, and almost illegible at the end of each sentence — was indistinguishable.

"Obviously, the letter to Kuhn is fraudulent," said Franz, bending down to examine the heavy black script. "Someone is playing a malicious joke on me."

"Obviously," Jakobsson replied.

Christian and Helene moved closer to see the letter, Christian's panic rising, but Smith kept them at a distance.

"I'm afraid it's not just the matter of the letter," said Smith stoically. "Two of your employees confided — after not much pressing — that they heard you make pro-Nazi statements in the office. And one claimed to have seen you spit on an American flag. Any recollection of using the Stars and Stripes as a spittoon?" he asked, running his hand back and forth on the desk, causing even more papers to fall.

"You are gravely mistaken," said Franz, no longer succeeding in keeping his temper in check. "I love this country. My wife and I chose to build our lives together here and to have our son right here in Wisconsin. I am as much an American as I am a German."

"No," said Smith. "You are not an American and will never be."

Helene stared at him as if he had taken her country club membership and pitched it in an incinerator.

"We could hunt through your house for contraband, but we have enough to arrest you right now," Smith said to Franz, the agent's forehead beginning to sweat as the warm air of the Langes' house caught up with him.

"You intend to arrest me because of false information. A forged letter. Now. At four o'clock in the morning in front of my wife and son," said Franz.

"Yes," said Smith flatly. "Yes to the arrest. As for the grounds, you can argue what you want during your trial."

A trial, thought Christian. So there was a

chance for his father. He, with his elo-
quence, would be able to explain everything.

"But this is all hearsay," said Franz.
"Clearly someone planted these forged
materials in my office. A competitor. Or a
disgruntled employee. Isn't that obvious!"

"Are many of your employees disgruntled?" Jakobsson asked from across the
room. "And the handwriting. Identical to
yours. The same slant, written with a left
hand," he said, walking back over and moving the paper closer to Franz's face.
"There's a smudge here made by the side
of your hand, just as there is on the other
letter."

"It is not impossible to forge someone's
writing. To smudge a letter with the side of
a palm!" Franz said, pushing the paper away
angrily.

"And how would you know that?" asked
Smith.

"Because I know that, just as you do.
Because of common sense."

Jakobsson laughed and looked at Helene,
who was standing with her back to the wall.
"Mrs. Lange," he said, "your husband is not
the only one who brought us to this house
tonight. You did, too."

"What?" asked Helene, stunned, reaching
out for Christian, who was across the room.

"Did you make a wire transfer of eight thousand dollars to a Mrs. Jutta Köhler on the eleventh of October, 1942?" Smith asked her, having trouble looking away from her dress, which had loosened at the neckline after it had been tied in haste.

"Did I what? Do what? Send money to Jutta?" she said, rushing to her husband's side. "How do you know Jutta?"

"She is your cousin. Jutta Köhler, maiden name Braun. You grew up together near Aachen, Germany," said the agent, not explaining how he knew who Jutta was or that Helene had sent her money. "She has two daughters, a husband, and an elbow that has been broken twice. So answer the question. Did you send Mrs. Köhler eight thousand dollars?"

"Yes, I did. Yes," Helene replied, flustered. She looked at her husband, who was quite aware that she had sent the money. He had allowed it, in fact, since he was the one who earned and meticulously managed all the household's money. "But I did so legally. It was when I was on a trip to New York," she reminded Franz. "I sent it through the German consulate there. If it was meant for anything corrupt, why would I have sent it through the consulate?"

Smith shook his head.

"I don't care if you sent the cash by paper airplane. Your cousin, as I'm sure you are aware, is a member of the Nazi Party," he said. "You supporting her financially is you supporting them."

"A Nazi? No. Jutta is just a housewife. The wife of an elementary school teacher. She makes her own clothes and bakes bread for the church every Sunday. She has never done a thing out of turn in her life," said Helene, starting to panic. "Her husband lost his job because he *wasn't* in the party. Jutta was in need of money, and we have it to give. Why should I not send some to her? I could not refuse her. Franz?" she said, looking desperately at her husband.

"Wasn't in the party?" asked Smith. "He's since joined. Probably got his job back, too, and not needing your money anymore."

"Mr. and Mrs. Lange, you'll be leaving with us right away," said Jakobsson, cutting the conversation short. "We will come back for your son in the morning. Pack your things tonight," he told Christian. "And don't even think about running."

"For him?" said Helene, her eyes full of tears. "But he must come with me!" she screamed, pulling him closer.

"He can't," Jakobsson barked. "He'll be going to the Milwaukee Children's Home."

"But you don't need Christian!" Helene protested, her shock edging toward hysteria. "You can't take him! Franz, do something!" she shouted.

"We aren't arresting your son. Control yourself," said Smith. "He's a minor, so he can't live here alone, can he? We'll bring him to the Children's Home in a few hours. And he'll stay there until . . ." His voice trailed off, and Christian knew that Smith didn't know anything more definite. Until the war ended? Until he turned eighteen? "Until" was open-ended for him now.

"But you can't put him there! In that awful place with those street children!" said Helene, growing more frantic. The ribbon on her neckline had slipped totally open, exposing her ample flesh.

"I don't think you understand, Mrs. Lange," Smith said, his voice more sympathetic than Jakobsson's as he eyed her body.

"She understands perfectly," said Franz, putting his hand on Helene's back. "She just doesn't want to be separated from her only son, and neither do I. Can't there be another way? I am contributing to the war effort for this country, my adopted country. If you arrest me, what will happen to my company and all my employees? Have you considered that?"

"We've taken care of it," said Smith. "Spoke to a second in command. Or was it a third? Whoever it was, he assured us he'd keep your company running. Maybe better than you've been running it."

"But where are my parents going?" Christian broke in, finally finding his voice while his father looked as if he might choke over what he'd just heard.

"Prison, for now," Smith said, with his back turned to him.

With that, he deftly handcuffed the elder Langes, not letting them hug their son before their arms were locked behind them.

"You can't arrest me like this," Franz protested, twisting his hands. "You haven't followed any sort of protocol."

"There is no protocol," said Smith. "You, as a German citizen, have no rights at all. That's what happens during war."

"We will take this," said Jakobsson, unplugging the expensive E. H. Scott radio in Franz's study.

Helene, despite her handcuffs, suddenly turned and began to walk up the stairs. Smith instinctively reached for her arm to stop her but she shook him off and kept going, screaming about the upstairs radios. He hurried after her, grabbing her arm firmly, but Franz shouted in a panic.

"Leave her! She's pregnant!"

"Suddenly every German woman is fragile and pregnant," said Smith, stopping on the stairs and reluctantly letting go of Helene.

"She *is* pregnant!" Christian confirmed, running to his mother.

"Yeah, I got it, she's pregnant," said Smith, not even glancing at Helene or her neckline after he succeeded in getting her back downstairs.

Christian gripped her shoulders and thought of the night his parents had told him about the baby. They had called it the happiest of accidents, as doctors had always told Helene that after Christian's difficult birth she would not be able to have more children. But here she was, in her forties, pregnant again.

He kissed her wet cheeks, draped her coat over her shoulders, then watched as his parents were pushed toward the door.

The sun was just starting to lift over the horizon as the agents walked Franz and Helene out of the house. The neighbors were not in their beds anymore, were no longer breathing their collective breath. They were driving their cars slowly down the road, noses to the windows, watching Franz and Helene Lange being taken away by the FBI. And in the light of day, they

would watch as their son was driven away,
too.

CHAPTER 2

Emi Kato
January 1940–May 1941

Despite her fluency in English, Emi Kato had never been drawn to America. "A country as old as a toddler?" she'd said to her father in 1938 when he disclosed that they might be posted there after Vienna. "I won't like it — not enough history. Strange accents," she'd added, as they sat surrounded by an icy winter day in Vienna and the warm comfort of their large eighteenth-century apartment and its three marble fireplaces. "Why not Paris?" she suggested. "I've always wanted to live in Paris."

"I speak English and German, like you," he'd reminded her. "They will never send me to Paris. You'll have to find your own way there. Maybe in the freight hold of a banana boat," he said, eyeing her wrinkled white school shirt. After teasing his daughter playfully for a few moments, pushing her to try an American accent, his tone grew serious.

"If I am sent to Washington, we will go," he said. A year later, they were in the nation's capital.

Emi had never set foot in a place as untamed as America and though she wouldn't admit it to her ever-curious father, she was intimidated by the vastness of such a country.

"You? Your English is perfect. I'm afraid no one will understand me," said Keiko on the boat over, one of the most luxurious they'd traveled on yet. "British English with a Japanese accent and grammatical errors. I won't even be able to buy bread."

"I'll buy the bread," said Emi.

She had grown used to being the mouthpiece for her mother over the years, a habit that started on her father's first assignment in London, when Emi was only five years old. There she was sent to a British school for girls, where she wore a uniform so starched by the family's *amah* that she had to wet the collar down or her neck would itch until it turned purple. After school, Keiko and her *amah* would pick her up and drag her to piano lessons, as Keiko assumed it was what Western girls did. She forced Emi to practice until she was far and away her esteemed teacher's best student.

After lessons — because Keiko's English was still poor despite a year in London, while Emi had picked it up like a child catching a cold — she dragged her mother by the hand all over the city. For three years, Emi spoke and lived like a Japanese child with her parents, but like a British one in public. Then the Katos moved to Berlin and Emi was put into German school, where she continued to float to the top. She learned German, just as she had learned English. And just as she had led her mother around London, she did the same in Berlin.

By the time she was sixteen and had reached Vienna, she was fluent in German, which was a pleasant surprise for her parents. Somewhat unintentionally, Norio and Keiko Kato had raised a fiercely independent, worldly young woman. Emi could tell that her parents, though they had started bringing up marriage and children after she'd reached twenty, were proud of the way she'd turned out. By 1939, Keiko's English was near fluent, but Emi knew that she still liked it when her daughter spoke first when they entered a restaurant or a shop, always enjoying her daughter's upper-crust British accent.

As they made their way from their first-class cabin to the dining room for dinner on the boat that night, Emi took her mother's hand, happy that they were still packing her up like a little suitcase wedged between them.

Though Keiko had been trying for years to have Emi crop her hair like she had, chin length and waved in the front, Emi still wore hers long and straight, refusing to change it. She wasn't sure why she was so uncompromising about the cut; perhaps she liked the rebellion more than the hairstyle. On this cool night on their ocean crossing, she had put it up for dinner at her mother's insistence and was wearing one of her best dresses — that part she didn't mind. After two years in Vienna, she was used to formality, and despite resisting her mother's plans for her hair, had come to enjoy the nice affairs her father's job allowed them.

But Washington was not Vienna. The Kato women soon learned that in America, the diplomatic world was far less extravagant than in Europe.

It took Emi and Keiko some time to adjust to their new landscape after their arrival in 1939. Though they both thought it would be very much like England, the language was the only similarity they felt. The people were much more outspoken, and the city did not have the cosmopolitan flair that London had. "For all the embassies being here, it doesn't feel very international," said Emi, who was always looking for faces that resembled hers.

In two years, Emi grew to like the city as much as someone whose heart was somewhere else could. She made a few friends at her all-girls Catholic school in a Maryland suburb, but she did not bother to get close to anyone. On the family's first posting abroad, to London, Emi had made many friends, too young to realize that she would have to give them all up in a few years. In Berlin, the Katos' next posting, she was accepted at her all-girls school with the same kindness and genuine fascination she had received in London, but she became more reserved with her friendships as her heart still stung with the pain of leaving her British community behind. And when she moved to Vienna, she had reached an age where all she wanted was a small circle of friends. But when she met Leo, that circle tied itself into a knot. All Emi wanted was Leo.

In Washington, though her classmates did not treat her with hostility or spite, they all took a few months to warm to her presence, and the reception never heated past tepid.

The girls' indifference, compared to what she had encountered in Europe, bothered Emi at first, but she soon realized that she preferred to return to her apartment near the National Zoo after school and dream about Leo anyway. So Emi went to school, was civil with her classmates who were civil to her, but after years in Washington, she still did not have any true friends.

Leo and Emi wrote to each other every Friday, though the letters did not always make it across the ocean. Still, Emi read the ones she received until the paper was nearly translucent. She took them to school, she read them in the bath. She was never without a letter from Leo somewhere on her person. The Katos' apartment in Washington overlooked the south part of the zoo and Emi could sometimes see giraffes milling around their small sandy enclosure while she bathed, letter from Leo in hand. It was her favorite thing about the city.

"You shouldn't spend all your years here locked in your room," Keiko advised, eyeing Emi's letter resting on her floral coverlet and her glossy pictures of Vienna's landmarks hanging on the wall. It was January 1940 and Emi was leaving the apartment much less than she had when they'd first arrived, choosing to spend her time with the comfort of her memories.

Emi looked at her mother skeptically. "And you?" she asked.

"Yes, I know. I don't go out *that* often, either," Keiko admitted.

"Almost never unless you're with father," said Emi.

"But the world doesn't need to see me. You're young and beautiful. And unmarried. Don't waste those fleeting things locked up in here staring at pictures of a city across an ocean."

"No one thinks I'm beautiful here," Emi said plainly, flipping over onto her back and kicking off her stiff school shoes. "In Europe we were interesting. The Japanese family. People wanted to get to know me, would seek me out at school. Here, everyone speaks to me with caution. First they're skeptical, amazed that I can speak English. Then their eyes follow me around the restaurant, or wherever I am, like I'm some exotic bird they've never seen before. I can tell they don't know what to make of me and their conclusion is mostly the same. They don't want to speak to me, but if I stay quiet and try to blend into the wallpaper, they won't talk about me."

"You're exaggerating as usual," said Keiko, but Emi could tell by her voice that she was experiencing similar reactions from the Americans. They had previously talked about the stares they had received, the comments, though Keiko was hesitant to ever speak ill of anyone, even strangers. But she had been willing to talk about her shock at the treatment of Negroes in America. "They hate them," she'd said to Emi one night when they'd returned from a family dinner in a hotel and seen a young Negro man berated by a white woman outside the restaurant, slapped across the face in the middle of the sidewalk. "They forced them into this country and yet despise them for still being here. They like their dogs better. Even the ugly dogs."

Emi had agreed, as shocked as her mother was at the racial divides in America. "A bit like us and the Koreans," Emi pointed out.

"Oh no, Emi, I don't think so," Keiko had replied, refusing to admit that the Japanese had their own brand of bigotry. "Besides, it's not like that in the diplomatic community. We are open-minded, curious people. Educated. Especially the wives," she said smiling.

"But I'm not in the diplomatic community," Emi reminded her. "I'm at a small school in Maryland with people who have known each other since they were babies.

Maybe it would be different if we lived in California, where there are many more Japanese. Erika Adachi said it was much better there. They used to live in Los Angeles — she and her American mother — while Takeo was at the consulate."

"You are almost done with school, Emiko, for good. And we are not going to California," said Keiko. She folded one of Emi's dresses and sat on her bed, too. "I admit, sometimes I do wish your *amah* Megumi was still with us. More for my sake than yours. Her English was poor but she was so tough. Stubborn, too. I think she'd do much better with the stares and the questions than I do."

Megumi had sailed back to northern Japan before the family left for Washington in 1939. In America, the diplomatic corps did not employ *amahs* as they did in other countries, and Emi had said goodbye to hers tearfully, knowing that at seventeen, she was too old for one anyway, but not wanting to let her companion go.

"She must have given you your toughness," said Keiko. "Because despite your hesitation to go out and get to know the city, your annoyance with strangers' behavior toward you, you're the strongest person I know. Please try to remain that way."

"Okay, Mama," said Emi putting away her latest letter from Leo, making sure the exotic stamps weren't peeling off the envelope. She folded it and placed it at the corner of the bed, running her hands over the return address. "I promise I'll leave the house more."

Emi did start to venture out with more frequency after the winter of 1940 melted away, writing to Leo about the things she liked about Washington — the low marble buildings, the streets inspired by European grids, the humidity that reminded her of Tokyo weather. Sometimes they wrote to each other of war, of their fears about what was happening in Vienna, but they'd agreed to focus mostly on the good in their lives.

There was far more good for Emi than Leo in 1940, especially after she turned eighteen and graduated from high school that spring, but when Japan signed the Tripartite Pact in September, Emi couldn't help but write to Leo expressing her shame. He dismissed it as bad judgment on the part of the Japanese, and they tried to turn their correspondence back to their positive tone, but so much more was to come.

Pearl Harbor.

The attack on Hawaii in December 1941 changed the lives of every American with

Japanese ancestry. But first, it was the Japanese diplomats who were zeroed in on for dismissal.

Emi was too distraught to write to Leo about what was happening to them, but he still wrote to her, knowing to send his letter to her father at the Japanese Embassy instead of to their home. In the last letter Emi received from Leo, he wrote, "You have nothing to do with them. To me, you are still the good that exists in the world."

But the American people, especially President Roosevelt, did not agree. After Pearl Harbor, the diplomats' families were shut inside their apartments, while the men were at the embassy trying to understand their new position, living and working in an enemy nation.

"They'll treat us well," Keiko assured Emi the first night they spent alone. Emi, stunned and nearly silent since the news of the attack broke, was sharing her mother's bed, and trying to understand why Japan had made such a foolish choice. She knew quite a bit about Japan's history with America, as her father talked about little else since moving to Washington. She knew the Americans did not approve of Japan's recent occupation of southern Indochina, putting massive pressure on the Japanese to pull out. Japan had refused and the United States had frozen its oil exports. But Japan had not relented, moving deeper into Southeast Asia, occupying Saigon. Even with what she knew about the different power struggles, what she was most desperate to know was if her father had been aware in advance that the Japanese military was going to attack Pearl Harbor. Did he know before the bombs hit how much their lives — and the world — were about to change?

She could tell that her mother was thinking the same thing. "Try to get some sleep," she said, holding Emi close to her, curled up like they used to years ago, before Emi was a head taller. "No one will hurt us. They have to treat us well. They want to get their American diplomats out of Japan — alive — as badly as they want to send us back."

"What does a bomb do to you?" Emi asked, trying not to shake in her mother's arms. "How do you die? Do you explode? Are you burned alive? Is it instant? Or does your body melt from the heat, your organs slowly giving out one by one?"

"I don't know," said Keiko, stroking Emi's hand. "It can't be good, however it is. Let's just pray for the souls of the dead and hope that the Japanese are right. That there is an important reason behind the bombs and

56

gunfire."

Emi knew her mother would never say that the Japanese could be wrong, but nothing felt right about what was happening. She knew that the bombs and torpedoes had mostly killed military men, but the radio reports said civilians, too, had died. Emi imagined herself walking alone, peacefully, somewhere as beautiful as Hawaii, and suddenly being blasted to her death, burned alive. She reached for her mother, knowing sleep was not coming soon. They were both aware that the entire country was now incensed, with intense hatred toward Japan.

The women spent a week locked inside their apartment, and no contact with Norio was allowed. They left the building only for short walks in the company of an FBI agent named Mark Rhodes, who was assigned to guard them. As Keiko predicted, though their freedom was gone, they were treated very well by Rhodes, who liked to talk about his love of teriyaki chicken and his children who lived in the Florida Keys with their no-good mother.

After a long week, Emi and Keiko were transferred along with the other diplomats' families to the Japanese embassy on Massachusetts Avenue, a handsome Western-style stone building with a gold chrysanthemum adorning the front, where they were reunited with their husbands and fathers. The heavy steel gates were locked behind them as soon as the families were safely inside, since angry demonstrators had gathered nearby. The diplomats and their staff had not left the embassy since the news had broken.

"I'm in shock more than anything," Norio said to his daughter when she was finally allowed to see him. He looked desperately in need of a shower and a change of clothes. His eyes were bloodshot and his hair, usually pushed back neatly with Brylcreem, and styled with a small wave on top, was falling across his forehead in every direction.

"But why did we attack Pearl Harbor?" asked Emi. "Did you know they were going to? The newspaper said over two thousand people died. Two thousand."

"No, Emi. Not another word," said Norio sternly, his white shirt stained and his custom-made suit wrinkled at every crease. His body, tall and straight like his daughter's, was hunched with exhaustion. He repositioned his round metal glasses on his straight nose and repeated himself.

After a week in the embassy, living on top of each other and sleeping on makeshift beds, they were told that they'd be moving collectively to a luxury hotel in Hot Springs, Virginia, a rural town in the western part of the state, and that they would stay there until they sailed back to Japan. "But that could be in months," a State Department official warned.

"Months!" said Emi as she collected her things and tried to make her hair look less oily at the crown. Her mother gave her a small wool hat, and she pinned it on, and pinched a little life into her cheeks with her cold hands.

"They don't know precisely what will happen yet. Don't panic," said Keiko as she helped her daughter.

"I know what will happen," said Emi. "We are about to become the new face of public humiliation." Outside, they could see that a crowd had again gathered on the busy street, waiting to watch the imminent Japanese exile from the city.

When the embassy assembled everyone to leave, transferring them to idling buses to head to the train station, the demonstrators, mostly men dressed nicely in handsome winter coats and hats, let out a few angry shouts as soon as the front doors opened. Their hateful tone threw Emi off, the jeers causing her to trip over her mother's valise, but it was nothing like what they faced when they arrived at Union Station.

Emi had worn her nicest traveling dress and cashmere coat with a fur collar, the same one she had worn when she'd first set foot on the luxury steamer to the United States. Her hair was dirty but covered and her shoes were shined, the heels not scuffed at all.

But all the people watching them at Union Station seemed to care about was the shape of their eyes.

She could see kids pulling their eyes at the corners, making them thinner and then laughing hysterically while their parents did nothing, at best. At worst, they shouted angrily at the group, drowning out their children's laughter, using slurs Emi had become familiar with in the past few weeks. Japanazi. Blast the Japs. Yellow peril. Emi heard them all, coming from people who looked like the girls she had gone to school with, or their parents. Behind her, her own parents walked next to each other, her father ignoring the jeers and commenting on the handsome gold and white coffered ceiling of the station. He even pointed out a few birds that had made their homes in the carved pockets of plaster.

The FBI agents hurried them through the large station, telling them to board the private train that would take them to the Homestead Hotel.

Exhausted from having to remain stoic in the face of such hate — something her parents excelled at and she did not — Emi closed her eyes once she was in her seat, imagining that she was the type of person who could have spit in her hecklers' faces. As sleep almost caught her, the corners of her mouth went up slightly. Wasn't she that person? A little bit? She thought back to 1938. To Vienna. She had been then. It was just that she would never do anything to harm her father's position. When she was with her parents, in the presence of the ambassador, she knew to play the part of the obedient daughter. That's what they expected of her and she understood why. But in those moments where she was tried, and alone, she *was* the person who could slap someone right back.

Emi fell deeply asleep as the train whistled into Virginia, not waking up until the wheels slowed for their descent into Hot Springs.

"What a strange place," Emi said as she looked out the window at the bare oak and maple trees, their branches frozen and unmoving against the gray sky. "Why would they put us out here? There's nothing but trees."

"I believe it's called the countryside," said her mother. "Not 'nothing.' "

"They'd put us in a cave if they could," she heard one of the wives say, an American with soft blond curls and a wonderful command of Japanese. "But then the American diplomats might get thrown into a ravine in Tokyo. So instead, we are here. You'll see. It's actually a very luxurious hotel. I stayed here with my parents as a girl."

Her husband told her to stop gossiping, and before the train had come to a stop, the entire Japanese diplomatic community was on their feet, trying to ignore the fact that there were FBI agents and State Department employees hovering around them.

"I'm sorry to say," the senior State Department official in charge announced before anyone had stepped off the train, "but we don't have enough cars for all of you." He ran his fingers through his gray hair nervously. "There are some people — people who live in town — who are waiting outside . . . who have come to watch all this. So for everyone's safety, the men will walk together to the hotel and the women and children will take the cars." They heard the train doors open and they were told that they could all disembark.

"The diplomats have to walk? Past all

those people?" Emi asked her mother incredulously.

"Emiko, we are being interned! The Americans are not going to send Rolls-Royces for
the men," one of the Japanese wives said to
Emi. She started to laugh until her eyes
were watering, the tears moving straight
down her face until they got trapped in her
waxy red lipstick. "I'm sorry," she said, waving her hand in front of her mouth. "I'm
just very anxious. I don't mean to bark at
you."

Her mother put her hand on Emi's back
reassuringly. "They'll be fine," she said, as
they all tried to carry their luggage and
themselves off the train.

As the women and children loaded into
the cars, they could see a large group had
indeed gathered to watch them, these far
less sophisticated in appearance than the
Washingtonians. They were in southern,
rural America and that alone scared Emi.
"Not again," she grumbled to her mother
as she waited to climb into a car with her.
"The people in Washington already made it
perfectly clear that it's a miracle I can see
out of the slits in my face. I don't need to
hear it twice."

"Do not complain," said her mother. "In
fact, do not say another thing until we are

locked in a room together inside the hotel. No sound at all."

"The pretty ones are always obstinate," said an older woman who was already in the backseat.

Emi looked at them both and frowned. Out of the corner of her eye, she could see another car idling with the back door open. The three oldest Shiga children were crammed inside. "I'll ride with the Shigas," Emi said turning around, squeezing herself into the backseat with them. Unlike Emi, the Shiga children had never lived in Japan before. Their mother was Canadian and they had spent most of their short lives following their father on postings or in Ottawa with their mother.

"You don't fit, Emiko Kato," said Mirai Shiga, the youngest, who had inherited her mother's Canadian diction and curly hair.

Emi pulled her onto her lap, closed the door, and opened the window, resting Mirai's arm on the ledge.

"Better now?" she asked the little girl.

"Better," said Mirai, leaning back comfortably against Emi's long frame.

The car was in a line, waiting for the others to start driving, and Mirai was starting to wiggle on Emi's lap.

"You're moving because you're freezing,"

her sister Anna said to her, pointing at the open window. "Close it before we all die."

"No," said Mirai stubbornly, letting her arm dangle out of it as the car finally roared off.

Emi and the Shiga children all looked straight ahead out of instinct as they drove close to the crowd of townspeople. Even though Mirai was just five years old, she was already trained to act with decorum when insults were being fired at you.

"Don't worry," said Emi as the car puttered slowly in line with the others. "They're all staying quiet. Not like in Washington."

But just as Emi finished her sentence, she felt something small and sharp hit her neck. She put her hand to it, wondering if something in the car had stabbed her, perhaps a piece of metal in the seat.

"Ow!" Mirai suddenly screamed, wrestling herself off Emi's lap and falling on her older sister. Emi felt another sting and then another before she had the sense to roll the window up. Right next to her on the seat was a piece of gravel. Someone in the silent crowd was pelting them with it.

"What was that?" asked Anna, looking at her little sister.

"I don't know," said Emi, answering for her. "It's the wild countryside out here. Just things flying through the air. Don't worry. The window's closed now."

Mirai climbed back into Emi's lap. A small red mark on her cheek started to show and she rubbed it against Emi's coat. "I don't like the countryside," she said, putting her thumb in her mouth.

"Me neither," said Emi, relaxing only when the crowd was far behind them.

"Are you scared to go to Japan?" Mirai asked Emi as the beautiful, sprawling brick hotel came into view. It had several buildings attached together, the largest a ten-story tower dotted with loggias, all brick with white accents, so thick and shiny that they looked frosted on. It looked far better than the prison Emi had imagined.

"No, not scared," said Emi, hugging her. "It's home to me. I just wish we were going back under different circumstances."

"Are you Japanese? I thought you were an English like our auntie. You talk like an English," said Mirai.

"And you speak like a Canadian. It's the curse of the diplomat's child," said Emi, pointing to the hotel. "In Berlin I knew a Japanese woman who learned English in Australia and she sounded quite wild. So sounding British, or Canadian, isn't so bad."

"My Japanese is bad," said Mirai.

66

"No it's not," said Emi, who had heard her speak Japanese when they'd been living in the embassy together. "And you'll improve once we're all over there."

The Japanese diplomats and their families stayed at the Homestead for four months, eating well and living in peace. Though there was hardly any school for the children, and all their parents' bank accounts were frozen, making money an eventual problem, they were allowed to move around the grounds with relative freedom. Emi and the other young people took advantage of their isolation and went on snowy hikes, explored the old halls, and went swimming in the enormous swimming pool as soon as it was warm enough. Emi was even allowed to play the hotel's piano, something she did on a near-daily basis.

The first night she had played, Ambassador Nomura himself had sat to listen, swaying gently to the Debussy piece and then requesting some American jazz.

"You play incredibly well," the ambassador had said when she was done. "No, that's an understatement. You play like a professional musician."

Emi thanked him politely before leaving him in the company of her father.

As Emi had hoped, her father had promised her that he, and even the ambassador, had not known that Japan was planning to attack Pearl Harbor before it happened. It came as an enormous shock to them, as Ambassador Nomura had been trying desperately to negotiate with the Americans, to keep the two countries from going to war with each other. "Sadly, diplomats do not have as much sway as we think," said Norio to his relieved daughter.

After months of their Virginia hotel life, the diplomatic community was finally told that they had a sail date. They would leave for Japan on June 10, 1942. But before they did, they were all being moved to yet another luxury resort, where the German diplomatic community had been housed, the Greenbrier in White Sulphur Springs, West Virginia.

The hotel in West Virginia was much like the one in Virginia, sprawling, elegant, historic, and very isolated. High in the Allegheny Mountains, the resort, like the last one, originally beckoned visitors to its hot springs.

"Like *onsen*?" Emi had asked her mother when they arrived, imagining the beautiful Japanese baths in the mountain towns outside Tokyo.

"Not as nice," said Keiko. "And you have

to wear clothes. You know the Americans."

But, they admitted, the hotel was beautiful. All white and built in the classical revival style with four wide columns out front and long wings on each side. Emi approached it with much less trepidation than she had the Homestead.

The Germans were very happy to have the Japanese there, and Emi felt that suddenly their luxurious prison became mostly cocktail parties with the German diplomats, which her parents occasionally let her attend, especially if she had been babysitting the Shiga children the night before. Emi was surprised that many of the American wives of German diplomats were terrified to go to Germany. Some had never set foot in the country and weren't fluent in German. Other wives were very pro-Hitler, which surprised Emi less. Those she avoided entirely, though she did spill a champagne cocktail on one particularly anti-Semitic woman, who was so drunk that she didn't even notice.

"Why did the government decide to ally themselves with the Germans, again?" the eldest Shiga daughter, Anna, asked the next day. Though only fifteen, she had been at the cocktail party the night before, too, and had heard the drunk German woman call

Jews "as disposable as table scraps."

"Because the Germans don't mind the fact that the Japanese are in Manchuria, unlike the U.S., and the two countries think they can protect each other against Russia. Plus, the fascism that Germany is touting appeals to some of Japan's militarists. My father is not in line with them. Neither is yours, I hear," said Emi, sipping her cold orange juice by the pool, which was helping to soothe the painful throat she'd woken up with. She hadn't been feeling well since they arrived in West Virginia, but she chalked it up to a change of air, and to finally acting her age, out late at the diplomats' parties.

"It was more of a rhetorical question," said Anna, picking up her novel and rolling her eyes. "Are you a diplomat in training or something? Doesn't all that political talk bore you?"

"Wouldn't that be something," said Emi coughing, the movement hurting her back. "There's never been a female Japanese diplomat. I doubt there ever will be. I love Japan, but it's a very sexist country. You'll see. It's not Canada."

"Why couldn't you be the first? You're stuck up enough. And smart enough," Anna added with a wide smile.

"Thank you, Anna," said Emi, choosing

to ignore her first comment. She coughed again, reaching for her chest. "I think I'm allergic to White Sulphur Springs," she said, surprised to see a trace of blood splattered on her hand after she coughed.

"You are sick," said Anna.

"Maybe. I don't feel very well," Emi said, reaching for her forehead. She tried to stand up, to find her mother, but her body crumpled to the ground, the back of her head hitting the slate tiles.

When Emi woke up, she was in a car lying flat in the backseat. She made out the silhouette of a man she didn't recognize, reached for her mother, and, reassured that she was there, fell back asleep. When she finally woke up, she was in a hospital.

"You have tuberculosis," said her mother, dabbing her daughter's watering eyes. Keiko was wearing a medical mask over her nose and mouth and a cotton net over her hair. "You're going to fight it, of course, and you'll be fine, but we won't be able to go back to Japan with your father in a few days. Everyone is leaving the Greenbrier and because you're very contagious, they won't let you on the boat. You're too weak to travel and even if you weren't, they don't want you anywhere near the ambassador."

Emi sat in bed, her eyes and head heavy,

and tried to understand what her mother had said. After months of purgatory, she was still not going home.

"Can I say goodbye to father before they leave?" she asked hoarsely.

"Maybe from a distance," said Keiko, fixing her daughter's white bedding.

"But I can say goodbye to you here?"

"Emiko!" said Keiko, shocked. "I'm not leaving you. I'm going to stay here with you, of course. I would never leave my sick child. What a wild idea."

"I'm twenty years old. I can be on my own," Emi protested with a raspy, weak voice.

"You won't get rid of me so easily," said her mother, reaching for her hand. They both noticed a few specks of blood on Emi's palm and Keiko cleaned it with her handkerchief.

"I suppose there are worse places to spend a few months than the Greenbrier," said Emi, her body feeling heavy and hot. "It's prettier than the last one. What was it called? I can't think; I'm so tired."

"No," said Keiko, looking away from her daughter, at the stoic guard outside the hospital room. "We are not allowed to stay at the hotel without your father. We are being sent away."

"To prison?" said Emi, her eyes closed, her mind drifting away with her pain.

"No," said Keiko. "To Texas."

CHAPTER 3

Christian Lange
January 1943

Christian had arrived at the Children's Home without fanfare. Though he had left his River Hills house in the early morning, he had spent the day at the small FBI office in Milwaukee, alternating between filling out paperwork and sitting idly on a cracked green chair. He had finally been driven to the Home late at night, where a guard took him to a boys' dormitory, told him to go to sleep, and said he would learn more in the morning. He was given a creaky metal bed in a corner and had climbed under the blankets with his clothes still on, afraid to turn on a light. But he slept deeply and undisturbed until he woke up with daylight flooding his eyes, sweat on his chest, and a pain in his abdomen.

He pointed his toes and lay still and quiet. The blanket over him was woolen and thick, the kind that would scratch painfully if not separated by a sheet. His mattress was thin yet lumpy, nothing like home, but at least it felt clean. Christian looked around at the other beds. He was in a room with five other boys. It smelled like it, he thought, putting his hand on his throat to keep himself from coughing from the acrid, sweaty stench of male teenage sleep.

There was something about being an only child that Christian had always found civilized. His closest friend growing up in River Hills, Baxter Novak, had seven brothers and sisters, each louder and rowdier than the next. And though their house with six bedrooms should have been big enough to contain them all, it felt to Christian that there was always a child about to drown in a bathtub or break their leg bounding off the furniture. At night, the few times Christian had agreed to sleep over, it was never so silent you could hear your own heartbeat, like at his house. With ten Novaks in the house, plus him, someone was always awake. There was even a sibling who sleepwalked, plodding straight down the stairs every night.

"Her subconscious probably just wants out of that crowded house," Christian had told his mother one night after he'd sworn to himself that he'd never sleep there again. He was helping Helene make dinner and was washing the salad until it squeaked. "She's probably heading for the front door every time, but all their belongings get in her way."

"Growing up in Germany, I always believed that the rich had few children and the poor had many," Helene had replied. "Or at least that's how it always seemed, and maybe part of the reason why they were richer."

"The Novaks are Catholic," Christian had reminded her, and they'd gone back to preparing dinner, the only noise in the house their knives on the cutting boards and at one point, the sound of his mother giving him a kiss on the cheek, as she was prone to do.

Suddenly, he ached for that peace and quiet and for the assurance of parental love. He let himself turn from his back to his right side so he could take in the room and groaned at the pressure on his already strained bladder. He was thinking desperately about relieving it when he felt a shoe hit his cheek.

"You awake, Adolf?" asked someone with a too-loud voice.

Christian weighed his response before

answering: "I would be, wouldn't I? I was just hit in the face by a shoe." He sat up in bed, the mattress barely doing a thing to keep the coils of the bed from digging into his flesh, and felt sweat inside the waistband of his pants. The shoe had fallen next to him in bed and he picked it up and examined it — light brown leather, with the sole worn deeply on the inside.

"That's *my* shoe. Bring it back here now, kraut. Right away," said the boy, who Christian could tell was significantly smaller than he was, judging by the size of the worn-out Oxford shoe and the short, stocky frame just sticking out of the bedcover halfway across the room.

Because things were already dismal, Christian got out of bed and brought the boy his shoe. He should have thrown it back at him, but he was smart enough to know that he was currently in need of friends. He dropped the shoe on the white iron framed bed, but it bounced off when it hit the shoe thrower's leg. Both of them watched it fall to the floor and neither moved to pick it up.

"And why have you joined us at such an advanced age?" asked the shoe thrower, looking up at his morning's entertainment.

"Not exactly sure," said Christian, shrugging. His bladder was starting to hurt terribly.

"I'm exactly sure," said the shoe thrower, loudly. "You're here because your parents are Nazis. There's one other kraut kid here. A lot younger than you. Sickly looking. Her parents are Nazis, too. Big-time Nazis. Sprinkle baby Jew parts in their cereal."

"Sure they do," said Christian.

"They do. Poor kid. But she's just a pawn in all of this. Like you. 'Course you're older, so who knows? You could be involved in the krauts' plot to take over America. But not her. She cries constantly. Like a starving dog."

The shoe thrower was making no move to get out of bed, even though the boys around them were all standing up and heading out of the bare white room, adorned with nothing but a cross, in the direction of what Christian assumed were the toilets and showers. He wanted badly to follow them, but the shoe thrower was still engaged.

"Want to know what brought me here?" he asked, putting his hands behind his head as if he were lying in a beach chair instead of in the boys' cottage at a children's home.

"Sure, why not?"

"My parents died. Both of them. I've been here for ten years."

"Ten years? Jesus Christ. I'm sorry," Christian said, his eyes still following the other boys.

"Don't lament on my behalf, sauerkraut. I'm almost eighteen, so I'll be getting out of here soon. My birthday is in ten months, five days and —" He turned his head and looked at the black plastic clock on his pine bedside table, identical to the others in the room. "And twenty-three minutes." Behind him snow was falling in large flakes, too wet to turn the ground white, but pretty to watch. Christian could see the small bare trees of an apple orchard beyond their dorm and half-frozen horses with blankets on their backs in another field.

The shoe thrower tossed back his covers and stretched his muscular legs. "Bring any liquor in with you?" he asked with a grin.

"Me?" said Christian, looking at his brown leather bag across the room. The floors were tiled, big and rust colored, and freezing against his feet. "I barely brought a thing with me. Definitely not liquor."

"Then you're useless. Get lost."

Christian felt a burning in his groin and backed away from the shoe thrower suddenly. "I have to . . ." he said.

"You got to use the can? Back there. Hurry up, don't piss near my bed, kraut."

He motioned Christian away and watched as he struggled to make it to the restroom.

Two days later, Christian opened his eyes and saw a low, gray sky, the color of freshly poured concrete. He watched the clouds move across it as fast as airplanes. He couldn't remember why he was on the ground, or where this ground was, but his mind felt pleasantly fuzzy. Then he saw Jack Walter's face come into view, leaning down until his fat pink ear was almost on Christian's nose. Suddenly he remembered exactly where he was. He was at the Milwaukee Children's Home, and Jack Walter, the shoe thrower, had just knocked him out with one punch. But it was a sucker punch, so it didn't count. Where he was from, people didn't walk up to you with a smile and then deck you with all of their weight behind their right fist.

Christian held his breath, sure that Jack was checking whether he was dead or not, and then when he saw the look of panic spreading on Jack's face, he lunged up and bit his ear.

"You feral son of a bitch!" Jack screamed, losing his balance and falling onto the frozen ground himself. "You bit off my ear!"

"Me?" said Christian, standing up and trying to ignore the cloudy pain in his skull.

"You just punched me for no reason. Is that what you do around here? You just punch people in the face and then place bets to see if they have a concussion or not?"

"No, but that's a good idea," said Jack, holding his bloody ear. "You'll be dead soon enough, kraut. Just like your parents. I'm just trying to speed things along."

"This is Wisconsin. My parents aren't getting beaten in some cell till they bleed out."

"Think what you want. *I* think the feds would have shoved you on some relative if they thought your parents were coming back. But instead of cohabiting with a fat aunt, you're here. I bet you hear the death knell soon, just like them."

"For a boys' home bruiser, you've got quite a vocabulary," said Christian, brushing off his coat and battling a rush of nausea. Though he knew he should hate Jack Walter, there was something about him that he liked. Maybe it was that he offered distraction, or that although he liked to throw shoes and punches, he also liked to be around Christian, and he was the only one at the Home who did.

"You're grim," said Christian, his ears still ringing. They both let their ailments settle and turned their attention to some of the older girls sitting in the field just a few yards away, close enough to watch the boys fight, far enough away that they didn't feel the need to stop them.

"I've slept with all of them," said Jack, giving a wave in their direction.

"Sure you have," said Christian smiling as they made retching sounds at Jack.

"I have," said Jack. "Okay, most of them. The pretty ones definitely, which after a few drinks is all of them. Actually, I lost my virginity not far from where we're sitting. I'm surprised there hasn't been an earthquake since. All that . . . passion," he said laughing.

"When was that?" asked Christian, who felt a slight surge of jealousy that someone in a children's home had lost their virginity and he hadn't. "Yesterday?"

"Years ago," said Jack, his laugh stopping abruptly. He pointed to a field behind them and said, "The Home sits right on the Monarch Trail. As in butterflies. They fly through the tall grasses all around the Home and then stop, as much as a butterfly can stop. Thousands come, all right here, next to these buildings, covering acres and acres. But they're smart enough not to stay in Wisconsin. They're flying from Canada to Mexico. It's really beautiful. Maybe you'll be here long enough to see it," he said, stretching his wide calloused hands up to the sky.

"Maybe," said Christian.

"It's during the summer," said Jack. "It's the best part of the summer."

"So you made love to a butterfly," said Christian, trying to keep his head still.

"No," said Jack, still looking up and smiling at the memory. "I made love to a beautiful girl. Patricia Talbot. She looked like she was made of corn and rain, just a pretty Wisconsin girl. And we decided that the first time we should have sex was when the butterflies were migrating, flying all around our naked bodies. Because if we couldn't leave, at least we could be surrounded by creatures who fly. Who are completely free." He closed his eyes and said, "It was the best day of my life."

"What happened to Patricia Talbot?" asked Christian. "Can I take her off your hands?"

"If you can find her," said Jack. "She was adopted. Fourteen and adopted. Doesn't happen often, but like I said, she was really pretty. Some woman adopted her whose daughter had been around the same age when she died. I never heard from her again. I'm not mad at her for it. She'd been here since she was six because her parents decided they had too many kids to feed. Just dropped her off like she hadn't lived with them for six years. Washed their hands of her. I hope she never sees them again. Or this place. Or even me."

"The butterflies sound nice," said Christian. "Kind of stupid, but nice."

"No, said Jack, grinning again. "It was amazing."

"I could use some amazing," said Christian.

"Don't hold your breath," said Jack. "Because if your parents are in prison," he said sitting up next to him, "bad times are ahead for you, kraut. First, your house will be looted. They'll take everything, down to your mother's underwear."

"My house in River Hills?" said Christian, hugging his knees into his chest, hoping it would ease his need to vomit, which had just hit him more sharply. "Everyone there is already rich."

"So what? You think the River Hills rich are above greed?" said Jack. "The rich are the worst kind of criminals, because they don't need anything but they take it anyway. Trust me, you're getting looted. Hope you're not too attached to your stuff. Bet you had some nice things; you've got that rich boy smell." He wrinkled his stubby nose. "I can smell River Hills on you. I should punch you again just for being from there."

"You smell like a thief," said Christian, grabbing Jack's right hand and squeezing it until Jack couldn't move his arm. "You want my address? You can go and loot it yourself. Bring your magical butterflies with you."

He let go of Jack's hand, the effort of twisting it only making him feel worse. This time he was sure he was going to be sick.

"No, thank you," said Jack, flapping his bruised wrist. "I like my things brand-new. Even the things I steal."

"How discerning of you," said Christian before vomiting.

Though Christian suffered through his first week at the Children's Home, getting sucker punched and going to the infirmary with a concussion (thanks to Jack Walter's right cross), he did not break down to the extent he'd feared.

It was the staunch belief that his parents were innocent that kept him from folding into himself. They would be questioned and tried, but then they would be let go, with an apology. He was sure he'd be leaving the Home within a week.

Lying in bed, Christian imagined his parents thinking about him. It comforted him to envisage their worries and prayers meeting somewhere in the air in Milwaukee, knotting together, because they were suffering at the same time.

After dinner at their long dining table, which was sectioned off by age, Jack came up and stuck out his leg to trip him, but pulled it back when Christian went to pin it down with his foot. The boys around them pushed back their plastic chairs and stood to see if a fight would break out.

"Let me say it for you, so you don't have to bother," Christian said. " 'Get out of here, dirty kraut.' "

"That's right!" said Jack, laughing and hurrying to catch up with him. "Listen, you dirty kraut, I'm sorry I gave you a concussion. I was just trying to present you with the gift of a little shiner to remember your time here by. I guess I don't know my own strength. I have grand plans to become a boxer, or a philosopher, when I get out of here. What I won't do is end up dead in the war. Not for me an early death. That's just for you."

"Forget it," said Christian, ignoring Jack's death sentence and thinking only about how Jack had ten months left in the place and no one to go home to.

As Jack had mentioned on Christian's first

day, he wasn't the only one whose parents had been arrested for un-American activities. There was also Inge Anders, the most nervous little girl to ever sleep on the other side of the orphanage.

When they were all outside a few days later shoveling snow after Christian was allowed to resume physical activities, Jack called out to a thin girl wearing a boy's winter coat. She was playing with other children in a pile of insect-infested firewood in front of the administration building. The building itself was quite beautiful, as the orphanage had originally been built as a college. The words over the door frame spelled out "administration" in Gothic letters, as inviting as one could hope for an orphanage. Christian's eyes moved up from the children to the steeply sloped roof and the rows of rectangular windows below them, their thick panes divided into squares. It was a much more attractive building from the outside than in.

"Hey, little kraut! Come over here," Jack yelled to the girl. "I've got another kraut for you to meet. Still a kraut, just a bigger one."

Inge hesitated for a moment, then dropped the wood she was holding and ran over. She stopped right in front of Christian, her big green eyes fixed on him, her brown hair falling out of the hood of her coat in messy curls.

"This is him," said Jack. "I told you about him before, when you were crying yet again. Christian. He speaks German like you. And some English, too."

"Bist du Deutscher?" Inge said, her mouth quivering and her little hands pulling at her hood. She looked as if just a small gust of wind could knock her down and pull the tears out of her.

"Ja, ich bin Deutscher. Amerikaner, aber meine Eltern sind Deutsche," he explained. I am American, but my parents are German.

"Are your parents going to die, too?" she asked.

"No. They're not going to die. Do you think your parents are going to die?" Christian looked at Jack, sure that he had fed her that worry.

"I don't want my mother to die!" she screamed, her tears the exclamation point to her yell.

Christian was going to ask about her father — didn't she want him to live, too? — but Inge threw her skinny arms around him, lost in her big coat, her head coming just above his waist, and kept crying.

Surprised, Christian left his arms rigidly by his sides until Jack shouted, "Hey, hug the poor little kraut!"

"No one is going to die," Christian said, finally hugging her back. "They're questioning lots of people's parents, not just yours and mine. There's no reason to worry."

"Are they questioning Jack's parents?" she asked.

"Jack doesn't have parents," Christian said quickly.

That made her cry even harder.

"But what if my parents did something bad?" she asked, whimpering and holding on to Christian. "Something bad enough so that the men want to kill them?"

"Are your parents in the Bund?" asked Christian, wondering why she was wearing a boy's overcoat. He imagined that they had dragged her out of her house with very few of her things. She was too small to spend hours alone as he had. Maybe it was the same agents who had done it to him, fat Smith and pompous Jakobsson.

"What is the Bund?" she asked, looking up at him with wet eyes.

"Never mind. If you don't know what it is, then that's probably a good sign." He put his hand on her hood and noticed how little her head was. "How old are you, Inge?"

"Seven and a half," she said.

"Was there no family for you to go stay

with instead of coming here?" he asked, feeling sorry for her even if he didn't feel comfortable consoling her.

She started to cry again, and Jack punched him in the shoulder.

"No one wanted me," she said through sobs. "Auntie Aleit and Uncle Heinz are in Germany, and Mama and Papa's friends said no."

"Of course people wanted you," said Christian. He looked up at Jack, who appeared to be debating whether to hit Christian again.

"I didn't used to be here. I was with Mama," Inge explained. "They took Papa somewhere, and then they took me and Mama to a home in Milwaukee. It was full of nuns."

"Sounds like a convent," said Christian.

"That's what it was. A convent."

"And why aren't you there anymore?"

"They made me leave," she said. "They said Mama had turned crazy and it was dangerous for me to be there. They said I couldn't stay with my Mama, and one of the nuns, she took me here in a car that smelled like a dog."

Christian looked at Jack, who was spinning his finger next to his head to indicate Inge's mother's state of mind.

"I don't want my mother to die!" Inge started screaming. "No! No, no!"

"No one is going to die," Christian said.

He picked Inge up and, with Jack, brought her back inside the big brick administration building, where the youngest children slept. He stood outside the cramped director's office with her head against his shoulder, not daring to move until she had calmed down. When her breath was regulated and she had fallen asleep, he dropped her off with the sympathetic warden of the girls' side of the home.

After that, Inge followed Christian like a shadow.

CHAPTER 4

Christian Lange
February–March 1943

Despite their violent first encounter, Jack Walter and Christian became fast friends, their relationship founded on daily fistfights and insults. Almost everyone Jack had been close to for the last ten years had aged out of the Home, for as soon as a boy turned eighteen, he was gone before the candles on the cake could be blown out. And now Jack had just months left himself until it was his turn to live on his own. Christian Lange and his trials were a welcome distraction from his countdown, but it didn't last long. After a month and a half at the Milwaukee Children's Home, Christian finally got news of his parents.

"Sit down, please," said Mr. Braque, the head of the Home, pushing aside a pile of books and yellowing newspapers to make room for Christian in his office. Everything about Braque was gray — his eyes, his hair, the pallor of his skin — but his gentle demeanor made the children forget about his dusty coating. "What a trial you have gone through these past weeks, knowing nothing of your parents' whereabouts. Of course, every child here has their own cross to bear, but I have been thinking about you often, Mr. Lange, and I'm happy to say that you now have a destination beyond our old walls."

"I do? Do you know where my parents are, then? Where have they been?" Christian asked, letting the emotion he had been repressing for seven weeks rise up in his throat, making him croak out his words. He had thought of them without pause, but he'd barely talked about it. Except for Jack, the boys his age didn't bother to make friends with someone whose time at the Home was limited. And with Jack, he didn't feel it was right to dwell on his sad story, since Jack's circumstances had been much harder. So all of Christian's worry had stayed coiled inside his gut.

"Your parents, I am told, were both questioned, tried, and then sent from Milwaukee to a prison in Stringtown, Oklahoma." Braque spoke as he continued to clear his desk and chairs, placing his reading materials on the ground, as the floor-to-ceiling bookshelves were already overflowing. The room was barely bigger than a bathroom, and with all the files on the children housed there, too, it could barely accommodate Braque and one visitor. "If you're bad in pairs they have to yell at you in the cafeteria," Jack had told Christian when they had indeed been yelled at together for fighting.

"A prison? So they were found guilty? Why would they send them so far away?" Christian asked, following Braque with his eyes as he bobbed around the small room.

"The prison, from what I was told, is no longer a prison but a housing center for people like your parents. But they are not staying in Oklahoma much longer. They're going to South Texas, and you'll be leaving us tomorrow to join them." He reached in his pocket for a handkerchief and dusted the crucifix on the wall before turning around to gauge Christian's reaction.

"Texas?" asked Christian, trying to hold himself together. He stood up, his foot slipping on a newspaper that, like all of them, had a headline about the war. "Why would I need to go there?"

"You're being sent to a place called Crystal City," Braque said. "They told me it's an internment camp, but a family internment camp, where children and their parents can be together."

"We're being interned?" asked Christian, addressing Braque, who had finally sat down. "Like the Japanese?"

Braque let Christian have a moment and then cleared his throat and continued. "It's important to note that you will be going to Crystal City as a voluntary internee. Your parents were forced to go there, but technically you are volunteering to go there. Or more precisely, your parents are volunteering you. But you don't have the option to say no, unfortunately, because you are still a minor. So once you are inside the camp, you can't leave again until they release you. You're essentially a prisoner. From what I know, based on other camps, they're not too much better than a prison. Of course there are nicer accommodations and fresh air, but there are barbed-wire fences, watchtowers, men patrolling with guns."

"Guns? Like they're going to shoot me?"

"No, they're not going to —"

"Why would my parents subject me to that?" Christian interrupted. "Why won't they let me stay here until I turn eighteen?"

"I'm not sure," said Braque, looking at Christian's desperate face. He handed him the handkerchief that he had just dusted the crucifix with. "But I can think of one good reason why."

"I can't," said Christian, thinking that, all of a sudden, getting shoes thrown at him in Milwaukee sounded like a vacation.

"Well, I imagine," said Braque, "it's because they love you."

The only person who saw Christian off from the Children's Home was Jack. And he wasn't seeing just Christian off, but Inge, too. She was also headed to Crystal City, and Christian had been tasked with making sure she got there safely. They hadn't left the Home yet and her hand was already in his, holding on tighter than a child on a roller coaster.

"This is for you," said Jack, giving Christian his shoe as they stood outside the boys' cottage, their faces red from the cold. "You can hit yourself in the face with it at night to remind yourself of the good times."

"Your shoe?" said Christian. "I can't."

"Sure you can. I may be a sad orphan, but I'm due to get another pair. My big toes can't breathe in those, and Braque owes me at least that for babysitting you."

Christian took the shoe from Jack, tying a knot at the end of the frayed lace, and put it in his traveling bag. "I'll take it if you promise me one thing. You'll like it, I swear."

"Try me."

"When you're out of here, can you go to my house and see if there's anything left? If there is, maybe change the locks?" He reached into his coat and handed Jack Walter his house key. "Nine thousand River Road."

"There's not going to be anything left in your house."

"Maybe not, but check for me, okay? Sleep there if you want, while you sort out your non–Children's Home life."

Jack nodded and took the key. "If you haven't been looted, then I'm the man for the job. I'll sleep right in your parents' bed, pretend I'm the mayor."

" 'Course you will," said Christian. "And will you write to me in that awful place? Something like, 'Hey kraut, you're probably going to die soon.' "

Jack laughed his good-natured laugh and agreed. "Yes. But only because I have absolutely nothing else to do but count down the days until my eighteenth birthday and punch anyone new who comes into my room."

Jack gave Christian a fake, slow punch to the jaw and waved goodbye. It was the kind of stiff wave a boy who was always being left was used to giving: devoid of emotion but jovial enough to show that he wasn't being tortured at the Children's Home.

It wasn't until Christian was at the station with the Home's assistant headmaster, Mr. Klimek, that he was told anything about his trip. Maybe Braque had not wanted to scare him with details, but Klimek had no such qualms. He was the least liked person at the Home, and all the students made sure he knew it. It wasn't that he had ever done anything truly menacing; he just didn't have the right personality for children, especially children desperate for stand-in parents.

"Crystal City, Texas," said Klimek, leaning against the station wall, his right leg up and slightly bent, the way they always described detectives posing in the radio shows. "Braque told me about it. Little shit town near Mexico with scorpions on every block. How much did he tell you?"

Christian squinted at him and said, "Nothing."

"Wanted to spare you the truth. I don't see it that way. I think you should know what you're getting into. Mexicans everywhere. They hate whites down there. Especially German ones. But don't worry too much, son, your parents will be there, too, so you won't suffer alone."

Christian looked down at Inge to see if she was listening. Her hand was still attached to his, but her mind seemed to be elsewhere and her eyes, usually big as a doll's, were closed.

"I almost forgot. You have to wear this," said Klimek, taking an identification tag out of his pocket and giving it to Christian. He gave him Inge's, as well, and stood back as Christian inspected them and put hers in her hand.

"It's got to be around your necks on a piece of string," he corrected him, pointing at Christian's collar.

Christian stared at him. "You got string?" he asked.

"Why would I have string?"

Christian kept looking at him, to see if he was kidding, his hand starting to hurt from the pressure Inge was putting on it.

"Don't just stare at me and do nothing. You best figure something out for you and the girl. Quickly," Klimek warned. "It was an INS agent who gave them to me. He had a gun and everything. Bet the train will be crawling with them and I wouldn't want to get on their wrong side by not having your tag on a string. Pretty simple request that you can't seem to follow."

Instead of arguing, or asking how he

should have intuited that he bring string, Christian reached into his bag and took out Jack's shoe. He took Inge's tag and tied each end of the lace to a little hole on either side. He leaned down, took the shoelace out of one of his own shoes, and did the same thing. On Inge, the tag fell where it should, but his barely made it around his neck.

Once the tags were straightened, Klimek reached out his hand for Christian's and gave it a firm shake. "Could be worse, kid," he said with a forced smile. "And don't forget all your friends at the Home."

"Right. I won't. Thanks," said Christian, thinking of everyone but Klimek.

"I'll wait until you are both safely on. But you better go talk to the agents now and figure out the details. You're almost eighteen. You should start doing these things on your own."

Christian wanted to remind Klimek that he had only been at the Home for seven weeks, and not for ten years, but he held back. He was aware that he was far more babied by his mother than any of the children at the Home had been by Klimek or even the kindly Braque.

He wasn't sure if it was the shoe constantly thrown against his cheek, Jack's fist against his nose, or his concussion, but he knew that the punches he endured in the Home had done him some good. Tucked in between the snoring of orphans, Christian had realized how much his parents coddled him. He knew they doted on him, but he hadn't fully understood the extent of it, since that was the norm in River Hills. Perhaps now, Christian thought, he was more prepared to be a man who fended for himself, who might one day make love under a canopy of monarch butterflies and whose spirit didn't break from having to share a room with others. Even someone like Jack Walter.

On the train platform were other children, all with mothers, who were going to the camp, too. Christian stopped and asked one of the mothers whom he should speak to before he boarded the train, and she pointed to a young man flirting with one of the teenage daughters about to be shipped off.

"He doesn't seem to mind her German background, does he?" she said, holding her own little boy by the hand.

Christian shrugged and headed over to the agent, who looked barely older than he did.

"Names," said the agent, his brown hair glued to his head with so much pomade that it resisted the winter wind like a helmet.

He looked right at their name tags but

waited for Christian to say their names.

"How old are you?" he asked Christian after checking his list.

"I'm seventeen. Doesn't it say so there?"

"Yeah, it does. I was just hoping you'd lie and say eighteen so I wouldn't have to check on you two the entire train ride down." He flipped the pages of his list back over. "But I guess you didn't think about me, did you? Fine. You don't have seat assignments, but you'll be in car twelve. It's full of mother hens, so I won't bother to check on you very often. Just make sure that she," he said, pointing at Inge, "gets to San Antonio looking happier than that." He looked down at Inge's tear-and-mucus-streaked face disapprovingly.

Christian said he'd do his best and moved down the train.

"Will you sit with me? The whole time?" Inge asked. "I don't want to be alone. Not for one second. Will you stay with me? Do you promise? Say promise."

"I promise," Christian said with a compassion that surprised him.

In front of car 12, it was the same scene as in front of car 4: women and children, and INS agents wrangling them. They all wore tags that had been affixed with string instead of shoelaces. No one had boarded yet, and Christian could no longer see Klimek, who he was sure had gone back to the Home the second they were out of his sight.

Christian tried to make small talk with Inge, but she was more interested in crying than talking, so they stood there, letting themselves slowly freeze from the toes up. After fifteen minutes, their breath was forming clouds so thick they lingered in front of them like cigarette smoke before dissipating, and Christian's hands, his right still intertwined with Inge's bare left one, had gone numb.

"Sorry we don't have gloves," said Christian. "Braque asked us to leave them for the other children since we're going to Texas. We won't need them there. It's very hot."

"I didn't have gloves anyway," Inge admitted. "I did when I arrived, but I traded them to Nadia Sitko for her jelly bears."

Christian was going to ask what a jelly bear was and how Nadia Sitko had smuggled them into the Home, but Inge's lip was already wobbling.

When an INS agent finally directed them to, they boarded the train, which smelled like sweat even though it was still empty and 26 degrees outside.

Inge and Christian were the only ones not

laden down with suitcases and trunks, so for the first hour they just sat and watched the chaos, trying to stay out of the way, sitting tightly together on the dirty cloth seats. Women screamed in German at their children, who ran through the train banging into the luggage and each other. Before anyone was settled, the train was well out of Milwaukee, heading southwest for the trip through Illinois, Missouri, Arkansas, and then into East Texas before turning due south.

For another hour, Inge continued to sit next to Christian, not talking, not answering him anymore, but still holding his hand tightly. Then, finally, when they were approaching Springfield, Illinois, and the still beauty of Lake Michigan was far behind them, she leaned over and fell asleep against his shoulder. She would stay like that for the next three hours, her mouth slightly open, her head bobbing off him only to be placed gently back on by Christian's careful hands.

As the landscape turned from snowy and wet to just cold and then less cold, Christian's thoughts returned to how easy his life had been until then. He'd been preternaturally good at everything a teenager in Wisconsin needed to be good at. He was book-smart enough, but not too smart to draw attention, he drove a nice car that he worked on with his dad even when it didn't need work, he excelled in sports, and he was very well liked by girls and their mothers. And because of the success of Franz Lange, usually by their fathers, too.

But the way he was driven out of town by FBI agents — it had changed everything. He knew that people in River Hills now believed that his parents had been arrested as foreign enemies, which meant he was implicated as well.

He was only a semester away from graduating from high school and had plans to attend the University of Wisconsin and maybe walk on to their football team. He was going to apply in the spring, knowing that he'd be accepted handily. His father had been donating money to the football team for years, and Christian's grades were strong enough even without his father's money. But now, college seemed out of reach. Would he even be allowed in after the country had declared him an enemy?

He tried to let his confidence in his parents' innocence rock him back to sleep, but halfway through Missouri he heard the word, and he knew sleep would evade him for hours.

Hitler. It was said once, and then five minutes later he heard it again. Then again. The conversation was in German, but he could understand it perfectly.

"There will be many who support the Führer there."

"I know," said a woman diagonally across the aisle from him while her very young children climbed all over the seats. "My husband is one of them. He was able to write to me and said that when Fritz Kuhn is released from prison, if there is still war, he will be transferred to Crystal City, too."

Christian had known who Fritz Kuhn was before the FBI agents had accused his father of writing to him. He was the head of the German American Bund. Christian first heard him on the radio when he spoke at Madison Square Garden in 1939. He had dubbed President Roosevelt's New Deal "the Jew Deal." Franz, listening with him, had described Kuhn as one of the biggest idiots that Germany had ever produced. "And we have produced plenty," he remembered his father saying. Since his speech at the Garden, Kuhn had been arrested and imprisoned for embezzlement and tax evasion and the Bund had lost the following it had in the late 1930s. But that was not the case for everyone, it seemed.

Christian tried to ignore the conversation as he looked out on the America he had never seen. The train's speed transformed it into brilliant streaks before his eyes.

At night when the children were quiet and Christian could hear only the mothers' rhythmic breathing and the train's thundering wheels, he let the fear of what lay ahead of him set in. He squeezed Inge's little hand, this time letting her comfort him. If a child of seven and a half can endure all this, then I better be able to, he thought to himself. But then the sun came up and the babies started to cry for food, and he suddenly felt not very different from them.

After thirty-one hours of travel, the train was seventy miles outside San Antonio and the landscape was bone-dry. This was winter in a part of the planet where the soil felt like sand between your fingers and the air lay hot and dense in your lungs.

"I don't like it here," said Inge, when she finally woke up. She pressed her snub nose flat against the glass. "It's all the same color. It looks like a place that will make me sneeze."

"I don't like it, either," said Christian, as the world they knew went out of focus for good.

"Give the little one this candy," said the

woman who had been talking about Hitler, offering a slightly melted butterscotch in a foil wrapper. "She is your sister?"

"Yes," said Inge, before Christian could say no. She reached out and grabbed the candy, shoving it in her mouth. Christian nudged her, and she got up to give the woman a hug of thanks.

For the last thirty minutes, Christian wrestled with his own anxiety while he tried to persuade Inge there was nothing to worry about.

And then it was over. They were in Texas, and the doors opened with a loud, tired groan onto the San Antonio train station. Christian looked out the window, with Inge peeking out from behind him. Together, they saw that the platform was packed with American men in uniform.

"Are they all here for us?" she asked, climbing over his knees.

"They can't be," said Christian, trying not to stare at the men, who all seemed to be around his age. Instead of the exhaustion and dread that were caked onto Christian's face, they appeared buoyed by the glamour of the uniform, the heroics of war, perhaps even the probable death that was looming for them.

"Follow me," an agent said, nudging

108

Christian's foot with his own. He ushered them off the train and told them to walk as fast as they could, giving Inge a firm push forward when she paused to look at the stained-glass windows of the station.

"I want to see my mother," she said, startled.

"You will. She's going to be waiting for you," said the agent.

They passed the soldiers, who eyed them suspiciously, and were hustled to a parking lot.

"If these soldiers find out all these broads are Germans, they'll harass them all the way out the gate," he heard one INS agent say to another. In the distance Christian could see an Army bus and people standing in front of it.

"Wait here. Your parents are coming," the guard told them, but Inge was already off and running.

Christian could see his mother, one of two women in the group of fathers. She'd grown visibly pregnant instead of just soft around the middle. She beckoned for him to run to her, and without thinking, he did.

"You're finally here! My baby. My always baby. They promised me you were in good hands at that orphanage in Milwaukee, but I cried myself to sleep over it every night," she said, her arms tight around him. "Were you okay? Do you promise me you were all right? No one tried to hurt you?" Christian thought about his concussion and the shoe thrown at his head with a pitcher's gusto every day and said that he was fine.

"But I wish they had let me go with you instead," he said, relaxing into his mother's hug. "Was it awful where you were? Were you with Dad?"

"All that is for another day," she said. "You're safe, and you're here with me. That's all it takes for me to feel happy again." She let her son go and explained that she and Inge's mother had shared their worry night after night. "But I knew you would take care of the little girl on the train. That's the kind of heart you have. I told Elke Anders that you would."

"That's him, there," Christian heard Inge saying behind him in German. "Big kraut. He held my hand for two days on the train and only let go when I asked him to because someone gave me a candy."

"Don't say kraut!" her mother replied, shocked.

"Jack Walter said I am little kraut and Christian is big kraut and now that we are gone from the Home there is no kraut left, so who will he call kraut?"

Her mother smacked her hand and told her never to say that word again. Then she walked over to Christian and threw her arms around him the way his own mother had just done. With her thick brown hair and thin frame, she looked like a movie star in shabby clothing.

"You are an angel, Christian Lange. Inge's angel," she said, in tears. "Helene, your boy . . ." She touched his face. "I'm so thankful."

"I was happy to watch her," said Christian, who was soon transferred from her arms back to his mother's arms. "She gave me something to think about on the trip."

"How are you feeling?" he asked his mother as they all made their way onto the bus.

"I'm tired. My back is sore. But without you here, it's been this baby who has kept my sanity."

Since the night the agents had come to the house, Christian had grown even more thankful for the baby. At first, he'd been shocked, and distressed at what a baby might do to the calm of their lives, but now he appreciated the hope it was giving his parents. Something good for the Langes, despite what was happening outside the womb.

"What's the camp like?" he heard Inge ask her mother as they settled onto the old bus's vinyl-covered bench seats.

"Oh, it's all right, *Schätzen*. There's a swimming pool and lots of other children to play with. You'll like that. And since it's so warm here, you can start swimming very soon."

"Like summer camp," Inge said, smiling.

"Yes, *Schätzen*. That's what it's like. Summer camp in March."

CHAPTER 5

Emi Kato
August 1942–March 1943

Norio had explained to Keiko that as much as the Japanese Embassy had pleaded with the U.S. State Department, the Americans would not let her and Emi stay at the Greenbrier hotel alone. The American government was removing all their staff — the FBI agents, the State Department employees — from West Virginia as soon as the Japanese diplomats sailed in June. The only place where Emi and Keiko could go besides prison was an internment camp. And the government had decided that they'd be going to a largely female camp in Texas.

"But why can't we just go back to our apartment in Washington?" a very weakened Emi asked her mother from her hospital bed.

"Your father said it's not an option. They don't trust us to be there without surveillance. We have to go to one of these camps."

"But what is an internment camp exactly?" Emi's chest still felt like there was a hot iron on it and despite the nurses' constant doses of medicine and fluid, she was still coughing up blood at night. Her breathing was very labored and she couldn't walk to the bathroom without having to stop to rest — how was she going to make it to Texas?

"I don't know what an internment camp is precisely," said Keiko, "but I know that the Japanese-Americans are being sent to them. Whatever it is, it won't be for long. And we won't leave until you're better. That they promised me."

A week later, Emi was told that her father would be coming to the hospital but that he wasn't permitted to be in the same room as her. He would stand outside the building and she would be allowed to wave at him from her window.

They waved for ten minutes, Emi crying as she held up a piece of paper that read, *ai shiteru, otōsan.* I love you, father.

"What if he doesn't make it back to Japan? What if the boat is bombed? This will be the last time I ever saw him, through an American hospital window. Not even able to touch his hand," said Emi through her

114

coughs and sobs.

"Don't think that way," said Keiko, with tears in her eyes. "Do not let war — or illness — turn you into a pessimist."

"I don't think war is producing many optimists, Mother," said Emi, watching her father get into a car.

After one month in the hospital, the women were told that Emi was healthy enough for them to travel to the internment camp in Seagoville, Texas. They were assured that it would be a short stay and that they would soon head to Japan and be reunited with their family.

The Kato women were used to long journeys, but they'd had the luck of always doing so when they were healthy. While Emi was no longer contagious, she still needed to take medicine for six more months and was a very weakened version of herself on their train ride down to Texas. The government officials had toyed with letting them travel to Texas alone, without FBI accompaniment, but in the end, they sent a sullen agent with them. In healthier times, the presence of the man would have bothered her immensely, being treated like a criminal when it was only her place of birth that was the problem, but Emi was barely awake for the entire journey. She absorbed the noises and the smells — children complaining about the hard bench seats, women eating noodle salad and days-old rice — but her eyes stayed closed, as her mother's hand rested on her forehead, monitoring her temperature.

When they finally arrived at the camp, the first thing they both noticed was the barbed wire surrounding the buildings.

"But the buildings themselves are not bad looking," said Keiko, smiling at her weak daughter. "It looks like an American college."

Emi stared at the long two- and three-level brick buildings that seemed to have grown out of the earth, as there was nothing else for miles around them but dirt, a water tower, and some dry, browning shrubs.

"If you say so," said Emi, following a man in a sand-colored cowboy hat who worked at Seagoville and was barking orders at them.

Emi spent the first two weeks of their time in Seagoville in and out of sleep, still fighting the illness that had grounded them in the United States. On their fifteenth night there, her fever spiked, but by the next morning she had a clear head and a clear chest and was able to walk around the camp for the first time.

"I hate it here," Emi declared, sitting on her creaky twin-sized bed in their tiny stark room after her mother had taken her on a tour of the camp.

"I don't think you're supposed to like it," said Keiko, sitting on her bed, which was less than three feet away from Emi's.

"What a small, unpleasant room," said Emi. "I'm glad I've been asleep for two weeks. Do we know how much longer we're here for?"

"Your father and the embassy staff are doing their best to get us on the next boat to Japan. But it's not as easy as it sounds. We have to travel with others who are repatriating. Thousands of others. We can't just row there on our own, can we?" Keiko smoothed and folded her clothes, though they were already neatly folded and placed on the only shelf in the room.

"Have I received any letters from Leo?" Emi asked. "You did send him our address before we left the hospital? You promised you would."

"Yes, I did," said Keiko. "But like I told you at the Homestead and at the Greenbrier, America has cut off mail exchanges with many countries. That must be the reason that the last letter you received from Leo was just after Pearl Harbor. And it's a miracle that it made it through. You're lucky it arrived at the embassy — and that Leo had the foresight to mail it there — before we were all sent away."

"But perhaps when we are back in Japan?" said Emi, reaching under her pillow for an old letter from Leo that she had received the month before the Pearl Harbor attack. "Then our letters might reach each other?"

"Perhaps," said Keiko, placing her clothes back on her shelf.

Emi coughed again, her lungs rattling, and shook her head in disgust as she watched her mother try to occupy her time. "If I hadn't fallen ill, we would already be back in Japan. Instead we are in a women's correctional facility in awful Texas."

"Internment camp," her mother corrected her.

"The irony of that term!" Emi exclaimed, pushing her own unfolded clothes onto the floor. "Camp. Like someone would choose to be here so they might do a spot of canoeing."

"Emi, quiet down," said Keiko. "You're not well yet. Listen to your voice. You don't even sound like yourself. And this acting out. It's not like you, either."

"I heard you," said Emi, her face defiant. "You thought I was asleep, but I heard you speaking to the woman next door. Setsuko something. She said that this camp, Seagoville, used to be a minimum-security federal prison. Then they just ripped down that sign and replaced it with one that said internment camp. So technically, we're being jailed. We are in a prison."

"Emi, you should be onstage. Truly," said Keiko, shaking her head at her child. "Are you really sick, or have you just been pretending to sleep for two weeks so you can eavesdrop on my conversations?"

"Why are there so many women from South America?" Emi asked, ignoring her mother's criticism. "Setsuko said she was from Peru. Why are they interned? It sounds like they weren't even in this country until a few weeks ago."

"They're going to exchange them for Americans in Japan," said Keiko. "They all will be sailing to Japan, too. Probably with us."

"But that's quite odd, isn't it?" said Emi. "They don't even live in America. Why should they be punished because the United States and Japan are at war?"

Keiko motioned for her daughter to move over in her little bed and sat down next to her, straightening her thin pillows.

"I don't know," said Keiko. "I really don't

understand a thing of all this. But we are here now and what's important is that you're healthier. We just have to endure, Emi. We will be home very soon."

"Endure," spat Emi. "We have to endure because the Americans are afraid we'll turn into spies. Dangerous dragon women."

"Enough, Emi!" said her mother sternly, standing up and leaving her daughter alone in the room.

Emi spent the next few months at Seagoville trying to get her strength back: forcing herself to go on long walks around the camp, eating all the meals — as unappetizing as they were — and adapting to the Texas heat.

She had started to resign herself to the fact that they might be stuck in Seagoville for more than a few months, and though she remained guarded and sullen, she fell into the routine of the camp — the constant roll calls, the hours spent with her eyes closed, the ability to tolerate boredom.

"Your daughter has fence sickness," she had heard her mother's neighbor, and now friend, Setsuko say one morning. "Outside of camp, we would call it depression. Have you noticed how she barely eats? She's even thinner than when she arrived. She doesn't participate in any of the activities or sports;

she just stays here and sleeps or wanders around the periphery of the camp alone. You should be more concerned, Keiko," Setsuko advised.

"I've tried to encourage different behavior," her mother had said, "but she refuses. In here, she wants to be a ghost. I'm just happy that she's healthy again, so I let her. Maybe I'm being too tolerant."

"You are," said Setsuko, slowly closing the door. "The depression could stay with her longer than she's in here."

Emi grumbled and turned around in bed, her eyes still shut. She wouldn't be depressed when she left the hell she'd been placed in. She would be herself again. But until then, living as a ghost suited her just fine.

In March 1943, when the heat of Texas was starting to fire up again, Emi and her mother were woken up by an INS patrol guard. He came into their room, which they were sure was forbidden for male guards. The very young agent was wearing his beige uniform with pride and holding a clipboard against his thin chest in a commanding way.

"Is this the room of . . . I mean are you . . . ?"

"Yes?" said Keiko, coming toward the door of their small room, a blanket held over her nightgown.

"Are you Keiko Kato?" he asked, pronouncing both her first and last name incorrectly.

"Yes, I am," she replied politely. "I'm Keiko Kato and this is my daughter, Emiko Kato," she said smiling at Emi, still in bed. "Is there something wrong?"

"Nothing wrong," he said, moving back to the door frame when he saw that the floor near Emi's bed was covered in her clothes, including a slip. "Just here to report that you're both being transferred," he said looking down at his sheet.

"To Japan?" asked Emi excitedly. "Finally!" She sat up in bed, not caring if the guard saw her in her nightgown.

"No. To Crystal City," he clarified. "New camp just built 'bout six hours southwest. Right on the Mexican border. Bet you can even see the line from there."

"I don't think it's an actual li—"

"But why on earth?" said Keiko, silencing her insolent daughter and walking over to the man, dropping the blanket on the floor. "We've been here for seven months already. Why move us now? Surely we will be heading to Japan soon."

"All the families with children are being transferred to that camp. Built specially as a family camp and it just opened up to the Japanese. There've been Germans there a few months now." He looked down at his clipboard and pointed. "Says here that you, Keiko Kato, have a child named Emiko Kato, age one. That you?" he asked looking at Emi.

"Do I look like I'm *one*?" she said angrily. "I'm *twenty*-one."

"Right," he said reading his paperwork again, rearranging the pages. "Still looks like you're going. This comes from Washington so there's no reason to argue. When it comes from up high, it's like the word of God."

"But when are we going to Japan?" Emi asked her mother, ignoring the man she had deemed a buffoon the moment he started to speak. "We've been here for so long. I don't want to go to yet another camp. I want to go home!"

"You might like it better there," the guard said, his voice high and friendly. "Crystal City. I heard they built a swimming pool. For everyone," he added.

"She loves to swim," Keiko said quickly, looking at Emi to make sure she wasn't going to reply. "And when will we be transferred?"

"Today," said the guard, looking confused.

"That's why I'm here. You weren't gathered in the mess hall where you're supposed to be, so I was sent here to see why. You and the other families leave on the buses in an hour." He looked at the Katos' confused faces and said, "Am I the first one to tell you?"

"It's fine! Perfectly fine," said Keiko, smiling, her voice still managing to sound bright. "We will be ready in an hour. Thank you very much," she said as the man backed out of the room. "I'm sure Crystal City will be just lovely."

Emi fell backward onto her bed but Keiko stopped her before she could say anything. "Do not talk. Just put your things in your bags and nod your head yes to everything I say. Maybe the new camp will be better. Maybe the people from that camp will leave for Japan quicker. You don't know and I'm tired of you always speculating the worst. Ever since you got sick you've been impossible. I know you miss being in contact with Leo, and living in a civilized place with food that doesn't taste like animal droppings, but I am fed up with your wretched attitude. So just, for once, don't question everything, and step in line like the rest of us. Have some reverence for your mother."

Emi raised her eyebrows but didn't say

another word until they were gathered with the other families about to be transferred. Every family but theirs had small children.

For the first week at Crystal City, Emi continued her habit of speaking to no one but her mother. But it was much harder at Crystal City since there were so many young people interned there, and at the start of Emi's second week, she couldn't outrun them anymore.

As she exited her house, heading for the showers, she heard a cheerful voice call after her. She stopped and turned to look at the teenager jogging her way in knee-length plaid shorts, smiling like she was running down a boardwalk instead of a fenced-in dirt path.

"I know you. You live on my row. You just arrived, right?" the girl asked, wiping her brow animatedly. "Were you at Heart Mountain before coming here? Manzanar?"

Emi just looked at her, surprised. She knew the girl appeared as she did, with dark hair and Japanese features, but she seemed so overwhelmingly American that Emi didn't know quite how to respond.

"I'm June Miyamoto. I live right over there," she said pointing. "Right by you."

Emi noticed that her bluntly cut bangs were sitting a few centimeters too high on her face, like she'd been trimming them herself for the last few months.

"No, we were at Seagoville," said Emi. "It's only six hours away. We were two of the first women brought there when it opened in April."

"Wow, where are you from?" June asked, peering at Emi's mouth as if she was possessed.

"Japan," said Emi. "Oh, you mean the accent. By way of England, I suppose."

"That explains it," June said smiling. "England. I'd like to go there one day, but not today. They probably hate us as much there as they do here." She made a line in the ground with her shoe as she spoke. "Seagoville. Is that all women?"

"Almost," Emi confirmed while watching the Japanese schoolboys play American football. It was shocking to Emi how, like June, they seemed so un-Japanese. She hadn't known many Japanese-Americans in Washington, just a few of the diplomats' children, but they led such different lives that they didn't quite qualify. It shocked Emi to think that the American government considered these fenced-in children dangerous. Aliens. They seemed almost like caricatures of American teenagers to her. She was sad for them as they were in for an awakening when they got to Japan. The Japanese children were not at all as carefree.

"I am tired of being hated. California was a mess when we left. It was awful. No one wanted to sit near me at school, my father's crops were stolen every night. I didn't want to come here, but it didn't feel safe there, either."

"There had to be a better solution than this," said Emi looking around them, wondering if all *Nisei* children were as perky as June. She was saying how upset she was, but delivering it with the cheer of a bandleader.

"Do you go to the Japanese school?" June asked Emi, who explained that she had graduated from high school. "I go to the Federal School here, thank goodness for that," said June, showing off a perfect dimple and straight white teeth. "I wouldn't survive a day in the Japanese school."

"Probably a bit stricter than the American program."

"You should spend a day at the Federal School. You'd get a kick out of it, and you look young enough," said June. "You've just got to see it. Our teachers sound so weird. They have this drawl," she said turning the word into three syllables. "And of course no one knows anyone else, so it's a mess. It's sad to start your senior year with strangers."

"I moved all the time," said Emi. "I sympathize."

"All the classes are for idiots," said June laughing. "I'm in my last year and I have to take an earth science class *again*. I should be taking chemistry but O'Rourke won't let us have chemistry because he's certain we'll mix some noxious gases and firebomb the camp out of retaliation. Banzai Japan and all that. They're incredibly paranoid and that paranoia is forcing me to be dumb."

"I'm not at all surprised," said Emi. "They're all so blinded by hate. Afraid children are in cahoots to bomb this place. Why bother? There's nothing of beauty or importance to ruin here."

"I like the pool," said June smiling.

"A swimming pool doesn't quite make up for the rest of it," said Emi, sadly.

"It will all go back to the way it was," said June, hugging her, much to Emi's shock. "Too bad I won't be in America to see it."

When Emi and June parted ways, Emi thought about how her circumstances could be even worse if she were a little younger. What a place to finish high school, she thought. Or to be five years old.

Despite June's unexpected friendliness, Emi's nerves were still shaken. She knew that her mother was frustrated with her behavior, but she didn't know how else to be. Since being forced onto the train to Seagoville, she had a rage and a restlessness that she couldn't seem to lose.

In bed that night, she screamed as a lizard crossed over her sunburned back.

"I can't do this anymore," she said, standing up. "I miss Father. I miss Leo's letters."

"Is that why you're awake?" said Keiko, sitting back on her bed. "We've already spoken about this, many times. You can try again from Japan. The chances that you'll be able to get a letter through from Tokyo are far better."

"I'm not betting on it. We haven't received letters from any of the friends we've written to in Japan. We've barely even received any letters from Father, and he's sending them from the Ministry of Foreign Affairs," said Emi, exasperated.

"Things are going to have to change with you," said Keiko, making room for Emi on her bed. "At this camp, the women your age don't just sit in the corner and mourn themselves. Everyone works here. You will, too. I have spoken with the director and you will be working at the hospital as a nurse's aide starting this weekend. You just need to keep busy. Eventually you'll see that things could be much, much worse. I know they're not ideal now, but . . ."

"I just hope he doesn't think I'm dead," said Emi. "Leo. Or that I don't care anymore."

"He's far too intelligent for that," said Keiko. "I'm sure he can guess why his letters are no longer reaching you. And you're far too intelligent to be spending all your time thinking about a boy. You're on your own for a few more years, Emiko. Unmarried. Free . . . relatively free," she corrected herself. "You don't want to be like this, do you?" she asked, pushing up against the wall so her tall daughter could fit.

Emi didn't answer, letting herself drift off to sleep, the faint rattle in her chest the only noise they could hear.

CHAPTER 6

Christian Lange
March 1943

For a few miles they rode through the outskirts of San Antonio, full of buildings with stepped massing and flat roofs. The architecture was the opposite of the Midwest, everything brown and beige, sucked dry of moisture.

When the bus finally pulled up to the Crystal City camp and Christian saw the barbed wire and the watchtowers, the men patrolling on horseback and the signs warning internees that escape attempts were punishable by death, he knew that even little Inge would realize it was nothing like summer camp.

"It's enormous," Christian said as the dense rows of buildings came into view. They were composed of squat houses that looked too depressed to grow any taller, like malnourished children.

131

"There's the swimming pool," said Inge's mother, pointing to a large circular area in the distance.

"And there is a hospital and schools, even a German school where both of you can study."

"Is there an American school?" Christian asked.

"There is, but you can't go," said his mother, her tone indicating that he shouldn't ask why.

"Where's Dad?" he asked instead, as the bus drove past the two watchtowers near the entrance. They looked like very tall lifeguard stands, with flat roofs and small terraces where the guards patrolled. One was out, with a gun slung over his shoulder, its barrel reflecting the sun.

"Your father wanted to come, but they said there wasn't room enough on the bus, plus he had to work. You'll see him at home," said Helene. "Temporary home," she added. "Because all of this is temporary, Christian. I promise you."

"If you say so," said Christian, looking at the sprawl of buildings. In the distance he could see the houses, all small and identical. "One of those," he realized, "is where I live now." The thought made him shiver even though early spring in Crystal City

132

brought temperatures in the high 80s.

When they all stepped off the bus, Inge looked from Christian to her mother, not sure whose hand to hold. She settled on both and dragged them toward an official who was set up at a small wooden table with a registry book in front of the camp's triple-winged main building. Behind the fence in front of them, Christian could see a smattering of people. None came to the fence to observe the new arrivals.

"There are also Japanese and Italians here," his mother explained. "And many South Americans. They barely speak English at all."

Out of nowhere, a strong gust of wind blew the official's pages, and with it, a thin layer of orange dirt seemed to settle on everything. Coming from the Midwest, Christian had never experienced the dust of the Southwest. And this version, produced from the grainy golden dirt of Texas, felt like powder in your hands and, he could already tell, fire in your lungs.

When Christian was registered in the book, Inge had to let go of his hand, as she still had to wait her turn, and Christian and his mother passed into the camp through the barbed-wire fence.

He was craning his neck to look at the

buildings — a quickly fabricated sprawl in the desert — when he heard his name. His father was hurrying toward them in a pair of stained pants. Gone was the pressed and starched Franz Lange of River Hills.

"Christian, you're here," he said, giving him a sideways hug and hitting him affectionately on the shoulder. "Thank God you made it safely. Your mother has been so worried."

"Fine place you've gotten us into," said Christian, letting his father give him his version of a hug.

"It's not ideal," said Franz. "And a very strange combination of people. Communists and Nazis living on the same block. Whoever thought that was a good idea should be put out to pasture. But we won't be here long. Let's walk this way, to the German side," he said, heading toward the group of people who had been watching the bus arrive.

As they got closer, Christian suddenly realized they were all Japanese. He looked at them, stopping in mid-stride. He had never seen Japanese people in such numbers, and he couldn't hide his surprise.

"Why are you staring like that?" asked his mother, catching him.

"I don't know," he said, turning away, embarrassed. "I guess I've never seen them all together."

Christian diverted his gaze to the ground, but not before he had eyed a group of Japanese teenagers with interest and felt his mother's hands on his back again.

"Stare at the barbed wire. At the men with guns who are trained to shoot us if we try to escape. Stare at the cardboard-box houses we are living in or the scorpions in the shower. But don't gape at them. They are in the same situation as we are. Probably worse."

"I'm sorry," said Christian, trying to comply. He took one last glance at the crowd and noticed a pair of feet going by — a girl's feet, in pink shoes. He looked up, thinking they would be attached to a young girl, one close to Inge's age, but instead they belonged to a stylish teenager, only a bit younger than himself.

They walked past rows of little houses, which Christian thought looked more like garden sheds than homes. The roofs barely sloped and the brown walls looked very thin and nailed hastily together. Some people had tried to make their exteriors more cheerful, adding a few plants out front, while others had let their circumstances dictate and were treating their places like camping tents. When Christian reached his family's house, it was obvious that they were in the second group.

They stepped inside, and his mother pointed to a suitcase by the door.

"Before I left Wisconsin, they let me go home, with an escort, to pack some of our things, your things. I have them here." She brought Christian over to a large suitcase and unzipped the top. "I wasn't able to bring much. Just clothes, really. But I did manage to bring your football. The one that was autographed by that boy you and your father like so much." She dug through the top of the case and produced it. It needed some air but the Don Hutson signature was white and clear. Christian turned it over, fitting it between his thumb and pointer finger, ready to throw a pass to no one.

His mother leaned over and kissed him on the cheek. The small laugh and smile lines on her face that had barely been apparent in the fresh air of Wisconsin were creased more deeply, and her lips felt cracked.

"This place will age me five years in five months," she said, sighing.

"I doubt we will be here for five months more, Mrs. Tomato Soup," his father said, trying to cheer up his wife. He crossed the room and opened his arms for Christian to throw him the ball, which he did, even though the room wasn't more than ten feet long.

"It's not a very big space," he said to Christian, trying futilely to mask his misery. "And we have to share it with another family. But we are surviving."

"It's awful is what it is, Franz," said Helene, taking the ball out of his hands. "And for what?" she snapped, losing the composure she had been radiating since she picked up Christian at the station. "For eight thousand dollars sent in all innocence to Jutta? For lies told about you? I am sure it was Martin who made that convenient call to the FBI," she said, her lip curling as she mentioned Franz's deputy at Lange Steel. "It had to be. He saw the perfect opportunity to take your company. Report you as a Nazi and then Lange Steel is his. Your hard work. Your years of sacrifice. Now that you're here, he's free to take it all from you."

"For the hundredth time, it wasn't Martin," said Franz. "He's my oldest friend in America. He would never do such a thing. I'm sure we'll have a letter from him any day now."

"You keep believing that, Franz. Please, do. But it's always the one just a notch below you who pulls you down."

"It could have been someone in the neighborhood," said Christian, remembering the cars moving slowly down their street when he left their house.

"Yes! Exactly," said Franz. "It could have been."

He put his hand around his son's broad shoulder and said, "Come, I'll show you around." They turned the corner and he said, "Unfortunately, we all have to sleep in the same room. And your poor mother with the baby." He shook his head at the two beds in front of him, both twin size, and said: "We only have two. Maybe they can bring us another one, or you and I can take turns sleeping on the floor. At least it's warm here. It's not like having to sleep on the floor in Wisconsin."

They both looked down at the dusty floor, and neither said anything about the two lizards scampering under the first of the twin beds.

"Just tell me this is all their mistake," said Christian, sitting down on the closest bed.

"Of course it is," said his mother, who had followed them. "Do you believe we did this? That we are spying? Nazis? Sweetheart, you don't really think that," she said, growing visibly upset.

Christian and the rest of America had been hearing about the Nazis, and Nazi barbarity, for more than a decade. In the early thirties, since much of the campaign for what Hitler announced as a new world order was centered in Germany, Christian, though very young, had paid attention to it when it was in the news. He knew that Germany meant his family, him. He listened to the radio reports fearfully, but as he grew up, he went from being a little boy who was scared of something beyond his grasp, to a young man starting to understand the horrors. In the summer of 1942, Christian read an article — from the *New York Times* but reprinted in the *Milwaukee Sentinel* — that reported on a killing center in Poland, targeting Jews. He'd spoken about it with his father, who'd said that it was hard to know what to believe. The media, the American government, didn't even seem to know. But at the end of 1942, when the Allies joined together to denounce the killing of the Jews in Europe by Nazi hands, Christian started to believe every word he read about Nazi atrocities. By 1943, he understood that even normal Germans were involved in the cruelty, but it still felt very far away.

Stuck in Crystal City, he was forced to confront what it meant to be a German. Maybe the FBI agents were right. Perhaps

Jutta and her husband were Nazis. And what about on his father's side? It was certainly possible. The young men would at least have to fight for Germany. And what did that mean? Killing the Allies, or worse.

"I don't think you're guilty," Christian replied to his mother, honestly. "I just haven't seen you since that night with the agents. You've never had a chance to explain. And now we're here in this place."

"There is nothing to explain," said Helene. "Except a grave American mistake."

Christian raised his eyebrows and reached for his mother's hand. He believed her, but that did not change their circumstances. "What are we going to do, stuck in here?" he asked, looking around the cramped room.

"We are going to live our lives as well as we can. Nothing is forever. Certainly not this," said Franz.

CHAPTER 7

Christian Lange
March–April 1943

A week later, Helene started to feel the baby kick. Christian was walking back from his second day at the German school when he saw his mother approaching. She had a smile on her face that belied her dismal surroundings. Christian had planned to tell her how his German abilities did not extend to writing essays in the language, but when he saw her happiness, he decided to delay the bad news. Within just a few days of his arrival, he'd learned why he couldn't attend the American school. The elected spokesman for their side of the camp was intensely pro-German and anyone who sent their children to the American-style Federal School was deemed a traitor. There were whispers that one family's food had been withheld for several days because their daughter, who spoke no German, enrolled there.

"Put your hand here," Helene said when she'd reached Christian. She placed his right hand on the top of her stomach. She was wearing the dress that was given to women when they arrived, and Christian thought it made her look plain and home-spun, definitely more Mrs. Tomato Soup than Mrs. Country Club.

They waited a few minutes, but nothing happened. Christian started to fidget, and his mother laughed at him. "Do you have somewhere to be? Wait to feel the baby."

So they waited. Mothers walked by them and smiled, teenagers coming out of school slowed down and whispered, and finally, when Christian was about to pull his hand away, embarrassed, the baby kicked.

"I felt it!" he said, pressing his hand harder against his mother's belly.

"I told you it would be worth the wait," said Helene, her voice full of delight.

Christian thought of the tiny body inside his mother bursting with life. He imagined the growing organs, the heartbeat, the developing brain and he felt sorry for it. He wished it could be born far from loaded guns and barbed wire. At least it would have love, he thought, looking at his mother's joyful face.

Helene kissed her son's hand and walked off, letting him catch up to the other boys who were making their way from the school to the German mess hall, where they worked prepping the next day's milk delivery. Internees in the camp woke up to a bottle of fresh milk on their stoop every day, one of the measures that the camp's warden took to show that he was going well beyond the laws of the Geneva Conventions. The camp, it was whispered among the internees, was one President Roosevelt took great pride in, and the guards didn't want any suicides or fence jumpers to ruin his vision. "They want happy prisoners," his father had told him. "So just remember, it could be much worse."

For Christian, sharing seven hundred square feet with another family and sleeping on floors with scorpions did not make for a happy prisoner. The view of miles of barbed-wire fencing him in did not help, either. The orphanage had changed him — he felt it in his newfound patience. Even gentleness. The way he felt toward Inge, had guarded her on the train, he was sure the old Christian would not have been as kind. But it didn't mean he was elated about his circumstances.

Then there was the camp's segregation. In two days, Christian had learned how bad it was. Though he had seen the large group of Japanese internees when he came in, invisible lines kept them apart inside. The Germans and Japanese, despite being allies in the war, occupied separate sections of the camp, ate in separate facilities, worked different jobs, and played different sports. The only places where they mixed were the hospital — as illness never discriminated — and the swimming pool. The few Italians were sprinkled among the Germans, but they kept to themselves, too.

Work would help keep Christian's mind off things. That's what Franz Lange had said when he explained that he was working in the camp's central utility building. A classmate named Kurt Schneider had told Christian he should volunteer for the milk prep job before he was given a much more painful assignment than washing and filling milk bottles. In the camp, all the men and older boys had their jobs assigned by Joseph O'Rourke, the camp commander. Kurt said that if he told O'Rourke that he was already a milk slinger, he'd let him remain a milk slinger.

"You caught up fast," said Kurt as soon as Christian was next to him again. They spoke

English, as Kurt's German was so poor that he was only in the fourth-grade class in the German school despite being seventeen years old.

"So your *Deutsch* is good enough to put you in twelfth?" asked Kurt, taking long strides to keep up with Christian's.

"Yeah, I grew up speaking German at home. I'm decent. My writing's not, but I'll survive."

"Lucky you. You might have teachers who aren't completely stupid. My teacher is a pig farmer. And the tenth-grade history teacher is an electrician. Only teaches the history of the lightbulb. Most of the German teachers didn't even go to school. I heard the kindergarten teacher used to be in prison." Kurt grinned at a passing group of girls and whistled. Christian stopped walking and Kurt shrugged. "You got to try with all of them, then maybe it will work with one of them. I don't look like you, Hollywood. All tall and blond. I need a different approach."

"Working the odds," said Christian, moving again. "I respect that."

"Anything to keep your mind occupied in this place. You don't want to get fence sickness. You'll be in the hospital for something while you're here. Everyone is. Just don't make it for fence sickness." He stopped in front of the mess hall and looked down the road to where a group of mothers was standing. "Was that your mother you were talking to before?" he asked. "She's a —"

"Don't elaborate or I'll have to knock your teeth out," said Christian. He had no desire to knock anyone's teeth out; he just felt it was obligatory to say it, especially given his mother's current state. The thought of a fight made him think of Jack Walter the shoe thrower and he wished he were still in his room at the Home instead of fenced in in Texas.

"Come on, Tarzan," said Kurt. "I'll introduce you to Herr Beringer, who can put that aggression to work moving dairy products."

As soon as Beringer saw Christian's size, he was very happy to enlist him into his milk prep ranks.

"You're lucky you came to me first or you could have gotten one of those piss-crap after-school jobs that O'Rourke has been handing around like gumballs since the Wisconsin train came in," he said. "They might have put you out working the crops with the Japanese. Big kid like you. And it's only getting hotter. You want to till soil in a hundred and twenty degrees with mountain

146

lions and black widow spiders lurking around you? Trust me, you don't. Lucky you found the milkman before that happened."

Christian started to thank him, but Beringer shoved a crate of empty milk bottles into his hands instead. "Wash these until you can see yourself in 'em. They'll be refilled and delivered by the men tomorrow morning. You boys can't work the first shift — you've got school. So just wash 'em and put 'em over there." He pointed to a corner of the room that was filled floor to ceiling with empty, crated milk bottles.

"We get paid for this?" Christian asked Kurt as the two started washing in four large metal sinks. "I thought you couldn't use money in camp."

"Paid? I guess we get paid," said Kurt. "If you call ten cents an hour getting paid. We barely use money in the camp. Instead they issue us fuzzy green fake coins, about five bucks' worth a month. You can buy some junk with them in the store. Cigarettes. And drinks in the beer garden."

"As in beer?" asked Christian, filling the first sink with soap and the second with cold water.

"Definitely. This is prison. The old men feel sorry for us. They'll pour you as many as you can pay for. And then if they're drunk enough, which they always are, they'll slip them to you for free, as long as you'll listen to them talk about the war. Germany's going to win, in case you didn't know."

Christian was on his tenth set of a dozen bottles, soaping them and scrubbing them with a sparse bottlebrush, when he heard a high-pitched scream. Kurt let his already clean bottle bob in the soap as they listened. It was followed by a louder scream, and then another, before everything went quiet. The screams had come from somewhere outside the mess hall. Beringer dropped the milk bottle he was holding, which smashed on the floor. He jumped up and ran out the closest door, followed by the boys.

Christian went out last, as he was by the farthest sink and was the least comfortable around Beringer. When he got outside, he could see everyone gathered in a circle around something.

"What is it?" Christian asked a younger boy who was also hanging back.

"Someone got hit," he replied.

"I know who it is," Christian heard Kurt say. "It's that woman from near the school. It's Christian Lange's mother."

Christian pushed in front of the other boys, shoving them so hard that one of them fell, cutting his hands on the fragmented milk bottle shards that were all around the loading area of the mess hall.

Christian, his shirt and pants wet from the washing, looked at his mother lying on the ground. She was faceup, her legs dirty and limp, her eyes closed. Terrified, he held his breath as if he were about to plunge into a pool before he dropped down next to her. He put his hands on her face and checked to make sure there was breath. It was faint but there. His eyes traveled down, and he saw that there was blood all over the bottom of her dress.

A daytime guard, one of the many who patrolled the camp in their big blue pickups, stood there. He bent down next to Christian, his stiff blue jeans full of dust, his hands dirty. "I didn't see her," he said, frantically. "She just came out of nowhere. I don't know what happened. I just didn't see her." He put his ear against Helene's nose to see if she was breathing.

"She's pregnant!" screamed Christian, pushing the guard away from his mother. "How the hell can you not see a pregnant woman?"

"I don't know. I just didn't," said the patrolman again. He had taken off his cowboy hat and was holding it over his stomach. "I swear I didn't swerve to hit her,

I just didn't see her." He kept repeating his line to the boys around him while Christian tried to wake up his mother.

"She's not lying in the middle of the road!" Christian screamed from his position on the ground after he had gently shaken Helene again. "She's on the side, she's where she should be, but you hit her anyway! You might have killed her and the baby."

"Shit," said the guard, looking at Helene's protruding belly and the blood on her dress. "Let's put her in the back of the truck. Quickly. I can get her to the hospital faster than they can get up here."

Christian kneeled down again and picked up his unconscious mother with the help of the guard and Beringer. They loaded her onto the truck's flat bed and Christian sat next to her battered body. "They could both die," he said softly. The baby his parents had wanted for years, the mother he had never successfully detached from: they could both be dead.

"What can I do?" asked Kurt.

"Find my father," said Christian. "Franz Lange. Get him to the hospital. Tell him what happened. Q section, duplex Q-45-B. We share with the Kalbs."

Kurt took off running while the truck sped

away and Christian held his mother's slack hand. "They could both die," Christian repeated to the guard.

"Your mother is alive," said a nurse once they had arrived at the hospital and his mother was unloaded onto a stretcher by the staff.

She walked him inside the small hospital to a chair near the front door. "You can't come in with her, but we will find you as soon as we know anything, I promise." She'd explained to Christian that she was a nurse from the United States Public Health Service, as was Dr. Oliver, the physician in charge. Christian saw some young Japanese-American women in white uniforms go into his mother's room and the nurse explained that they had trained some of the internees as orderlies and nurses' aides. "We've had more illnesses than we imagined and they make things run smoother. Don't worry, your mother is in qualified hands."

When Christian's father arrived fifteen minutes later, sprinting to the hospital door, the nurse said she would bring him straight back to Helene's room. He didn't stop and comfort his son, just shouted his wife's name until the nurse quieted him and let him through.

Christian sat in the tiny waiting room for

an hour, but when he heard his mother screaming so loudly that he was sure the sound carried back to the mess hall, he ran into her private room. As short-staffed as the hospital was, there was no one to stop him.

He didn't knock on the door, but flung it open, only to see the doctor holding a tiny, blood-covered baby in his arms, still attached to his mother by the thick spiral of umbilical cord. It was a girl, as his mother had prayed for, and she was dead.

"Christian, get out of the room right now," said his father, seeing him first, but Christian didn't move. He just stood there staring.

The baby girl was going to end up nothing but a bloodstain on an internment camp hospital floor. A dead baby, just twenty-four weeks old.

"The American killed my child!" his mother was screaming at his father in German. "He's a murderer!"

The doctor didn't quiet her, but continued the delivery, cutting the cord and handing the baby to the nurse.

"Don't look, Christian!" his father shouted again, but his son couldn't divert his gaze. The baby was pale blue, with tiny bulging eyes and translucent hands. She looked amphibian. Christian kept staring as the nurse wrapped her in a thin white blanket and tucked it over her face while the doctor delivered his mother's placenta.

The nurse turned away from Helene to take the baby out of the room, but Helene reached out for her, almost falling off the metal delivery table.

"I want to hold her!" she screamed. "Take that blanket off her and give her to me!" She was kicking her legs hard and one of the Japanese-American women had to press her forearms against them to keep her from thrashing herself off the table.

The doctor and the nurse looked at each other and finally placed the dead blue baby on Helene's almost bare chest, still wrapped in the blanket. Helene unwrapped it and held the little girl tight against her, but the baby's head flopped to the side, her limbs hanging unnaturally, covered in thick vernix.

Helene started to sob loudly and lose her grip on the baby. But she fought off the nurse's attempt to take her.

"I want to hold her, and I want to name her!" she shouted. "And I don't want her buried in this desert hell!"

Christian closed his eyes, stunned, and saw the baby's dead eyes, gray as stones, following him around the room. He imagined her pale face that would never smile, her cold cheeks that would never be kissed.

"Christian. I mean it," said his father, moving to his mother's side. "Get out of this room. Let me be alone with your mother. Right now."

Christian turned and walked out. He didn't head to the chair at the front of the office as he should have. Instead, he just stood in front of the closed door picturing the baby's tiny dead face.

He could still hear his mother sobbing, and he instinctively moved to go back inside.

"Why don't you wait a bit?" he heard a voice say quietly from behind him. Surprised by the British accent, he spun around to see a young Japanese woman in a white uniform. She was holding a pile of folded bedsheets. "It's your mother in there?" she asked.

Christian confirmed with a nod.

"I heard what happened," she said, handing the sheets to another young woman who walked by. "I'm very sorry. But she probably wants some privacy right now. I know I would. I'm just finishing my shift. Why don't you walk me to the swimming pool and then come back here? I bet the air will make you feel better."

"The fresh Texas air?" asked Christian.

"It's better than in here," said the nurse. "Let's talk about something else than all this. At least for a little while. Then when you feel better, you can come back and ask to see your mother."

Not ignoring the fact that the nurse was very pretty, Christian nodded yes and together they walked out of the hospital.

"If you don't mind, I have to stop at my house to get my bathing suit. I didn't bring it to work today and I really want to swim before it's too dark," she said once the hospital was out of view.

"On the Japanese side?" said Christian, immediately realizing how stupid he sounded.

"Yes, of course," the nurse said, laughing at him. "Are you afraid to go?"

"No," said Christian, feeling foolish. "I'd be happy to walk you there."

"I'm sorry. I shouldn't tease you. I really am sorry for your mother. It's terrible what happened."

"Thank you," said Christian, suddenly surprised by tears. He wiped them away, even more embarrassed.

"I think you have to cry when a baby dies. I'm sure I'll cry, too, tonight when I'm alone. It's awful," she said sympathetically.

Christian looked at her and noticed how

high and sharp her cheekbones were. It was probably what everyone noticed about her first. It would have given her a severe look if she hadn't had such a pleasing face, softly curved at the jaw. He looked away before she noticed him staring and said, "Let's, as you said, talk about something else for a little while."

Realizing that she hadn't introduced herself, the girl stopped and said, "I'm Emi Kato. It's Emiko, actually, but everyone in America prefers to call me Emi. And I'm not a nurse. I'm just a nurse's assistant. An aide. The seamstresses dress us up like nurses, I think because they're bored."

"Which do you prefer?" asked Christian. "Emiko or Emi?"

"Emi is fine," she replied. "I'm trying to pretend I'm still living the same American life I was before I was fenced in here. The name Emi helps a little bit."

They both paused as two guards walked past them, guns slung across their shoulders. It was anything but the same American life.

"Does your side have a piano?" Emi asked after a few minutes of walking in silence.

"A piano?" said Christian, surprised. "Why would we have a piano?"

"I thought maybe the German school would. Or the beer garden. I asked the *Nisei* girls — those are the second-generation Japanese girls — who go to the Federal School and they don't have one there. I thought perhaps the Germans get preference for something like a piano."

"Why would we get preference?" asked Christian, his voice catching as three Japanese children walked past them, but not before looking at him with surprise. Emi didn't seem to notice.

"Because you seem more American to them. So maybe more worthy of a piano," said Emi.

"Because we're white? And that entitles us to music?"

"Do you have one or not?" she asked.

Christian looked down at her hands, which were long and slender. The hands of someone who had spent years of her life at a piano, he guessed. "No. Well, I don't think so anyway. I've only been in school for two days and I don't play, so I haven't paid attention. But we don't really have anything, do we, so why would we have a piano?"

"Morale, perhaps," she said, pausing as an elderly woman said *konbanwa,* good evening, to her.

"I don't think they care very much about our morale. Yours or mine," Christian argued. "If they did, they wouldn't have put us in a sandbox full of scorpions and sharp-shooters."

"Sharpshooters?" Emi asked, following Christian's eyes up to the closest watch-tower.

"Them," he said pointing. They could make out two men in the tower waiting to see if one of the internees was stupid enough to run. "Sharp like accurate. So if we try to escape, they won't miss when they shoot at us like dogs."

"Let's try to avoid that," Emi said. "I think your mother has gone through enough."

At the mention of Helene Lange, both were quiet again.

Christian finally said, "I'd like to hear you play the piano."

"Then having a piano would help."

"I'll find one," said Christian, realizing how Emi had gone from pretty to beautiful with every step. He looked at her hair, straight and clean despite the dust of the camp, and imagined running his hands through it. Then he imagined running his hands through it while she lay next to him. He stopped himself before he imagined anything further, embarrassed that such lustful thoughts could cut through his grief. "Were you interned before Crystal City?"

The wind had picked up and Emi was

busy gathering her long hair to one side of her neck to keep it out of her eyes. Christian was already sure that if he could just watch Emi wrestle with the wind for the rest of his time in the camp, he would never get fence sickness.

"I'm not American. I'm Japanese," she said after her hair had been tamed. "And my father is in the Foreign Service, so I was interned right after Japan bombed Pearl Harbor. My mother and I were in Seagoville, near Dallas. And before that, I suppose I was interned in a different, much more pleasant fashion." She paused and looked up at the sunset, which was starting to spread all over the sky in a way that seemed unique to South Texas. "There was a piano and a group of talented musicians in that place," Emi added. "And there was wonderful food. But that's a story for another time." They had reached what Christian imagined was Emi's family bungalow. It wasn't a double like his. Emi's family had its own small space.

She was in and out in two minutes, but in those two minutes, the sun had turned from pink to red and was spreading like paint behind her little house.

"So. The piano," she said, putting her bag over her shoulder and starting to walk again.

"I'd like it if you came over to our side," Christian admitted. "I'd like to see you not play the piano, because I don't think we have one."

"Don't be silly," said Emi. "Watching someone not play the piano is just watching someone being alive."

"That doesn't seem so bad given what happened today," said Christian. "Will you come and not play?"

"I won't promise anything," said Emi, turning the corner toward the big round swimming pool.

"That's a promise in itself. To not promise anything."

"Don't try and trick me," she said smiling. "Plus, it's easier for a German boy to come to the Japanese side than it is for a Japanese girl to go to your side. And even harder for me since I'm not *Issei* or *Nisei*. I'm just passing through."

"But you could try."

"I could."

"Why don't you tell me that 'story for another time'?" he asked, slowing his steps as they got closer to the swimming pool, which was designed and built by the internees. "I don't think I should go back to the hospital yet."

"It's not very exciting, but I suppose that's

welcome after what you saw today. I was just going to say that before Texas, we were interned somewhere quite beautiful."

"You weren't imprisoned?"

"Imprisoned?" she said laughing. "The entire Japanese diplomatic corps? If the American government treated the Japanese diplomats and their families badly, word would travel to Japan and the American diplomats over there would be treated badly in retaliation. There were no harsh conditions. After the bombing, we had to sleep at the embassy, on just mattress bottoms. The kind without tops. Does that make sense? There must be a better way to say it. Mattresses with just the springs," she said, making a bouncing gesture with her hands.

"Box springs," said Christian.

"That's it. Spring boxes."

"Box springs," said Christian again, fighting a smile. "And after the box springs?" he asked as Emi frowned at her mistake.

"The box springs lasted a few days and then we were escorted out of the embassy by FBI agents. There were people on the sidewalk when we left, some taking our pictures, others yelling at us. Yellow this and that. You know the insults. But they would have been even more irate if they knew we were taking a train to Hot Springs, in

Virginia, and staying at a nice hotel called the Homestead. It wasn't bad at all. The food was good, and they let me go swimming and play the piano. After a few months there, we were transferred to the Greenbrier hotel in West Virginia. That was beautiful, too, and the last place I played the piano because I became very sick and couldn't travel soon after."

"Sick?" asked Christian. "What was wrong?"

"I contracted tuberculosis. I was very contagious, so they wouldn't let me travel to Japan, not on a boat with so many important men. But my mother stayed with me. We are the only two associated with the embassy that are still here in the United States. They didn't close all the consulates right away, but eventually, those people made it on board, too. The MS *Gripsholm*. A Swedish ship. That's what they sailed on back to Japan." Emi looked over at the pool, which was almost empty. She said she should hurry before it closed, but Christian didn't want her to go yet.

"Were the diplomats angry that they had to live in hotels, cornered off, and then be shipped away?" he asked, more interested in the way her lips moved than the answer.

"I think most saw it as what had to be

done," she said. "We aren't wanted in this country. We are the enemy. It isn't a matter of *Issei, Nisei* — first-generation, second-generation Japanese-American. Almost none of us are American citizens. Some of the wives and children are foreign, but the men are employed by the Japanese government. It's not safe for us here; we have to return. So now my mother and I are waiting for the next boat."

"And until then you are here, volunteering at the hospital and going to the Japanese school," said Christian.

"I'm not going to the school," Emi replied. "I'm twenty-one. I haven't been a student for quite some time."

"But you must have gone to an English-speaking school recently. Your very proper English — despite your box springs — is perfect."

"Since my English impresses you, do you want to hear my German?" she said, smiling modestly.

"Natürlich spreche ich auch Deutsch. Glaubst Du mir das nicht?"

"I certainly do believe that you speak German," he said. "I believe you can do just about anything."

"But let's speak English here," she said. "I don't want everyone to know that I speak

German. Then they'll figure out that I'm eavesdropping on the German nurse's aides at the hospital."

"Kein Deutsch mehr," said Christian, promising to keep her secret. "I'm not even going to ask why you speak German."

"Good, then I can volunteer that story the next time we meet. Hopefully I'll see you again before I'm sent back to Japan."

"Do you know when that will be?" asked Christian, his heart already dropping at the thought.

"No, I don't. But none of us know when we're being repatriated. That's one of the hardest parts of being here, I think."

"What do you mean?"

"Almost all of us will be sent back," said Emi. "You to Germany. The Italians to Italy. It's not just me and my mother on the next Swedish boat."

"Me to Germany?" echoed Christian. "Why would I go to Germany?"

She stared at him incredulously. "Why? Because that's what happens. You're being traded for Americans overseas. An American in Germany will come here, and you will go there. That's why they are allowing families to be together here, because they've agreed to be repatriated. Didn't your parents tell you?"

Christian stood there, staring at the beautiful Japanese girl with the British accent, in a starched white uniform holding a bag with a bathing suit and a towel. He was too shocked to say anything more.

"You should go back to your mother now. I'm sure she wants to see you," Emi said after the silence between them had grown heavy.

"I should," said Christian, backing away. After a quick goodbye, he ran back to the hospital thinking about Emi Kato. Her confident beauty. Her spring boxes. How she was going to look in her bathing suit. He had felt ashamed that she had taken his mind off his mother, off the dead baby, but he felt a little less bad now that he knew what his parents hadn't told him. They were being sent to Germany.

When he reached his mother's hospital room, he didn't see the frozen eyes of the dead baby girl anymore, only Helene and her desperate grief. She gestured to him to come closer and when he sat down next to her, she put her hands on his head and cried about her baby, the man who had killed her, and the country that had made him. After holding the little girl's limp body against her chest and feeling just her own heartbeat when there should have been two, Helene Lange had started to hate America.

CHAPTER 8

Emi Kato
March–April 1943

Keiko stopped in her tracks as she reached the front door of the little house in the D Section of the camp near the Karate Hall. "Is that my child?" she said looking at Emi sitting on the front steps, her long shorts folded just below her knees, her white shirt billowing out above them, almost two sizes too big. "It can't be. My child doesn't sit on the stoop. She goes directly inside and lies on her bed pretending she's dead so that no one will socialize with her. So who, then, is this?"

"I don't pretend I'm dead," said Emi, moving over on the step to let her mother up. "I just rest my eyes. I'm recovering from tuberculosis, remember?"

"Of course," said Keiko compassionately. "But I have seen you swim twenty laps in the pool, barely coming up for air, your legs kicking so strongly that your whole body is almost out of the water. So I was under the false assumption that your lungs were healed."

"They work differently underwater," Emi protested. "My gills must help. And who says I'm out here to socialize. It's just a little less hot today. I thought I'd enjoy the weather."

"You enjoy it then," said her mother, putting her hand on Emi's shoulder as she made her way inside.

Emi listened for the latch closing on the door and pushed her feet out into the sandy road. It was true that she hadn't tried to make friends, but who was there to make friends with? She was one of the only women her age at Crystal City, too old for the school-aged crowd, yet not identifying with the young mothers, who were always trying to comfort their crying babies and little ones.

She knew that the high school children, especially the *Niseis* in the Federal School, did many things together, trying their best to pretend they were still out in the real world. She just didn't have the heart to join them.

As Emi put her head down to avoid saying good evening to two older women walking past, she heard a voice very near her call out her name.

"I was wondering who lived there," the man continued, his West Coast accent noticeable. Emi looked up and saw that it was her neighbor, a middle-aged man always dressed in ill-fitting clothes. She'd seen him sitting in front of the little house he shared with his wife and daughter many times. "I live right here. Right next to you," he pointed out. "So close you can probably hear me snoring. I'm John Sasaki."

"I've seen you before," said Emi, offering him a tiny smile.

"And I've seen you before," he said as he approached her, "but you've never stood still long enough to say hello, always running through the front door avoiding everyone. I didn't want to be the one to interrupt your misery. But here you are, sitting happily tonight, so I dared to say hello."

"Do you think I'm miserable?" Emi asked, looking up at him. She wondered if she should stand out of politeness. She started to and he motioned for her to stay where she was.

"Yes, I do think you are rather miserable. Am I wrong?" he said in a fatherly voice.

"Not exactly," Emi said. She was looking at his hair, which was short and streaked white in the front. The streak was so even that it looked painted on. "I have been pretty miserable. I was supposed to be on the boat back to Japan in June last year with my father. But I came down with tuberculosis and my mother and I had to stay behind. We weren't supposed to be interned."

"None of us are supposed to be interned. We just are interned," said John, tucking in the hem of his short-sleeved button-down shirt, which was sticking out on one side.

"Of course. It's just that if I hadn't contracted tuberculosis, I wouldn't be here. Looking at all that." Emi pointed out to the fence. She knew that none of them merited being locked away like they were, but she had felt like she and her mother's circumstances were more unjust than most. It was a selfish way to think, she knew, but it was a thought that had looped around her brain since they arrived and no one had been able to stop it yet.

"No one likes that," said her neighbor, pointing to the fence in turn. "But I don't think you should be too desperate to sail off to a country at war, either."

"Do you think it will be that bad in Japan? That dangerous?" she asked, leaning back on the stair above her.

"Yes, I do," said John. "I think it will be

worse than anyone can imagine. So don't let that terrify you too much," he said, nodding to the fence again. "My son is fighting right now," he added. "Training to fight, anyway. He's in Mississippi with the 442nd. That's the all-Japanese-American combat team that was just formed."

"All Japanese-American?" said Emi surprised. "Why would they want to fight against Japan?"

Both Emi and John stayed quiet for a moment as two guards walked past them, not bothering to greet any of the internees.

"Because they're American," said John when they'd passed. "Physical features do not ally you to one country or the other. It's where you were raised, what you were taught to believe, don't you think? And he, and I, think Japan is wrong in this war."

Emi shrugged, not in the mood to get into a political discussion.

"It sounds very brave of your son," she said tactfully. "Especially since the Americans put his family here. Does he speak Japanese?"

"A little," said John. "But it won't make too much of a difference. I've been told that they'll head to Europe eventually."

"Then I hope the war ends before your son is shipped over there," she said, her voice quieting. "I was in Austria just before the war broke out. I would not want any of my loved ones to go there or anywhere else in Europe right now."

"I have faith," said John, and Emi noticed the small cross around his neck. Many of the *Issei* and *Nisei,* she noticed, were Christian. Some very devout.

"So tell me, Emiko Kato," said John, sitting down next to her. "Why are you in such a good mood today when you've been so discomposed since you arrived here?"

Emi thought back to the way Christian had stared at her when they'd reached the swimming pool. As if he'd found something he'd been looking for for a long time.

"I don't know. Something terrible happened today, actually. I shouldn't be happy at all. I feel a little guilty that I am." She looked up at John's pleasant round face and said, "A pregnant woman on the German side was hit by one of the guards' trucks and lost her baby. I was working at the hospital when it happened. The poor woman. She was screaming and screaming in pain."

"I heard about that," said John. "Another death in the camp when it should have been new life." He looked at Emi and said, "That can't be it then. So what happened after the baby died?"

"I suppose . . ." said Emi, her voice lingering as she thought about Christian's glowing face when they'd spoken German together. "I suppose I helped cheer someone up after the baby died."

"Sometimes the sullen are the best at cheering others up," said John. "With the frown you've been carrying, I'm sure you were excellent at empathizing with his grief."

"Did I say it was a him?" said Emi.

"Just a guess," said John, taking a step back toward his house. "A word of advice: if you don't try to make the best of a bad situation, you'll never survive."

"Fence sickness?"

"No. Just regret. Trust me. It's worse."

CHAPTER 9

Christian Lange
March–April 1943

When Christian walked into the family's shared house, his father was sitting alone, looking as if he had just been punched in the ribs and was trying to remember how to exhale. At the creak of the cheap plywood floor under Christian's feet, Franz looked up at his son with red-rimmed eyes and gestured for him to sit in the room's other wooden chair. Neither chair stood without wobbling.

"Your poor mother," said Franz, his voice hoarse. "You shouldn't have come into the room. Seen your sister —"

"I can't talk about that right now," said Christian, interrupting him. "I need to clear the air before I can talk about that."

"Someone just died and you need to clear the air?" asked Franz. "What is wrong with the air?"

"Germany," said Christian, doggedly. "Why didn't you tell me about Germany before I got on the train to Texas? You knew where I was. You could have written to me. Asked me what I wanted to do, asked me about repatriating —"

"Excuse me?" said Franz, standing up. "*That* is what you expect me to talk about? Now?"

"I know it's not the right time, but why didn't you tell me that we're all going to Germany?" Christian pleaded. "That we — that you — agreed to be repatriated to Germany? In the middle of the war? Can you imagine what you're sending us to?"

"Your sister just died!" Franz shouted angrily. "How did I raise such a disrespectful son? You should not be speaking to me about such a petty thing at a time like this. You should be at the hospital apologizing to your mother for barging into her room while she was in the midst of her tragedy, then try your best to prove that she can one day be happy again with just one child. With you."

"I'll do that," said Christian. "And I've already spent time with her today. But first please tell me about Germany. *Please.*"

"What would you like to know?" said Franz, sitting back down, exasperated. He put his hands in his graying blond hair and grew even more frustrated when several strands came out in his hands.

"How about what will happen to Lange Steel?" said Christian, his blue eyes locked with his father's. "You always said it would be my business one day. That I would run it with you and then without you. Is that possible if we go to Germany? And what about college?"

"All that will still happen," said Franz, shaking his head. He sat straight and rigid in his chair even though he was only in the company of his son. Christian hated how his father maintained his pompous air, as if they were sitting in his study in the River Hills house instead of a shack. He looked at him with visible annoyance but his father just sat up taller and prouder as he spoke.

"We did write to you while you were at the Home but our letters obviously never made it up to Wisconsin. They must have been thrown away by the censors," he said. "Both your mother and I did write."

"Did you explain about Germany in those letters?"

"No," Franz admitted. "We worried you wouldn't come to Texas if we did and we were desperate to have you here. Your mother, especially. You know that. You are her world. Now, more than ever, she needs you. Aren't you glad you came? To be here for her after something so devastating happened?"

"I am, but that doesn't mean I want to go to Germany."

"Is it not better than being here? At least we will be together and not behind barbed-wire fences, falsely accused of crimes against this country. My parents have been notified about our arrival — they have their house waiting for us in Pforzheim. We will be living with war, yes, but not in the way you're afraid of. We'll be shielded from the worst of it. This, what happened here, will be the worst of it. That INS man, that murderer, is the reason the baby died. That Lora died," he said, using the name he and Helene had chosen when the baby still had a heartbeat. "And he's not going to be arrested," Franz said, his anger rising with the color in his face. "O'Rourke came to explain," he said of the head of the camp. "There will be no trial, nothing. O'Rourke said that they've already concluded that it was an accident. So that's all. The guard keeps his job driving that truck that hit her and killed Lora, and your mother has to see him all over camp."

"There must be someone else you can appeal to?" said Christian, picturing the guard's pinched, sun-weathered face.

"Me? A prisoner?" said Franz. "I can't yet. For now we can only control so much."

"Like going to Germany."

"Yes, like going to Germany," Franz replied angrily. "We won't be there for long, just until the war is over. And that will be soon. Very soon."

"You know that how, Dad? Do you have some inside line to Roosevelt?" Christian said, tense with anger. "You have no idea. The war could go on for five more years. And just because Oma and Opa are wealthy and plan to put us up in some vacation house doesn't mean we'll be safe in Germany. Bombs don't discriminate based on bank accounts."

"The war will not go on for five more years. That's a childish thing to think. The end is near, Christian, I am sure of it. The night before we left Wisconsin, there was news that the Red Army was still swelling by millions. I know that means the war is coming to an end. Russia is changing the course of the war."

"Even if that's true, then what?" asked Christian. "We go to Germany for the remainder of the war and try to survive. What about Lange Steel? You're just going to leave it? Do you even know what's happening there?"

"I've now had a letter from Martin and he's assured me that he is running it as it should be and is acting president. He will relinquish that title as soon as I am back. I still own Lange Steel, Christian. The government may have frozen our bank accounts but they can't shut down our businesses forever. Not when there are other people to run them in the interim. Martin just sent me the recent figures and they were heavily blacked out, but if Martin is sending them to me, it means they are good. Lange will be waiting for me — and thriving — when I return."

"You're so sure the Americans will let us all back in," said Christian. "Even you and Mom, who are not citizens. They imprison us here and then after the war they will just let us sail right back over. Let me enroll in college just like nothing ever happened. Why would they spend all the money repatriating us if that were the case?"

"They say there's a chance we won't be allowed back in. They have to say that," Franz said. "But it will all be different after the war. These ideas that have emerged during the war years will feel antiquated. You'll see."

"You don't know anything for certain,"

said Christian, watching his father cringe at his disrespectful tone. "Lange could go under. Martin could run it into the ground or find a way to take it from you forever. The war *could* rage on for five more years. Or we could all go to Germany and die as soon as we're on land."

"Let's assume I know a little more than you," said Franz. "And I know this: Your mother said she couldn't live without her only son and that she would do anything to have you with her. Would you have wanted her to rot in Oklahoma? This was the only way to have us all together. Maybe you don't understand, but you will when you have a family."

"I understand," said Christian, flatly. He had managed to push his anger down to a level that his father might tolerate, but he was still livid at his parents for mishandling the news. It was just another way of theirs to protect him; he who they believed still couldn't handle the realities of the world at seventeen.

Franz nodded and offered no apology, instead saying, "This conversation should have happened after your mother was healthy again."

A siren interrupted their argument. It was the signal for the count, which happened three times a day — morning, noon, and night — with every internee in the camp rushing to their houses to have their names checked off by guards. Christian and his father went outside, Franz explaining to the guard assigned to their row that Helene was in the hospital.

"We'll check your story," the guard replied without sympathy, moving on to their neighbors.

After the count, Christian left his father and tried to shake off some of the pain of the day. The baby was dead. He was going to have to move to Germany until the Americans decided to let him back in. And he knew that was an if, not a guarantee. He would have to experience the war firsthand. But for now, he had the very fresh memories of the hour he'd spent with Emi. That would have to be enough to carry him till tomorrow.

He took a roundabout way to the hospital, past the camp's orchard of orange trees, letting the sweet aroma fill his lungs. A few Japanese men were back tending to the trees, finishing their shifts for the night, and Christian watched them prune the small branches for a few minutes. Quietly he observed the precision with which they worked. None of them wore gloves, instead letting their bare hands move the clippers slowly, diligently. Christian was surprised with their carefulness, their effort and apparent pride of work. They were essentially grooming their prison and Christian doubted he would have done the same. Already on his first day of dishwashing, he had barely scrubbed the bottles, just soaped and rinsed as fast as he could. Good enough to not get yelled at, said Kurt. He stayed a minute more, listening to the older men speaking Japanese and the younger men his age speaking English, and decided that the next day, he would put a little more care into washing milk bottles.

When he arrived at the hospital, a sympathetic nurse brought him to his mother's room — unfortunately, still the same room Helene had been in when the baby died.

"Christian. You came back," his mother said when he walked in, holding her arms out to him as if he were much younger. Her face was ashen, with a blue tint around her nose. She gave him a weak, closed-mouth smile and told him not to look so worried.

He sat on the floor next to the bed, reaching up to hold her hand. "I'm sorry," he said, squeezing her cold fingers. "I'm so sorry."

She held on to his hand and cried. "You're

my only blood relative in our little family now," she said. "I chose your father, but you are made from me. Flesh to flesh."

Christian nodded as she started crying so loudly that a nurse came in to administer what Christian assumed was a sedative. He rested his head against her shoulder, bending backward until his spine hurt.

He hated seeing his mother's face so lifeless. When he was younger, Christian used to sit quietly in his parents' bedroom and watch his mother play the violin, her eyebrows moving up like a sunrise, every part of her full of life, animated. He had once overheard a conversation between his parents, his mother telling his father how much their little boy enjoyed her violin music, how musical he could be. She could tell by the way he would keep time with his little foot, banging it against the leg of the chair he sat in. She suggested that they buy him a violin and that she could teach him. That she'd enjoy it. But Franz wouldn't hear of it.

"Too feminine," he'd said. "This is America. He has to only do the things American boys do. Football and baseball and driving cars."

"He's eight," Helene had replied, disappointment apparent in her voice.

Christian had still never played a note on

the violin, but after the conversation, he had played football and baseball with more effort than ever before, and never missed a day of his mother's violin practice, his foot keeping the beat even louder as he grew into a teenager.

After the quiet had gone on so long that it seemed to interfere, Helene looked down at Christian and asked, "Do you want to go to Germany with me? I know we didn't talk about it when you came, but I assume you know all about it now. Maybe not telling you was a mistake. But you can't fault me too much. I just wanted my son with me. But you do want to go, don't you? Our family, together, no matter where or how?"

"Of course I do," Christian answered, standing to kiss his mother's cheek. "Together, no matter where or how."

CHAPTER 10

Christian Lange
June 1943

When the calendar flipped to June, a heat wave engulfed the camp that astonished even the Japanese from Southern California. It made life behind fences even harder to bear, with the only relief being the swimming pool, and that became so crowded after school and work hours that it was often body-to-body.

The next time Christian saw Emi was on a day like that. He had started to go to the pool every night after the evening roll call, but he never saw her and instead had to pretend to be reading the German books assigned to him in school. On his fourth visit, in mid-June, she was there, too.

He had almost given up looking for her and was about to jump in the water when she walked out of the Japanese changing room wearing a navy blue bathing suit. Her long, thin legs, her small breasts, her straight, athletically built torso, and the balletic grace with which she carried it all turned heads as she eyed the deep end, but she looked at no one in particular. She bent over, her long hair sweeping down her shoulder, and dropped her towel before diving cleanly into the pool.

Christian could see her hair flowing behind her as she swam underwater, the German and Japanese children in the pool parting for her, something they never did for him. At the end of the pool, despite the fact that it was a circle instead of a rectangle, she executed a precise flip turn and swam back to the other side. She only made it halfway before she had to come up for air. Inhaling deeply, she pushed her hair out of her face and took it around to one shoulder, finally letting Christian inspect her back, her vertebrae showing when she arched. He imagined running his hand down her spine, pushing away water droplets until they evaporated from the heat on her very pale skin. He thought about what she would smell like when he first leaned over her, the way her arms would feel as he pulled her close to him, what she would think when she first felt his lips on her skin. He imagined her eyes closed, her body smelling of chlorine and the sweat that came from the eternal summer days of Texas.

When she got out of the pool after re-adjusting her suit, he badly wanted to fol-low her, to sit near her, but none of the older Germans sat near the Japanese, so he stayed put at the rear of the pool's thin concrete surround, his eyes fixed on her despite the sun's glare in his face.

Suddenly, he felt a wet slap against his back.

"Hey, Lange. You got a crush on someone? That Jap over there? Sure looks that way to me," said Kurt, coming around from behind him.

Christian looked up to see Kurt in his bathing suit, his skin still a pink-tinted white. He was pudgy in all the wrong places, but his cheerful, pleasant face made it easier to forgive his ample midsection. He took out a glass bottle of water and drank a few swallows before pouring the rest on top of his head and shaking it out like a dog, spray-ing Christian.

"You're the kind of person that says 'Jap'?" Christian asked as Kurt arranged himself on his towel.

"Nah, I just wanted to piss you off. Be-cause you have a crush on that Jap. You should see your face."

187

"I definitely do," said Christian, lying down again. "Have a crush on that Jap*anese* girl. Know anything about her?"

"I know she's a rich kid," said Kurt with his eyes closed against the sun. "Real high-class. Her dad is a diplomat or a general or something. I also know you're not the only one to have a crush on her — on the Japanese or German side — and that she's what . . . twenty? Twenty-five?"

"Twenty-one."

"Fine. Twenty-one. Well, that means she's not going to want anything to do with an American kid like you. Look at all those eyes on her. You should give up now. There are plenty of girls at the high school who are in love with you."

"Are there?" Christian asked, surprised.

"Sure there are. Are you really that stupid or are you just being humble?"

Christian shrugged, still looking at Emi.

"You're just bad at reading women," said Kurt. "Lucky for you, I have a gift for it. Now things aren't great for me because I'm in fourth-grade *Deutsch,* but who am I not to help out my fellow man, especially my interned fellow man of pure German stock? But that one," he said, raising his head and looking at Emi, "is not in your orbit. Plus, they separate the sides for a reason. I bet

O'Rourke will come running if you try something with a Japanese girl. Mixed-race anything is mighty illegal in Texas."

"There are mixed-race people here," said Christian.

"Then they are illegal," said Kurt. "Texas probably doesn't even acknowledge them as human beings."

They watched Emi as she dove into the water again, this time making it down the pool and back without coming up for air.

"I forgot to say before, but I'm real sorry about your mom," Kurt said when Emi had climbed out of the pool again, silently greeted by her coterie of Japanese admirers. "Real bad luck."

"Is that what it is?" asked Christian, still watching Emi.

Kurt shrugged and tried to kick a passing lizard. He kicked the concrete instead, making his toe bleed. "Whatever it is, I'm sorry."

Christian nodded his thanks and they watched the kids playing in the deep end; the youngest seemed to have forgotten that they were fenced in, simply enjoying being in cool water on a hot summer afternoon.

"Maybe it's easier to be here if you're young," said Kurt. "But at our age? Have you ever been more bored? Now you've got your crush to amuse you, but even that's not enough, is it? I want to drive a car. Run on the road. Go to a school where I'm in eleventh grade. For Christ's sake, I'm in a German class full of nine-year-olds. Can you imagine? I want to be in a class where I can stare at pretty girls. Instead, all I daydream about is jumping that fence and running as fast as I can from this place."

"They'd kill you," said Christian flatly.

"That doesn't happen in my dream. Instead I sprint right out of town like Jesse Owens, I'm never caught, and I'm hailed a hero. Also, there's a girl out there waiting for me. An innocent American of pure Irish origin who doesn't even know about these camps and would never think that a dashing fellow like myself could find himself trapped like cattle."

"Instead you are hailed a hero by Herr Beringer and his dishrags," said Christian. "I've seen how many bottles you can get through in four hours. You're the Jesse Owens of dishwashing."

"Lucky me," said Kurt, rolling onto his well-padded stomach, his cheek on the rough concrete.

"We all need a skill," said Christian. "At least tomorrow's Saturday. I need the weekend to figure out how to get Emi Kato to fall in love with me. You can help me brainstorm at work."

"No, I won't be there tomorrow," Kurt mumbled, his mouth half-open. "I don't work for Herr Beringer on Saturday. Haven't you noticed?"

"Don't you?" said Christian, thinking back. "Why not?"

"Because I'm Jewish," Kurt said, his eyes closed. "Beringer lets me work Sunday instead."

"What?" said Christian, sitting up. "You're Jewish?"

"Yeah," Kurt said. "And I'm the kind of Jew that doesn't work on Saturday. Is that a problem?"

"Of course not," Christian replied. "I'm just wondering why someone Jewish would be stuck here with us. I thought they were imprisoning us to protect the rest of the Americans, especially the Jews."

"Bad luck is why I'm in here," said Kurt, seemingly appeased. He closed his eyes. "Like everyone else. Well, most everyone else. There are definitely a few Nazis among us, but I try to stay far away from them."

"Yeah, you don't have to be Jewish to know that."

"And what about you? Why did the feds flag the picture-perfect Lange clan?" asked Kurt. "Too good-looking and successful?"

"Haven't I told you already?" asked Christian. "My dad's vice president ratted us out, I'm sure of it. It's the only explanation that makes sense. He's probably praying that we die here or that we all get blown apart in Germany, then the whole thing can be his. Greedy ass. But you're the Jew. Your story has to be more interesting."

"The beginning, you can probably guess," said Kurt. "My father came to America to escape the anti-Semitism in Germany — it was already getting worse in the twenties — and then in '42 he gets arrested here for suspected Nazi activity. Him. Who was raised Orthodox. It would be laughable if it wasn't so depressing."

"What was he doing that got him arrested? I know those FBI agents are stupid, but that's a whole new level."

"From what I know it was just fear. And that canceled out reason," said Kurt, propping himself up on his elbow. "My dad was a math teacher in Germany but he couldn't find work in the United States. He looked for almost a year while we lived with his sister above a laundromat in Queens — two bedrooms for six people and a kitchen that always smelled like burning rubber — but nothing. So he took a job delivering newspapers to the German-speaking community in New York. Not great pay, but steady. We moved into our own place at least. Then war broke out, and I guess some of those Germans he was delivering the paper to were FBI suspects, which made my father suspect by association because he dealt with them every day. They thought he was hiding messages, running information."

Kurt sat up and wrapped the towel around his feet, pushing it in between each toe. "I don't like the bugs crawling in there, makes me paranoid," he explained, not seeming to mind the bugs near his head. "It was that or some asshole just ratted him out for fun," he said. "Maybe they said he was a fake Jew. Who knows? When was your father arrested?"

"Five months ago."

"Only? Mine was arrested right away, like the Japanese. He was cuffed during the raids after Pearl Harbor. Me and my mother and sister just joined him this year when they opened this family camp, but we aren't repatriating like most of the people here. For obvious reasons. At least the United States knows not to send their Jews to Germany right now to die on arrival."

"Do you believe what they say is happening to the Jews in Europe?" asked Christian. "That Hitler wants to kill every single one?"

"I believe every word," said Kurt. He pointed to Emi, who was watching them, but she turned away as soon as Christian looked at her.

"I do, too," said Christian.

Kurt squinted across the pool again and nudged Christian. "You've got happier things to think about. She's looking at us again. You," he said, this time nodding subtly in Emi's direction. "I'm going to go before I have to observe your embarrassment. Tell me later about how your marriage proposal failed."

Kurt stood up and headed to the German changing room while Christian looked at Emi. She stared back at him and motioned with her head in the direction of the large citrus orchard east of the pool. Christian mouthed the word *orchard* and she gave a tiny nod, which caused him to jump up fast, leave his only towel on the pavement, and push his way into the changing room as fast as the children coming out of it would let him.

Hoping to get there first, he put on his clothes hastily, threw his wet bathing suit over his shoulder, and started toward the orchard.

He knew that instead of going to the orchard to meet Emi, he should be going home to check on his mother, to sit with her. The day before when he went to see her, she was staring intently at a blank wall, reaching her hand out to it. When he asked her what she was looking at, she'd simply answered, "Lora." "Let her be," his father had said, motioning for him to leave again. When they had first arrived, his father had spent many nights at the German beer hall, trying to charm his way to the top of the internment camp heap as if he were still at the River Hills Country Club, but since the baby's death, he had stayed with Helene. Christian stopped for a moment to look at the sky, thinking of his beautiful, quiet mother.

When he started for the orange trees again, he was immediately stopped in his tracks by a pair of big green eyes, shining in the dark like an animal's. They belonged to Inge.

"Big kraut!" she said, rushing up to him and throwing her thin arms around his waist. "It's been so long since I've seen you."

"Really? I thought I saw you yesterday after school," said Christian. "Where is your mother?" he asked looking for her.

"Oh yeah," Inge said smiling, ignoring his

last question. She let go of his waist and slipped her hand in his. "Where are you going?" she asked.

"I can't tell you," he said, watching her happy face cloud over.

"Why not?"

"Because I'm not supposed to be going there."

"Oh good. Can I come too, then?" she asked, jumping up and down, her brown curls springing like a doll's.

"Absolutely not."

"You were more fun in Wisconsin," she said, but kept her hand in his as they stood on the dirt road. Together they listened to the faint sounds of their desolate corner of Texas, so different from the booming noise of the children's home where they'd met.

"I saw your mother at the hospital," Inge said finally. "The baby died, so she was crying."

"You saw her?" asked Christian, surprised.

"My *mutter* went to visit and I went with her. She told me the baby died and that I should hug your mama tightly."

"I'm sure she appreciated it," said Christian, noticing how much happier Inge seemed now that she was with her mother again. Perhaps, he thought, there was some good in pushing families back together in

Crystal City before expelling them from the country.

"Oh, she did. She braided my hair for me, too, because it looked messy and I like it to look neat. She cried while she was doing it, but it was a really nice braid, the kind that starts at the very top of your hair. Then I gave her a shoelace to put on the end like a bow."

"It's remarkable what we've done with shoelaces these past couple months," said Christian, smiling and thinking about Inge with the shoelace around her neck in Milwaukee. It already felt like so long ago. "The baby was a little girl," Christian explained. "So I'm sure my mom appreciated you letting her braid your hair."

"That's sad. Little girls should never die," said Inge.

"I agree," said Christian, starting to worry about the time. He didn't want Emi to be alone in the orchard. "I have to go, Inge," he said, putting his other hand on her head. "And you should get home, too."

She gripped his hand tightly, before finally relenting and giving him a hug.

"Good night then, little kraut," he said, giving her a push toward her house.

"Good night, big kraut," she screamed before running away.

Christian hurried to the orchard, which wasn't fenced in. He slipped easily inside the line of trees and waited by the corner where he could see the swimming pool. He was wiping away the chlorinated water still dripping down the back of his neck when he felt a hand on his shoulder. Emi's perfect hand.

"You beat me here," he said, as she had come from farther inside the orchard.

"Of course," she said, her wet hair tied up tightly on her head. "And you're loitering by the edge. Not the best idea. The guards patrol here all the time."

Christian followed her until they were swallowed up by trees. "I'm glad you asked me to come here," he said, still feeling the warmth of her hand on his shoulder, though she'd moved it as soon as he turned around.

"Did I ask you here for *those* kinds of reasons?" she said, giving him a half smile. "Or did I just nod my head toward the orchard? Maybe I want you to help me pick oranges."

"That's fine," he said, flushing from embarrassment. He reached up and pulled an orange from the tree, placing it in her hand.

"We'll see," she said, pulling off the thick peel. She let the juice run down her hands before putting a piece in her mouth.

"I watched you dive into the pool," he said as he studied her. "It was perfect, like a knife slicing through the water."

"Every time I dive in the deep end, I get nervous," she said. "I can't help but think about the day Sachiko and Aiko drowned."

"Who?" asked Christian, not aware that anyone in camp had died before Lora. "People died here?"

"No one tells you much of anything, do they?" Emi said, wiping her sticky hands against Christian's T-shirt sleeve. "You know that some of the Japanese and Germans here were living in South America. Their countries made an arrangement with the United States to have them deported."

Christian shook his head yes. His father had explained why a group of the German internees spoke Spanish.

"Right before you came, two Japanese girls from Peru drowned in the deep end of the swimming pool. I saw it happen. Dozens of us did. But no one could get to them in time. The bottom of the pool is so slippery, it just wasn't possible. We tried to edge over to them while holding the ropes, but we were all too slow. Even the lifeguards."

"They died right there in front of you?"

Emi nodded. "One of the girl's mothers tried to kill herself the night it happened,

199

and the other was close to breaking, too. Those mothers are still here. They didn't even let them go home after that."

"That's awful," said Christian, his mind going back to the image of dead Lora in his mother's arms. "Who else has died here?"

"They were the only ones to die so far. Besides your mother's baby. At a camp in Fort Sill, Oklahoma, I was told that a man jumped the fence and they shot and killed him, but that hasn't happened here, yet. Everyone is aware that trying to escape means death."

"Is your mother doing better?" Emi asked, reaching up for another orange. She, Christian quickly realized, did not care too much about the camp rules, and as the daughter of someone prominent, she probably had more leeway than the others.

"Not really," said Christian. "She's very angry at the driver who hit her, but she's angrier at America, I think. If we weren't here, if she hadn't gotten run over, then Lora — that's what she named the baby — would still be alive. She keeps saying that to me. What if, what if. And all her what-ifs end with her holding a live baby instead of a dead one."

"She's probably right, unfortunately," said Emi, her voice sympathetic. "The baby would be alive if you all weren't here. If the Americans weren't so scared of their own shadows." She looked at Christian and said, "Not Americans like you."

"She doesn't look the same, either," said Christian. "She's pale and sick and spends the day staring at nothing. I was terrified to go to Germany when I first heard about it, but am less scared now. My mom needs to get away from this place. She's already dreaming about Germany, and you know it takes a lot for a person to long for a country fighting a war."

"Especially because she's already lived through one," said Emi.

"That's strange to think about," said Christian, realizing that his parents almost never talked about the Great War.

"Japan and Germany fought against each other in the Great War. And now they're allies. Does a country really go from hate to love in twenty years? I don't think so. It's just money, power, expansion by any means necessary, and we all have to sit idly by."

Christian's stomach turned at the thought of it. War. They were going to be sailing into war. He, who had up until a few months ago thought hardship was a football game that ended in defeat, a cold winter that you weren't quite dressed for, or a girl who wasn't as interested in you as you hoped. Those were the little wars that Christian had waged. Now he was going to be dropped into Nazi Germany. He knew how unprepared he was and that nothing, not even a children's home and an internment camp, was going to change that.

"And you?" Emi asked, picking up on his anxiety. "Are you ready to go to Germany?"

"Me? Of course not," said Christian, rolling an orange in his hand. "I've heard that Americans who speak German are easy targets. I won't have to fight for Germany, because I'm American, but the Nazis will probably throw me in prison for that exact reason. That's what some people are saying, anyway. They worry we'll be seen as on the wrong side of the war. Or they'll think we're spies. Kurt keeps telling me that that's the most likely scenario, and that they'll cut off my toes one by one and feed them to me. I'm trying not to believe him. Whatever my fate is though, it's lose-lose. They hate me here, they'll hate me there. I can't think of a corner of the world that would want me, us, the German-Americans, right now. It's like I want to run somewhere safe but there is no somewhere safe."

"It might be the same for the *Nisei* in Japan," said Emi. "I hope not."

Christian ran his foot through the dirt and checked over his shoulder to make sure they hadn't been spotted. It was nearly dark, so he was starting to feel safer. "I've only been to Germany three times, so I don't know my family there well at all. The FBI agents who came to our house accused my mother's cousin Jutta of being a Nazi. I only remember her looking and smelling like cooked potatoes, but I suppose anyone can change. My father's family, I don't know. I assume the Americans did their homework, but maybe they found one Nazi in our family tree and that was enough to arrest us. Maybe my father's side is littered with them. My dad, he keeps saying that we will live with his family and somehow their lifestyle will shield us from the realities of war, but I don't believe him. War puts everyone on equal footing."

"I lived in Austria in 1938," said Emi. "With my parents. And it wasn't even war yet, not officially anyway, but it was already horrible. The chaos didn't put everyone on equal footing. For some it was much worse."

Christian was about to respond when they saw a beam of light circling the watchtower nearest to the orchard, on the edge of the north fence.

"Time to go," said Emi, moving quickly

toward the southern boundary with Christian behind her. "Let's wait until the light passes again and then run toward the pool."

"You go there. I'll make it home," said Christian. He reached for her hand and she let hers rest inside his. He waited another moment to gauge her reaction and brought her hand up to his lips and kissed it.

"Let's watch each other swim again tomorrow," he whispered.

"I can't speak to you there," she replied, bringing her face closer. "You know people will talk."

"I know. Let's meet underwater then. Where no one can see us. You swim one way, and I'll swim the other, and for just a few seconds, we'll meet in the middle."

Emi smiled. "Okay. Tomorrow evening. Head to the pool right after roll call." She squeezed his hand just as the light shined over their feet and then they both took off running.

CHAPTER 11

Emi Kato
June 1943

For the next week, Emi and Christian met underwater every evening. Emi would do her flawless dive into the pool, with her legs pin-straight and her toes pointed, and then she'd swim four lengths. When she did her second flip turn, Christian would jump sloppily in on his side before doing a messy breaststroke toward her. Their eyes open, they'd watch each other approach, then brush hands quickly under the water, making it look like an accidental touch in a crowded pool. Then Emi would swim through the groups of laughing children, gliding through with very little splash, before getting out to lie on her brown towel, bleached in so many places that it looked polka-dotted, and watch the sun melt over them, their orange and pink painting.

After seven days of touching hands in the

pool, without any mention of them meeting again in the orchard, Emi decided it was time she bring it up.

She had wanted to see him again, alone, since the night he kissed her hand under the orange trees, but her longing for Leo kept her from doing anything more than brushing Christian's fingers in the pool. It was June 1943 and she had not had a letter from Leo since December 1941. The lack of any communication with Leo had made her so much lonelier and the camps even harder to bear.

And now, there was Christian. He had come into her life at a time when her depression had started to feel permanent. There he was, standing in the hospital with his movie star looks and raw desperation over his mother and dead sister. He had looked at Emi in a way that made her blood go warmer, just like it used to with Leo. She realized she was desperate for companionship, and for the feeling of being wanted, rather than all the hate and apathy she'd been surrounded with since Pearl Harbor. Really, since they'd come to America.

The next time they were at the pool together, nine days since meeting in the orchard, Emi pushed her thoughts of Leo away and motioned to Christian as subtly as she could. She pulled her wet hair over her right shoulder, wrung it out, and stared at Christian until he turned and looked at her. She mouthed *orchard,* like he had done the first time they'd gone, and made the outline of an orange with her hand. She quickly flashed nine fingers and then put her hands behind her back, lying back down on her towel, propped up only high enough to see Christian's reaction. He looked up at the clock near the bathhouse, which read seven thirty, then nodded yes and left the pool. She watched him go, his tall, tan body bathed so perfectly in an American summer. She wished that she were observing him somewhere else, on a beautiful beach or a neighborhood pool without curfews and patrols.

She breathed in deeply. Somewhere in the camp, something was burning. It smelled like smoke in winter, refreshingly out of season. She inhaled again, thinking of how fresh the air used to smell in Europe when it was cold. Stale and old. The best air in the world.

There was something different about that night. Something was going to happen, something more than touching hands in the pool. The fire in her nose felt like it matched the rest of her. It was desire — she admitted to herself as she breathed slowly in and out, transported by the smell of burning — the kind of physical craving that could stamp out misery in any circumstance.

After the darkness started to take over, and it was almost nine, Emi got dressed slowly and walked carefully toward the orchard, feeling like someone young and beautiful for the first time in so long.

Alone, in their corner, Emi waited for Christian, sitting on the ground in one of the homemade camp dresses with seams that looked as if they had been stitched by knitting needles, her back against an orange tree. She smiled when she heard him coming, and was very aware of how her pulse had quickened. When he was in view, a small flashlight in his hand, he extended his other hand, calloused from his hours of dishwashing, to help her up.

"Are you looking at this ugly dress?" she said, as his light shined on it. "I used to wear my nice clothes when I got here, but I realized there was no point. I might as well save them for when I return to Japan, since I doubt I'll have anything new for a long while. My father has informed me that I won't need my nice clothes there, but at the very least, maybe I can sell them. So for now, this." She looked down at her dress, the outline of her body just visible in the lamplight. She had lost ten pounds the month after she was diagnosed with tuberculosis, but working at the camp hospital was helping her gain it back. Being on her feet all day was building muscle and she was finally feeling strong again.

Christian started to protest about her dress, but she hushed him.

"One day we're going to get in trouble for being here. It's more a matter of when than if. But let's just keep enjoying it until we do. It's invigorating to be doing something a little risky, don't you think?"

Christian took a step closer, keeping the flashlight angled down toward the ground, making sure the guards could not see the light.

"Even if you'd said we're going to get shot instead of we're going to get caught, I don't think I could stop coming here with you," said Christian. "Not after these past few days spent underwater."

"Really?" Emi said, playfully. She knew from the first time she walked to the pool with Christian that he might fall in love with her. It was like Leo. She could tell that her differences were interesting to him, even pretty.

"Touching my hand was enough to make

you fall in love with me?" she said, reaching out for his hand, which he gave her eagerly.

"I didn't say that," said Christian, his change of tone showing his embarrassment.

"You wouldn't have wanted to know me a few months ago. When we were in Seagoville, I was the worst version of myself. I was anything but optimistic." Emi leaned against his shoulder, her thin frame against his broad one, and tilted her head back, exposing the length of perfect skin on her neck. Christian leaned down and kissed it, causing a rush of warmth to shoot from her heart up to her head. It was hard to keep quiet from the joy it brought her.

"Look at the camp lights, they're almost pretty," she said in response, trying to calm herself. "Let's try to imagine they are stadium lights or theater lights. The bright lights of Texas." She turned to him. "When my father told us we were moving to America, I never thought it would mean this."

"Of course not," said Christian.

"I still think about the boat ride over here. I wasn't convinced I would like America yet, but it was one of the most glamorous experiences of my life. Beautiful cabin, well-dressed women mingling happily on deck. I loved that boat. I've done some of my best thinking on the deck of a ship, but especially that particular ship."

"I think the nice things, the memories, matter even more during war," said Christian.

"Aren't you sentimental," said Emi. "What are you holding on to, then? Besides my hand," she said, looking down at their fingers, interlaced again, both their nails short and brittle, their skin dry and his sun tanned.

"Well . . . as juvenile as this may sound, I've been thinking a lot about how much peace I've had at home with my parents all these years," said Christian, holding her hand tighter. "That I've been lucky, because I know so few people have what I've had. My mother didn't. My dad, maybe, but there was a strictness that came with his privilege growing up in Germany. My parents have done a good job giving me more than I need while not sacrificing the time they spent with me. They've coddled me too much, I understand that now, but always with good intentions. As a boy, I was practically sewed to my mother's hand, and she still makes me feel that way. It's weird, but some of the happiest times I've spent with her have been sitting in our kitchen — we have this big kitchen in Wisconsin. Even on rainy days it feels like it's sunny. Anyway, we didn't do anything special. It was just a very warm room and my mother always made me feel like it belonged to the two of us."

"Your poor mother," said Emi, thinking of the day she'd helped discharge her. "I hope you have that sense of happiness with her again soon. Even if it's in Germany."

"Germany. I won't have any freedom there," he said flatly, "but we have freedom here. Not real freedom," he clarified as Emi looked at him questioningly. "But here with you, hiding among the trees, it feels something like freedom."

"Do we have something?" she asked, her blood going warm again. She looked up at his face, less and less visible as the sky went from dark blue to black, and put her arms around his back. Without letting reason start to hum between her ears, she tilted her head up and kissed him. Caught by surprise, his lips were stiff at first, but in seconds they had relaxed into hers and the kiss turned into the perfect moment she hoped it would. She had kissed him, and he had kissed her back, but soon after that initial touch of flesh, it was him, desperately moving his mouth against hers, holding her firmly, and more confidently than she thought he would. She wanted to write off his age, but she was even younger when she'd first kissed Leo and she'd felt very grown up.

"I don't know," he said, his face very close to hers. She could still make out the stubble on his chin, very pale, but there, and the small freckle he had under his right eye. His face, she realized, had become very familiar. He ran his hand across her cheek and said, "Kiss me again so I can see what we have." Emi, who even in flat shoes was only a few inches shorter than him, tilted her head up and kissed him. "Emi," said Christian, holding her bare arms, her skin sticky with the evening humidity. "We definitely have something."

Chapter 12

Emi Kato
August 1943

Emi rolled over in bed, hugging her flat pillow and thinking about the orange orchard and the hours she was spending there with Christian. Night after night, after they finished dinner on their respective sides, they would escape to the trees, lips and bodies against each other as soon as they came together in the dark. Emi flipped over on her back, wearing, against her will, her nice cotton nightgown, far too well made for the Texas heat. When she went to the orchard that first night, thoughts of Leo had accompanied her. They'd promised each other, when they separated in 1939, that they would find a way to be together forever. What was she doing then? Running off after dark with someone else?

But now, when she went to meet Christian, no thought of Leo came with her. Leo who had become a ghost — and perhaps one who no longer needed her.

Maybe it wasn't right, but she was happy. She was finally happy. Not wholly and completely, like she had been in Vienna — she would never again be that innocent and naïvely in love — but at least she wasn't always looking over her shoulder, relying on her memories to get through each day. For the first time in four years, the present was more important than the past. Happiness now, guilt later, she told herself as she got out of bed.

Back in the orchard that night, life felt like it was normal again. The new normal. One where danger seemed a little further away and intimacy was unbreakable. So it didn't surprise Emi when three days later, Christian didn't just brush her hand in the pool, but grabbed it and pulled it above the water for everyone to see. "I've decided it's time to stop caring about getting into trouble," he said as she lowered her hand back under the water.

"Really?" she said smiling. "Because you sure are courting it right now." She was happy that Christian wasn't ashamed of her, but she was scared that the gossip would get back to her mother, who had yet to say a thing about Christian. Emi assumed she knew, that some in the camp had seen them together and had told her. But Keiko seemed to be erring on the side of discretion, probably thinking more of her daughter's happiness than her own.

"I have a surprise for you," Christian said, just above a whisper. "But you have to come to the German side to get it. Meet me by the water tower on Airport Drive. Just past the Japanese market at the usual time." The usual time didn't have a number attached to it. It was thirty or so minutes after roll call was completed, when the sun was starting to sink low in the sky.

Before Emi could answer, Christian was underwater again, and she watched him as he swam choppily through the pool and then pulled himself up, heading toward a reclining Kurt.

That evening, Emi watched the emotionless guard check her and her mother's names off the list yet again, then she ran to the water tower in her best pair of shoes. She'd been on the German side plenty of times before. It was impossible not to crisscross the camp, for while the houses were grouped together by nationality, the public areas like the Japanese market and the German bakery were built close to one another.

She saw Christian standing near the chapel, looking slightly guilty. His blond hair was combed and he was in what looked like clean clothes. She watched him for a moment, staring along the dusty road trying to spot her coming. She was happy that she had reached him without him seeing her arrive. She liked to be the one to startle him.

"Is it a real surprise?" she asked as she approached.

He turned around to look at her. "I think you know what it is by now. But let's just pretend you don't. Come on." He motioned for her to follow him across the road to the chapel.

"Is the surprise in the chapel? Is the door open in the evening?" she said, trying to look past him. She knew it was a piano, she couldn't imagine what else it would be, and she felt silly for not looking in the chapel before.

"Yes, it's in the chapel," Christian said, reaching for both her hands and holding her still.

"Is the surprise that you're going to try to convert me?" Emi said, walking in.

She let Christian lead her to the back of the chapel, where he started to open a little door to a storage closet. He hesitated, put one hand over her eyes, then opened the door wide. "It's an empty chapel with an out-of-tune —"

"Piano!" Emi exclaimed, pulling his hand away. "I was hoping it would be."

"You knew it would be," he said, opening the dusty black lid. "But thank you for acting surprised."

She pushed past him and sat down on the bench, leaning over and placing the side of her face on the keys. "How did you find out it was here?" She had played so many pianos in her life, but she was as excited to play this cheap one as she had been to play antique Steinways in Austria.

"I asked O'Rourke if there was a piano at camp and he laughed at me and asked why I hadn't been to church yet. I guess it's played on Sundays and then rolled back in this closet. Sorry I didn't figure that out before, but I did get permission to come in here this evening. I told him it was so I could play, so let's hope he doesn't ask me to give a recital or anything."

Emi ran her fingers across the keys and played a few chords.

"Is it okay?" Christian asked, sitting down next to her.

"It's very out of tune, and it's not the grandest piano I've ever played, but it's perfect." She hummed a few bars, then launched into a well-known Mozart tune. After a few chords she stopped and said, "That doesn't feel right. Not when you went to all this trouble. I'll play my very favorite for you." Her favorite. The song Leo always asked for. She didn't know if it was she who loved it or if it was her favorite because it reminded her of him.

She put her fingers on the keys and then started to laugh, lifting them again.

"It's funny, I haven't played the piano in over a year. I feel like I'm breaking a law."

"Who cares if we are," said Christian, pushing on one of the keys.

Emi moved his hand away and began the familiar piece, much slower and more emotional than the Mozart. She felt Christian's eyes on her as her thin fingers stepped easily across the keys. When she was finished, she rested her hands in her lap, her eyes alight. "Chopin, Opus Ten, Étude number three," she said, before he could ask. "It's been my favorite for a long time. It's not very hard to play, but difficult to perfect, so that's why I keep playing it. Plus, everyone seems to like it." The Hartmanns, at least, did.

"Play it again," Christian said, placing her hands back on the keys.

"The same one?" said Emi grinning up at him.

"Yes, please."

"There's orange dust everywhere," she said, blowing on the keys. "You can really see it on the black keys, like sand between someone's teeth. You can't escape it. Even in here." She wiped some off with her shirt hem and launched into the étude again, elbowing Christian out of her way. He stood up and watched her from above, and when she was done, she exhaled happily. Emi played five more pieces and finished with a jazz song by Cole Porter. As soon as she had stopped playing, Christian lifted her up from the bench and held her close to him, humming the tune as they started to sway.

"Isn't it illegal to dance in church?" asked Emi, looking around and tipping her head back.

"No," said Christian laughing. "What gave you that idea?"

"I don't know. Churches always seemed quite stiff to me."

She rested her cheek against his shoulder as he hummed "I Get a Kick out of You," which she'd just played.

"If you had to fight for one side, who would you fight for?" Emi asked as he held her tight, starting the song over again, adding the words in.

"The Americans, of course," said Christian, looking into her eyes. "I'm American."

"The Americans? Would you?" she said surprised. "You'd fly over Germany and drop bombs on your relatives? Or fly over Japan and drop them on mine?"

"I never thought of it that way," he said, slowly. "That's depressing."

"It's true, isn't it?"

"I just feel more American. I feel ninety-nine percent American. It's only recently, with what's happened to my family, that the one percent slipped away. I'm angry at this country now, at the government, at O'Rourke. All this," Christian said, looking around the simple chapel, "is an awful thing to do to innocent people."

Emi was about to answer when they heard a loud bang behind them. They turned around and looked, paranoia growing between them, but there was no one there.

"It must be outside," said Christian, "but let's leave anyway. We're probably pushing our luck with the time." They slipped out the back and, clasping hands, ran toward the orchard out of instinct.

Safely hidden in the trees, Emi collapsed to the ground. "Today was very memorable," she said, looking up at Christian and smiling. "Thank you for that surprise. For a few moments I forgot where we were."

He fell to the ground, too, rather clumsily and took Emi's hand. "It scares me how much I like you," he said. "I know I'm not supposed to say things like that, and I never have before, but caution seems like a ridiculous line to follow in here."

"I'm glad you like me," she said happily. She stretched out her legs so her feet were resting in his lap.

"Oh," he said laughing. "You're glad *I* like you? There's nothing there on your end?"

"You're not bad," she said, before she sat up and kissed him gently on the mouth.

"Kiss me again," said Christian, pulling her close to him.

When he let her go, he looked at her face, which she knew was more freckled from the sun than when he'd first met her, and said, "I know you think I'm a bit of a dumb kid. Seventeen. Wisconsin. All that."

"I've never been to Wisconsin," she said smiling.

"It's not Austria."

"Let's not talk about Austria," she replied.

"All I mean," said Christian, reaching for her hand, "is that despite my age, and where I'm from, and this dopey wide-eyed look that I really can't get rid of. It's genetic," he said, smiling and pointing to his big blue eyes. "Despite all that, I really like you. I've kissed other girls . . ." he said. "But it always felt a little out of expectation. That I should like a certain girl, because she was pretty, or interesting, or liked me. But this — you — it's very different."

"Because you're imprisoned," said Emi laughing. "Less choice."

"I'll have you know that I am a highly desired member of the German school's class of 1944," Christian said, laughing at himself. He plucked the pebbles in the dirt and threw them into the darkness, holding on to Emi with his other hand.

"I don't doubt it," said Emi, lying back on her hands.

"Don't lie down," said Christian, reaching for her. "Let's weave deeper through the trees."

"Weave?" she said standing. "And then do what?"

"I don't know," said Christian. "Eat oranges."

"Eat oranges," she repeated slowly, and she let herself be pulled gently inside the rows of trees. They walked back a few feet, as quietly as two excited people could do, and he kissed her as soon as they were partially hidden among the branches.

With that kiss, she knew his attempts at restraint were gone and so were hers. He put his hands under her shirt, feeling the muscles, the bones in her back, slowly and respectfully, but she was already pulling at his shirttail, trying to untuck it.

Suddenly, knowing what they were about to do, she was thinking about the last person to kiss her, to touch her in that way. Her body went cold from the memory. It wasn't Leo. That boy, he had been the opposite of Leo. She stopped kissing Christian as she tried to push the image of what had happened in Vienna back into the depths of her mind. If she died in Japan, or en route to Japan, at least the last person she'd kissed would be someone she cared for.

Christian laid his shirt on the ground and Emi on top of it, asking too many times if she was comfortable.

She wasn't comfortable, but she was comfortable with him.

"Even though nothing is perfect," she said as he kissed her neck, "everything is."

"Because here it's just us," he said, his clothes off, resting on her, still breathless. "You can take some of the humanity away from people, but not all of it," he said, holding her tightly.

Emi knew that her time with Christian

was finite. But that limitation helped her get over her fear of imagining a future with him. Her future had already been promised to Leo Hartmann, and she and Christian, they could only exist in Crystal City.

Emi's life was different after that night. She was locked in an internment camp but everything else seemed to have been unlocked again. Her heart, her physical being, was thriving.

She had slept with Christian, on the ground in the orchard of an internment camp. How crazy, she said to herself the morning after it had happened. How wild and crazy and wonderful.

And how fleeting, she thought as she walked to meet him in the orchard two weeks later. Just like everything in her life had been lately.

Emi kissed Christian after they had their clothes back on and rested against one of the trees, trying to position herself around the roots. "We're leaving tomorrow," she said, not looking at him. "My mother and I. We're boarding the train to New York in the morning." She'd wanted to say it days ago, but the words refused to travel from her mind to her lips. Now she was out of time. In less than twenty-four hours, she would be gone.

Christian didn't move, didn't bend his head to look at her, and she thought he'd misheard her, but when she peered up at him, she knew he hadn't.

He sank down next to her. "How can you find out one day and leave the next? They can't make you just disappear like that. You need more time."

"I didn't just find out today," she admitted. "I found out a month ago. But I thought if I told you it would upset you. You knew I'd be leaving sometime, just as you will leave, but you didn't need to know when."

"I didn't need to know, but maybe it would have been better," he said, moving his hand away from her body.

"Perhaps," she said, sure that it wouldn't have been. "But then we would have spent the last few weeks focusing on me leaving instead of on us being right here. Present. Together."

She could tell that Christian was trying to agree with her, trying to remain stoic, but it wasn't his nature. He, she had learned early on, wore his heart on his sleeve.

"I should be your shoulder to cry on," he said, pretending to dust off his old blue T-shirt. "But we both know that I'm too crazy about you to be that person."

"Crazy good?" she said laughing.

"Crazy great," he said smiling back. "But heartbroken, too." Christian threw his body back in the dirt and let out a helpless cry, looking straight up at the never-ending Texas sky.

"I suppose it doesn't matter if we get caught anymore," said Emi after putting her hand over his mouth. "But don't be broken. You only feel that way because you had nothing to do here but fall in love."

"That's not true," he protested, wrapping his arms around her so tight that she had to wiggle out of his grip so she could breathe. "Not every young person in camp is falling in love out of boredom. This was different."

Yes, she admitted to herself, it was different. It was, like he had said, something.

"It was — you are — very important to me," she said, tracing around his sad blue eyes with her fingers. "And we will write. As much as our hands will let us. Maybe the letters will even be delivered. I know I'm going back to our family house in Tokyo. It's in a neighborhood called Azabu. It's a really nice place to live, full of houses with quite a bit of space, and shops selling housewares and things, a few noodle restaurants for when the men come home from work and little schools down one-way streets. Best of all, there isn't any barbed wire. I'll give you my address and you will give me your address in Germany. In Pforzheim. Do you know it?"

"Unfortunately," he said, holding her hand so tightly that it was beginning to sweat. "I will write to you," he promised. "But it doesn't feel like enough." He sat up, dusted off his pants, and said, "You don't know what you're returning to, and I definitely don't know what Germany is going to be like, but whatever the circumstances," said Christian, "I want to see you again. I have to."

"How will we do that?" she asked, letting her body fold into his. "Because I don't think I'll be allowed to return."

"Not here then. Somewhere else."

Where, she wondered, would two people like them ever be welcome again?

"You're a dreamer," she said, kissing him. But wasn't that always what her father said of her?

"Am I? I feel I'm a realist," he said, his gaze growing more intense.

"Do you know where Japan is?" she asked, stretching her arms wide. "Across an ocean. And who knows how long the war will last? Or if America and Japan will ever have good relations again?"

"I don't care about any of that," said Christian. "All I know is that we will see each other again and it will be wonderful."

"It's wonderful now," she said, taking his hands and wrapping his arms around her even more tightly. She'd been sure that every moment in the camps would be misery. But sometimes, the world surprised her.

"Okay, then," she said, leaning against him and closing her eyes. "Please come and find me. Life is long. I hope."

CHAPTER 13

Christian Lange
September 1943

At 10 A.M. on August 30, Emi was gone. Christian swam in the pool and reached out under the water for her invisible hand, he went into the silent orchard, and every night he walked past her empty house on the Japanese side. Unlike most of the families in the camp, Emi and her mother had not shared with another family. Perhaps, thought Christian, they were given preferential treatment. The windows were open, the two stumpy cactuses planted outside still growing — it looked as though the Kato women were home, quietly living their imprisoned lives. Christian knew how he appeared, dawdling outside an empty house on the Japanese side every night, but he was long past caring. A week after she'd left, he walked up to the door and slipped inside.

The small house smelled like a hot day in

Texas, and a hot day in Texas meant Emi. He ran his fingers over the thin walls — the paint raised in places, the brushstrokes apparent, as if applied as hastily as possible — and sat on one of the twin beds. One of them was hers. He saw a makeshift broom in the corner, abandoned.

At the pool the next day, Kurt kicked back on the pavement beside him, his skin dark from spending every afternoon outside, and said, "Don't be upset. What did you expect to happen? She's twenty-one, Japanese, far better off than even you, and she's going back to a country being shredded by war. Just be happy you knew her. Think about me. What have I known since I've been here?"

Christian shrugged and turned his face up to the sky. He rolled to the side, grabbed his shoe, and dropped it on Kurt's head because, with that comment, Kurt had really reminded him of Jack Walter from the Children's Home. He missed Jack more than he had expected to.

"What in the hell is wrong with you?" asked Kurt, picking up the shoe and hurling it into the pool.

"And that was the one with the shoelace," said Christian, watching it bob up and down in the water.

That night after roll call, he went to Emi's house again, but this time, he heard a man's voice call out to him as he walked up to the door.

"You miss her?" asked a middle-aged man standing in front of the house next door holding the same kind of rough broom as Emi's.

"Who?" said Christian, not sure what else to say.

"Who!" said the neighbor, amused. "Emiko Kato, who else? You two weren't very good at hiding. But it was nice to see at least one thing grow in this desolate place. Love between two young people."

Christian smiled at the thought and started to open the door, but the man spoke up again.

"This is the last night you can come here," he warned. "Another family is moving in tomorrow. So take your time tonight, but don't come back."

"Thank you," said Christian, adding, "I'm Christian Lange."

"I know who you are," said the man, introducing himself as John Sasaki. "And I'm sorry for your mother and her baby. Terrible thing."

"Does this side know about that, too?" Christian asked.

"Of course we know. The camp news-papers leave a lot to be desired, there are barely any books to read. What else is there to do but gossip? I think we all know everything. Even the sad things."

"I guess so."

"It's being cut off from everything that's the worst part, isn't it?" said John. "I don't know any of the current troop movements in Europe, and my son is fighting over there."

"For the Americans?"

John frowned. "Of course. I'm American and so is he. Just like you are."

"I'm sorry," said Christian, embarrassed. "That was a stupid thing to say. I hope your son is okay."

"That's the one thing they would tell you in here," said John, relaxing again. "That your son is dead."

"I suppose so," said Christian. He thanked John for the update on the house and opened the Katos' door.

Once inside, Christian immediately no-ticed an envelope on the floor that had not been there the day before. He bent down to pick it up. It was addressed to Emi and was post-marked from Japan. Ignoring his qualms, Christian stuck his finger in the flap of the envelope and opened it. Like all the mail that came into the camp, it had been opened and resealed, but unlike the letters he'd received from Jack, this one bore none of the censors' black marks. It was short and written in Japanese. Christian studied the characters, as Emi had taught him a few simple kanji, but he didn't recognize any of the writing.

Deciding to take the letter anyway, he put it back in the envelope and walked outside. John Sasaki was still there, watching him. "Done already?" he said, eyeing Christian suspiciously.

Christian shrugged and tried to hide the letter, but John spotted it. "Stealing something on your way out?"

"It's just a letter I found on the floor," said Christian, wishing he had hidden it.

"And I'm sure you opened it," said John, walking over. He took the letter from Christian and scanned it. "Would you like to know what it says?"

"Of course," said Christian, looking over John's shoulder at the inscrutable text.

John smiled and said, "You're going to be happy."

Christian took the letter back and looked at it as if all of a sudden it might translate itself. "What does it say?" he asked.

John pointed at the last character. "In

Japanese you read from right to left." He traced the vertical text with his hand and said, "Beginning here it says, 'You sounded very much in love in your last letter, Emiko-chan. And I will never be the one to criticize you falling for an American. I am, after all, the one who brought you there. Despite the geography of Japan, the world is not an island.

" 'Since you asked in your last letter, I'm still doing just fine, though the house is silent without you. It misses you very much, just like I do. I will write more soon, but I just wanted you to know that even the architecture is longing to see you.' "

John looked at Christian and smiled even more broadly. "It's from her father, of course," he said, pointing at the name at the bottom of the letter. "This says 'father.' Or more like 'papa.' That's a better translation." John put the envelope on top of the letter and pointed to the sender's information. "Norio Kato. That is her father. And it looks like he's sent the letter from the Foreign Ministry in Tokyo. Probably increased its chances of arrival here. Though certainly of being read by censors, too. Looks like they were humane with this one. Didn't black out a thing."

"Does it really say that?" said Christian,

grabbing the letter back, barely hearing John's last words. "It says that? Love? About me. Are you sure? To her father? Can you check again?"

"It does," said John, keeping his grip on the envelope. "Looks like you made a bigger impression on Emiko than you're aware of. But that's how it is with women like her, a reserved Japanese woman from a certain echelon of society. She probably kept her feelings closer to the heart than you did."

"Could you write down the translation?" said Christian, holding the letter more carefully, afraid to crease it, the words on the page starting to float under his gaze. "I don't want to forget what it says."

John went inside to fetch a pen, then jotted down his translation of the contents on the back of the white envelope. On the front he translated the address of the Ministry and Emi's father's name.

Christian read what John had written. "Very much in love." He knew he would think about the letter every day until he saw Emi again.

"What will you do with it?" John asked.

"I don't know," said Christian, smoothing it. "Keep it, if you don't mind."

"Of course. Stealing a letter about oneself is not really stealing."

Christian put the piece of paper back in the envelope and said, "Maybe one day I'll get to Japan. When the war is over and the world is normal again."

"Who knows if that will ever happen?" said John. "And what if the world is even harder to travel around in after the war? If I were young and in love like you, I'd try to do something now."

"I have to repatriate with my parents to Germany," said Christian. "And even that's not happening anytime soon. They keep saying end of '44. Maybe '45."

"There is a way you don't have to go to Germany," said John, gazing at the Katos' former house.

"Which is?" said Christian surprised. His heart started to beat faster as he watched John, still poker-faced.

"It's simple," said John, turning his attention back to Christian. "Enlist."

CHAPTER 14

Emi Kato
September 1943

Emi looked out the window of the train that was humming along from San Antonio to New York. Four hours into the journey and she had already grown tired of looking at desolate landscapes and the run-down houses that lined the tracks. She thought about what she used to see from the train windows when she lived in Austria: the artfully constructed buildings, picturesque villages, the imposing mountain range near Vienna. She hoped that at the end of the war, some of that beauty would remain.

After two nearly sleepless nights, kept up by crying, snoring, and other people's motion sickness, Emi finally saw hints of New York in front of her and felt the sting of longing for her former life. What a way to come into the city, she thought. She had made the trip many times from Washington with her parents before the Pearl Harbor attack, as there was a Japanese consulate there. She had always worn new clothes for the trip, and they traveled in first class. Now that lifestyle was gone. Emi and her mother were arriving in New York as part of a trainload of people the Americans hated — even though many were American themselves — ready to be traded for 1,340 people the country deemed far more important.

In Japan and Germany there were Americans that the government cared for, that they wanted returned safely: Missionaries, teachers, journalists, POWs. Japanese-Americans and German-Americans would go in their places, even though many had never lived in their so-called mother countries. The government found their heritage suspicious, and that was enough to send them into war-torn nations to get the more valuable Americans back.

It was September 2. The ship they would soon board — the MS *Gripsholm,* the same Swedish vessel her father had traveled on — was not expected to reach Japan until November. The Japanese passengers, including 169 from Crystal City, would be traded in the port city of Goa in Portuguese India, switching ships in the process. They would transfer to a smaller Japanese ship, the *Teia Maru,* and the Americans coming from Japan would board the *Gripsholm.* But before the *Gripsholm* reached Goa, it would travel to Brazil and Uruguay to pick up more Japanese who had not been interned in America but were still being traded. After the trade in Goa, they would make stops in Singapore and the Philippines before finally reaching Yokohama.

As New York City came into focus, Keiko passed Emi a bowl of rice with pickles on top that she'd packed for the journey. She handed her two chopsticks, which were wrapped with a few other utensils in a white towel, and told her to eat. She was no longer wearing the homemade dresses she wore in the camp or on the first days of the train journey, but one that she'd worn to embassy lunches in Washington. Emi eyed the pretty scalloped neckline and Keiko said, "I couldn't bring myself to wear rags for our arrival in New York City. I haven't lost myself just yet." She ran her left hand across the stomach of her dress and pushed the food toward Emi again.

"All we've eaten the whole year is rice," said Emi, reluctantly accepting the bowl. "My body feels like it's made of small white grains."

"You should be thankful," said Keiko. "The people in Japan are starving, some to death, and that's where we're headed. The boat, the *Gripsholm,* it won't be the way you're used to traveling. Who knows what kind of food we will have? It could all be spoiled. So eat the small white grains while you can."

"I'll try," said Emi. She put the bowl down on her lap and turned away from her mother, listening to the conversations around her instead. Two women appeared to agree that they weren't nervous to return to Japan since the country was winning the war.

"What do they know?" said Emi, rolling her eyes at her mother. "Our access to the news is severely restricted. No one really knows how well or badly Japan is doing. If you listen to the Americans gossip, the Japanese are losing, and fast."

"Don't think of speaking like that around your father," said Keiko, looking disapprovingly at Emi. "The government is sure that Japan won't lose."

"Everyone loses sometimes."

"Not this time." Keiko took Emi's bowl and said quietly, "Since you're already so combative, maybe this is the right time to finally talk about that American boy. Christian."

"What?" said Emi, trying to look shocked.

"Oh, Emiko. Let's just speak plainly, please," said Keiko leaning tiredly against the window. "You know that I was aware of your relationship with him since the night it started. I was just polite enough to let you do as you wished. You're twenty-one years old; too old to be policed. Besides, when he came to Crystal City, you were finally happy and I was sick of having such a sad child. I should have thanked him before I left."

"I appreciate you not saying anything all these months," said Emi. "Not intervening."

"I know you do," said Keiko, gently. "But you do realize it was the talk of the camp, don't you? At least on our side. I tried to silence the rumors, even if they were true. Mostly, I just didn't want it all to get back to you and ruin your joy."

"You think it was true? What people were saying about us?" said Emi, wondering why she had waited for so long to confide in her mother. She forgot that when her father wasn't around, her mother could be decidedly more modern.

"I know it was true," Keiko replied, gesturing to Emi's food again. "I've seen you in love before."

"That was a long time ago," said Emi.

Keiko moved seats and sat next to her daughter. "Was it? Only for someone so young would that seem like a long time ago." She smiled and readjusted one of the hairpins struggling to hold her hair in place.

"Christian, he was nothing like Leo," said Emi. "He was really just a pleasant distraction."

"I don't think so, Emiko," said her mother, still looking out the window and away from her daughter. "I think you're lying to yourself if you really believe that."

"Perhaps," said Emi, leaning against her mother, bending her neck to an uncomfortable angle. "I didn't think I had the capacity to feel anything for anyone but Leo. Ever. Maybe I was wrong."

"Our hearts aren't built like that," said Keiko. "It's a romantic notion to think so, but for the most part, they have a large capacity to love." She reached over and fed her daughter a bite of rice, as Emi still hadn't touched her food. "Many of our neighbors, they suggested I interfere. And if he had just been a distraction, a nothing much, I might have. But I could tell he meant something to you. That he was bringing you a joy that no one else had been capable of since Leo. I couldn't bring myself to rob you of that."

"I did finally feel happy," Emi admitted. "He was different." She looked at her mother and smiled. "Christian, he managed to pull me out of my — what did you call it?"

"Ungrateful haze," said Keiko laughing.

"Yes, that's it. He pulled me out of my ungrateful haze. The one I've been in — according to you — since we left Europe. But Christian doesn't matter now. We are going back to Japan, he will go to Germany in a few months —"

"No. They say the German repatriation voyage won't be for another year," her mother corrected. "He'll be in Crystal City much longer than we were. Well into 1944."

"Well, I am not convinced that we're headed anywhere better. At least bombs didn't fall from the sky in Texas."

"Tokyo will be safe for us," said Keiko. "Your father said we shouldn't be afraid. Like I said, people are starving, but we won't be. The government will take care of us."

"He would say that if there were corpses falling from the sky. He knows how you are. He doesn't want to scare you and he wants us home."

"Emi, your father has a high position in

Prime Minister Tōjō's government. That will give us preferential treatment. Haven't we always had preferential treatment?"

"Yes. We will get to eat the day-old rats instead of the week-old rats. How wonderful. And I don't know why you think father is so loyal to the government. I don't think he even believes we should be fighting."

"Watch what you say!" Keiko hissed at her. "You're not in an internment camp anymore. You're on your way back to Japan, a country you will be loyal to when you arrive."

"Of course I'm loyal," said Emi. "But that doesn't mean I think we are right. Any country that aligns itself with the German Reich can't be right."

"Emiko, we've gone over this," said Keiko, exasperated. "You are Japanese and you will act like it starting right now. You will be as loyal a patriot as the soldiers fighting the war as soon as your toe is on that boat."

When the train finally chugged to a labored stop in New York and disgorged its passengers, Emi and Keiko took a walk along the platform to stretch their legs and revel for a moment in the absence of barbed wire.

"It's a strange feeling, isn't it?" said Keiko. "To be almost free."

"I don't feel free," said Emi, looking out at the New York skyline. One of the armed guards helping to herd them to the port pushed her shoulder and told her to move up and join the line. They had to be questioned and searched before boarding the massive ship.

They all piled into a row of buses that blew gray smoke and seemed to have only a few miles left in them. "This is a prison bus," she heard a man say, pointing to the words "Correctional Facility" painted inside. Emi gave them a quick glance but the bus turned a corner, jostling the passengers, and there it was, the boat that would transport them to a country at war.

When they had lined up again on the dock, Emi stared up at the enormous freighter with the words GRIPSHOLM SVERIGE printed on the side and DIPLOMAT written above that, all in bold block letters. This boat, it was clear, was not to be blown up. Sweden was a neutral country and the boat was to sail fully illuminated at night, a Christmas tree of the sea. O'Rourke had told them not to fear for their safety on board, that as long as they took care of their health, they would arrive back in Japan in good shape.

"Only to be killed there," one of the

246

Japanese-American teenagers had said, loudly, but O'Rourke had ignored him. What happened to them once they were on Japanese soil was not his concern.

Finally, after they had all passed the questioning process and had their belongings pawed through, they were led on board the ship. At the train station, Emi and her mother were told they would have to share a cabin on the *Gripsholm* with another mother and daughter coming from Crystal City. All four would sleep on bunk beds, the younger women on top. Emi and Keiko knew of the other women from the camp, but they weren't friendly with them. They certainly would be by the time they disembarked, thought Emi, when she saw the size of their cabin.

She and her mother started to unpack as best they could in the tight quarters and when their cabin mates walked in — Chiyo Kuriyama and her daughter, Naoko — they exchanged pleasantries before Emi's mother excused herself to the deck. Naoko, who was as petite as Keiko, followed her out, saying she too was feeling claustrophobic. Emi hoped that Naoko's mother would follow and that she could be alone in the room for just a few minutes. But Chiyo sat down on her bunk, her trousers wet at the bottom, and watched Emi unpack more of her things. They made small talk, much to Emi's annoyance, and then Chiyo, apparently unable to resist, brought up Christian Lange.

"I heard about you and that foreign boy," she said, as Emi folded and refolded the same dress.

"What do you mean you 'heard about me and that foreign boy'?" Emi said defensively, not turning around to look at her. Her mother had said that she and Christian were the talk of the camp, but even if that was true, it was so impertinent to relay the gossip back to its subject. Japanese women may have gossiped behind closed doors, but they always took pains to hide their rudeness. This Chiyo, thought Emi, must have been in America too long.

"You two weren't very subtle, were you?" Chiyo said, pushing her hair out of her eyes. It was cut to the chin in a blunt, practical style. "He was just a baby, too. I understand you were bored in that place, we all were, but I doubt your relationship with that *child* is something your father would be happy to hear about."

"On what occasion would my father hear about my friendship with an American boy?" Emi said with a cold stare. "Are you planning on speaking to him? Because I'm sure he doesn't have the time to speak to you. He's working right under the foreign minister now. He's extremely busy."

"I'm well aware, Emiko-san," Chiyo said haughtily. "You and your mother did such a good job advertising your so-called high position all through the camp for the last few months. But circumstances change during war. The rich aren't so rich anymore. The important not so important. You'll see when we get back. Your life won't be the way it was."

"Of course it won't," said Emi, although she was starting to feel she might be as naïve about the state of Japan as her mother was. "None of our lives will be."

"I would be more careful if I were you," Chiyo warned. "An unmarried woman of twenty-one. Keep acting as you are and you will remain unmarried. Or worse. You know what I'm speaking about. Now that would bring such shame on your *honorable* family."

"You're not me," Emi said. "And I certainly am not seeking your advice. Thank you. I'm going to join my mother now."

She didn't bother to bow goodbye, instead reaching for the door and pulling it shut loudly behind her.

Despite what women like Chiyo expected

of her, what her parents sometimes expected of her, Emi knew she would never become a subservient married woman. She was going to be as interesting as the world would let her, even if it meant dealing with the scorn of women like Chiyo.

Being interesting to Emi used to mean excelling at everything in her grasp — school, languages, love, the piano. She knew she would never play in sold-out concert halls — Japanese women never did — but she was good enough to play somewhere, elsewhere. For so many years, the world had felt open to her. But with the war, all of that had changed. There weren't pianos to play, or languages to learn, but she still knew she wanted to be more than just another submissive woman supporting the empire. Even in wartime Tokyo, there must be some way that she could do things differently.

When Emi reached the deck, she took a moment to savor the breeze, so welcome after her months in the blazing heat, then set out to find her mother. The ship had just pulled away from the dock, but the deck wasn't crowded. The passengers hadn't bothered to gather there since they didn't have anyone to wave goodbye to. Even the strangers on the dock seemed happy to see them go.

Emi spotted her mother leaning against the south railing, once again holding food. She offered some to Emi when she came up. *"Gohan taberu?"* her mother asked, pointing to the dish of rice leftover from the train.

"I can't have anymore," said Emi, holding her stomach.

Keiko finished eating, and they both watched the New York skyline receding. "I never want to see this version of America again," said Keiko.

"I'm sorry I got so sick. You should have gone back with father in '42," Emi replied, switching back into English.

"Nihongo o hanashite, Emiko," said her mother, reminding her to speak Japanese as they had been doing since they left Crystal City.

Emi closed her eyes and let the ocean spray hit her face. She thought of all the sea crossings she'd made in her life. How lucky she had been — and then how unlucky. And now, would she be lucky or unlucky in Japan? Each time she and her family returned to Tokyo after one of her father's assignments, she felt a certain calming of heart, and she had come to realize she enjoyed the periods between assignments as much as the assignments themselves. Japan would always be home. But now home felt anything but calming.

"Are you thinking of him?" asked her mother, breaking into her reverie.

"Of Christian? No," said Emi. "I was, earlier, when I was downstairs with that woman. I can't say I like her much. She's very rude."

"I didn't mean Christian," said Keiko. "I was speaking of Leo. You once said that you would never be on a boat again and not think of Leo Hartmann."

"Did I say that?" Emi asked. She remembered her voyage from Vienna back to Tokyo, crying in her mother's arms. That long journey was haunted by Leo. "Well, he was — is — someone who gets inside your head."

"Or your heart," said Keiko, patting her shoulder and leaving her daughter alone with her memories.

PART TWO

CHAPTER 15

Emi Kato
September 1937

Emi's peripatetic adolescence crossed with Leo Hartmann's stable one in Vienna in September 1937, two years after she and her parents had arrived in Austria. In 1937, the country was run by an extremely conservative government, which it had been since 1932. But that fall, the city started to feel different. Emi's father said it had the beginnings of a tornado about to strike, with the city changing color, just like the sky does before a storm. When Emi had arrived in 1935, she was aware of the country's Austrofascist regime — her father never allowed her to arrive in a country without a solid grasp of its history and politics — but she also knew that the Jews were not being violently persecuted like they were in Germany. Some German Jews — prominent actors and musicians — were even seeking refuge in Vienna. In those early days, when she was discovering the city, she could not have imagined how the tide would turn just two years later.

It was a very hot September in 1937, and on her walk to her school, the Gymnasium bei St. Canisius, Emi was sweating in her short-sleeved cotton blouse paired with the requisite long navy blue skirt issued by the prestigious Catholic school. As she was switching from an all-girl institution to a coeducational one for her two last years, on her insistence, her mother had brought her to a conservative Austrian seamstress to fit her uniform and now the skirt fell down her slender hips perfectly, though no one would have called the cut flattering.

On her walk that day, she noticed that there was already a small rip in the shoulder of her new blouse. She would ask her *amah* to repair it when she got home, but until then she couldn't help but stick her finger in it, which made it bigger and bigger, so that half her left shoulder was visible by the time she entered the centuries-old school building.

It was in this state that Emi encountered Leo Hartmann for the first time.

Two years later, when she'd packed her clothes to leave Vienna, she had put the white school shirt in layers of tissue paper at the top of her trunk, the hole still there, unrepaired.

Emi was in the music room practicing the piano as she was told she could when she interviewed for her position in the eleventh-grade class. When she came to tour the school with her parents, she had sat with the music teacher, who, after listening to her play two notoriously difficult Brahms pieces, had given her permission to use the piano for as long as the school stayed open in the afternoons. Emi immediately took her up on her offer. Three days a week she had to travel outside the inner city to piano classes with a renowned conservatory teacher, but on days when she didn't, the thought of practicing away from her apartment, especially away from her mother, who made her play every song twice as many times as she would have liked, was too tempting to pass up.

Leo thought he could hear piano music when he turned the corner away from his chemistry classroom, where he'd stayed late to clean up a glass tube that had shattered on the floor. It wasn't his fault that the tube had fallen, but he was the one tasked with sweeping up the tiny shards. When the music grew louder, he continued toward it, wondering if his mind was deceiving him. The building had soaring stone ceilings and wide marble floors, and the combination often caused strange sounds to echo through the halls, especially on hot days when the thick walls seemed to shift. When Leo reached the door of the music room, he was happy to discover that it wasn't just an effect of the wind that he'd heard. He leaned against the door and listened. His mother played the piano quite well, but he recognized instantly that she didn't play nearly as well as whoever was playing here. When the music ended, he opened the door slowly and looked at the slight girl with long black hair sitting on the piano bench.

"I'm sorry," Leo said in German when she smiled at him.

"Did I startle you?" Emi replied, looking at him with interest.

Leo shook his head no.

"Really? Because you should see the expression on your face," she said, her amusement apparent. "You look as if I were a cat playing the piano."

"Do I?" Leo started to laugh. "I'm sorry. How embarrassing," he said, walking into the music room. "I was just surprised to see you. You weren't whom I was expecting. Not that I know whom I was expecting." He paused to think about it and admitted, "Just not you."

"Let's hope I'm a pleasant surprise," said Emi, standing up. She noticed that her skirt had turned sideways, and without embarrassment, pulled the button around to the front. "Did you enjoy the piece? Chopin, Opus Ten, Étude number three. In E major," she added.

"I know the piece," said Leo. "I only heard the end, but you played it very well. It pulled me all the way here from the chemistry room."

"Good!" Emi smiled at him and then sat down again and pressed on a few of the black keys quietly as he looked at her.

"Are you a student here?" he asked, after he had offered her his hand and introduced himself.

"I am," said Emi, "but I just started today. Which is why you haven't seen me before. My name is Emiko Kato. Emi Kato. If you had seen me, I think you'd remember . . . being that I'm not Austrian. I stick out a little bit."

"Do you?" he said neutrally. "Either way, you sound Austrian."

"That's wonderful to hear," said Emi. "I've worked very hard to keep up my German. My parents will be thrilled when I tell them."

"Did you not grow up in Austria?" Leo asked, resting his arm on the piano. Emi looked at it, stocky even under his neatly pressed white school shirt. He had an athlete's build, thick and muscular but without making him look inelegant. And he was the perfect height to look her square in the eye, just a few inches under six feet, as tall as she was. She was sure that most people first noticed his eyes, wide and green and bright, but she looked back down at his arm, feeling a sudden urge to place her hands on top of it and keep them there for a while. She realized, when she was inspecting the curl of his brown hair, that she hadn't answered his question.

"No," she said suddenly. "I'm not from Vienna. I've only been here two years. My father is in the Japanese Foreign Service. We're Japanese. You might have guessed that already, or you might be thinking that all Orientals look the same and that perhaps I'm Chinese or Korean."

She raised her eyebrows and Leo shook his head no.

"My father is the consul general at the consulate here," Emi went on. "Prior to Vienna we were posted in Berlin for four

years, and we were in London for a few
before that. I've tried not to let my German
slip away. I like speaking it."

"I'd say you succeeded," Leo said, looking
at the sheet music in front of her. He flipped
through a few pages, then stopped suddenly.

"What are you doing right now?" he
asked, sitting down beside her with such
animation he almost bumped her off the
bench. "You must come to my house and
play the piano for my parents. Will you?
They are classical music enthusiasts, especially interested in the piano. It's an obses-
sion of theirs. My mother plays, she has all
her life, but nowhere near as well as you.
They'll be your biggest fans. Will you come?
Please? You can call your mother and tell
her where you are as soon as we're home.
And my father's driver will see you back to
your apartment. Do you live near the
school?"

"I live on Berggasse. Right near Sigmund
Freud," said Emi. Besides her home in
Tokyo, it was the most beautiful place she'd
ever lived, big and light with four large
bedrooms, though they only needed two.
Her mother had pointed out that a two-
bedroom apartment wouldn't have enough
living spaces for entertaining on a diplomat's level. They were on the third floor of

a soft limestone building and the elevator to reach it was an ornate moving cage of wrought iron. Emi often took trips on it, up and down, just to amuse herself.

"Now he's an interesting man," said Leo. "Freud. My parents have known him for years. But you don't need any psychoanalysis today, do you? You should come play for my parents instead. It will be much more fun. I'll come, too, of course. I won't just kick you off with some strange driver to be taken around the city. He's Hungarian on top of it. A very solemn fellow who's missing a finger on his right hand," said Leo, lifting up his hand and hiding one of his fingers. "But he's a good driver."

Leo made a steering motion with his fingers on a fake wheel, his dark hair flopping forward. "Please say yes."

"If you would like me to, I will," Emi answered, delighted. Having started school later than the rest, she'd worried she would find it hard to make friends. And in her new school, she knew, she was the only non-Austrian and would indeed stick out.

Leo slung Emi's bag across his shoulders and showed her the shortcut to the front of the building through the chapel. It was still as hot outside as it had been when Emi walked to school that morning, but they didn't have far to go. Leo's nine-fingered chauffeur was waiting outside the front door in his black driver's suit and matching brimmed hat. He opened the door of the expensive car for Emi and they got in on either side. Leo made small talk with him as they pulled away from the school. Then he turned and made a clownish frown at Emi. "You'll see," he whispered, "a very solemn man." And it was true. The only words the driver uttered the rest of the ride home were a string of expletives when a young woman tried to cross illegally in front of the shiny black Mercedes, its long, elegant frame curved like a slide over the wheels.

"This is quite a car," said Emi, leaning back into the beige leather seat.

"It's a little too much for a ride from school," said Leo. "But my father insists. He is almost as passionate about cars as he is about music. Race cars, chauffeured cars, boxcars, all of them."

"Boxcars?" asked Emi, confused.

"Don't worry about boxcars," said Leo. "They're not very relevant to your lifestyle."

When they arrived at Leo's, Emi quickly understood that the Hartmann family did not own just a floor of a townhouse apartment like the one her family was living in on Berggasse Strasse, but the entire building. This did not much surprise her after the chauffeured Mercedes.

Leo's glamorous mother greeted them at the door and managed to hide most of her surprise when she saw her son emerge from the car with a teenage Japanese girl with a hole in her blouse.

"This is Emi," Leo explained, as Emi moved her hair over her shoulder to cover the hole. "She just started at the school today. Her father is a diplomat from Japan — the consul general. I barged in on Emi playing a Chopin piece in the music room this afternoon. The very same one you've been playing for years. Étude number something. The sad one."

"Étude number three!" exclaimed Hani Hartmann. She clasped her hands, diamond rings on four out of her ten fingers, and started to hum the melody, reaching out for her son's hands and doing a few waltz steps, though the piece wasn't a waltz. Emi liked the way her curls bounced around her face, just like Leo's, though hers were a dark red and very coiffed.

"She speaks perfect German," said Leo. "Don't let appearances fool you. But we Hartmanns would never be so mindless as to be surprised by a foreigner speaking German, would we?" he said, winking at Emi.

Looking from son to mother, Emi was sure she had never met two more charming people in all of her life. The Hartmanns, she could tell from the start, were going to be wonderful.

"Of course she speaks perfect German," said Hani, ushering Emi into her house. "A diplomat's daughter. Such a pleasure for the afternoon. I am of course Hani Hartmann, Leo's mother," she went on, kissing Emi on both cheeks and squeezing her thin shoulders as if they'd been acquainted for years. "And you are most welcome in our home. Come with us, right here and up the stairs," she said as Emi and Leo followed her up the marble staircase into the expansive foyer, the ceiling as high as the two-centuries-old ones in the school classrooms.

"The piano is just through there," said Hani in a happy singsong voice as they made their way along the hall. She gestured down another long hallway, the walls expertly hung with ornate oil paintings. "But you must both be hungry — thirsty? Let me just ask Zsofia to prepare you something appropriate to eat in this unseasonably hot weather. It's just too warm to eat cooked food."

"Zsofia. Also Hungarian," Leo whispered to Emi. She turned to look at him and he executed another silly frown, which made her lips twitch.

"What Emi needs to do is call home and tell her family where she is," said Leo, gesturing to the phone in the hallway. "You don't want me to have kidnapped her, do you?"

When Emi had told her *amah* where she was and assured her that she was safe, relaying the Hartmanns' phone number and address and promising to be home for dinner, Leo asked her if she was ready to play for his mother.

"*Mein* Froschi!" said Hani. "How rude! She hasn't even eaten or had a drink of water. Come to the sitting room, both of you, and have some refreshments first."

"Froschi?" Emi asked, curiously, wondering why his mother had called him a little frog.

"Leo!" Mrs. Hartmann clarified, laughing and putting her hands over her small mouth, unable to hide her smile, all red lipstick and white teeth. "Of course, Leo. Forgive me," she said, turning to her son. "I call him Froschi," she explained to Emi, "but he told me I was forbidden to use that embarrassing name in front of his friends. What a bad mother I am," she said, putting her freckled arm around her son affectionately.

"Please excuse her," said Leo, not seeming a bit embarrassed. "She has an affliction, you see. She still thinks I'm five years old and that this handsome, manly body is just an evolutionary mistake."

"*Mein lieber* Froschi," Hani said, laughing and kissing him again, leaving a trace of red lipstick on his left cheek. "*Froschi,* as in frog," she explained. "When he was a baby he was always smiling and sticking out his little pink tongue as if he was trying to catch a fly. Exactly like a frog. Despite that, he was the cutest little baby. Just rolls of fat and a head. But that name, I'm afraid it stuck."

"I like it. It's a good nickname," Emi said, happy that Leo was no longer just rolls of fat and a head. "And I'd love to play now. I'm sure your piano is better than the one at school."

"Perhaps a little," said Hani, poker-faced. She led Emi through the long, dark hall to the piano, which was in a separate music room with a sweeping view over the Ringstrasse. Hani opened the lid and gestured to Emi to join her.

The Hartmanns' piano wasn't just nicer than the piano at school, it was one of the nicest pianos in the world: a hand-painted, rosewood turn-of-the-century Steinway, which Emi knew were made only on commission in the company's Hamburg factory.

She sat down on the polished bench, wanting to embrace the keys, to breathe in the piano and the memory of all the hands that had ever played it, but she managed to just rest her fingers on it carefully and smile up at the Hartmanns as if it were an everyday occurrence for her to play such an instrument.

She took a deep breath and launched into the piece, quickly forgetting the opulence of her surroundings and focusing only on the notes, simple and unfussy, but some of her favorite ever written. She played the étude with more emotion than she had felt in months, transported by her company, the instrument, and the happy afternoon. Above her hung a Fragonard painting, but she wouldn't know that until weeks afterward, when Leo's father, Max Hartmann, took her on a tour of the apartment, explaining each of his paintings with a curator's eye.

Emi had practiced almost exclusively on Steinways when she'd lived in Germany, but never in her life had she played on an instrument more beautiful than the Hartmanns'.

After she had finished playing, letting the étude's last hopeful note linger, Hani looked at her with tears in her brown eyes and shook her head. "What a gift you have. What a tremendous gift. Look at me," she said, wiping her eyes. "Joy. Tears of joy."

She walked over and sat next to Emi on the piano bench. "You must come back and play for us, Emi. Come every day that you and your family live in Vienna. I beg you. Froschi went off to school with a leather bag and some books he won't read and came home with a concert pianist. What a very memorable day."

That hot September afternoon — filled with the charismatic Hartmanns, Hungarian servants, Fragonard paintings and clothes that needed to be mended — was the start of Emi's days in Austria playing the rosewood Steinway for the family. Sometimes she would play for Leo and both of his parents; sometimes she would come in the evenings and provide the entertainment for a dinner party the family was hosting. But no matter how many people were there, she was always just playing for Leo.

After a few weeks, she called him Froschi, too, and after a few months it was *mein* Froschi. Leo quickly became hers, and everything that Vienna would come to mean to her was tied up in him.

CHAPTER 16

Leo Hartmann
September 1937–November 1938

Leo Hartmann was a good son. He had been an easy baby to take care of, and in later years he was certainly going to be a good man, Hani Hartmann would say to anyone who would listen, but mostly to him. Ever since he was old enough to understand, she'd told him that she'd thought she would have more children but after she had him — with his wild brown hair and bright green eyes — she knew she could never love another baby as much.

"It would have been selfish to have more children," she'd told him when he was younger and would ask why he didn't have any siblings. "How could I have loved anyone even half as much as I love my Froschi? When you were a baby you had the fattest little hands and I would squeeze them and saliva would bubble out of your mouth like a hot spring. I'd pray for you to stay small forever. Sadly, it didn't work," she'd say, kissing the top of his head, which got harder for her to reach every year. Leo would roll his eyes at his mother whenever she spoke in her sentimental way, but secretly he was glad he was the only one. He couldn't imagine having to share his mother's love with anyone else.

The kindness that Hani Hartmann appreciated about Leo, and that he learned to appreciate about both his mother and father, was also highly regarded by their community in Vienna. Having old money, made in honest ways, was something that caught people's attention, but what held their attention were the Hartmanns themselves. Perhaps it was the smallness of their family, coupled with the largeness of their home, but the ornate rooms were never empty for long. Both Hani and Max — Max especially — came from prominent Jewish families that had been in Austria for more than a century. The Hartmanns had been chocolate tycoons for several generations, as Leo's grandfather had founded the largest chocolate factory in Vienna in 1850. Max, surprisingly the family's rebel, had opted not to continue in confectionery and had gone into banking, where he did exceedingly well. He kept his stake in the family business while allowing his enterprising younger brother, Georg, to run it. Hani, who came to Vienna from Linz when she was eighteen years old, did not grow up with the level of wealth Max had, but she was from the Baum family, a name that Max's mother happily approved of. Even if Hani had sprung from the gutter, Max would have married her. Her joie de vivre was even more intoxicating than her looks and together, they agreed, they would live a wonderful life.

While Max didn't work at his family's factory after he went off to the University of Vienna to study economics, he was still monetarily and emotionally invested. If a worker was down on their luck, between roofs over their heads, they were invited to stay with Max and Hani Hartmann. If one had a family member moving to town, needing shelter before they embarked on their own, they stayed at the Hartmanns'. And there was always a handful of Hungarians coming and going, friends and relatives of their staff who needed a few days in Vienna without spending their own money. Max and Hani's open-door policy made them popular not only within the city's Jewish community, which they were fairly active in, but among the blue-collar Viennese employed at the Hartmann chocolate factory.

That same openness, the charisma that came effortlessly to the Hartmanns, worked on Emi right away.

It took only one afternoon for Leo and his parents to captivate her, and it took only one more for her to realize that at their school, in 1937, she was the only admirer Leo Hartmann had left.

It wasn't always that way. Since few things appeal to children more than a rich classmate who also has a never-ending supply of sweets, Leo Hartmann had been surrounded by friends as a child. They were as attracted to his peaceable temperament as they were to the chauffeured black car he came to school in. But in 1937, Austria was no longer the country of Leo's youth. Emi was the only non-Austrian at their Catholic school, but Leo was the only Jew.

"I thought I'd tell you before everyone else did," Leo said to Emi outside the stone building before her second day at the school began. On warm mornings, the students lingered outside, soaking in as much of the sunshine as they could before having to sit silently in the cold Gothic building. Leo looked at Emi's pretty figure, her subtle profile, and wished they could spend the day there together.

"I don't mind if you're Jewish," said Emi, sitting close to him. "Our ambassador to Germany has a German-Jewish wife, Edita. And she's fascinating. They've already come to see us in Vienna twice."

"A Jew fascinating? Our classmates would disagree," said Leo looking around them. "But I'm very happy to hear it." He had hoped that someone as worldly as Emi would find a difference in religion something intriguing rather than worthy of revulsion.

"Why do your parents have you in a Catholic school?" Emi asked. Her eyes were on the priests who had started to usher the children inside. "Isn't that strange?"

"It's the best in Vienna," said Leo. "There used to be other Jewish students, quite a few, but none of them came back for this school year, except for me. I think everyone has been waiting for me to go, too — looking very forward to my exit — but I'm still here. As you saw, my parents like the best of everything. Even if it means that I'm a little uncomfortable sometimes."

The morning bell rang, and Leo and Emi walked inside with the rest of the students. As she headed up to the girls' side of the building, he stood below the stairs, watching her long thin legs move gracefully in her ugly skirt. "Can you play again today? The piano, that is," Leo called after her.

Emi turned around and shook her head. He noticed that she was wearing a new blouse, without a hole in the shoulder. He'd wanted nothing more than to put his hand on her skin through that little hole the day before, and was sad to see that it was no longer an option. "Lessons," Emi said. "Always lessons. But I'd rather play in your music room."

"Maybe you can take your lessons in our music room?" he suggested. Emi promised she would ask her teacher, but as she told Leo the next day, the request was flatly denied.

"It turns out he's an awful man," said Emi the following morning as they gathered in the courtyard before class. "He said he knows who your father is and won't teach in 'Jew houses.' "

"At least he's honest," said Leo trying to smile.

"He's an anti-Semite," said Emi. "But my mother won't let me stop taking lessons from him, even if I tell her. He's a very talented anti-Semite."

"Don't tell your mother," said Leo. "It will only worry her." He tried to look as happy as he had the morning before, but he was sure Emi could see his strain. He hoped that her mother was as open-minded as she was.

"I'll come to your house and play without him," she said, putting her hand right next to his, so that their fingers touched. "Every free moment I have."

"I doubt you have that many," said Leo. "I've seen the way the girls speak to you, asking about Japan and living all over the world. I'm sure you'll have many invitations soon and my piano will be just as forgotten as a child's music box." He pretended to cry, though he was smiling and Emi reached up and touched the front of his curly hair, causing him to reach for her hand out of instinct. She held his and he looked at her intensely.

"What is this funny timepiece?" she asked, breaking their gaze. She moved his sleeve and ran her hand over the slightly domed glass of the watch. The cogs were visible underneath and the numbers were mismatched, raised Roman numerals.

"I made this with our Hungarian driver, Zalan, when I was a child," said Leo, happy to talk about his strange but beloved driver. "His father was a watchmaker and when I was a boy, and rather lonely, he and I used to work on this. See," he said, taking his watch off. "It says here on the back of the dial, 'Made by Leo Hartmann.'"

"It's quite ugly," Emi said laughing. "But I like that you still wear it. It should also say, 'made by nineteen fingers.'"

"It's not ugly," said Leo, holding it up to get a better look at it. "It's unique. And it has never quit on me."

"And you've never quit on it," she said, and covered it up with his sleeve again. "I seem to quit on everyone. Since we started traveling, everywhere I've been, I've never been very good at keeping people," she said.

"Because your life is so transient?" he said, reaching for her hand again.

"Exactly. What's the use of getting close to someone, even a friend, if you won't see them in a matter of years? I should get a watch to keep me company instead."

"You shouldn't always be thinking about the future," said Leo laughing. "Don't you ever just appreciate the here and now?"

"That's what I'm trying to say," said Emi. "With you, I think I do. I'm beginning to fall for the here and now."

While life tucked inside the Hartmanns' home together was as peaceful an existence as Leo and Emi could imagine, things at school were not as simple. The girls' and boys' sides had Mass together every afternoon, and though both Leo and Emi skipped communion, no one bothered Emi about it, while Leo was the object of increasing scrutiny for sitting it out. As the weeks went on and the calendar moved to the end of 1937, that scrutiny turned to anger.

"I'm beginning to understand why you're a little uncomfortable at school," Emi said when Leo explained why he preferred to walk through the halls on the girls' side of the school. What he didn't tell her was that he often found himself bleeding from the nose or mouth after classes, especially sports class.

He tried his best to hide his reality from Emi, going to the bathroom after he'd been punched in the face and cleaning up as best he could. He had bought more than a dozen white school uniform shirts and matching sweaters and kept at least one of each neatly pressed and laundered in his bag, in case the ones he was wearing that day got ripped or bloodied.

But as he started getting fists put to his jaw more often, the reality of his school day was harder to hide from her. And then one day in October, he could hide it no longer.

When he noticed her brown eyes peeking in at the boys' chemistry classroom door, he knew she had been heading to the music room and stopped just a few steps past it. She must have heard the glass shatter, he thought, the test tubes that were being thrown at his feet by his usual aggressor.

"Look what I have for you to pick up today, Jew," Fritzie Dorn, one of the most popular boys in the school, and one who spoke with reverence about the Hitlerju-gend, the Hitler Youth, yelled at Leo. "You shouldn't have knocked down another tube. Such an ugly, clumsy Jew."

Leo counted his breaths, made sure there was a long calm pause before he said, "I didn't knock it down. You did."

Fritzie laughed, told Leo that their after-noon routine was just starting, and threw a large beaker at Leo's feet, the shards spray-ing up to his eyes. Leo felt a small piece of glass tuck into the corner of his left eye, but he refused to close it, letting it sting until there were tears on his cheek.

"And that's another one," said Fritzie. "Two glass tubes broken, and all over the floor. Too bad there's no broom to sweep it up," he said. "And no dustpan. Just your little Jew hands." Fritzie crunched his polished black school shoes on the glass, his toes smashing it nearly to dust. "Now if you can pick that all up and not get a single cut, then I'll let you leave chemistry tomorrow without any broken glass to pick up."

Without making a sound, or looking at Fritzie or Emi by the door, Leo got on his hands and knees and started gathering the tiny pieces of glass while Fritzie moved a few feet back, sat on a table, and watched him with amusement. He started swinging his big legs, hitting Leo's back every few kicks with the tip of his leather shoe and reciting some edicts that Leo imagined he'd learned from pro-Nazi literature. Leo stayed unmoving against the blows, trying to keep his spine neutral, focused on cleaning up the glass as best he could.

He was reaching for the tiny dust that remained, the powder that he was pressing his sweaty fingers against to pick up, when he heard Emi breathing too loudly. Why was she still there? He grew anxious but didn't look up. He knew not to.

Fritzie looked up immediately and Leo could practically hear him smile before he declared, "Jew boy! You have an audience. The Japanese girl!"

"What are you doing to Leo?" Leo heard Emi ask, her voice steady, not panicked. When Fritzie didn't answer, Leo guessed that she wasn't talking to him. She was addressing the school's chemistry teacher, who was in the room with them, watching Leo.

He was doing nothing, as usual, to stop Fritzie's torture of him.

"It's no concern of yours, Miss Kato," the teacher said to Emi, while Leo only dared to look up to the teacher's knees. "Go back to the girls' side, right now." The next thing Leo heard was Emi's feet taking off down the hall. A minute later, after her footsteps were out of earshot, he heard a much better noise. She had started to play the piano. Loudly, angrily. Hard enough to break the strings.

It wasn't until a month later that Leo brought up the incident. It was the end of November, and they had plans to go to the Prater amusement park in Vienna's second district before the weather turned too cold. As they walked to the park, arm in arm, Leo pulled her back a little, motioning for her to slow down. He wanted the afternoon to feel long and easy.

Leo had liked Emi from the first moment she pointed out that he was staring at her as if she were a cat playing Chopin. Most of the girls he knew would not dare say such a thing, even if his tongue was on the floor. But he'd learned quickly that Emi said whatever was on her mind, and it was usually something intelligent and a little daring. He liked that she was confident, and talented, yet very self-contained. He had written it off as a Japanese trait at first, but he soon concluded that it was more of an attribute particular to Emi. It was apparent from the first week they spent together that she didn't need him, or the world, saluting her as he imagined many young women would have liked. She seemed to move through life as her only critic, her opinion of herself, and her expectations, the ones that mattered most of all. But she had assured him that she did need him, and that made him like her even more. Of all the students at their school, many who wanted to be close to her, she had picked him.

They waited in line for the Ferris wheel and when it came, Leo took Emi by the hand, his bare fingers sticking to her leather glove, and helped her climb into the little, swinging compartment. When they were almost at the top, he leaned over and kissed her softly, knowing he couldn't avoid the subject of the chemistry room any longer.

"Thank you for playing the piano that day," he said when his lips lifted from hers. "I think I could endure anything if you provided the music."

"Leo, I didn't know what to do," she said, starting to cry. "I should have marched into the room and stayed there until they let you stop."

"You can't cry after I've kissed you," said Leo, wiping her tears with his index finger. "Please don't. I can handle a lot. It isn't my school, or my city anymore, but it will be again one day. I just have to be patient and wait."

"Until then you will pick up broken glass with your hands while that malicious Fritzie Dorn kicks you and the teacher looks on gleefully?"

"Yes," Leo replied. "And probably worse. But I don't care about any of that, especially not now."

"What do you care about?" Emi asked, her voice anxious. "Because I couldn't do it. I could not just get on my hands and knees and pick up glass while being kicked by Fritzie."

"It's surprising what a person can endure," said Leo, pointing out the view of the city. "My parents are happy that I'm still in the school, and while some of the things that happen to me are unpleasant, I'm not in any real danger."

"Aren't you?" asked Emi. "Because I saw Fritzie's face. He looked ready to kill you. And he's in the Hitlerjugend. You've seen the boys wearing the pins around school.

There are more and more of them."

"This is still Austria, not Germany," said Leo. "We don't have to live in fear of actually being killed."

"But for how much longer?" said Emi, reaching for Leo's arm. "It's not a secret that Hitler wants Austria. He is desperate to fold it into the Third Reich. And then what? All his policies against the Jews will become law here. Your father won't be able to work. You won't be at school. You listen to the radio and read the newspapers, Froschi. Don't pretend you don't know."

"Of course I know," said Leo, leaning against the cold metal wall of the Ferris wheel compartment. He thought about an article he had seen that morning about the further implementation of Aryanization laws in Germany. If the Hartmanns were there rather than in Vienna, their factory would not be in their hands anymore and his father would have been dismissed from his job at the bank. Generations of work would have been sold to a non-Jew for a song. "I know, but Hitler isn't in Austria. Our government still wants to keep him out. So I'm focused on that. And more importantly, I'm focused on you."

"I need to be more like you," said Emi, her face still contorted with worry.

"No," said Leo, moving to her side of the bench, even though it made their little compartment unbalanced. "You need to be you. What I care about is you. What allows me to smile as some fat brute kicks me and the teacher laughs away is you. As long as I have you, everything will be fine."

Emi threw her arms around Leo, kissing his face, his neck, until the Ferris wheel had come back down and she had to scoot quickly to the other side of the bench. Leo fixed his collar and paid the attendant to let them ride again. "This is what's important," he said and kissed Emi without stopping for two more rides up and down over Vienna. That was the day that Leo and Emi finally said the word. *Love.* And once it was said, it was repeated during every quiet moment, between every kiss.

Emi had told Leo that she needed him more than he needed her when they met in 1937 and she was brand-new to the school, but things took a turn in 1938 when one word started dominating every conversation: *Anschluss.* Nazi Germany's annexing of Austria. At the start of the new year, the Hartmanns and many other Jewish families were still confident that the young chancellor Kurt Schuschnigg, who was a fascist but was still pro-Austria, could preserve the country's independence, despite the mounting power of Adolf Hitler and his determination to unify Austria and Germany. But everything changed on the twelfth of March when the Nazis plowed through the Austrian border. The fate of the country was sealed when Hitler drove through Vienna two days later.

Leo and Emi, like all the Austrian children their age, were at school the following day when they heard the tumult in the street. They ran to the windows and listened to the mayhem of raised voices, followed by elated shouts and screams. Then they saw the rush of people. Hitler, they were told by their teachers, would be addressing the people at the Heldenplatz, one of the city's main squares, in a few hours. It was within walking distance of their school.

Granted an early dismissal, the students started running toward the square, including Leo, with Emi reluctantly in tow.

"What are you doing?" she said as they ran through the crowds of people. Almost all of them were holding small red and black flags, the swastika emblazoned brightly in the center. "We can't go to the square. *You* can't go there. Hitler's going to speak! It's not safe!"

"They're all going," he said pointing to

the students from their school.

"They're not Jewish!" she shouted back. "Some of them are in the Hitlerjugend. Look at their armbands! And the flags," she said, swastikas waving all around them. "They're salivating for this moment. We should be hiding, not running toward loaded guns."

Leo looked out at the street they were on and noticed that in most of the shop windows, huge swastika flags hung. They were also draped across government buildings, and hanging from lightposts. The image of Nazi Germany was everywhere.

In the days leading up to the Anschluss, the bullying that Leo endured crescendoed and nearly broke him. It wasn't just Fritzie Dorn and the chemistry teacher, it was every child in school. His clothes were stolen in gym class, and if it weren't for his habit of carrying so many uniforms, he would have been stuck in the changing room naked. Even some of the younger girls were spitting near his feet and then smiling at their bravery. They didn't dare spit right on him, but as Austria changed, so did their proximity to his face. They were clearly feeling more and more confident that they should be targeting the school's only Jew.

"I need to see it," said Leo, pushing past a

group of laughing children. "I'm not just running away from this like a coward."

He felt Emi pull her hand away from his. He looked at her as she stopped in the middle of the street, which had been closed to cars that morning after Hitler drove through. "I wish you would act like a coward instead of an idiot. We shouldn't be here and you know it," she said. "Your parents are going to worry about you until they're sick. They will hear what's happening and how close we are at school."

"I haven't run from my aggressors yet," said Leo, looking down at his hands, which were marked with dozens of little cuts. "I don't want to start today. Come. We'll be all right." He took her hand again and pulled her into the crowd.

They could see in the distance, a hundred yards away, a podium set up for Hitler on the balcony of the ornate Hofburg Palace, with rows of Nazi flags hanging crisply below it. Emi tried to drag Leo back toward city hall, but so many people had pushed into the square that it was almost impossible to move. There were men climbing everything that was climbable, all clambering for a view of the Führer. Just ahead of the crowd were tight rows of German soldiers, all identical with the ropes around their chests and their black helmets. Beyond them, Leo and Emi could hear a band playing, and the troops were pacing back and forth, walking with their legs straight, in perfect time to the songs. Leo felt Emi reach out for him as the crowd jostled them even more and the clanging of cymbals got louder. As the metal crashed, the crowd started screaming *"Sieg Heil!"* and reaching out their arms in front of them in the Nazi salute. Leo put his lips to Emi's ear and was about to tell her not to worry, when he was drowned out by an even louder chant of "We want to hear our Führer," and the noise of German bombers flying in formation above them.

Leo looked at the enraptured faces, fanatical with excitement. Maybe they weren't as safe as he thought, but it was a nightmare he couldn't turn away from. He had to see these people — the ones who had worked in his father's factory, who had benefited from his family's charity — shed tears of joy over Hitler. He took Emi tightly by the hand and whispered, "No one is going to think I'm a Jew if I'm with you." They walked through the crowd, past a large group of men, being careful not to push them, and watched as boys their age tried to climb on the statue of Prinz Eugen of

Savoy to get a better view.

Leo eased up as Emi reached for his shoulders. "You don't know that," she said quietly. "I am not your guaranteed savior just because I'm obviously not Jewish. People know who your father is. They might recognize you. Let's not get any closer," said Emi, stopping by the statue, which was already surrounded.

Leo held Emi tight as he watched the faces of the people around them. He was trying to stay still, though he wanted to get as close to Hitler's podium as he could. Old and young, male and female, everyone around him was rejoicing. Did they know what it meant to be German? Leo wondered. Did all these people, his countrymen, really support the Führer so blindly?

He started to whisper as much to Emi when he felt her pinch him.

"They're looking at us," she whispered, glancing very carefully over to a group of men to their right. Leo noticed that though they were wearing what was probably their best winter clothing, it was dirty and worn. Suddenly he felt very conspicuous in his cashmere coat. He unbuttoned it to show his Catholic school uniform and Emi quickly did the same.

Leo turned his head to the side, with a

happy smile on his face, and looked at the men, once his clothes were exposed.

The oldest of the men, his gray hair uncovered, reached over and handed Leo one of the flags he was holding. *"Sieg Heil!"* he screamed out, his arm stretched in front of him.

Leo took the flag, looked at it, and out of instinct dropped it on the ground, grabbed Emi, and pushed through the people as fast as he could until they were a safe distance away.

"Leo! What are you doing!" she screamed, ripping her hand out of his. "You're going to get yourself killed! And me while you're at it!"

Leo stood with his hip against hers and suddenly the noise of the crowd drowned out his apology. The Führer had just arrived, in an imposing, stretch, white open-top car. They could barely make him out, but even from a distance Leo saw Adolf Hitler standing up in the front seat, his arm extended straight as a bayonet. He was in uniform, wearing a red armband bearing a swastika. The crowd was ecstatic, the shouts of *"Sieg Heil!"* nearly deafening.

"I don't understand why we are here," said Emi, sounding close to tears. "You've seen him, now can we go? Maybe that man followed us, Leo." She turned around, glancing nervously behind her.

"I need to see it, to hear them," said Leo. "I need to know how much hate there is in this country for me. Not just in the chemistry classroom, or in the little hallways of our school, but here on the street. I want to see the people who are going to try to kill me. Your words, right?" He knew he was scaring Emi with the determination in his voice.

"We've seen it!" she screamed.

"Yes, we *are* seeing it," he whispered. "All these people who want me dead. We are seeing it right now."

He knew he sounded bold and careless to Emi, but what else could he be? There would be time for panic and fear later.

"I'll never let anything happen to you," Emi said, as she gripped his arm. He reached for her hand, trying to reassure her.

"Until today, I believed that. But now . . . Do you think you can do anything against all this?" They watched as two women in front of them threw flowers in the air and wept happily.

Emi said yes, but Leo could only see her mouth move, unable to hear her over the ecstatic screams of the men and women around them. He closed his eyes and kissed her forehead. After that, he finally let her pull him out of the crowd and straight home.

Leo knew that Emi was desperate to make good on her promise of keeping him safe, but as the difficult year raged on they both knew it was almost impossible. And after November 9, the first night of the horror that would become known as Kristallnacht, they agreed that no one could keep him safe. In the two days of anti-Jewish violence, the Hartmann chocolate factory was set on fire and almost every window broken with rocks or hammers. The manager of the factory disappeared that night, and though Leo's parents had their Hungarian staff search the city for hours, there was no trace of him.

"He is one of what?" Hani had screamed to her husband as the terror raged on. "Dozens? People are being taken already, Max! Abducted from the streets. We have to think about leaving. No, we have to leave. Immediately." She started running around the house, putting her things in suitcases while Max tried to calm her, but Leo could tell no one was calm.

Jewish homes and businesses were being destroyed one after the other and the synagogues were burning like haystacks, the firemen doing nothing to save them. They just stood and watched them, consumed by flames, sometimes trying to save a Christian-owned business if it was being affected by the blaze. When the spontaneous mobs of SA and citizens weren't breaking glass and lighting fires, they were arresting Jews like the factory manager.

"Dachau, Max," said Hani, crying, Leo sitting at her feet. "That's where they're all going." They heard a pounding on their door, shouts, and they all ran up to the top floor of the house, locking themselves in the attic as they had done the night before.

When the sun had set on the second night of violence, though they were too terrified to leave the house, the Hartmanns opened their doors for Jews trying to escape the street. The factory manager's wife, Lina Kofman, was one of them.

"Egon was taken to Dachau, I know it," she said, gripping Leo's shoulders when he'd opened the front door just enough to let her inside. Her black hair was covered with a scarf that was tied so low that he had to ask her to raise it, to see her face, before he let her in. "He will die there!" she yelled when she'd reached the Hartmanns' stairs. Leo gave her his arm, which was shaking.

"People aren't dying in Dachau," said Leo, repeating what his father had told him.

"It's a work camp."

"A camp where they work you to death," said Lina, breathing heavily. "They say it's for communists and socialists. Egon isn't one of those things! But now they hate the Jews even more. I know he's there, he will die there," she said, crying as Leo led her upstairs.

That night, the Hartmanns' synagogue, Leopoldstädter Tempel, was torched. Hours after that, the word *Juden* was painted in black, tarry letters on the side of their house. Max had the Hungarian driver paint over it in white the next day, but it didn't stay covered for long.

Against his family's wishes, Max went outside the next morning to inspect the damage to their house, and seconds after he was on the street, he was pulled to the ground by the Sturmabteilung, the Storm Troopers. Leo and Hani watched from the window as they threw him against the still-wet paint. Four men circled around him and forced him to clean it off to expose the word *Juden* again, only allowing him to use a toothbrush and his tongue to do so. They then beat him and left him on the sidewalk unconscious.

Leo had tried to run out of the house, to help his father, but Hani would not let him, instead closing the curtains and forcing them both to stay in the attic until it was quiet outside. Ten minutes later, Leo checked the window and ran out to get his father, who was badly beaten but alive. It was a miracle, said Hani, crying over her husband's raw face, that he was left there and had not disappeared like the factory manager. They must have thought he was dead.

That was the last day Leo went to school. The last day of Emi and Froschi in the music room or waiting for the black car driven by the nine-fingered Hungarian.

CHAPTER 17

Emi Kato
November 1938
After Kristallnacht, Emi was forbidden to set foot in Leo's house.

"It's too dangerous," her father had explained after he'd spoken to Max Hartmann. The two men had met several times before when the Katos, realizing that Emi's best friend in Vienna was an Austrian boy, had invited the Hartmanns to dinner to make sure there was nothing untoward going on between them. The Hartmanns had returned the gesture, inviting the Katos not just to dinner, but to several of their musical soirées. To no one's surprise, everyone got along very well, as anti-Semitism had not gripped Japan and certainly held no sway over the Katos. As for the Hartmanns, they were already taken with Emi and pleased to be able to host a prominent diplomatic family. The Katos figured out quickly that Emi had a romantic relationship with Leo, but they were relieved to find in him a boy who was thoroughly respectful of their young daughter, even in awe of her.

"It wasn't my doing, Emiko. Leo's parents don't want you in danger. They've forbidden you to visit them at home, for your own safety," Norio told his daughter, who had spent the three days after Kristallnacht alternating between stunned silence and tears, though she had tried not to break down too often in front of her parents. "You'll have to practice the piano at school or here, never at the Hartmanns'. And you're not to walk in the city alone anymore. You will always have to be with your *amah* when you're not at school."

"But then I'll never see Leo," Emi said, her brow creased with worry. "His parents have taken him out of school. When will I see him if he's not at school and I can't visit them?"

"Your seeing him is not the Hartmanns' concern right now," said Norio. "Don't be so selfish. They need to figure out if they can save their family's business and how they will manage without Mr. Hartmann's salary, as his employment at the bank has been terminated. Their house could be seized, their assets frozen, their possessions stolen. Mostly, they need to determine how they can leave Austria. The situation for the Jews in this country has become dire, Emiko," Norio went on. "Their companies are being liquidated, they are being banned from public places and worse. They are simply disappearing. It's no longer about mistreatment, it's a matter of life and death. I hate to speak so somberly, but you should be aware of the horrors that are occurring around us."

"I *am* aware!" said Emi, getting more upset. "I saw what they did during Kristallnacht."

"Then please, let the Hartmanns take care of their affairs without having to worry about you running around their house crying," he said firmly. "When they have things in order and are leaving Vienna, we will find a way for you to say goodbye to Leo. Maybe at the consulate, where we can have some measure of protection for them. And you."

"I need to see him again," she said, trying to keep herself together. "Please help me. You can arrange it, can't you?"

"I just said I would! Things are going to get so much worse, Emiko. This part of the world, it's starting to scare me. You've seen the lines of Jews desperately begging for exit visas in front of the police stations, the foreign consulates. Not all of them will be able to leave. Nazis have even blockaded the University of Vienna. The Jews are all over the streets, being forced to do the most terrible things. And what can I do? Yesterday, I spoke to Ambassador Togo in Berlin about the situation here and there. In October he was replaced as ambassador to Germany by Hiroshi Oshima, who is very pro-Nazi."

"Replaced? But what will happen to Ambassador Togo and Edita?" asked Emi, anxiously.

"He's been reassigned to Moscow," said Norio. "Which is fine. Not a demotion. But Oshima, he is an army general. A hawk. He's been in Berlin since 1934, serving as the military attaché when we were there, and he met with Hitler personally the following year. I remember the pride he took in his tête-à-tête, speaking about it for months afterward. He will be no friend to the Jews."

"Why would anyone replace Togo with a man like that?"

"I know Oshima has been maneuvering for the position for years, but perhaps Shigenori and Edita wanted to leave," said her father solemnly. "I would not want to keep my Jewish wife in Berlin at such a time."

"Vienna will become just as bad as Berlin," said Emi. "I can feel it."

"Which is why you must leave the Hartmanns alone," said her father sternly. "Let them focus on how to escape Vienna safely. I mean it, Emiko."

Emi nodded respectfully and turned to leave the room. She was definitely not going to heed her father's order.

When she returned to school after Kristallnacht, Emi expected other students to be as shaken as she was, but life went on as usual. If anything, many seemed more animated, displaying an enthusiasm that matched the chaos roiling the city. Emi was alone in her solemnity and fear.

On the first Friday after the terror in Vienna, Emi made her way slowly to the school's music room after classes were over, dragging her hand along the wall, imagining Leo's hand at the end of it reaching out for hers. Instead, she heard footsteps behind her and turned to see one of her classmates trying to catch up with her. A tall, heavyset girl with fine blond hair always parted straight down the center, Kersten had once seemed eager to be friends with Emi, but this afternoon she had a grimace on her face. As she approached her, she cut in front of her so that Emi almost tripped trying not to crash into her.

"Watch where you're going!" said Kersten, laughing.

Emi looked at her, and immediately saw the pins on her shirt. Kersten was part of the Hitlerjugend. Before the Anschluss, there were members of the Jugend at her school, but it was mostly an underground operation. Now it was the only youth group that the government allowed and Kersten, it seemed, had jumped into service immediately.

Emi had never felt a pull toward Kersten, even when Kersten had been very friendly to Emi when she first arrived. Her father, she knew, was one of the city's most prominent doctors, but he had also been active in the Christian Social Party, one of Austria's most right-wing political factions. Kersten was often repeating his rhetoric, especially the criticism of the heavily Jewish Social Democrat Party, which Emi knew Leo's father had been a member of.

Emi wasn't surprised at all that Kersten was one of the first girls at school to wear the Hitlerjugend insignia on her uniform.

"You better apologize to me," said Kersten, her hand on her shoulder, feigning pain. Her hair was in two braids, one on each side with the bottoms rolled intricately together. Other than her too-thick build and her scowl, she looked like the perfect image of Aryan youth.

Emi righted herself and said, "I'm trying to go practice in the music room. Can you move, please?"

"And my apology?" said Kersten, her foot in front of Emi.

"You certainly won't get one from me," said Emi, speaking to Kersten's pins rather than her face.

Letting the apology drop momentarily, Kersten said, "You're going to practice all alone without that Jew? Can you even play without him anymore?"

"Leo Hartmann," said Emi, trying to move around Kersten. "Of course I can."

"You shouldn't see him again," said Kersten, still blocking her way. She spread her feet wider so Emi could not get around her and leaned in closer to her nervous face. "In case you were thinking about it. It's too dangerous now."

"I know," said Emi, standing still. "My father said the same thing."

"And he's right." Kersten flashed Emi a disingenuous smile and said, "I'm just warning you because we're such good friends, and I think as a foreigner you don't understand what is happening in this country. I just want to help keep you safe."

"Don't understand?" echoed Emi. "I don't think you have to be Austrian to understand what Adolf Hitler is doing. And Kersten," she said, taking a bold step toward her, "we are not such good friends. Especially not now," she said, pointing to the swastika patch on her arm.

Kersten shook her head. "Everyone our age of Aryan descent has to join now. It's an honor. You do not understand the good that's happening in Vienna because of Hitler, not like an Austrian does. If you did, you would never have gotten caught up with Leo Hartmann in the first place. You wouldn't have been seen around Vienna kissing him. You don't understand Austria and all we've suffered at their hands. So you went and ripped your clothes off with some dirty Jew. Do you want to end up with Jew babies at a time like this?"

"What?" asked Emi, teetering on her heels, feeling faint. "You have no idea what I did or didn't do with Leo."

"Oh, Emi, please. Don't play chaste now. We *all* know. But *you* should know that it's illegal for you to be with a Jew," said Kersten, ignoring Emi's disgusted face.

"Why would it be illegal for me to be with a Jew? I'm not Christian. I'm not even

Austrian."

"Because it's disgusting! Against nature. Like making love to a dog," Kersten exclaimed. "See, like I said, you have no idea what you're doing. You made a big mistake, and now the whole school knows you as the Jew lover. You better start going out with another boy soon so you can try to save your reputation. Everyone wanted to be your friend at first, but you ruined it when you ran off with Leo Hartmann day after day." She took a few steps toward Emi. "But that's all over since this school is rid of him. Now you can fix your Jew-lover problem."

"I'll be leaving the school next year," said Emi. "So you can all remember me by whatever name you want. Go ahead, yell 'Jew lover' in my face. I don't care." She sidestepped around Kersten and rushed toward the music room, but Kersten yelled back at her before she could make it around the corner and out of earshot.

"He's going to die!" she shouted. "Leo Hartmann is going to die. He has the red *J* stamped in his passport now and my mother says that's the kiss of death. And no one will care but you."

Emi looked over her shoulder and said, "Thank you for your concern, but you have

no idea who is going to die. You are not
God."

"No, I'm not," said Kersten. "But you
don't have to be God to know that all the
Jews in Austria will die. Don't you listen to
the radio? Jews have finally bitten off their
own big noses. After all these years of taking our jobs and our money, they've written
their own fate with their greed. Now Hitler
has decreed that the Jew must go and no
one wants to stop Hitler."

She paused and looked at Emi, tilting her
head. "I take it back. Leo Hartmann will
die and *no one* will care, not even you,
because you'll be back in Japan."

Emi and her family were due to sail back
to Japan in March 1939, four months off.
She stared at Kersten and shook her head
no.

"At least you were able to play their
piano," said Kersten. "Though don't feel so
special because I've played it, too. We all
used to go to his house when we were like
you. When we didn't understand the plague
of the Jew."

Emi thought she saw Kersten hesitate,
perhaps reminded of a good memory from
her time at the Hartmanns', but the moment quickly passed. Kersten scowled and
continued. "Too bad you're leaving so soon,

Emi. If you waited long enough you'd be able to have their piano for yourself. You do play it so well. Everyone will take from the Jews when they're dead. With all their money, the Hartmanns' house will probably be first on the looting list. That beautiful house will be stripped bare."

Emi blinked back her tears and shouted, "Leo Hartmann is *not* going to die!"

"He is, Emi," said Kersten, softly. "They're all going to."

Kersten left Emi standing in the hall, her tears running down her face onto her blouse. She wiped her eyes and glanced at a clock hanging in the classroom next to her. The music room was just a few steps away, but her *amah* was not due to meet her at the school for two more hours, after Emi's practice was over. Instead of going into the music room, Emi took the shortcut out through the chapel that Leo had shown her on her first day and ran all the way to the Hartmanns' house.

As she turned the corner onto their street, trying not to trip over her own feet, she could see that there was still black paint all over the right side of the façade's ground floor. This time *"Alle Juden müssen sterben"* was scrawled in thick letters over layers of painted-over words. All Jews must die.

Emi put her hands over the letters, only able to cover the word *sterben,* "die," and closed her eyes. Before anyone could confront her, she wiped her hands on her skirt, as the paint was still wet, and knocked on the Hartmanns' door. After a minute of waiting and no answer, she started to shout Leo's name.

"Get away from that dirty Jew door," a woman scolded as she passed, hitting Emi's back, but she did not stop and Emi pounded on the door again. After several minutes, Zalan, the Hungarian chauffeur, finally opened the door, his hand with four fingers held behind his back. He was not in uniform.

"You're not supposed to come in," he told her, his dark eyes looking at her with suspicion. "Mr. Hartmann's order." Emi was about to protest when he said, "But I told them you wouldn't go away, so here I am. You have five minutes, and then I will drive you home. Not the same car. Horrible little car, but safer. Go," he said, holding the door open wide enough to let Emi in, then slamming it shut behind her and locking it.

Emi thanked him, clasping her thin hands together, and ran up the stairs to where Leo was waiting in the dark hallway. Every curtain in the house had been pulled closed, and only a few electric lights were on.

"You shouldn't have come," he said, wrapping her in his arms. "But I'm so happy you did."

"Five minutes," said Hani Hartmann, coming into the hallway, too. "I mean it. It's too dangerous for you here, Emi," she said, but she stopped and embraced her before hurrying into another room and closing the door.

"You can't stay here," Emi said, sobbing once she and Leo were alone again. "They'll kill you."

"We're not going to stay," said Leo, holding her shoulders, looking at her. "We have visas to enter Switzerland. The border is going to become much more difficult for Jews to cross, so we have to go soon. My parents are preparing everything now."

"But how will you get there?" asked Emi, trying to calm herself. "How did you obtain Swiss visas?"

"We paid for them, probably ten times what everyone else paid, which is why we already have them. Money will help us escape now, but they say that it won't help for long. Switzerland already doesn't want Jews. But they do want money. If we don't leave in the next few days, then we might

not ever leave. And if we can't leave Austria
—"

"Don't say it, Froschi!" she said, putting her hand on his mouth. "Don't ever say it."

"Okay," he said, kissing the inside of her palm. She moved it to his cheek and he whispered, "I won't say it."

Emi, her hand still on Leo, looked around her at the paintings on the wall. "What will you do with your house? With all these beautiful things?"

"We hope they can be shipped to us when we have a place to ship them to. Right now, we are hiding the best of them with friends. There are still friends, Christians, who will help us. Former employees at the factory who have known us for many years. But I don't know if any of our property will make it through all this. We have to be prepared for it to disappear. It's funny, I don't think any of us care about such things anymore. It's strange to me now, that my father spent so much time amassing art and furniture and everything. What for?"

"Because it's so beautiful," said Emi. "It's not wrong that he did."

"Isn't it?" said Leo. "It feels very small-minded."

"No," said Emi. "He was focused on being alive, and now when the focus is staying

310

alive, priorities change."

"Staying alive. I wonder if we will all make it through this."

"Froschi," she said, her voice strained and tired. "Please don't say that, *please.*"

Leo was about to reply when the carved oak door of Max Hartmann's study opened and he and Hani walked out together.

"Oh Emi," said Max, coming over to her. "I said not to come. You should not have taken the risk."

"I had to," she said. "I'm sorry."

"You are too brave right now," said Max, his eyes bloodshot, his face still heavily bruised, the bags under his eyes dark. "But it's not the time to be brave, it's the time to be safe. We will see you again, but now, you have to go. Please." He put his hand on her head and said, "May God keep you safe." He recited several lines of the Tefilat Ha'derekh, the Traveler's Prayer, explained what it said, and kissed her on the cheek.

"But I will see you again," said Emi. "Before you leave for Switzerland. I must."

"It's not possible anymore," said Hani, putting her arm around Emi's shoulder to comfort her. "We have to say our goodbyes. But we will call them 'when we meet agains' instead of goodbyes."

Max and Hani took her by the hands and

then left the room. She was alone with Leo.

"I will see you before you leave, despite your parents' wishes," she said, leaning against him. "I'll come here tomorrow. I don't care what happens. This can't be the last time I see you before you go."

"It has to be. If anything were to happen to you, and it was my fault —"

"But none of this is your fault!" she said. "You are the persecuted. The rest of this country, they have gone crazy with hate. They are the animals."

"It's the last time in this house in Austria," said Leo. "But I will see you again soon. Of course I will. That alone will be enough to keep me alive. Please don't worry. I know we will end up together in the end. Froschi and Emi," he said, smiling confidently. "Always."

"How can I do anything but worry?" said Emi. "Promise me we will see each other again soon. Look at me and say 'I promise.' "

"I promise," said Leo. "I promise." He kissed Emi and she held on to him until he whispered that she had to go.

"I don't want Zalan to take you back," he said. "I think it will be more dangerous for you in a Hartmann's car than on foot. Even the little car."

"I'll walk," said Emi. "You're right, it's safer. Tell your parents that I love them." She wiped her eyes, threw her arms around Leo, and said, "And you. I love you the most."

"I love you, too," said Leo. "Together forever. But with a slight, unplanned intermission in between forever." He kissed her and let her go.

Scared that if she touched him again she would never be able to leave, she hurried out their back door, happy that the glass was covered in intricate bars of iron. She looked at her watch. Her *amah* was going to be at the school in five minutes and Emi, on foot, would not be able to beat her there.

She hurried around to the front of the house and was about to start running toward the Ringstrasse when she heard someone scream her name.

Down the street, a tall blond girl was looking her way.

"That's her! There!" the girl shouted. She had changed out of her school uniform, but it was Kersten.

Emi turned in the other direction out of instinct, but not before glimpsing three boys from their school behind Kersten. As soon as they saw her lock eyes on them, they all began sprinting toward her.

Adrenaline pumping, Emi ran as fast as she could, turning a corner to the back of the Hartmanns' house again, but despite her speed, the boys reached her before she made it to the door.

She felt two grab her arms, and she screamed as one of them put his free hand over her mouth. They pulled her against the Hartmanns' house and then turned her around to face Kersten when she caught up. Emi was being held so tightly that she could only move her head and feet, so Kersten slowed down and sauntered up to her. She put out her hand, touched Emi at the top of her cheek, and ran her fingers slowly down her face.

"It would be so much easier for you if you listened to me," she said in a pitying tone. "I told you it was illegal to be with Jews. I told you it was dangerous to see Leo Hartmann again. But what did you do but take off straight here after school. I saw you leave through the chapel," she said. "Didn't you think someone might be watching you? And know exactly where you were going?"

"No," said Emi, her shoulders burning from her arms being pulled back behind her. "I was sure you had something better to do with your time than run after me."

"Oh, I didn't have to run," said Kersten.

"I knew you would be up there for hours, crying over Leo and his rich Jew parents. But I timed it perfectly. Just as we turned on his street, you came out, looking this way and that like a panicked little mouse."

"We heard all about you and Hartmann," said the boy who was bending her left arm. Emi recognized him as Erich Böhm. He was in the class below hers and blond as a field of wheat. "If you're so ready to be with the Jews, then your legs should open up very easily for us." Erich laughed and thrust his pelvis against her. He told his friend to take both her arms and stepped in front of her. He unbuttoned her coat, pushing it off her shoulders and letting it dangle on the ground. Her schoolbag fell with it and he yanked it off her, letting go of her for only a second, and kicked it into the street, where a taxi immediately ran it over. It bounced once from the movement of the cab, then lay in the middle of the street, like a flattened animal. Emi tried to lunge for it, but the boys holding her were far too strong.

"What? All of a sudden you don't like male company?" said the third boy, laughing. "That's not your reputation. I've heard you've taken it more than once." He bent back her arm even more unnaturally and Erich started unbuttoning her blouse, pulling at the pearl buttons until they were all undone. He moved it back onto her shoulders so that Emi's chest in her thin slip was bare in the nearly freezing weather. Then he ripped open her slip and bra, so that her body was exposed in the street. Emi screamed, trying to grab her breasts, but her arms were being held back too tightly.

"Let's all do it right here, against the Hartmanns' house," Erich said to the two other boys. He leaned down and fondled her breasts, biting them and pushing his hands against her nipples. "No one will come out to help her. They're too scared to leave. They can just watch from the windows. They'll love that. You're probably sleeping with the rich Jew father, too," he said, kissing Emi hard on the mouth. He shoved his tongue into her throat, moving it up and down, causing her to gag. She coughed loudly in his face, choking, but he didn't take a step back. When he finally pulled away from her mouth, he moaned with pleasure and pinned her back harder. Emi started to scream, thrashing her body back and forth, trying to escape. A clammy hand went over her mouth again, though she wasn't sure whose it was, and she felt her feet scraping on the pavement as she was dragged, trying to fight in vain against three boys. As Erich slammed her body against the wall and spread her legs open, she felt his hands in her underwear, pushing hard inside her. She screamed again, starting to thrash her head, the only part of her that wasn't held back. With her eyes watering and the taste of blood in her mouth, Emi felt one hand move from inside of her to the fly of his school pants. He opened it and then pushed himself in her, causing her to scream so loudly that both the other boys put their hands over her mouth at the same time.

As she tried to bite down on their hands while Erich moaned, she heard Kersten sigh and walk to them, grabbing Erich by the shirt and pulling him off of Emi.

"Leave her alone," said Kersten, looking down at Emi's feet, which were bleeding through her stockings, her shoes kicked off on the pavement. "Her father is a diplomat. It will cause too much trouble. If he wasn't, then I would say go ahead. She deserves to be raped in the street by all of you after what she's done."

"Get off of me!" Erich yelled at Kersten. "I'm going to finish," he said, moving toward Emi again.

Kersten got to Emi first and covered her with her body. "You will not. Go whack off in that end of the alley," she said, pointing down the road. "I don't want to see how little you have down there."

Erich moved a step back, zipping his fly as he went, and spit on Emi's stocking feet.

"I don't want to shoot it in a girl who has been with a Jew anyway," he said laughing and grabbing his crotch as the other boys finally let her go and ran off laughing with Erich.

Kersten lingered behind, smiling at Emi's appearance. Emi got up, covered herself, and ran back for her coat and shoes, Kersten watching her. She picked her coat up, threw it over her shoulders, fastening the buttons up to her neck, and then hurried into the road to get her bag, which was ripped along the side seam from the car's tires.

When Emi was on the sidewalk, holding her broken bag across her chest like armor, Kersten said, "I wouldn't bother coming back to school tomorrow." She walked over to Emi and pulled at her coat collar button, which was hanging on by a thread. It came off in her hand and she threw it into the nearby gutter.

"I told you Leo wasn't worth crying over," she said. As she walked away, she pointed to the Hartmanns' windows above them.

All the curtains were drawn, with no sign that the family had witnessed anything.

As soon as Kersten was out of sight, Emi leaned against the Hartmanns' wall and looked up at the big white house one last time before running toward school.

It never happened, she told herself as she sprinted through the street, her insides burning. She would never tell her family; never tell Leo. Everything about the day, except kissing him goodbye, would just have to disappear.

CHAPTER 18

Leo Hartmann
December 1938

It was four weeks and one day after Kristallnacht, and the Hartmanns were leaving the city at 11 P.M. to make the seven-hour drive to the St. Gallen border crossing with Switzerland. The man from their synagogue, who had helped Max obtain their visas so quickly, said that there was a compassionate border police commander there who had already let in fifty Jews during the first days after the attacks. But they had to cross before 7 A.M., when the day guards came on. They were much stricter with the Jews.

The three Hartmanns watched as Zalan loaded up his own small car, having exchanged his for the Hartmanns'.

"Will we have to ride in the trunk?" asked Hani, looking at the cramped space.

"No," said Max, putting his hand in hers.

"We have visas for Switzerland and enough money to pay off everyone who might stop us."

"They don't even care about our money," said Hani. "They just want us gone. Preferably dead. There's no bribe to outweigh that kind of hate."

"We're doing everything we can," said Max. "We're fleeing, aren't we? I'm leaving my brother in charge of too much, leaving all my family burdens on him. We should be staying months longer. Waiting until our staff leave. Even the Christian ones."

"You gave them more money than they make in a year. Helped them obtain exit visas. We've done all we can. Staying in Vienna, in Austria, is a death sentence," hissed Hani, opening the back door to the little white car and crawling inside. "Your brother will leave before the spring. He promised. As will my family."

Leo tried to ignore his parents' conversation, helping the chauffeur — one of the only members of the Hartmanns' staff who were not Jewish — with their bags instead. He knew they had to escape Austria, that they were lucky to have Swiss visas, but he was heartbroken about leaving Vienna. His life, his house, everything he had ever known was about to fade into the distance behind him. And Emi, too. The unlikely girl that he'd fallen very much in love with.

At five past eleven, the chauffeur signaled to Max that they had to depart if they wanted to stay on schedule. Zalan was going to return to Vienna and try his best to keep the Hartmanns' house and possessions from being seized by the Nazis. If he succeeded, and if the Hartmanns never came back, it would all be his.

The family sat as stiff as corpses as the car made its way out of town. Once Vienna was behind them, they spent half the trip nodding off, only to be jolted awake at every stop, when the worrying would begin again. But as the sun started to rise, a half hour before they reached the Swiss border, nothing had gone wrong. So it was with confidence that Max handed his family's papers and passports to the young guard they encountered at the point of entry at six o'clock in the morning.

Stern-faced until he saw Hani, the guard took the papers and made small talk in German until he opened Max's passport and saw the large, red *J* stamp. Then he looked at Max's visa again and announced, "These visas are not valid."

"Of course they are," said Max, trying to take his passport.

The border guard pointed at the *J*, then flipped through Hani's and Leo's passports and saw that they bore the incriminating letter, too. "Your visa is not valid for a Jew and certainly not valid for three Jews. You will have to leave now." He waved toward the road and turned away.

"Of course it is valid, Jew or not. This is an entry visa into Switzerland," said Max, pointing at the paper, his eyes, as green as Leo's, wide and pleading. He started after the guard, but Leo caught him by the coat.

Turning back to Max and pulling out his gun, the guard said, "My orders are to use my own discretion, and my discretion tells me that this country already has too many Jews and we are not letting any more in." He spat on the ground near Max, then eyed Hani and added, "Even beautiful Jewesses."

Max started to protest again but the guard roared, "Enough!" and lifted his pistol to Max's face.

"But we must cross!" insisted Max, oblivious to the risk. "Who else can I speak with?"

"Let's leave, Father," Leo urged from behind him. "Can't you see what is in front of you? This is not the man we were expecting."

"That's right! Listen to your son," said the guard. "You want to speak with someone else, *Jude*? You were expecting some Jew lover? You don't think I have absolute authority here?"

The guard turned and shouted for another officer who was reading a newspaper in the nearby guardhouse. Reluctantly, at his second shout, the man got up and strolled over, his expression unchanged. Leo hoped that this guard was the one they had been told about, and as he approached, he could feel his parents' desperation also. The younger guard asked him if he had the authority to reject the three Jews trying to enter Switzerland.

"You can do whatever you want with them as long as you don't make me come outside again," he said yawning, showing off a mouthful of yellow teeth and not even glancing at the Hartmanns.

"Turn your car around there," said the young guard smugly, pointing to a wide stretch of road. "Leave right now or I will report you. I'm sure the Germans will be happy to see you back in Vienna. They'll know just where to send you so you never return."

"Could we buy the right visas?" asked Max in a last attempt to cross. He took his hat off of his thick gray hair, respectfully. "We will pay any price."

"How much?" said the young guard.

Max handed him five thousand perfectly ironed reichsmarks and the guard laughed. "I don't want reichsmarks! And even if you gave me a million of them, I wouldn't let you in." He put the money in his pocket and said, "No to your bribes, no to your Jew visas. Now turn around before I report you to the Gestapo."

Max, finally seeming to understand the clout the juvenile guard could exercise, motioned for Hani and Leo to get in the car.

"We will try to enter Switzerland at another crossing," he said when the border was out of sight.

"But they will just pass word to each other that we already tried," said Hani tearfully. "You heard what that little fascist said. He was going to turn us in. We can't risk it again. Especially not today."

"Where should I drive then, sir?" asked Zalan, and Max told him to follow signs for Lienz.

"Olis Benn gave me the address of his parents' house in case we had trouble at the border," said Max, mentioning a man who had worked in the family's chocolate factory for thirty years. "Quickly, Zalan, please," he said to the chauffeur. "Get us to this address without incident."

The little car sped back east through the countryside in the increasing sunshine, driving without stopping, straight toward their destination in the mountains.

"We helped Olis when his wife died," Max told Leo. "Financially. He had three children and no one to tend to them. He said if he could ever repay us." Max broke off to tell the driver to be careful. He turned back to Leo, squeezed against Hani in the backseat, and said, "I thought very little of it at the time, since he was a factory employee and I had so much more. But perhaps he sensed what was coming for the Jews more clearly than I did. Things can change quickly, fortunes can turn, so always be kind, Leo. Be kind to everyone. If I can give you any advice, that is it."

"Max, he doesn't need life lessons right now," Hani snapped. "He is always kind. He's a wonderful son." She kissed him on the cheek and they all fell silent, looking out the dirty windows as the car weaved its way through the rolling countryside, beautiful in its bare winter form but menacing in its quiet.

After two hours, Zalan announced that they'd arrived. Or so he thought. Leo looked out and saw a long driveway leading up to a very small farmhouse. The house was bright white, but the paint was peeling and the shingled roof sagged on the left side, moss growing plentifully between roof and walls. Already, although the car windows were closed, they could smell farm animals.

"I'll park around the back," said the Hungarian, maneuvering the car to a more secluded area near the matching white barn.

Before they were out of the car, the elderly couple who owned the house were outside, the husband holding a pitchfork and walking slowly.

"Let me speak to them first," said Max, opening his door. Leo watched him walk over with a smile, explaining in a loud, clear voice who he was before he reached the Benns.

"They seem to recognize his name," said Hani. Relieved, she pulled the scarf off her curls and sighed loudly. "The man has put down that weapon."

"That's not much of a weapon," said the chauffeur. "Especially not when it's being brandished by an eighty-year-old farmer."

"Did Papa give a lot of money to Olis Benn?" asked Leo.

"Enough so that his parents should let us sleep in the barn for a night or two," said

Hani, opening the car door when Max waved to them. "Even if they don't like Jews."

To the family's relief, the Benns were kindly people, seemingly indifferent to Nazi propaganda. They brushed their white hair and changed out of their field clothes after the family came into the house and thanked Max repeatedly for his generosity toward their son and grandchildren.

"Of course you will sleep in the house, not in the barn," said Alfred Benn, Olis's father, through a gap-toothed smile.

When they were seated in the living room, on a faded velvet couch, Leo looked at the wooden cross on the wall, family photographs hung around it. And then he noticed the piano.

He walked over to it, put his hand on top, and looked at his parents.

"Do you play, son?" asked Alfred. "Please, feel free to play."

"I don't, my mother does," said Leo, looking at Hani. But he wasn't thinking about his mother, or music. He was thinking about Emi Kato and her father.

"We should ask Norio Kato for help," he said to his father. "If we could get in touch with him, with the Japanese Consulate, maybe there is a way he can help us get across to Switzerland."

Max looked at his son, surprised. The Benns stood up to leave them, seeming to understand that this conversation was more important than the piano, and Hani sat on the piano bench, a smile starting to appear. She looked at her husband and said, "Yes, Max, you must."

"It's a good suggestion, Leo," Max said after a pause. "Let's call their house if the Benns will allow it."

He left the room to consult with their hosts and returned quickly, smiling. He nodded at Leo.

"It's all right," he said. "But you should be the one to call, Leo. Emi's father might find it harder to say no to you."

That evening, when Leo guessed that Norio Kato would be home, he dialed the operator and was connected to the Katos' residence. The phone rang several times before Norio picked it up and said hello in Japanese.

"Mr. Kato, this is Leo Hartmann," said Leo, trying to keep his voice calm and steady. When Norio immediately asked what was wrong, he guessed he hadn't done a very good job of it.

"We didn't make it across the border to Switzerland," Leo told him. "The border guard threatened to turn us over to the Gestapo, but we were able to flee and are now in the countryside. We are in Lienz at a friend's home. They've been kind enough to put us up for the night."

Leo paused, then said urgently, "I'm sorry to bother you, Mr. Kato, but I'm afraid we are desperate for help. Without someone intervening, they won't let us into Switzerland, even with our visas, or with bribes. We tried that as well. Nothing has worked."

There was a pause on the other end of the phone, then Norio assured him, in his always-formal German, that he would do what he could. Everything he could. Leo explained where the house was, gave him the phone number, and Norio said he would call back within three days.

When Leo hung up, his mother lunged for him, wrapping herself around him.

"Can he do something?" she asked. "I don't want to have to try to enter Switzerland again without help. It would be like walking ourselves over a cliff. You were right to think of him, Froschi."

"Let's not relax into thinking he's saved us yet," said Max.

"You said Switzerland was a certainty!" said Hani, looking at her husband angrily. "That with what we could pay, we would

330

never be turned away. But now we are without anything, we could die here —"

"He will help us," Leo interrupted. "I'm sure he will. He said not to move from this house. That he will contact us in a few days."

"I will stay here, then," said Max, putting his hand on the phone. "I won't move from the telephone."

"Don't touch it," said Hani. "You could rattle it by accident. Keep it from working."

"I'll be fine," said Max, settling back onto the couch. "You should both see what help you can be to the Benns, Hani. They are very kind to let us stay here. And now we might need to stay longer than one night."

Hani nodded, her eyes tearing up.

"Not yet, Hani," said Max. "If we don't hear from Mr. Kato in the next three or four days, we will have to leave. We can't continue to impose on the Benns. It's obvious that they are scared having us here, even if they are too kind to say so. Then you can cry."

"And where will we go?" asked Hani. "To the border again? We can't go back to Vienna."

Leo put his arm around his mother, then walked to the front window, where the gingham curtains were pulled close. The Benns had told them they could stay as long as they needed to, provided they did not leave the house. They did not want their neighbors, however distant, to see strangers. The Hartmanns' car was hidden in the barn and Alfred had taken out their things after it was dark.

By their third night in Lienz, Max was whispering with his driver about what other Swiss entry points they could try and Hani's head had acquired a permanent droop, making her neck ache. Leo took over his father's position near the telephone.

As the late evening turned to the quiet of night, Hani and Max were so caught up in their discussion of other scenarios of escape, most of them impossible, that Leo was the only one to notice the lights of a car pulling slowly up to the house. Impulsively, he abandoned his post by the telephone and ran outside. When Hani saw him, she screamed, and Max ran after him. He grabbed Leo by his shirt collar, accidentally choking him as he dragged him back inside.

"You're not to leave the house!" Max said as Leo coughed. "You could be shot running at a car like that. What are you thinking?"

But before Leo could answer, they saw the distinguished figure of Norio Kato walking up the path from his car.

Max sprang to open the door for him, apologizing for their behavior and welcoming him inside.

"I thought it was safer if I didn't call," said Norio. "I'm sorry I startled you."

Leo looked out to the car, hoping Emi was with him, but only Norio and a chauffeur had made the journey.

"I have a solution," said Norio, when they were all sitting down. "It's not Switzerland, but in many ways it could be safer. If you can leave with me, immediately, I will explain everything on the road. Right now, we need to get you to Italy. And in two days, you will be sailing to Shanghai."

CHAPTER 19

Leo Hartmann
December 1938

Norio had explained to the Hartmanns how he had obtained visas for them to enter Shanghai — with the help of the Chinese consul-general in Vienna, Ho Feng-Shan — but the Hartmanns did not grasp the extent of what the consul-general had done until they boarded the ship. There the three words they heard more than any others during their first day at sea — the first of the thirty days it would take them to reach Shanghai — were Ho Feng-Shan.

"You don't need a visa to enter Shanghai, which is under Japanese rule, but you need a visa for another country to leave Austria," Norio had informed them in the Benns' house. "The Chinese, for now, are willing to grant these visas. And if you have boat tickets for immediate passage out of Europe, even better. The boats are few and only leave from Germany and Italy. They go via Japan and several other countries, a month-long journey, but they are all booked for the next year. You can imagine why. And if a ticket can be bought, a round-trip must be purchased, for as chaotic as Asia is right now — Shanghai especially — these boat companies will not guarantee that they can deposit passengers there. It's a disaster at best, but one worth trying. It helps if you lie to the boat companies and say the tickets are for Japanese diplomats. Then suddenly, doors open." He reached into his coat pocket and handed Max three tickets for a boat called the *Potsdam,* leaving from Genoa. In his other hand were three visas for Shanghai. "They should have been stamped directly into your passports," he explained, "but they should still work."

Hani had reached out for them, holding hers up to the lamp to read it over and over, as if she couldn't believe it was real. Finally, she'd put it down and said, "Oh, Mr. Kato, I will never be able to repay you for this." She broke down into tears, and Max had to keep her from hugging the esteemed diplomat, still dressed for a day at the office.

"I know China and Japan are not on the best terms right now," Max had said, reaching out to shake Norio's hand. "So for you to go to the consulate for us —"

"Yes, so kind," Hani had said, interrupting her husband. "On top of the kindness your daughter has shown to Leo. Please let us repay you financially. You must accept at least double what you have paid. When our chauffeur is back in Vienna he will bring you the money. Our accounts have been frozen, but we have some means —"

"Of course that is not necessary," Norio had said, stopping her. "I did not do much. It was mostly the Chinese consul." He'd pointed to Ho Feng-Shan's name on the visas. "I have learned since obtaining these that he has already issued many visas for Jews this year, and hopefully will grant many more."

They could take few possessions with them, Norio had instructed. Their luggage — and their persons — would be searched for contraband many times, and they should not attempt to bring anything of value, although Hani would be allowed to bring her wedding ring and a watch. Norio had had all their travel documents processed in advance, getting around barriers with bribe after bribe, and he promised to try to get the family money when they reached China, either out of their frozen bank accounts or through his.

Just an hour after Norio had arrived, the Hartmanns' chauffeur was on his way back to Vienna while Norio's driver ferried him and the Hartmanns to Innsbruck, where the family were to catch an express train to Genoa.

The drive to Innsbruck took just under three hours and there was very little time for emotional goodbyes at the station, where the train stood ready to depart. But Leo lingered for a moment with Norio.

"There will never be anyone in my life like your family, Mr. Kato," he said. "If we don't survive this ordeal, please tell Emi that she was very important to me. Tell her that there is no one else like her in the world, no one as interesting, as curious, as talented. I am quite embarrassed professing my love to her father like this, but I miss her very much already. She has made the last two years wonderful, when they could have been very difficult."

"I know she would echo your sentiments, Leo," said Norio, bowing. "Now please, don't miss your train, and make sure you take care of your parents. It's always harder for the older generation to leave their country behind than it is for the young."

Leo nodded and ran onto the train, where Gestapo officers were already checking papers, clicking their black boots intimidatingly. They looked, and looked again, at the family's visas and boat tickets, finally tossing them back into Max's lap and moving on to the next passengers. It wasn't until they were nearing the Italian border that the family started taking deep breaths, and when they crossed into Italy a cheer was heard throughout the train. They were out of Austria.

On December 15, just thirty-five days after Max Hartmann had been beaten unconscious by the Sturmabteilung, the SA, the family was far enough out to sea that they could no longer make out European land.

"Good riddance," Hani had said to her son, hugging him and her husband on deck. "It wasn't home anymore."

At dinner their first night on the Potsdam, they sat with a couple with two small children who told the Hartmanns to eat everything they could on the luxurious boat because Shanghai, they had heard, only had food for the Japanese.

"You are here because of Ho Feng-Shan," the wife said.

"Yes," said Hani, smiling at Leo. "And a few other benevolent men helped us, too. But the Chinese diplomat, he is issuing visas for Jews. Many, many, we heard."

"It was the tickets for this boat that were harder to get," said the husband. "We are only here because the father of another family was killed by the SA the week before the boat was set to sail. There was a wife and two children, as well, so there was room on the boat for four. Their travel agent called us to inquire if we could pay for the tickets and leave at once since we were on the top of the waiting list."

"No!" said Hani, reaching for Leo's hand.

"Yes," said the man, "we were very lucky."

The Hartmanns looked at the couple's two young children, who did not seem to understand how they'd been granted passage, and excused themselves from the table.

Leo and his parents went onto the deck, where they took out and studied the map Norio had drawn for them of the ship's route. From Genoa, they would go to Port Said in Egypt, then sail through the Gulf of Suez, the Red Sea, the Gulf of Aden, and the Arabian Sea to the Indian Ocean, before docking in Bombay and again in Ceylon. From there it was the Orient: Singapore, Hong Kong, and Kobe, Japan, before heading south to Shanghai.

"I used to feel far from home when I was across the city," said Leo, watching the stream of white left by the boat as it churned slowly through the water.

"I want to be far from home," said Hani. "And I never want to return."

CHAPTER 20

Emi Kato
September–November 1943

She hadn't thought of it before she let her mind wander back to Vienna, but Hani Hartmann looked quite a lot like Christian's bereaved mother, Helene. They both had striking red hair — Helene's straight and Hani's a bit darker and curled — though Emi had never been sure if those curls, or the color, were natural or not. They had freckles that made intricate constellations on their arms and were both mothers to only one son. She hoped that Hani Hartmann had not spent the last few months covering her freckles with tears, as Helene was likely still doing as she sat by her window looking out at Crystal City.

There wasn't, thought Emi, a soul with russet-colored freckles on the MS *Gripsholm,* except perhaps the captain, but Emi hadn't seen him yet. He was busy navigating their immense vessel straight down the Atlantic coast toward South America.

Emi turned around at the railing and looked at the people on the deck with her instead of out at the ocean. They were all ethnically Japanese. Emi realized that she wasn't used to that kind of homogeneity anymore. Even in the internment camps, the populations had been mixed. Now she was headed back to a country that was filled with Emikos and Keikos; there would be no Christian Langes or Leo Hartmanns. How strange, she thought to herself, to have been involved only with foreign men. Chiyo's gossip down in the cabin was still eating at her, but if she could blame anyone, she thought, it should be her father. She hadn't asked to be dragged all over the world. There were no Japanese boys for her to fall in love with in Vienna, and in that city, you had to fall in love with someone. It was too beautiful to waste, especially for the young.

Though the first night on board the *Gripsholm* went smoothly, despite the small cabin and the poor company, the water turned choppy as soon as dawn broke over the horizon on their second day at sea. The Swedish crew members came around to each little room handing the passengers big bars of chocolate, which they said had been reserved as a surprise for when they reached their halfway point in the voyage but were being handed out now instead, as they had rough days ahead. The passengers were advised not to eat the chocolate yet, to wait until the water was calm and there was less danger of seasickness, but Emi unwrapped hers and devoured every morsel in big, starving bites. She hoped the sugar would help settle her stomach, which was starting to feel like a mixing bowl. Emi was well-versed in seasickness from her many long boat trips, but some of the *Nisei* children, who had never traveled on a boat for such a distance or on one that size, did everything wrong, eating too much and staying in their cabins instead of going up to the deck to breathe the cold sea air.

The weather turned worse on the third and fourth days, and all Emi could hear for forty-eight hours was the sound of bathroom doors opening and closing, waves splashing against the ship like slaps in the face, and the collective groan of over a thousand green-faced people trying not to be sick. When the boat finally settled, on their fifth day at sea, it smelled of vomit, cleaning fluid, and chocolate bars, as Emi was not the only one who failed to heed the crew's warning.

That night the dinner on board, which was eaten only by the hungry few, including the well-traveled Katos, was beef stew with the thick, Italian-style noodles that few of the Japanese were accustomed to eating. Emi wondered if they might all be sick again, but her stomach proved stronger than her confidence, which could not be said of Chiyo and Naoko. It took two weeks for them not to look green in the face.

It was during the third week at sea that the monotony of being trapped on a ship set in for Emi and her mother. The mornings and afternoons started to run into each other, then the days were hard to tell apart and whenever someone mentioned the day of the week, Emi was always surprised. Everything was blue when the sun was out — the sky, the water, the décor of the ship — and at night everything was black. Blue and black, blue and black, a two-colored world floating past her. Emi started to come up to deck less, choosing instead to sleep and rest the days away. Lying in her narrow bed with too many metal coils sticking in her back and not enough blankets, she thought often of Christian and what they'd shared in Crystal City. She wondered if Leo had had any indiscretions since he'd left Vienna. Had he also been desperate to find some joy in a difficult time?

The MS *Gripsholm*'s first stop on their eighty-three-day voyage was Rio de Janeiro, logistically a challenge for the understaffed Swedish crew, who had to bring on board nearly a hundred more people — Japanese who had been living in Brazil for years, sometimes generations — who would also be traded in India for American citizens. But despite that task, the crew informed the passengers the night before they docked in Brazil that they would be allowed to leave the ship, unsupervised, for several hours. And not only were they allowed to leave the ship and walk around the city, but they would all have time to go up Rio's famed Sugarloaf Mountain by cable car, akin to flying for people who had spent more than a year behind fences.

Emi, thrilled at the prospect, leaned against her mother and said, "Freedom." Together they stayed on deck, well positioned as the sprawling metropolis came into view. They looked down at the craggy coastline, the low houses that seemed to go on forever behind the tall apartment blocks lining the sparkling shore, the dots of palm trees and the white boats, which looked so small below them, and heard each other's breathing slow down.

345

"Can you imagine?" said Keiko as the anchor dropped. "It took a world war, a year and a half of internment, and a long ride on a Swedish boat to allow us to see such a place."

"It's very pretty," said Emi, smiling and pressing her hips into the railing, as she was apt to do. "But I don't think it was worth it."

"I don't, either," said Keiko, holding her daughter's hand as she leaned out even farther.

When they were in the slow-moving cable car with the vibrant city beneath them and Rio's iconic mountains in front of them, Keiko said, "Let's appreciate being in a country that isn't at war. Let's remember every minute of this."

"I'll come back and see Rio under different circumstances one day," said Emi when they stepped out of the cable car. "I'm sure of it."

"I don't doubt my daughter's will, ever," said Keiko. "I learned that a long time ago. You're a stubborn child, but that's not a bad trait in a modern young woman, especially one these days."

"I don't feel very modern," said Emi. "Look at me, going back to Japan to do what?"

"To stay alive. To help your parents stay alive," said Keiko, sadly. "You're still a modern woman, just one hindered by war. Trust me, you are far luckier than I was. I was taught that the only reason to better myself was so that I might marry a remarkable man. No one told me to be remarkable myself. But your father has been telling you to be since the day you were born. And you know what? I think it worked," she said, looking at her daughter with pride.

The boat did not drop anchor again for several weeks — weeks that Emi spent mostly with her eyes closed, letting herself dream about the past, knowing that it would be those memories that would make her future bearable.

When the *Gripsholm* finally docked again, it was at South Africa's Port Elizabeth in early October, but the weather tricked them into thinking it hadn't been thirty-seven days since they left New York.

This stop, the crew warned before the ship pulled into harbor, would be far less pleasant than Rio. They were told that here they were only allowed to walk onshore close to the dock.

As the boat crept up the coast of Africa, slowing as Port Elizabeth came into view, the crew expressed surprise to see the port fully illuminated.

"We were told we would be coming in dark," one said to Emi as she stood back on the deck, this time having no desire to be at the front of the boat. "Maybe you'll be let off for longer than we thought."

But it wasn't to be. While the crew said they could stay on land for four hours as they took care of administrative duties, almost none of the passengers did once they confronted the WHITES ONLY signs dotting Port Elizabeth like the signs many had seen all over California after Pearl Harbor.

"Are we considered white here?" Emi asked her mother as another mother pulled her child away from the large sign. Keiko didn't answer. She sighed, told her daughter to stretch her arms and legs, enjoy stable land for a few minutes more, and then they were going back on board.

Her mother was right, thought Emi. They had heard enough about such signs from the *Issei* and *Nisei* in Crystal City. They didn't need to be subjected to them, too, even if they were meant for a different race.

On the forty-fourth day, after the forty-fourth sunrise and the forty-fourth breakfast of weak tea, too-soft rice, and dried fish, India was supposed to be on the horizon. Emi, her mother, and the Kuriyamas stood on the deck together looking for a dark line to indicate land. Chiyo had not grown any friendlier to Emi as the trip wore on, using every moment they were alone together to bring up the expectations facing Japanese women in wartime, as if it were an honor to be deprived. But Keiko had pleaded with her daughter to remain civilized, since they were in such tight quarters. They were on a boat, Keiko reminded Emi, where rumors traveled fast. If Chiyo wanted to start talking about Norio Kato's rude, promiscuous daughter on board, word would certainly get back to Norio Kato and the Foreign Ministry staff as soon as they docked in Yokohama. Out of respect for her parents, Emi was polite. She smiled at the women when she rolled out of her bed and let the Kuriyamas use the bathroom first both mornings and evenings. She spoke of nothing unpleasant, and even when she was privately burning with contempt for them, she always managed to make banal small talk. The result was that by the time they reached India, Chiyo's harassment, while still biting, had been less constant.

They saw nothing but blue sky and dark ocean all through the morning on what they called India day, but just before lunch was served, a young boy whose hair had clearly been cut with the aid of a soup bowl screamed *"Riku — Riku ga mieta!"* and everyone on the deck rushed to where he was standing to see if they, too, could see land. Emi squinted and tried to find a high perch so the midday sun wasn't blocking her view. After a few seconds, she saw it. India. The word *riku* flew around the boat, drawing passengers up from below deck like a magnet.

"If we weren't prisoners, this would be much more exciting," Chiyo said to Emi, and for the first time, she agreed with her.

Their destination was the port of Mormugao in Goa, a Portuguese territory on the west coast of India. Arriving in Goa meant much more than being able to walk on solid ground for a few hours. It meant the day of the switch. The Japanese and Japanese-Americans would disembark from the *Gripsholm* and the people the U.S. government deemed "real Americans" would be loaded on. The passengers on the *Gripsholm* were told that the whole process would only take a few hours, so they wouldn't have time to see anything in Goa besides the port and their new ship, the *Teia Maru.*

"I don't think anyone on this boat wants to waste their time sightseeing now," said

Chiyo. "This certainly isn't a pleasure cruise."

"I'd have to agree," said Keiko. "I think we are all just ready to be in Japan and not on these choppy waters. I don't know how much longer my stomach can take it."

"It better get stronger quickly, Kato-san," said Chiyo, her expression indicating that she was enjoying Keiko's admission of weakness. "After we trade boats in Goa we have to travel around the southern tip of India to Singapore, then on to San Fernando Bay in the Philippines, then to French Indochina, which I hear has the most beautiful cranes, though I doubt we will see any. Then we are to go on to Hong Kong, then Shanghai, and finally Yokohama. Would you like to see a map? I have one in our room. It's still a very long journey. How many days?" she asked her smirking daughter.

"Very many more," said Naoko. "At least thirty."

"Did you hear? At least thirty," she said to Keiko. "So time to toughen up, Kato-san. There are no servants to wait on you here and certainly not on the next boat, run by the Japanese. Unless you think that's what we are. Your servants." She executed a deep bow in the style reserved for the highest dignitaries, and then righted herself and gave Keiko a pitying look.

"Come, Emiko," said Keiko, pleasantly. "Let's go down and finish packing our things."

"If we are rooming with the Kuriyamas on the *Teia Maru,* you can just leave me in India," Emi whispered to her mother as they walked away. "Contracting typhoid and dying alone seems less painful than another month with that pair."

When the boat finally pulled up to the shore the morning of October 15, the salted warm air wafted up, smelling foreign and thick with humidity, unlike that of even Washington, D.C., or Tokyo. Would anyone try to run from the boat and stay in India? Emi wondered. She looked out at the dark-skinned men on the dock, most of them shirtless and barefoot, busily trying to maneuver the giant ship into position, and was jealous for a moment that they got to live in a peaceful country. Maybe, she thought, she should be the rogue passenger who stayed in India. Keiko's hand brushed her shoulder and Emi remembered that even though she was twenty-one, as an unmarried woman she wasn't free to make her own choices.

The *Teia Maru* had not yet arrived, so the

public spectacle they were destined to create was still modest. All the same, by the time they'd been at anchor for an hour, the crowd of Indians at the dock was growing. The Portuguese officials in Goa, who were helping with the transfer, managed to keep most of the civilians back, but a group of teenagers broke away and ran onto the pier closest to the *Gripsholm,* waving their hands and screaming. From that moment on, the chaos of the day was in full swing.

When the *Teia Maru* finally appeared, Emi saw illuminated crosses along the sides, the same as they had on their boat, to help keep them safe from enemy submarines. The men in charge of the switch, all Portuguese military men, didn't waste any time. They made sure the ships were docked end to end and a short metal walkway was placed between their decks. The *Gripsholm* passengers were instructed to walk onto their new ship without speaking a word to the Americans leaving the *Teia Maru.*

"Avoid eye contact," the Portuguese officials suggested. "It will be much easier if you look down."

When everything was as organized as possible, the passengers from each ship crossed in two horizontal lines, like ants on a log, with just a few yards separating them on the wide walkway.

It was impossible, Emi and the rest of the passengers immediately realized, not to make eye contact with the Caucasian faces streaming past them. Do they know where we have spent the last year? Emi wondered to herself. Were they in internment camps, too? Do they want to go back to America? She stared at them as they passed by in their tight, orderly line, almost all looking back at her with friendly, exhausted faces. "These are the kind of Americans who would not put Japanese people behind barbed-wire fences," she whispered to her mother. "They chose to go to Japan. They've lived like we have."

It took more than two hours for all the passengers to make it onto their new boats, but no happy sounds floated out from the Japanese arriving on board the *Teia Maru*. The Japanese boat, built by the French a decade before, was thoroughly inferior to the *Gripsholm*. It was smaller, much dirtier, the facilities were rudimentary, and it had a capacity of only seven hundred. One thousand five hundred and three Americans had just disembarked from it and almost that many Japanese had boarded. Emi sighed and leaned against the wall, trying to avoid having her feet trampled and suitcases pushed into her body. The *Teia Maru* was as packed as the swimming pool at Crystal City after sunset.

As the boat pulled away from the dock that evening, the passengers heard singing from the *Gripsholm*. Many of the Americans being repatriated were missionaries, and Emi knew from attending Christian church at her schools in Europe and Washington that religious Westerners all knew the same songs. It seemed to be the case on the ship, too, for even as the *Teia Maru* sailed farther away, the singing on the *Gripsholm* grew louder, as if more people were joining in. Emi could still hear the song even when their faces were blurred: "In Christ there is no East or West, in Him no South or North, but one great fellowship of love throughout the whole wide world."

"Maybe they're singing that song to us because they've seen their luxurious new boat and feel sorry for us on this rowboat," said Emi.

"You complain too much," her mother replied crossly, but Emi could tell that she was just as disgusted by the *Teia Maru* as her daughter was.

When the two went down to their cabin, they saw immediately how much worse this leg of the journey would be. Theirs was a room for two, but four would apparently be sleeping in it, as a pair of straw pallets had been placed on the floor, shoved tightly against the narrow beds. Keiko said that Emi would have to sleep on one of them, even though they were in the room first, and she propped one pallet up temporarily against her own bed to make room for the other passengers, who soon arrived. Emi looked up to see the downcast faces of Chiyo and Naoko Kuriyama.

"Of course," hissed Emi to her mother when they had unpacked their things and left the cabin. "Why don't they just have me sleep next to a horse?"

The other problem on the *Teia Maru* was that while every cabin had a small washbasin — with the water on for two hours a day, from six to seven in the morning and from five to six at night — there were only two real bathrooms on their ship. After just a few hours at sea, the ship smelled worse than a stable.

But Emi and Keiko soon discovered that they were lucky to have a room at all, for many of the men did not. In good weather they had to sleep on straw pallets on the deck; in bad, they were in the hallways. This was problematic not only for them, but for everyone on board because of the threat of fire. As there was so little to do during their long, tedious days at sea, many passengers chain-smoked, and while they were ordered to throw the cigarette butts into the water, they often missed and the straw pallets continuously caught on fire. Adding to the unpleasantness of the journey, the Japanese crew had surprisingly miscalculated how much rice the Japanese passengers would eat compared to the Americans, and by the time their eighty-three-day trip was coming to an end, the only rice that was left was infested with worms.

Because of the poor food and their inability to sleep well in their claustrophobic space, Emi and Keiko could both put a fist in their pant waistbands by the time they were three days out from Japan.

"Your father will be worried when he sees us starved like this," said Keiko as the two packed a few more things in their suitcases. Emi had been almost completely packed for the last week, desperate to finally be off the boat. She wondered if she would be able to stay on deck when Japan finally came into view or if the desire to be on familiar dry land might impel her and hundreds of others to jump off the boat and try to swim ashore.

She turned to sit on her straw bed, as beds

were the only place to sit in their cabin. As soon as she was somewhat comfortable, and her mother next to her, the door opened and Chiyo came in. Emi had stopped bothering to smile at Chiyo now that the trip was almost over, as the older woman had become much more unpleasant on the *Teia Maru* than she was on the *Gripsholm.* If the Japanese coastline didn't lure Emi into jumping ship, she thought, the prospect of getting away from Chiyo surely would.

"Oh, you're both here," Chiyo said as she closed the door behind her. "I was just finishing my lunch on deck when I thought how sad you must be, Emi, now that we've almost reached Japan. I know how you feel more comfortable around *gaijin.* Now that one cook on the *Gripsholm,* the young one with the blue eyes, he reminded me a bit of the boy you had the affair with in Crystal City," she said, dropping her packet of cigarettes on the bed. "I imagine you miss him. The boy from Crystal City, not the *Gripsholm* cook."

To Emi's surprise, her mother responded before she did, her voice calm but resolute.

"Kuriyama-san, I do think this arduous journey is going to your head. You are speaking as if you have some intimate knowledge of my daughter's life, which you do not. We have just been unlucky enough to have to room with you for nearly three months and this must have you thinking that you know certain things about our lives. But let me take this opportunity to correct you. You do not know a thing about my daughter, or me, other than the positions we sleep in. If you are entertaining the idea that it would be amusing to spread wild rumors about Emiko when we are back in Japan, I will take this opportunity to remind you that we are not returning to the Japan we used to know. People, especially *ordinary* people, are so powerless when a country is at war, and they wouldn't want to find themselves in an even more difficult situation just because of a rumor they'd taken pleasure in spreading. So, Kuriyama-san, what was it again that you said about my daughter?"

Chiyo looked at Emi with disdain and frowned at both of them. "I said that it was an honor rooming with her for the last eighty days and that I will cherish the next three."

"What a thoughtful thing to say," said Keiko, standing up. "Emiko and I were just going to go take some air. I'm glad we were able to see you before we left the room. Have a pleasant afternoon."

Emi and her mother left in silence and walked up to the most private part of the deck near the roaring engine. Emi turned to her mother and started to cry.

"No," said Keiko. "You can't. Not here."

"Then where?" Emi asked, sniffling. "In our shared room? In one of the two bathrooms that have a line of a dozen people or more night and day? Where can I cry, mother?"

"You can't cry at all, Emiko," said Keiko. "Not over a woman like that. And besides, you know what she is saying is true. You did have an affair and you can't expect the bad apples of the world to ignore it. You made your choice and you are living through the consequences."

Emi wiped her eyes and managed to swallow the rest of her tears. "It was stupid of me, I know. Careless. But Christian, he was the only good thing that happened in over a year."

"I know," said Keiko. "But it's often the things you enjoy that have the most devastating consequences. Come," she said, turning to walk inside. "Let's not speak of it anymore. You can't undo it, and from the sound of it, you wouldn't want to anyway. It's been a long time since I threatened someone. It felt rather good. Let's just hope it works. And never, ever mention Christian Lange to your father."

"When have you ever threatened someone before?" asked Emi, ignoring her mother's last warning. It went without saying that Norio Kato was never to know the details about her time in Crystal City.

"Women," she said to Emi, "have fascinating lives before they become mothers. Perhaps I was a little bit different before I married your father and had you. A little more daring." She looked at her daughter and smiled. "A little more like you."

On the last three days of the trip, the weather cooperated and Emi and her mother decided to sleep on straw pallets on deck instead of in their room with the Kuriyamas. "Better to be cold than to be insulted," said Keiko as she reached for her daughter's hand.

"It is," said Emi. "And I suppose we should enjoy being outside, without worrying about bombs dropping on our heads. Here, we just worry about rain."

CHAPTER 21

Emi Kato
November 1943
Unlike in New York, where everyone had appeared happy to see them depart, some hurling insults at them as easily as they might toss a flower, coming into port in Japan was a heartening experience. The dock was packed with people desperate to reunite with their relatives. Before the passengers on the *Teia Maru* were close enough to pick out individuals in the crowd, they could see the sea of small flags waving in welcome.

"Perhaps the country will be difficult to live in when we arrive," said Keiko. "But here, from a distance, it's beautiful."

"Yes, it is," said Emi reaching up to fix her hair, caring for the first time in eighty-three days how it looked.

The thrill of returning to Japan was somewhat dampened by the inspection they all had to succumb to after they docked. Eager though they were to disembark and find their families, the passengers had to line up again in their orderly rows under the watchful eye of stern government officials, this time Japanese. Small wooden tables were set all around the deck of the ship and Japanese military men questioned them at length. The small man with a red and white armband assigned to the Katos was astonished to learn that Emi and her mother should have gone back with the diplomatic corps in 1942.

"But why didn't you come home with your husband?" said the man, looking at their papers.

"My daughter was very sick with tuberculosis. Here, we have her medical papers," Keiko said, pushing the stack of documents at him, though they were all written in English. "She could not travel. We were banned from the boat in 1942 as they were afraid she would give the ambassador and the other diplomats tuberculosis." The official took a long look at the yellow and pink papers, then stamped everything with an intricate red stamp before dismissing them to bow to a photograph of the emperor.

"How strange to see so many men in military uniform," said Emi when they had gathered their belongings, "and to see the military flag, the navy flag instead of our usual one."

"Things are going to be very different," said Keiko, walking slowly. "It will not be the Japan that we last saw in 1939. You read your father's last letter in Crystal City. It's a blessing that you are not going to school here, as all your time would be spent learning how to be more obedient. Never your strong suit."

"I'm surprised that made it past the censors," said Emi, knowing her mother was right.

"I'm sure they let in letters that seemed disparaging to Japan."

"But Father is loyal to Japan. He's working for the Foreign Ministry."

"Of course he's loyal, as we must be," said Keiko just above a whisper. "But you know your father. He will question everything, though he always wants what's best for our country."

"And not for the West," said Emi, trying to move ahead of a group of particularly slow women.

"The West is behind us now," said Keiko. "No longer a part of us. I am sure we will see much anti-Western propaganda at home, especially against America and England. For some of the diplomats, for you, that hatred may be hard to comprehend, but we must simply ignore it." Emi was about to protest but her mother interrupted her. "Instead of arguing, how about we try to get off this boat and never set foot on it again."

Emi shook her head in agreement and together the Katos walked down the metal plank to the dock, not bothering to turn around to see the ship one last time, and were instantly absorbed into the chaos. Despite the jostling and shoving of the crowd, Emi and Keiko stayed side by side, their angular bodies pressed together, weary legs braced, looking out for Norio Kato.

"There!" cried Emi after ten minutes battling the crowd. She pointed to where she'd spotted her father's profile. She had inherited her height from him and he stood half a head above the men around him. *"Otōsan! Otōsan!"* she called before realizing that everyone was screaming the Japanese word for father. *"Vater!"* she called instead, using the German word. *"Vater* Kato!" He heard it the third time, then spun round and saw them, his expression changing quickly from confusion to joy.

"There you are!" he exclaimed, reaching them first. "My family!" He gave his daughter a long hug and kissed his wife's head, making a happy humming sound as his lips touched her. Though public affection was not at all the norm in Japan, especially on such solemn occasions, Norio Kato had lived abroad for so long that different instincts guided him in emotional moments. Emi threw her arms around her father, not caring about any sort of cultural norms, and laid her face on his shoulder, something she hadn't done since they were all together in West Virginia in 1942.

"Father!" she said after she'd pulled away. "You look gaunt! Where is your belly?"

"Gone," said Norio, opening his coat buttons and showing off his flat stomach. "It looks better, doesn't it? Nothing like war to help take the pounds off a man. I've been trying to lose them since we left Austria." He sighed and helped his wife and daughter find their things, before going to reserve a taxi. "It's been a very difficult year," he said when he came back. "And Tokyo, you'll see, it's not the same."

He smiled, his cheekbones newly sharp, and commented that he wasn't the only one who looked as if he could use a good meal.

"The boat was dreadful," said Emi when they were in the car. She tied her hair back with the twine she had been using on the boat. "Like an animal transport. I've been sleeping on straw, Father, like a goat. I can't wait for my bed."

"You do still have a bed," said Norio. "But I'm afraid we don't have much else. We are all on rations here, as I'm sure you've heard," Norio warned.

"We've been told," said Keiko, "but what does that mean? What are they rationing? It can't be *all* the food?"

"What it means is that you won't ever eat enough to stay full. The fish especially is severely rationed. Mostly we eat dried squid. The rice ration is shrinking every month and things like sugar and vegetables have to be purchased on the black market, which as a diplomat I should not be touching."

"But are you?" whispered Emi.

"Of course," said Norio. "While I can. I don't want my women to starve."

"But aren't there other ways? Don't we have any money left?" asked Emi, surprised.

"We do. But it doesn't make much of a difference here now if you have money. There is just a shortage of food. Money won't make it grow."

As her first week in Tokyo sped by, Emi remained glued to her parents, staying by her father's side when he was home, which was only late at night, and spending her days in the kitchen and running errands in the nearly empty shops with her mother.

They were in the only house that Emi remembered living in in Tokyo. When she was a baby, they had lived in a smaller house, but ever since she was a mobile toddler and Norio's career felt more certain, they had lived in the spacious house in Azabu. Before they had been stationed abroad, it had been decorated in a typically Japanese style, with tatami floor mats, low tables, and futons. But after the family's four years in England, the house had changed. They slept on tall Western beds and brought back much of the furniture and art they had amassed in Europe. It continued to gain European influences with every one of Norio's postings, Emi and Keiko insisting that they could never leave anything behind.

The Kato women had not been to their house in Tokyo since before they'd left for Washington at the end of 1939. And still, they had only been in the city for a few months after arriving from Vienna. When Emi first walked through the door of the two-story wooden house, the smell of her childhood shocked her. As it was only her father there for the last year, she was sure that it would smell differently, but somehow, the scent of her past had permeated the rooms. Besides the smell, it looked quite the same, though with much less furniture, and Emi wondered if her father hadn't sold some of it in the years they were away. Her room, she was happy to see, with her large Western bed and deep purple quilt, was untouched. Right on her glass side table, where it was when she left, was a photograph of her and Leo at Prater amusement park, the Ferris wheel right behind them.

To her surprise, the picture made her think not of Leo, but of Christian. She did not have a photo with him, as cameras were forbidden in the internment camp. She would have to think of his face every day, so that she'd never forget it. Emi was happy that her father hadn't changed too much since he came back in 1942. But the house felt a little too still. As if only one or two rooms were lived in. He had a cook that made him every meal and another woman who kept the house tidy, but they too, it seemed, barely stepped through the parts of the house that were Keiko and Emi's domain.

As the days passed in Tokyo, and Emi started to feel the stark reality setting in of a country at war, her mother encouraged her to spend time with people her own age, to make it feel more like the Tokyo of her youth. Emi still had a few friends in the city, her childhood friends, but she had learned when she had been back in 1939 that there was a distance between them that she could never close, because she had lived throughout the world and they only in Japan.

During that sojourn in Tokyo, she had heard the father of her closest friend from childhood, Kiyo Ono, say that his daughter should approach Emi with suspicion now that she had spent so much time in Europe. When Emi had told her father he had tightened his lips and said he was growing more and more weary of the lack of individual thought in their country.

Keiko had suggested to Emi that she stop by the Onos' house when they'd gotten settled after a few days but Emi shook her head and said she preferred to stay with her parents.

"In Crystal City I barely saw you," Keiko told her daughter as they collected their rice ration a mile from their home later that day. "Now you are like my second skin."

"I'm sorry if I abandoned you there," said Emi, helping to strap half of the rice allotment onto her mother's back. "I didn't mean to." There was a tear in the thin paper sack and she tried her best to fix it by tying her scarf around it. She never in her life thought she would be anguishing over a few grains of rice.

"You were happy," said Keiko, shifting her weight to make the package sit straighter. "And I was happy for you. I knew what was awaiting us here. At least, I had an idea." She sighed and helped Emi tie the rest of the rice to her back. "Look at us now, trudging through the city like peasants, carrying rationed rice that is probably crawling with insects."

"But like you reminded me in Texas, we've seen much worse," said Emi.

It wasn't just rice that was rationed in Tokyo, but clothes and shoes and medical supplies like needles and bandages. Even cooking oil.

"Which is fine," said Keiko, "since we have no food to cook."

They sat around the table together that night, as Norio had promised to eat with them before going back to the office. Emi passed the limp vegetables to her father, which smelled closer to rotten than fresh, and asked him about his work.

"All I can say is that I spend far more time there than I do here, and I wish that wasn't the case." He put his chopsticks down on

371

his plate and looked at his daughter, sympathy creeping into his face for the first time since she came home. "Emi, before I go back to the office we need to be frank with you about the future here," he said, looking at her from across the polished table. He stood in front of his chair after his wife poured him more tea. Emi got up from the table and walked to the large living room wall. She put her arms against it and said, "I have missed this house terribly. I have missed living in it with you. I feel somehow very young again being here. The last time I was here I was only eighteen."

"Did you hear me, Emiko?" said Norio loudly, banging the porcelain teapot on the table. "I said we need to talk about your future here."

"What?" she said, finally looking at him.

"You'll only be spending one more week here, Emiko," he said. "You can't stay in Tokyo."

"Are we moving?" she asked, letting her arms drop.

"Not forever," he said. "And not we. *You.* You are leaving Tokyo. I've made plans for you to stay with the Moris for the remainder of the war. Do you remember them? Yuka Mori and her husband, Jiro. Yuka is your mother's cousin."

"An older, distant cousin," Keiko chimed in from her seat.

"Yes, but still family," said Norio. "They lived in Tokyo but have a summer home in Karuizawa. A small one — a cottage — but perfectly decent conditions. You went there once when you were a child, perhaps fifteen years ago, twenty at most. Do you remember?"

"No," said Emi curtly, trying to understand what her father was telling her. She shook her head vigorously. "Karuizawa? Are you saying that I just spent eighty-three days on a boat so that we could be reunited as a family and now you're sending me away after just a few weeks to live with our distant family? Don't you want me with you? Haven't you missed me?" she finished, tears falling.

"Of course I have missed you, and yes I want you here with us," Norio said, moving around the table to her. "But more than that, I want you to stay alive. I can't have you living here with us in Tokyo. The city will be bombed. It's not a question of if, it's when. Emiko, if anything were to happen to you, I, your mother, we would die with you. If not in body, in everything else. You will be much safer in Karuizawa. Many foreigners from neutral countries are there — the

Swiss, South Americans, Hungarians. The foreigners from Allied nations were interned in a camp near Kobe but those who weren't deemed threatening are allowed to live in Karuizawa in relative peace. There are many Jews there as well. And embassy staff. The entire Soviet delegation works in a hotel. Other embassies — the Spanish, the Portuguese, the Turkish — are in town. Over two thousand foreigners from neutral countries are living in Karuizawa now. Because of that, it's the safest place you can be in Japan. The Americans won't dare drop bombs there."

"But why would I go there? I'm not a foreigner. I'm not a Jew. No, Father," she said shaking her head. "I won't leave you. I won't go through this war without you. I've been without you for too long. And if I go, everyone will label me a traitor. No one is leaving Tokyo — please don't make me." She ran back to the table and threw her arms around her father's neck. "Let me stay with you here, I beg you. Please!" she said, looking at her mother.

"You do not have a choice in the matter," said Keiko, standing up and removing Emi's arms from Norio's neck. "The Moris are fascinating people. They used to live in England; he even raced luxury cars there.

374

You'll like them fine."

"I have no desire to live with an aging race car driver," said Emi, angrily.

"He was a diplomat first," said her mother, matching her daughter's frustration. "And that's beside the point. Your safety takes priority, Emiko, and we have a train ticket for you already. You leave in a week."

"But I don't even know them," Emi protested, fear in her voice. "What if I go to Sapporo instead," she said. "To stay with Megumi. If you pay her, I'm sure she will take me."

"We did think of that," said Keiko, who cared for Emi's former *amah* as much as she did, "but she already has her own family to look after. You would be a burden."

"And there is no guarantee that Sapporo will be safe from the Americans," said Norio. "Karuizawa will be unharmed. They won't target a town filled with foreigners."

"I've spent my life following you," said Emi, trying not to let her voice break again. "For the past year, I was a prisoner in America because of your job, Father. Because of you. And now you're sending me away? I am twenty-one. When will I be able to make my own decisions?"

"When you're married!" said Norio. "Until then, I decide. You will be going to

Karuizawa and you can thank me at the end of the war when you are still alive. Many people are leaving."

"Your father has made up his mind," said Keiko. "Now go and change that dress. That internment camp clothing all needs to be burned. Throw it in the garbage."

"We will come there to see you," said Norio. "We are allowed to travel and will visit you. Perhaps not often, but we will see each other, I promise. You will not endure the war alone, but you will not endure it here. You will see. People are going to start sending their children away as fast as they can when they realize what is to come."

"But you don't know what is to come," said Emi angrily.

"Emiko, from where I am standing, I have much more of an ability to gauge the temperature of our country. Our government. Let's just agree that what I say goes."

"I don't know why you are acting like an oracle of the war," said Emi angrily. "You do not have a direct line to the emperor."

"Emiko! How dare you speak to your father that way," said her mother, shaking her daughter by the shoulders.

"It's been you and me stuck together for the last year and now you can be rid of me so quickly?" Emi said to her mother, taking a step back. "Why don't you seem more upset? Won't you miss me?"

"You have to trust me on this," said Norio, calmly. "The army controls every aspect of the press. What you are reading in newspapers here, hearing on the radio — that is not really what's happening in this country. Even if the men in charge of running the newspapers haven't been brainwashed, they have no choice in what to write. Normal citizens like you do not have the opportunity to hear what I'm hearing. The failures of war are being suppressed to a point that causes panic in me, Emiko," he said, raising his voice. "Panic."

"But you usually tell me everything," said Emi. "You haven't spoken to me about this — not to this extent — since I returned."

"I am speaking to you about it now. With a candor that scares me. But everything scares me these days. I scare myself. The way this country is feeding lies about our war efforts and causing these innocent people to follow in their dangerous mentality. That terrifies me."

"But I want to stay. I don't care about the risk. I —"

"It was my idea," said Keiko, cutting off her daughter. "Sending you away was my idea." She shook her head, her frustration apparent. "Your father hasn't wanted to alarm you, but he hasn't been so kind with me. And with the small advantage we have getting to the truth also comes a tremendous responsibility to try to get you to safety. We don't know with absolute certainty that Karuizawa will remain unharmed, but your father tells me that it is without a doubt safer than Tokyo, or anywhere else in the country, so you are without a doubt going."

Emi could tell that her mother was angry with her, disappointed in her tone, but also very worried about her.

"Why don't you come with me, then?" Emi asked quietly.

"Your father needs me here," said Keiko, looking at her husband. "And we aren't worried about ourselves, we are worried about you."

"This is upsetting for you now," said Norio. "But if you were to see more of this city, of what this place has become, you would be thanking us. The blind patriotism in this country . . ." He sighed and pushed his chair away from the table. "I love Japan. I have made myself a servant of it. But I don't recognize my country. In the streetcars, people bow every few blocks. They bow at the Yasukuni Shrine and at the palace. There are soldiers everywhere, fancy Western clothing on women is frowned upon — we have no more freedom. And the limitless power of the military . . . it's just . . . it's a very changed place."

"I won't know, will I?" said Emi. "I'll be alone in the middle of nowhere."

"You don't want to know!" Norio shouted. He was not quick to anger but was used to a great deal of respect from his daughter. "Haven't you noticed that every night we have to black out the windows, that there are air drills constantly, and the thought of bombings colors everything we do in our daily lives? We now have cement water tanks that we are required to keep full so we can help put out a fire caused by a bombing."

He stood up and walked to the kitchen, coming back with a long pole tied with strips of faded blue cloth. "This is to put out a fire on the roof, and you've seen the piles of sandbags behind the house in case a bomb falls in our vicinity. Do you understand, Emi? We are going to be bombed here. You'll have to be trained to do a bucket brigade and learn how to climb a ladder and pour water on the roof in case of fire. All the women here are trained for that. Is that how you want to live? In constant fear?"

"And due to those annoyances, I am being sent away. Because you're worried about me having to bow when I take a streetcar."

"No," said Norio, closing his eyes. "I'm worried that you will be killed when you take a streetcar."

CHAPTER 22

Leo Hartmann
May 1943

"We treat you good, Jewish! Hurry up. Don't scare! We treat you good!"

Leo heard the insistent, Chinese-accented voice call after him as he hurried to keep up with his parents.

"Don't scare, Jewish!" the voice came again. Leo looked back to see a man hauling a rickshaw pursuing him doggedly along the crowded street. Long splinters flared from the vehicle's handles and the wheels wobbled, but the operator was in worse shape. His hands and bare feet were brown and calloused from years outdoors in the grime of Shanghai. The wind was whipping through the alley where the Hartmanns were walking in Hongkew, one of the poorest corners of Shanghai, but the rickshaw puller was in thin rags, his unrelenting physical effort the only thing keeping him healthy enough to stay alive.

Leo glanced back again, struggling to hold on to the pile of still-damp sheets and blankets he was carrying, and shouted in Chinese, "I'm sorry! No money!" He quickened his pace to catch up with his parents, who were almost out of sight ahead of him. During his first year in Shanghai, Leo had found it impossible to hurry past the begging children with rotting teeth and rashes on their faces, the men missing arms and legs, and other destitute souls of Hongkew, but by 1943 he had learned to focus on his own survival. It wasn't something that came naturally to him, given both his temperament and his comfortable upbringing, and he still gave what he could to those worse off than he was. But he could move through the city speedily now, a skill he'd found was a key to staying alive in Shanghai's slums.

He passed insistent vendors hawking stolen goods, women washing tattered clothes in rusting metal buckets in the street, messengers running to deliver the building materials tied to their backs, and then he stopped short before a post on which a number of identical signs had been pasted. He had passed such signs many times since February, when the signs started going up, and he had memorized their message. But they still never failed to chill him: the Japanese authorities who governed Shanghai were forcing all the Jews to move into the city's restricted area in Hongkew and they had just three months to evacuate their homes and relocate.

Rumors had circulated since 1940, when Japan formally joined the Axis powers, that the Germans were putting more pressure on the Japanese to isolate the Jews in Shanghai, but in the three years that the Hartmanns had lived there, no significant steps had been taken. The Jews in Shanghai knew that while the Japanese could be very cruel, their fury was mostly inflicted on the Chinese and that anti-Semitism was not something the Japanese authorities believed in.

"Maybe the Germans are exerting more influence over them," said Max Hartmann when he and Leo had first seen the signs. "But I doubt many have truly been indoctrinated. So many have said since we arrived that the Japanese believe that the Jews are very powerful. That they could be a help rather than a hindrance, so please don't worry too much," he'd assured his son as Leo reread the notice.

For the Jewish community, life in the city was difficult, but tolerable. And every day the Hartmanns thanked God that they were in Asia, not Europe, where lives were being extinguished as easily as two fingers pinching out a flame. News of what was happening to the Jews in Austria and elsewhere had trickled in, and while they weren't sure what to believe, they knew it was a miracle they weren't there.

Hani and Max had tried desperately to persuade the rest of their families to come to Shanghai once they realized their lives were not at risk there, especially in the early days when Ho Feng-Shan was issuing hundreds of visas, but no one had followed them. Some were afraid to travel such a distance, or did not believe that Austria would become more dangerous than it had been in 1939. Some, like Max's brother and his family, found refuge in other countries. And others, they were sure, were dead.

The Hartmanns had met many Jews who had arrived in China with the visas issued by Ho Feng-Shan in Vienna, as well as others who came with the help of a Japanese diplomat in Lithuania, Chiune Sugihara. Those with Japanese transit visas had traveled through Japan, many living there for weeks, even months, before making their way from Kobe to Japanese-occupied Shanghai.

The Jews in Shanghai had been poverty-stricken, yet their lives were steady. But things began to deteriorate rapidly in the spring of 1943, after those ominous signs went up on every pole and bare concrete wall in Shanghai. According to the decree, Jews who had arrived before 1937 could stay where they were, but those who had come after — most of the city's Jewish population — were to be corralled in a designated area, a small part of Hongkew.

The Japanese officials did not call it a ghetto, but that's what it was, Leo's parents told him. "I'm sure they won't kill us, but if they tell you where you have to live, control when you can leave, and force you to stay in one of the city's slums, then that is a ghetto," Max said.

The Hartmanns were warned by the Jewish community leaders that they would need passes to both leave and return to the restricted area, and that they would have to renew them every month, no longer free to move around the city. They had until May 18 to relocate, but housing was quickly becoming scarce, so they agreed to go sooner.

Leo ripped one of the signs off the post and let it fall in a brown puddle of filth on the ground. "The designated area is bordered on the west by the line connecting

Chaoufoong, Muirhead, and Dent Roads; on the east by Yangtzepoo Creek; on the south by the line connecting East Seward, Muirhead, and Wayside Roads; and on the North by the boundary of the International Settlement," the notices read. The area was less than two square kilometers and there were already one hundred thousand Chinese living there. They lived in dark, damp alleyways, sometimes a dozen in an apartment, full of filth and grime, lice and disease. The Jews were constantly being vaccinated by the Japanese, but they did not bother with the Chinese, not minding at all if typhoid spread through the alleys, killing generations. "It's the Chinese presence that keeps the Japanese from calling it a ghetto," Max had explained. But Leo wondered what difference that made. Everyone in Shanghai knew that, to the Japanese military, Chinese lives did not matter.

The rickshaw puller had finally given up on securing Leo's business, picking up a cigarette butt off the ground, and Leo left the signs and hurried faster after his parents and the Chinese men helping them move into their new room in Hongkew. The Hartmanns had spent the last three years in a one-room apartment on the other side of the neighborhood, but since it was not inside the new restricted zone, they had to cede it to a Jewish family who had come to Shanghai before 1937 but had been living in shabbier, more roach-infested quarters.

Leo ran as quickly as he could, with his arms threatening to give out under the weight of his load, and managed to catch up with his friend Jin, a Chinese teenager who had gone to high school with him for his last year of school in Shanghai. He was helping the family move and had brought the laborers with him, but they had gotten far ahead, impatient to earn a wage.

Leo took one of the cushions Jin was holding, as it was about to fall, and placed it precariously on the top of his stack of sheets, making it even harder for him to see in the narrow alleyways that made up Hongkew's mess of streets. Lines of strung-up laundry blocked the sun, as did the slum's low, packed-together buildings. The light that did make it through seemed to be sucked in by the hundreds of bodies zigzagging through, on foot, on bicycles, in rickshaws, and occasionally in something obtrusive and motorized. Shouting was heard constantly, day or night, and the first words in Chinese that Leo had learned were *Zǒu kāi,* get out of the way.

Leo steadied his stack and asked Jin why

the rickshaw puller would bother following a Jew living in the restricted area for a fare.

"Because you're white," said Jin, his British accent crisp and proper. "Plus, that's the only line the new rickshaw drivers can say in English. 'We treat you good, Jewish.' They didn't even know what Jewish was before 1939. Now they want your money."

"But we don't have any money," said Leo.

"You have more than they do."

Jin pointed to a mess of human excrement in the road and Leo stepped around it, used to such obstacles, since none of the buildings in Hongkew had flush toilets. He tried to move the bedding to the top of his head so he could see in front of him, but he didn't have the dexterity to keep his head straight under the weight.

"Before the Europeans and the Americans were put in internment camps, the coolies said, 'Take ride, sir,' and a few other phrases, but now most of the white people around this neighborhood are Jews," said Jin. "They had to learn a few more words. Maybe they'll be speaking German soon. Or Yiddish." Jin nodded to the next row of rickshaw drivers waiting for fares close to the Hartmanns' new apartment. They were thin as reeds, with clothes so ripped, Leo felt he could see straight through to their bones.

"Listen, they'll say the same thing." As if planned, another driver screamed out, "We treat you good, Jewish!" as Jin mouthed along and grinned. "Come on, Jewish," he said. "We better hurry or you know who won't treat you good? Your father."

The two young men, both in their early twenties, tried to skirt the chaos of people, vendors, and trash in front of them but got stuck behind a military car pushing its way through the narrow street. There were few cars on the roads, since most Westerners had been made to turn theirs in to the government. They moved closer to the rickshaw pullers to be out of the way. The pullers kept yelling at passersby, oblivious to the soldiers, until the car stopped in front of them and a Japanese officer climbed out and approached them. He bent to examine the worn carts, then took the pillows out of the rickshaw belonging to the oldest of the men, who was leaning on his cart as if he could barely hold his weight up otherwise. The officer was shouting furiously, and Leo turned to Jin for an explanation.

"The soldier — whose Chinese is surprisingly good — said the man is standing on the wrong part of the road. That the rickshaw line can only be so long and since he is on the end, he's at fault." Jin listened for a minute more and said, "He says he has the right to punish the driver by confiscating his pillows."

They watched as the officer took the worn seat cushions in his hand and ripped out the stuffing, letting it drop on the dirty road. The driver fell to his hands and knees, scrambling to pick up the cotton that was being shredded. Leo again looked at Jin for translation, as he had been doing almost every day since the two became friends at St. Francis Xavier's. They were two non-Catholics in a Catholic school, just as he and Emi had been.

"The driver. He's saying what they all say. That he's a nobody from the country and has nothing but the clothes on his back. No home, no family, and that he won't be able to eat tonight because of the officer taking his pillows and shredding them. No customers will ride on the bench without pillows when they can just climb into another rickshaw in the line."

Jin shook his head and gestured for Leo to keep walking. "People here, the Chinese and especially the Japanese, view the coolies as one step above animals. And even then, it depends on the animal. They are the faceless donkeys who keep this city going. And they're always going to be treated badly, no matter what we try to do about it. So stop staring and let's go."

"Their desperation," said Leo, walking on the other side of the car, away from the officer. "I'll never get used to it."

"Of course not," said Jin. "I've never lived anywhere but Shanghai, and I'm not used to it. To be sickened by their treatment is what keeps you human. Half the men here, they are no longer human beings. I may have more money than you, Jewish, but I get treated far worse than you do, money or not." Leo thought about the bridge between the International Settlement and Hongkew. There were two Japanese soldiers placed on it at all hours and while he was allowed to walk past them without any acknowledgment, as all Westerners were, Jin and the other Chinese had to bow deeply before the guards, every time they crossed the bridge. Even rickshaw pullers had to stop, suspend their loads, and bow. Leo shook his head in agreement and tried to look away from the line of men and their carts.

Before the war, Jin had been educated in the British school system. He had finished in the Catholic school since most of the British schools were being abandoned as the teachers were locked up in the Lunghua internment camp, a camp full of Brits, and a few Aussies, out of town on Minghong Road. They were corralled and imprisoned there by the Japanese after the bombing of Pearl Harbor. The Japanese authorities policed the British school, controlling the curriculum and locking up teachers at random, so Jin's father moved him to the Jesuits. Now Jin's role had gone from student to teacher, given the hours he spent every week writing down Chinese and English words for Leo. Leo's English had been poor when his family had arrived, and he'd had to improve it quickly. With Jin's help, he was able to finish school with far better than passing grades.

Jin looked at Leo and told him to hurry. "I know what you're thinking when you stand in the street quiet like that," he said. "Don't. It won't help anyone."

Leo nodded and resumed walking, but he couldn't stop his thoughts turning back to that awful day.

Two years before, when Jin and Leo were walking from school toward the French Concession, where Jin's father owned a very popular and sordid nightclub, they saw a poor Chinese laborer, his back permanently bent at a 45-degree angle, step on the heel of a Japanese officer's boot with his bare foot. The officer had turned and yelled at him, then slapped him in the face when he apparently deemed the man's apology not respectful enough. Then, in the shuffle of the crowd, the Chinese man had accidentally done it again, kicking the officer in the calf the second time. Irate, the officer spun around, took his pistol from his hip, and shot the man twice, once in each foot from less than a yard away. The Chinese man fell to the ground, screaming in agony, and Leo and Jin could see one of his big toes, severed from his foot, lying next to them on a pile of rotten vegetables. The soldier had walked away, stopping to buy a length of the delicious braided dough boiled in oil that was sold on the street. He ate it while watching the man scream and writhe in pain and then left the area whistling, as calm as if he were picking flowers.

"It's terrible to be a coolie," Jin said to Leo. He pointed at Max and Hani, who were within their line of sight again. "It's terrible to be anyone living under the Japanese, but at least we are all alive. That's what the world has come to now hasn't it? Living or not living. It's no longer living well, living humbly, it's just life or death. Even the coolie we saw that day. He could still be alive."

"A coolie without feet in Shanghai? I hope

he's not. I think he'd be better off dead," said Leo.

Leo had seen many people in the last few years who he hoped were just days from death. Children who had had their chests cut open under suspicion that they were hiding rice in their clothes, women so frail that they could barely stand under the weight of a baby on their hip, and old men who seemed suspended on the street somewhere between illness and the afterlife.

"Don't think that way," said Jin. "If that were the case, then half the city should be shot. Certainly every Chinese person in Hongkew."

"I'll focus on the glorious life all around us on Yuhang Road," said Leo of the road they were walking down, the road his new house was on. It was chaotic and pungent with the smell of filth, but it was the geographic center of the ghetto and couldn't be avoided. And like Shanghai so often was, on that day it was flooded, with fish bones and rotten vegetables floating next to his feet.

"At least there hasn't been a policed ghetto until now," said Jin when they passed more signs directed at the Jews stuck to a lamppost. "A restricted area," he corrected himself. He stopped to drop a coin in the hand of a young blind girl begging on the street. She could not have been more than eight or nine, and her bare feet showed signs of severe frostbite, probably years in the making. Leo reached into his pocket to give her a coin, too, but it was empty. Jin's father's nightclub was still thriving, even though most of the Brits were confined in Lunghua and the French hold on their concession was in peril. There were the Japanese and still enough rich Chinese who wanted women and alcohol in large quantities. Jin's father always had money to give his son, and luckily for Shanghai's poor, Jin often gave it straight to them.

When the Hartmanns had first arrived in Shanghai in February 1939, they stared from the deck of their ship with trepidation at the mass of buildings and people. They hadn't forgotten the hell they had left behind in Vienna, but their trip had been a thoroughly comfortable one. Norio Kato had bought them first-class tickets on the luxury liner. From the moment they boarded, they had a porter to tend to their needs, hearty meals at any hour of the day they pleased, and a staff that treated them with reverence, a welcome change from their recent treatment in Vienna. But what lay before them now?

"Before the war, Shanghai was known around the world as a mythical place," Max had told Leo as their boat docked, patting down his thick gray hair as if he had somewhere nice to be. Already, from a distance, they could tell that on land, it was pandemonium. "It was lawless, exotic. And there was a place for everyone — a section each for the French, for the Americans, and for the British. The neighborhoods for the foreigners are not separated by walls; the boundaries are just geographic. From what I've been told, everyone mixes with everyone else. And among it all, they hide drugs and prostitutes and worse. Now we are sailing right into it."

He winked at Leo and said, "Try not to lose your innocence too early."

Leo thought about the passionate afternoons he'd spent deep in the recesses of the Hartmanns' Vienna home with Emi, beautiful, naked, and very much his, and shook his head no. His innocence may have been gone in the physical sense, but he looked back on those days next to her as the most innocent of his life. As soon as they docked, he would write to her in Vienna. Tell her that they were safe now, the feeling of being thousands of miles from Europe the best feeling in the world.

Leo looked at his father and asked, "Where will we go, since we are none of those things?"

"We are going to a place called Hongkew," Max said, putting his hand on his son's dark hair, which was out of sorts from the wind.

"Hongkew." Leo said the word aloud for the first time soon after they were on land. It sounded mysterious and full of promise on his lips. He would soon see that it was a place of poverty and hopelessness, both for the Chinese who had long lived there and the Jews who had joined them.

The family's anxiety eased a little when they found a committee of Jews waiting to greet them and their Jewish fellow passengers. The new arrivals were all taken to a building where they would be put up for the time being in a warehouse-sized room full of bunk beds. They dropped their few things and then were shepherded by the volunteers to a soup kitchen.

There were two groups of Jews who had been in Shanghai for years, the exceedingly rich Baghdadi Jews and the Russian Jews. It was the Baghdadis, especially a banker named Victor Sassoon — the Third Baronet of Bombay and a Cambridge graduate who had been a pilot for the British during the Great War — who were looking after the

Jewish refugees. Sassoon had built the city's beautiful Cathay Hotel and much of its iconic Bund. Himself a Sephardic Jew, he hadn't lost his commitment to the community along the way. The Shanghai Jewish aid group was also heavily funded by donations from American Jews, and it was those donations that kept the arriving refugees alive and more or less healthy as they settled in and looked for work.

At the soup kitchen, Max and Hani had trouble accepting the handout.

"What is this?" Max asked Leo when they walked in and saw the spread of food. He was still wearing a nice traveling suit and all three Hartmanns realized right away that it was a mistake. The dress, it seemed, was closer to rags.

"They will feed us here for free," said Leo.

Hani reached for her husband in shock. "We should have brought more money with us," she hissed. "I told you. We left too much with our families. Will it even help them escape Austria?"

"There was barely any we could move," Max reminded her at a whisper. "Our accounts frozen, and everyone too scared to buy our possessions. I tried; you know I tried," he said, rubbing his red eyes.

"They weren't scared," said Hani. "They

just knew they could take our things for free as soon as we left. Why would they bother paying us?" Hani looked at the food with dread, but she finally managed to swallow her embarrassment, accept the meal, and thank the men serving it. "We used to give money to support such places in Austria and now we are eating in one," she whispered when they'd sat down with their tin plates. She uncovered her head, placing her hat on the table, and rumpled her curls a little bit. "We are the beggars. I'm not good at this, Leo," she'd said, her spoon shaking in her hands. "I'm very thankful, but I'm not good at it."

"You will be," he replied.

They got used to the handouts very quickly, as there was no alternative.

Having arrived in winter, they saw in the streets what it looked like to freeze to death. Dead children — babies — lay in alleyways, where they were thrown onto a garbage truck the next morning like day-old bread. The children who were alive were so emaciated, they looked as if they could crumble into ash.

"I would like to see a plump child," said Leo, looking down at a sickly little boy in short pants during their first week in the city. "Children shouldn't be so thin," he told Hani.

"I wish I could save them all," she replied. They both watched as the boy found his mother, also in rags. A newborn baby was tied to her back, the only member of the little family who looked warm. "It's amazing to me that women have given birth during the war," said Hani, looking at the bundled baby. "That there is enough optimism to bring children into the world."

The Hartmanns were to learn that it wasn't optimism that kept Shanghai turning, so much as a gritty will to survive. With the help of the established Jews, they, too, soon became cogs, rather than onlookers, in the city's churning life.

The American Jewish Joint Distribution Committee helped the elder Hartmanns find jobs, with Max hired as an accountant in a grocery store in the French Concession and Hani finding work playing the piano in a place she thought was a restaurant but that turned out to be an opium den. After she had come home for weeks with reddened eyes and her mind "feeling like a cloud," the family pressed her to quit, for her health's sake, and she took a job teaching piano to the children of a wealthy Chinese family, whose father had worked for Sassoon.

But as time went on, the poverty started to bite at their ankles — even for the resolutely happy Leo.

Three months after they had arrived, as they walked to their synagogue with other families living in their small apartment building, Hani had looked at her son and said, "Froschi, why do you keep touching your hair?"

Leo took his hand from his scalp, which he had been rubbing as they walked, and said, "I'm itchy. I think I need a bath."

Hani grabbed his hand before he could touch his head again and quickly examined a few strands of his curly hair.

"You have lice," she declared. "Turn around and go back to the apartment. You can't bring that into temple. We will find someone who will shave it off."

From that day, Leo never let his hair grow back, deciding that even if he could keep the lice at bay, his hair would never feel clean, so it wasn't worth having. Hani kept one of his brown curls in a bag. She wrote "Froschi's lice" on the bag and tucked it under a pile of dresses that she planned to sell when they fell on even harder times.

As the months went on, Leo thought he had grown used to the city, its sounds and strangers, but his body could not seem to adapt. Besides the lice, he had dysentery four times, which caused him to have accidents and wake his mother, who slept just a few feet from him.

"What's wrong?" Hani asked the first time.

"I missed the bucket," Leo said, looking at the soiled floor. "I'm sorry," he added, staring at the ground in shock.

"It's all right. We'll clean it up."

"I'll do it, Mother, you go back to bed."

Hani reluctantly crossed the room back to her bed and he used an old newspaper and the last of their boiled water in a tin thermos to clean it up. He placed it all in the bucket on their landing.

The next day an elderly Chinese woman took the night soil, as it was called, away. She did this every day, carrying the buckets through the hallways, their contents sloshing over the rims, to the street, where she dumped her foul load into the open sewers or onto a cart that came around to collect it.

Given the smell in their one-room apartment the entire next week, Leo had vowed to never have a mishap again, but the dysentery made that impossible. He guessed that it was from the consommé, the gelatinous rice porridge, which was always littered with vermin. Sometimes gray worms, other times hundreds of tiny flies. But it was never without pests.

In time, they discovered their problems were manageable. Hani and Max were able to keep working, and the family became accustomed to living on top of each other and without hot water or flush toilets. They learned how to sift their rice to remove some of the insects. They picked out rusty nails and dirt from the stolen noodles they bought from roadside vendors. And Leo finally enrolled in school, nearly a year after they arrived. He started at the Shanghai Jewish School, which was housed in a beautiful building paid for by Victor Sassoon. The students were served kosher lunches and they all worshiped in a large Sephardic synagogue. But then, to help make room for a wave of children who arrived in Shanghai from Lithuania, he transferred to the Catholic school, St. Francis Xavier's.

It was at his new school that he met Jin. As soon as Jin showed him kindness, Leo stuck to him like the lice he once had on his head, realizing how much he needed an ally in the city, particularly one who could navigate it far better than he could. Jin also got Leo a job as a janitor and drink runner in his father's club.

Liwei's was not the most expensive nightclub in the city, nor was it the most squalid. It was large and well decorated with just enough beautiful, disreputable women to always attract a crowd. The most upscale club in Shanghai was the Del Monte. The Park, Arcadia, and Farren's weren't far behind. Leo had never been inside those, but he'd seen the clientele they attracted and they did not live in Hongkew. There were such clubs in Hongkew, but they veered closer to whorehouses than nightclubs. The Little Barcelona was not far from his apartment, and he'd seen the women in high-cut dresses tending to the men outside, so drunk that they'd sleep draped across café tables like coats, lit cigarettes still between their teeth, burning their chins. But Liwei was Chinese, and with the club's Chinese name, they attracted the rich Chinese men who were afraid to socialize with Japanese military officers at the other establishments.

Like most of the nightclubs in the city that pulled their weight, Liwei's club was filled with taxi dancers, most of them White Russians who had seen better days. The women, all dressed as elegantly as they could with what little means they had, weren't paid by the club outright, but had a mutual understanding with the proprietors of how they would conduct their business. The patrons bought dance tickets in advance and presented them to the girl of their choice. She would then dance with them and if things proceeded from there, the club staff, especially Liwei, ignored it.

He knew that he wasn't able to attract clients with outdoor space, as Del Monte's was two floors and had an expansive garden, while his club was on the ground floor and had very few windows. But his wife had decorated it nicely enough — in red silk that had been tattered and resewn, dotted with high-gloss tables that Liwei kept shiny with animal fat. Plus, he told Leo when he first set foot inside, drunks appreciated the lack of light at Liwei's when the sun started to rise.

On his first night, Leo had been asked to dance by one of the girls, a stunning German named Agatha, even though he couldn't pay her. From her, he found out that almost all the money the girls made went to keep their gaggle of relatives alive. The men in the Russian families had a much more difficult time finding work than the pretty young women, so everyone pulled together to keep the women employed, the mothers making their daughters' décolletés lower so they all might be able to eat for a week.

"But I don't have a mother anymore," said Agatha, her body close to Leo's. "So I have to sew my own décolletés."

"You do a fine job," said Leo, trying his best to keep his eyes on her face.

Some of the women, Jin had explained after Leo returned wide-eyed from his dance with Agatha, turned to prostitution, others prayed for a client who turned into a husband, but most just saved their money and dished it out for their malnourished parents at the end of the night.

"They may look like tramps, but they're family to me at this point," said Jin, when he and Leo were left sweeping the club after closing on Leo's first night.

"But pretty little German Agatha doesn't look like a tramp," said Jin, watching Leo watch her. "At least not yet." Jin explained that while Agatha was German, she was in the minority. The Russians dominated Li-wei's. The White Russians had come in large numbers in the twenties, at the end of the Russian civil war, but they had been living as stateless since they made the voyage to Asia. With only League of Nations–issued passports, finding work was even harder. Meanwhile the French lived as if they were at a never-ending party before the war, as they benefited from extraterritoriality, which excluded them from Chinese laws. The Russians were not so lucky. But his father was always happy to assist a beautiful Russian woman in need.

The work at Liwei's was exhausting, but Leo learned that it was not without its perks. The scantily clad female employees adored him and Jin, and he was allowed to dance with Agatha at least once every night. Leo was also entitled to all the alcohol that was leftover in the customers' glasses. He sometimes abused the privilege, letting himself get drunk in ways he never had in Vienna.

"It's what men do in Shanghai," Liwei and Jin had advised him during his first week, both drinking down a combination of whatever was left that night, which Liwei called "bartender's choice."

When Leo's sense wasn't clouded by the Shanghai way of life, he would pour the dregs into bottles and bring them back for the men in his building. He didn't trade the booze for anything in particular, but if a family found themselves with a little extra food one night, and the slop of alcohol they were drinking had come from Leo, that food might find its way to the Hartmanns' table.

Finally making his way through the crowded street to his parents, Leo rearranged the load in his arms yet again as his father spotted them. He waved them over. "Here it is, Leo," he called, pointing to the concrete building behind him. It had been painted gray but now the paint was peeling off like a suntan. "Hurry, please!"

Leo stepped over another pile of human waste and coughed from the smell of something burning in the street. As the Jews had begun to move into the restricted area in February, a wave of typhoid had accompanied them, and the Hartmanns had already attended the funeral of a child killed by it.

Once Leo and Jin reached the house, Max nodded toward the stairs. "We're at the top," he said. "Five flights up. Attic dwellers." His voice was cheerful, but his forehead was dripping with sweat, despite the cold.

"How many families live in this building?" Leo asked as they climbed.

"Ten," said Max. "We know three of them." He rattled off the names and followed Leo, Jin, and his wife up the stairs, the laborers already ahead of them.

Leo dropped the bedding on the floor

outside their new apartment's door, opened it, and looked inside, trying not to let his heart drop at the sight. The room was large enough, but the windows had all been covered with black paint, leaving a dim electric light as the only source of illumination. The Hartmanns had sold almost all their furniture and had only their mattresses, one small table, and three chairs. There was a sink with cold water, an electric burner, and unlike in their last apartment, only one bathroom on the ground floor for the whole building to use.

"At least, all the way up here, we'll be safe from harm," Max declared when the laborers had gone. He was about to close the door to give them some rare privacy when a large Western woman in Chinese farm pants suddenly walked in. She was holding a knife.

Max took a step back, but the woman laughed and explained to him in German that she always carried a knife with her around the building, as she was suspicious of everyone in Shanghai, Jewish or not.

Her name was Eliza Behnisch and she was the first overweight person Leo had seen in Shanghai. She came from Berlin, she told the family as she sat uninvited on one of their chairs. She lived on the ground floor with her ailing husband, and she was taking it upon herself, despite her bad back and worse vision, to meet with all the new tenants to tell them how life worked in the ghetto.

"You'd better learn the rules of this place quickly or you'll find yourself on a concrete floor in prison," she warned the Hartmanns.

"Yes, Mrs. Behnisch, we wouldn't want that," said Max politely. "What are the rules, if you don't mind elaborating?"

"First, Mr. Hartmann, you have to get used to living like rats. Then when you're used to that, the rules won't seem so bad. There's a curfew, and it's enforced by the Pao Chia, a group of Jewish men who the Japanese have hired to act as the police. They must have very short memories of their own oppression because they can be real asses," she said, raising her eyebrows. "Also, us Jews have to wear buttons letting the world know we're Jewish. It's stupid because almost all the citizens of the Allied countries are in the internment camps, but we have to wear them anyway. The buttons are issued by a Japanese officer named Kano Ghoya. He likes to be referred to as king of the Jews. He has a small mustache like Hitler and is as sadistic as they come. He hits people. Spits in their faces. Even women. You'll see, Mrs. Hartmann. Pretty as you are, you'll still be spat on."

Leo translated what she'd said into English for Jin.

"I've met him, and she's right," Jin said. "Avoid him, his sadism, and his saliva."

"If you are caught outside the ghetto without a pass, you'll be thrown in jail, and the jails are full of disease, so that's on par with a death sentence," their new neighbor continued. "You need a pass to leave the ghetto to go to school or work outside it, and Ghoya issues the passes."

She looked at Jin and said, "But the Chinese can run freely."

Leo translated again, and Jin started laughing, shaking his head at Eliza Behnisch.

"Run freely! We haven't run freely since before the Japanese occupation in '37. They killed three hundred thousand people when they occupied Nanjing. Ask those people's families if their children are running freely. And it's no better here. Tell her to walk to the stadium and read the sign. 'No Dogs or Chinese.' Has she seen that? Or the children strangled to death by the Japanese soldiers for sport near the railway?"

He looked to Leo to translate, and Leo turned to the neighbor and said, "Yes. He agrees with you."

"I have to go to work," said Hani. "Leo and Jin, are you coming?"

After the three left, Hani walked the boys to the nightclub, saying hello in her poor English to Liwei.

"The offer to work in my establishment will always stand, Mrs. Hartmann," he said, after he had kissed her hand. "You wouldn't have to do anything untoward. Just chat with the city's lonely men. I am sure they would pay handsomely to see those funny freckles close up."

"My English. It is still unsatisfactory," she said politely, making the same excuse she'd been making for the last two years. She left to go to her job, and Jin and Leo went inside to wash glasses.

"I can't believe we live in that place now," said Leo as he washed. "I'm thankful we have somewhere to live, of course, but it still feels strange to be dirt poor."

"Everyone is poor," said Jin, shrugging. "War doesn't make anyone rich except the depraved. And they still have to loot."

"I'm washing dishes in a brothel. Are you sure I'm not one of the depraved?" said Leo, turning on the hot water and thinking of his house in Vienna, which he was sure was looted down to its studs.

"This isn't a brothel," said Jin. "There's

nothing for sale here except the alcohol. Plus, I started to work here when I was ten. If you're depraved, then I'm truly sick. Plus," he said, handing Leo a sponge, "from what you've told me, it's better than Vienna, yes?"

"Yes," said Leo. "We're very lucky. Bad as it can be, Shanghai is the Jewish Shangri-la."

CHAPTER 23

Emi Kato
December 1943

Emi did not look back at her parents after they brought her to Ueno Station in Tokyo. She took her two suitcases from her father, gave them to a porter, then walked to the platform where her ten-car steam-powered train was already waiting. Looking up at the train, with various stripes on its windows indicating first, second, and third class, she thought about her father's words: "I'm worried that you will be killed." A war was tearing her country apart — it was still her country, despite the war she didn't agree with — and her parents could die on a streetcar or somewhere worse. She regretted that she had parted from them flushed with anger. Once settled in her first-class seat for the five-hour journey, she opened her small bag, taking out her letter-writing box and stamps. She quickly penned a letter of apology to her parents, noting that she obviously needed to be sent away to grow up a little more. The time in the internment camp hadn't seemed to do it. She told them she loved them and that she was sure they would see each other again soon.

We have to, she thought to herself, her body aching at the thought of anything happening to her little family. Emi bit the inside of her cheeks, looked out the window, and decided that however good or bad Karuizawa was, she would handle her time there as gracefully as she could manage.

As she let her arm hang over her armrest, glad that the seat next to her was unoccupied, she remembered Christian telling her about his train ride to Crystal City, holding the hand of seven-year-old Inge for thirty-one hours. She smiled at the thought. Christian, more than she, had been thrown in the deep end with no warning. She had lived through Vienna, was used to getting certain looks in Washington. He was a golden boy living a seemingly perfect American life, until the government decided that his family wasn't American enough. She pictured Christian, walking around Crystal City as shocked as she had been before she started working at the hospital, before she met him. All the high school girls' eyes would follow him as he made his way between school and work, and eventually the orchard. All those pretty German girls, but he had chosen her. She hoped that he would write to her in Japan from Crystal City, and that by some miracle, the letters would reach her. She had told her mother to please send the letters down if he did, as she had given up on receiving anything from Leo, though she was still writing to him every now and then at the only address she had.

"If something terrible had happened to the Hartmanns in Shanghai, we would have gotten word," her father had told her in Tokyo. Emi liked to think that was true, but who would get word to them? Leo's letters were obviously being destroyed or lost en route.

When the train finally sputtered out of the station in a cloud of black smoke, precisely on schedule and accompanied by the sound of the stationmaster's whistle, Emi looked out the window as rows of houses gave way to a vista of endless rice paddies dotted with distant farmhouses. What would Christian be doing in Crystal City night after night at sunset? she wondered. She enjoyed the thought of him missing her, thinking about her in the swimming pool in her navy blue bathing suit, or in the orchard wearing less than that. She would continue to cry over Leo, especially with her uncertainty about his life in Shanghai, but not over Christian. Her mother had assured her that the officials in camp said the Germans were staying until late 1944. Until he left Crystal City, she was sure he'd be safe.

The atmosphere on the train was solemn, even in the luxurious first-class compartment with its hardwood floors and blue velvet seats that swiveled so that passengers could face to the front or rear. Soldiers went back and forth checking passengers' papers, not in order, but at random. The government issued travel permits, and no one could board a train without one. Emi's was tucked tight against her identification card. Her father had told her that foreigners' travel was severely restricted but that there would be some *gaijin* going to Karuizawa. That was where the government wanted them — all together, easier to watch.

As night fell, Emi was surprised to see that none of the stations the train chugged through were properly illuminated. Instead of electric lights, there were only fragile white paper lanterns, held by railway officials on the platforms. But the train did not stop at the smaller stations, steaming steadily ahead to the mountains and Yokokawa, where they would switch to electric power.

When she was just drifting off to sleep, the soldiers came stomping back into her car, jarring not only for the noise they made, but because they were the only people on the train who smelled clean. In their moss-green uniforms, their armbands stiff and proud on their biceps, they made it clear they were looking for anyone suspicious and that they alone defined what the term meant. Luckily for Emi, it didn't mean her. They walked by without a look in her direction and she pressed her face against the window, listening to her ears pop as they climbed higher.

Two and a half hours after the train left Tokyo, it reached the large station of Yokokawa, gateway to the Kiso Mountains. Though the passengers were not let off the train if they were not disembarking there, the enterprising locals knew they would be bored and hungry. Roaming vendors sold hot tea and rice balls wrapped with seaweed to the passengers, who awaited them with open windows, despite the exorbitant prices.

Worried about how much she'd get to eat in Karuizawa, especially without her father

418

to help her, Emi bought five rice balls and put them in her traveling bag. She looked out at the town, where if the streets hadn't been bathed in only soft lantern light she knew she would have seen a large statue of Kannon, the goddess of mercy. She closed her eyes and prayed to her for safety.

They were in Yokokawa longer than Emi had expected, to allow for the change of track and the switch from a steam engine to an electric-powered one, the train officials explained. The children had their heads hanging out the windows, despite the cold December weather, to watch the engine swap, craning their little necks as far as their mothers would let them.

As Emi finally slept, the train raced through the mountain towns, navigating more than twenty narrow brick tunnels before slowing to pull them up thousands of feet to the resort town of Karuizawa.

Emi's father had told her that it was Western residents that had made the town so popular as they fled there in the summer months to escape the heat of the cities. The altitude kept it cool, and according to Norio, Westerners found the active volcano picturesque. But it wasn't anywhere near as glamorous as some of the resort towns they had visited when in Austria and Germany, like Marienbad and Baden-Baden, he warned. There were a few hotels that catered to the rich, but the town was mostly dotted with modest summer cottages. The main draw was the weather, and the beauty of nature, not the architecture. Norio had drawn Emi a map, which showed that the town was originally a resting place for travelers going southeast to Tokyo and Yokohama or going west to Matsumoto Castle and Nagoya.

Emi's eyes were just blinking open when the train eventually glided to a stop shortly after midnight.

A porter arrived to help the women with their suitcases, a man too old to be doing such a job, while Emi stood and watched the groups of women — mothers and daughters, sisters — feeling, for the first time in many years, terribly alone. Her mother had been her companion ever since the war broke out, but here she was by herself. They didn't see eye to eye on everything, and they had gotten into arguments that they would not have dared engage in around Norio, but Emi could not have imagined her last few years without Keiko's companionship. She leaned against the open door, wishing she was leaning against her mother, and didn't move until the conductor warned that the train would be leaving.

When Emi stepped onto the platform, her lungs filled with fresh mountain air and she felt immediately calmer. Her parents had sworn she'd been to Karuizawa as a young child, but looking around she had no recollection of the station.

Emi stood for fifteen minutes on the dark platform, now nearly deserted, before walking to the entrance and waiting by the ticket counter instead. Her father had said Mrs. Mori was to meet her, but since Emi did not know what she looked like, besides an older Japanese woman, she would just have to wait and let herself be found.

After thirty minutes, it was clear that she was not going to be collected by Mrs. Mori or anyone else, and all the taxis that had been lingering in front of the station when the train arrived — the last train of the night — were gone.

The Moris, Emi concluded, had forgotten about her.

Emi knew very little of the Moris, besides the fact that Jiro had been a diplomat in London and Washington. His wife, Yuka, had gone to grade school in America. They didn't seem like the worst people to be dispatched to, sounding like older versions of her parents, but that made the reality even more preposterous to Emi. Stand-in parents when she could have just stayed with hers.

Emi had the Moris' address, but since it was very dark outside, she didn't trust herself to start wandering the town searching for the house. And even though she had been forced to live in it in America, Emi wasn't comfortable in the countryside. She looked at the address — which was no more than the house number, as was typical for Japan, as very few streets had names — and considered her options.

Emi took a few steps away from the station, turning onto what felt like the town's main road, the *ginza.* In the dark she could just make out a few small stores, some with signs outside in English. A photographer's store, a furniture store. Perhaps some proprietor would be open late and might know the Moris. She was about to pick up her suitcases and head to a shop where a light still burned when she heard a voice ask in heavily accented Japanese if she needed any help. She turned and saw two soldiers approaching — Germans, she knew immediately from the swastikas on their armbands. They walked up to her with interest.

Out of instinct she shook her head no.

"Are you sure?" the other one asked in German, gesturing that he was happy to pick up her bags.

Not thinking before she spoke, Emi responded in German that she could handle her luggage alone, but thank you. They both stopped short.

"Who are you?" the thinner of the two asked. "A Japanese woman speaking German?"

Emi guessed that the soldiers were not used to being treated with hatred or fear by the Japanese. Her father had warned her that she would be one of the only people in Japan who had seen, who understood, that the Nazis were torturing the Jews. Information was extremely controlled in Japan, Norio warned. When he had told their neighbors in Tokyo about Kristallnacht, what they had seen in Vienna, they did not believe him. The average citizens knew nothing about what the Nazis were doing to the Jews in Europe. All they knew were that the Germans were on the side of the Japanese, and that they were going to win, they were quite sure of that. Japan was a hierarchical society, her father had reminded her when she'd come back, and no one dared question what was proclaimed from the top, except those familiar with America and Europe. Men like him.

But Emi had reason to hate the Nazis, and she was terrified that that hatred was all over her face.

"We must know who you are," said one of the soldiers, his smile wide and friendly.

"Oh no," said Emi, still in German, but trying to backpedal away from what she'd just said. "I only speak a little." She picked up her suitcases and hurried away from the men as they called out for her to stop. Dragging the bags, she made it up the street and glanced behind her, relieved to see that they had not bothered to follow her. In Tokyo she hadn't had to interact with any German soldiers. Why had her father not warned her that they were in Karuizawa? Did he not know?

A store, closer to the station on the main street, had just turned on a light and Emi headed straight there. She put her suitcases on the ground outside and turned the door handle, which was locked. She knocked on the glass door several times, pressing her face against it, now afraid that she would have to spend her first night in Karuizawa on a bench in the train station or on the street with German soldiers. After her fifth loud knock, a second light came on and a man stepped out from the back of the store and walked toward the door. Emi was surprised to see he was a foreigner.

"Konbanwa," she said, greeting him when he opened the door.

"Konbanwa," he said back, offering to help with her suitcases. He spoke quick, confident Japanese with only a trace of an accent, which Emi thought might be Russian or Polish, certainly Eastern European.

He moved his slender body aside and let her enter, and she explained that she was just in from Tokyo and looking for the Moris, who lived at number 1462. "They never came to fetch me at the station and there are no taxis now," Emi concluded, apologizing for knocking at such an hour. "No taxis, but plenty of German soldiers walking the street," she added.

"Yes, you will see many German SS here," said the storekeeper. "So many that the notices printed in town are now written in both Japanese and German. For some in Karuizawa, it's unsettling."

"The Jews?" asked Emi, wondering if this man was Jewish.

He shrugged and didn't give any more detail.

He put a cloth over his cash register and started wiping down the counter. "I know the Moris, of course," he added, looking at Emi with red, tired eyes. "Their home is down a long dirt road a bit set aside from the others. It will be difficult for you to find on foot at night, especially with your luggage. All the roads in Karuizawa are dirt except for around the *machi*," he said, referring to the shopping area. "I would take you, but I'm afraid I still have a lot of preparations to do in the shop for tomorrow. It's Monday and that tends to be the only day we get business anymore."

Emi nodded. Her gut was gurgling, implying that now was the right time to panic.

"But my wife can surely drive you," he offered. "The children are sleeping. She can leave them." He called out, using a word in a language Emi was unfamiliar with, and a young Japanese woman came out from behind a door to what Emi could now see was the stockroom.

"This is my wife, Ayumi," the shopkeeper said, though he hadn't introduced himself. He explained Emi's predicament to his wife, a slight woman with a bit of a slope in her back, who smiled and nodded at Emi, telling her to follow her to their truck behind the shop.

"It's just a short drive to the Moris," Ayumi said as she helped Emi with her luggage. "I'm happy to take you. I've known them for many years; it's probably time I did them a favor," she said looking down at Emi's large bags. "Besides, you would only make it a few steps with these. You must be coming from Tokyo."

Emi nodded. "Mrs. Mori is my mother's cousin," she said, "but I've only met her once."

"You'll like her," said Ayumi, starting the truck and pulling out onto the main road. "Both of them are very interesting, though I don't see them in town much anymore. They are in ill health, I believe. I'm glad they'll have some company now. They never did have children, did they?" She looked at Emi questioningly.

Emi shook her head, though she had no idea about the Moris' family and her father hadn't said a word about their health. Emi wondered if she was being called down to Karuizawa to play nursemaid. Unsettled, she managed to say, "Yes, it will be better for all of us."

Emi looked out at the thickly clustered pine trees lining the dirt roads. Emi's father had told her that many senior European diplomats had houses there that they passed to each other with the changing of the guard. What she hadn't realized was how many of them had stayed in Japan despite the war.

"Is your husband European?" Emi asked Ayumi as they turned onto an even smaller road in the compact truck. Emi knew it was obvious that he was European; she just wanted Ayumi to be specific.

"He is, depending on your definition of European," said Ayumi. "Evgeni is Russian. There are a few Russians in Karuizawa now, but nothing like the number of Germans. They are everywhere. You saw soldiers tonight, yes?" she asked.

Emi nodded and admitted that she had stupidly spoken German to them.

"There are many soldiers," said Ayumi. "And you will see the Hitlerjugend, too. The Hitler youth. They parade down the street very proudly. They have matching brown shirts and coats and swing the Nazi flag like it's an extension of their arms. You'll see. But you, you speak German, you said?"

"I do," said Emi, thinking for a moment about Kersten and the beginnings of the Hitlerjugend that she'd witnessed in Vienna. "I lived in Germany as a child and then in Austria when I was older."

"The Germans have all the food. They even have their own bakery that makes dark bread," said Ayumi. "It's the color of mud, but it's delicious. They gave me a loaf once in the store when I was working without Evgeni. If you befriend them, they might give you one, too. They have many things to eat and we have almost nothing."

Emi stayed quiet for a few minutes as Ayumi detoured around several holes in the road, picturing Leo and what he would think of her if she took bread from a Nazi.

"Evgeni's parents emigrated to Tokyo following the Russian Revolution," Ayumi explained. "But after the earthquake in 1923 they went to Kobe, which is where Evgeni and I met. When the war broke out, we came here, and Evgeni opened the store."

"I've lived many places and met all kinds of people," said Emi. "Though I wanted to stay in Tokyo, I was happy to see a foreign face when your husband came to the door. It reminds me of the life I just left behind."

Ayumi nodded as if she understood, but suddenly stopped the truck and pushed the clutch into reverse, the wheels spinning loudly on the wet dirt.

"I missed the road," she said. "It's so hard to see between these trees at night." Ayumi drove fast down the narrow road but pulled up when they could just make out a light in the distance. "That's the Moris' house there," she said, pointing. "If you don't mind, I'll let you out here and help you with your bags. We had rain yesterday and Mr. Mori isn't known for keeping his road . . . well, I'll let you out here."

The two women got out of the truck and between them hauled Emi's large suitcases the rest of the way. Their shoes and pant legs were covered in mud by the time they reached the house, where the only visible light was a single lantern sitting on the front step.

"I'll go now," said Ayumi, backing away. "Let you three get acquainted."

Emi thanked Ayumi repeatedly as she headed down the road, bowing at her before she disappeared into the wooded darkness. She turned and looked at the house, which was two stories high, but much smaller than Emi's family's house in Tokyo. It had large sliding windows, which was nice for a summer house but not, she imagined, ideal in winter. The entire structure was covered in stacked, stained wood tiles, and its pointed, clay roof, layered in waved shingles, gave it a more European look than many of the houses in Tokyo.

Emi looked down at her feet, which were wet and growing cold. The bottoms of both her suitcases were covered in mud, too, as neither she nor Ayumi had been strong enough to lift them very high. She stood there and wished that her *amah* or her mother and father were with her.

She knocked on the door and waited. After a minute, she tried again, but still no one came. When she had knocked for almost five minutes, she reached for the handle and was relieved to find it open. She made her way inside and looked at the narrow staircase off to the right of the entry. Struggling to find a light first near the stairs, then in the living room, she almost tripped over a body on the floor, right in front of the fireplace, which held the last glowing embers of an evening fire. Emi looked down and saw, in the very dim light, that there were two bodies hidden under piles of blankets on two futons in front of the fireplace. They were as close to it as possible without being in it. She could make out the bodies only slightly, seeing a small protuberance under each blanket. She looked for the top of their heads, and soon realized that both the Moris' hair was covered by *zukin,* a thick fireproof hood that many now owned and Emi assumed was imperative if one slept with their head nearly in a fire.

Emi bent down, feeling very disrespectful, but having no other choice, and whispered,

"Excuse me . . ." When neither husband nor wife moved, she cleared her throat, kneeled beside them, and spoke loudly. "Excuse me!" she nearly shouted, standing up quickly so that she would not be on eye level with her hosts when they awoke.

Both roused, Emi stepped back and explained, before they stood up, who she was.

"Emiko Kato, of course," said Jiro Mori in a deep, sleep-filled voice. He removed four blankets and stood slowly. "I'm terribly embarrassed," he said, bowing. "We must not have woken in time to pick you up at the train station. Yuka," he added turning to his wife. "Were you not to rouse me when it was time to drive to the station to fetch Emiko?"

Emi was shocked at the sight of Mr. Mori. Not because he was in his sleeping clothes — he was far too bundled up to make anyone feel embarrassed — but because he was very old, much older than Emi had guessed from the way her parents had spoken about him, and frighteningly thin. Even though she couldn't make out the lines of his body, she could tell from his hollow face that he was gaunt everywhere. Emi had expected a distinguished gentleman, in good health, and just past retirement age. Someone very much like her father. Instead, the man standing before her, his head covered by the thick *zukin,* looked like he would be lucky to squeeze a few more months out of life.

Looking flustered, Mrs. Mori stood, too, similarly outfitted, and gazed at Emi like she was a ghost.

"How awful of us," she finally said, bowing to her guest, who bowed back much deeper. "I was to stay awake until your train arrived, but it seems sleep got the best of me. I'm terribly sorry."

"Nonsense," said Emi. "I should have taken an earlier train. It was rude of me not to think of the time."

"You must be hungry," said Mrs. Mori, stepping away from her futon and putting her hand on Emi's. Despite all her layers and the presence of a just extinguished fire, her hands were stiff and cold. "I'm afraid we don't have very much — we are at the end of our monthly rations — but there is some cold rice and fresh watercress."

"Oh, no," said Emi, ignoring the hunger pain in her stomach as Mrs. Mori switched on a light. Emi turned around and took the *onigiris* that she had bought during the train journey out of her bag and offered them to her hosts. "I have some food with me. Please," she said, handing one each to them, the last she had. "You must be hungrier than I am."

"Is this fish inside?" said Yuka, holding the paper-wrapped *onigiri* to her face.

"Salmon," said Emi as Mr. Mori started to smile.

"Salmon!" he said laughing, until his shoulders started jumping. "Where did you find these? In Tokyo?"

"Not far from," said Emi, thinking about her train journey. "Don't you . . . is there no fish here?" she asked.

"Not salmon," said Mrs. Mori. She bit hungrily into the *onigiri*. "But let's not worry about that now. If you aren't hungry, you must be very tired," she said. "I will show you the washroom upstairs and Jiro will set up your futon by the fire. Or what's left of it."

Emi couldn't hide her surprise and Mrs. Mori revised her statement. "There are bedrooms upstairs — private rooms — but it is very cold and you might be more comfortable downstairs with us."

"If you don't mind — perhaps just for tonight — I would like to sleep upstairs," Emi said, thinking that the only people she had ever been forced to share a room with were her mother and the Kuriyamas, and that was the American government's doing.

"Whatever will make you the most comfortable," said Mrs. Mori, finally untying her *zukin*. She started to walk up the stairs, very slowly, almost folded in half as she held on to the railing and made the short climb. Emi took one of her suitcases and followed the elderly woman up, one hand out in case she had to break her fall.

Emi barely slept that night, despite the heavy blankets Mrs. Mori laid out for her. The cold coming up from the floor, even though she was in a Western-style bed, was nearly unbearable and when she walked to the bathroom in the morning, her hands were as stiff and ice cold as Mrs. Mori's.

The sun had barely risen and the house was quiet when Emi returned to her room, which she soon saw was the Moris' bedroom. She tiptoed over to their dressers, afraid her steps might make the floor creak, and looked at the photos in silver frames positioned on top. She smiled and picked up one of Jiro Mori. He was in his late fifties or early sixties, very distinguished, and standing by a shiny race car on a gravel road. Wearing a handsomely cut 1920s-style suit, he did suddenly remind her of her father. The photo next to it was of Yuka Mori in New York City, though the photo was taken many years earlier, as revealed by her age and clothes. Emi put the frames down carefully, got dressed as quickly as she could, and made her way silently downstairs, only to see the two forms still under the blankets, unmoving. In the light of day, she saw that the sparsely decorated living room was handsomely done in a traditional Japanese style, with low tables and thick pillows for resting on. But it had all been pushed aside to make room for sleeping and a pile of firewood wrapped in a leather sleeve.

Not wanting to disturb her hosts, Emi slipped out the front door and headed, she hoped, into town. Once down the Moris' muddy lane, she was on the slightly wider road that she had come down with Ayumi. All around her were tall pine trees, thick and full, next to bare maple and larch trees. The dirt was drier and packed down on the road and Emi picked up her step, the sound of birds, more birds than she'd heard since she'd been interned in hotels on the East Coast, helping to wake her up. It was a peaceful, brisk thirty-minute walk into town, and Emi soon spotted the shopping street and headed to Evgeni's store. She hoped he was there at such an early hour, as she wanted to thank him and his wife for their kindness.

There was hardly anyone about, just a few men in a horse-drawn cart and some older Japanese women sweeping the stoops of the stores. Emi slowed down and watched the horses, their smell reminding her of the animals in Crystal City.

She turned her eyes away as one of the horses lifted his tail to relieve himself, but soon saw all the Japanese women who had been sweeping run over to the horse and start scooping up his dung.

"Kōzan!" one woman screamed, laying her claim to the dung and batting away another's hands.

"We are much hungrier in my house than you are," she heard another say.

"They don't eat it," said a man's voice over Emi's shoulder. "They use it to fertilize their tiny vegetable gardens. Manure is very hard to get now. So when the horses go, the women start running."

Emi turned around and looked at Evgeni, his thinning blond hair dirty and pressed to his scalp.

"I was hoping to see you," said Emi, smiling.

He gestured for her to follow him and put his key in the door of his store.

"You made it to the Moris' all right?" he asked, turning on the lights.

"With you and your wife's help, I did," said Emi, thanking him.

"We were happy to help," he said. "There's quite a lot to learn about survival here. It's a strange town now that it's overrun with foreigners. Many people, not enough food. You will learn in time where certain things hide — watercress, mushrooms, and strawberries in the summertime — and how to eat down to the bone. It's not ideal, but it's war."

Emi was formulating a response when she heard the store door open and a young white woman came in, closing the door loudly behind her. To Emi's surprise, Evgeni spoke to her in Japanese. Emi tried not to stare, but the sight of two Caucasian people speaking to each other in Japanese was too much for her. When there was a pause in conversation, Emi interjected and asked Evgeni why they were speaking Japanese.

"It must look strange to you," said Evgeni. "Especially since you are new to Karuizawa." He gestured to the young woman, vibrant and pretty despite her layers of thick clothes. "This is Claire Ohkawa. Claire Smith Ohkawa. She's married to Kiyoshi Ohkawa, who works at the Mampei Hotel. She is Australian and doesn't speak

Russian, and I don't speak much English. But we both speak Japanese. Quite well, I'd like to think."

Claire bowed to Emi, but Emi just blurted out in English, "You are Australian?"

"And you speak English!" said Claire, reaching out and wrapping Emi in an excited hug. "Oh, English!" she exclaimed. "Come and have a cup of tea with me at the hotel," she said. "I haven't spoken English in weeks."

"Well, I —"

"Oh, please don't say no," Claire interrupted her. "You must be new here or I would know you, and I know Karuizawa very well. We can be most helpful to each other, I'm sure of it. Come with me, I beg you."

"She's innocent enough," said Evgeni in Japanese, and Claire opened the door to let them both out, pulling her scarf up to cover her nose and mouth.

"Your husband is Japanese?" Emi asked Claire after she had explained to her why she spoke English and what she was doing in Karuizawa.

"Yes, Kiyoshi," said Claire. "He is and I love him, and I love it here. I never want to return to Australia. Not that it is even an option. It's true, it was much better in Japan before the war, but it will be like it was again. Soon, I hope. And Karuizawa is different from the rest of the country. The war hasn't hit us as hard here. There are food shortages, like anywhere, but everyone says we won't get bombed and I believe them."

"Who is everyone?" asked Emi, and Claire made a circle gesture with her hand indicating the town.

"I've endured a bombing," she added. "I was in Tokyo during the raid in '42. Everyone says it wasn't much, but it was still something to me. I was walking right down the street in the Ginza. The American planes were flying so low you could almost see the pilots' faces. And you know the strangest thing? They dropped notes from their windows. Some of them said, 'I love you.' I picked one of those up off the ground and waved it at the pilots. I still have it. It just shows you who is dropping bombs — little boys who don't know any better. If they had ever spent time here, in this great country, they wouldn't drop bombs on it."

"Do you think it's so great?" Emi asked, surprised to hear a foreigner speaking that way. She knew that many Japanese diplomats' wives who were foreign felt very isolated when they were in Japan.

"I do," said Claire enthusiastically. "Especially Karuizawa. Your father was right to send you here. You'll be much safer than if you were in a big city. If the Allies were to bomb Karuizawa and kill us all, it would be an international incident. There are so many foreigners from so many countries, like me. And then there are the Jews. A Jewish family owns that store right there," said Claire, pointing to a home furnishings store that didn't seem to have anything to sell but blackout curtains. "And while there isn't a lot of food, if you buy on the black market and befriend the right people, there is a little."

"If you befriend the Germans, you mean," said Emi as they made their way to the Mampei Hotel. They paused in front of it, and Emi admired its façade. With its criss-cross brown wood details on a white stucco background, it looked more Austrian than Japanese.

"I didn't say that," Claire replied before they walked in.

"I speak German," Emi admitted. "So I feel I might give in to the temptation of securing myself some bread, even though I would be very angry with myself for taking from the Germans."

"Why? The Germans aren't so bad. Some of the soldiers are quite handsome," Claire declared.

"They may not be so bad when they are in Japan, but when they are in Europe, they are inhumane," said Emi.

"Maybe these Germans are different," said Claire, seeming unmoved by Emi's words. "They don't bother me."

Emi stayed quiet as Claire gestured to two empty seats in the lobby. "Is it funny to be in a Japanese hotel full of Europeans?" she asked, as they watched the Caucasian men hurry through the hotel.

"No," said Emi. "The strange part for me is to be back in Japan during a war. I've spent very little of my life here and it's always been a peaceful, beautiful place to return to between postings. Now it feels as if I've come back for good, but nothing is the same. I miss what it used to be."

"Me, too," said Claire, telling her about the latest rations. "The Japanese and the foreigners sometimes get different food, but lately it's all measly portions and practically rotten. The bread that is rationed to foreigners isn't made of flour, but potatoes. And many say it's half potatoes and half wood pulp. That's if you're lucky enough to get a light-colored loaf. The dark loaves — they're not what the Germans eat. I've been told that ours are made of black flour and ground-up silkworms. And then the meat in the rations is almost inedible. Every cut I've been given was nearly rancid. So now I eat the Japanese rations, just like you. I don't think the government will poison their own people's rice. And I've been in Japan so long I prefer rice to bread anyway."

Emi nodded, horrified. She would ask the Moris what they were surviving on when she returned home. As Claire went on, Emi half-listened as she observed the people starting to fill the lobby. Most of them looked like diplomats, but there were also many Japanese, the majority in the very casual Western clothing that had grown in popularity during the war. They looked nothing like the well-heeled foreign visitors Karuizawa was known for. Emi wondered if those days would ever come back, or if this would be the look of the new Japan.

After she had shifted her weight to peer out the other door, Emi noticed what looked very much like a piano nestled behind a *shoji* screen.

"Is that a piano there?" she asked Claire, craning her neck further to confirm.

Claire looked, too, and nodded.

"Do you think I could play it?" Emi asked. "I've been desperate for a piano. I haven't played properly in almost two years. Just a few times when I was interned in the United States."

Claire glanced around. "In cases like these, it's better to just play and not ask, don't you think? If you play well enough, I'm sure no one will mind. This town needs something nice to listen to instead of the sound of their own fears."

Emi, conscious of her newcomer status, walked over to the piano as Claire looked on. She pushed back the screen and uncovered the instrument, then without checking to see if anyone was trying to stop her, she positioned her hands and feet and played a piece by Beethoven, one she hoped was pleasing and familiar to the mixed crowd.

When she was done, she heard clapping before she had even turned around. And when she did, she saw that many people had paused in the hotel's lobby and hallways to listen to her.

"Play another!" a Japanese man called out, prompting more applause.

Smiling, Emi nodded and turned back to the piano, this time playing a more difficult piece by Mozart. When she finished, she laid her hands on the piano, feeling an elation that she hadn't felt since she'd played with Christian by her side. She wished he were with her now. He would have liked to see her surrounded by people, clapping for her.

When Emi stood up and turned to rejoin Claire, she was cornered by a German military officer who had been listening to her play from just a few feet away.

"Good," he said to Emi in strained Japanese. "Good, good."

At the sight of the swastika on his armband, her heart dropped.

"Thank you," she replied in Japanese, taking a step to the side to move around him. She was about to motion to Claire that she was going to leave the hotel, but Claire came and joined them, introducing herself and immediately offering up that Emi spoke German.

"Deutsch, Deutsch," she said, smiling at Emi.

"Do you speak *Deutsch*?" the officer asked Emi, thrilled.

She acknowledged that she did and curtly explained why, before trying to move around him again, but he put his hand on her shoulder to stop her.

"Perhaps I have met your father," the man said, switching to his native language to introduce himself as Standartenführer Hans Drexel, acting German consul-general in Karuizawa. "You have such talent," he said flatteringly. "You must play at our New

Year's party. The German New Year's party. We can have this piano brought to my home and you can play for us." He leaned closer and said, "You play so well, and a beautiful Japanese girl like you will be a nice sight for the officers. Please come. We can offer you hot food. Enough so you'll be eating for hours. Until your stomach hurts."

Emi knew she should say yes, food was clearly never declined during war, but she did not want to play for the Germans. She was about to refuse when Claire said, "She will! Of course she will. And perhaps she will bring me back a little food, too. That is all anyone wants right now," she said, looking at Emi. "Hot, plentiful food. So if you can promise her that she will play."

"Of course I can," Hans said. "Then you will come, Emiko. Good. And you will uplift everyone's spirits."

Emi could only shake her head yes.

Chapter 24

Leo Hartmann
December 1943

For the Hartmanns, whose acquaintance with Japanese people had been limited to the courteous, kindly, German-speaking Kato family and their embassy colleagues, it was hard adapting to a world where the Japanese were the oppressors, the enemy.

Leo had at first tried to be polite to them, the occupiers, but when his friend Jin was spat on when asking for directions in broken Japanese, he had stopped. The men ruling Shanghai had nothing in common with the Katos. Leo explained as much to Emi in a letter when they first arrived, when their letters were reaching each other with ease. The last letter he had received from Emi was before Pearl Harbor but he still checked the communal mailbox outside their building in Hongkew, though he had no idea how Emi would even know they lived there. He still liked doing it, holding on to some hope that his past might still be part of his future. Most of that hope was gone, but checking the mail, that he could not stop doing.

"Just remember," said Max when they first saw a Japanese officer berating a Chinese beggar on the side of Nanking Road, "they may be isolating us, but they are not persecuting us. They are letting the Jews in when no one else is. They may be allies of Nazi Germany, but they are, in many ways, friends to the Jews. That doesn't make what they are doing to the Chinese right, but it's something to remember before we complain about our conditions."

But the Chinese, Leo knew, did not care if the Japanese treated the Jews better than they were treated in Europe. They hated the Japanese for what they did to them.

One of the few Chinese who did not appear to hate them was Jin's father, Liwei Zhang, as some of his nightclub patrons after the war broke out were Japanese businessmen.

Leo, who had been heavily shielded from the realities of sex until he was having it, was still surprised that his parents let him work in a nightclub six days a week, but money was money and Leo was bringing more home than Hani or Max was.

"I don't want handouts anymore," was Hani's answer when Leo had asked why she was letting him work in such a place. "You're not a child. You will make your own decisions. But I am sure that the son I raised will not go from Emi Kato to a Russian prostitute in a snap."

"A snap?" said Leo. "I haven't seen Emi since 1938, and I haven't received a letter from her since '41. I can't exist in a state of blind hope. Besides, if she really wanted to keep our childhood promises to each other, she would have found a way to contact me. With who her father is? This is Shanghai, which is essentially Japan." He saw his mother's face fall and started to laugh. "Don't worry, you know I still think about her often. We promised that we'd find each other again after the war, and who knows, maybe a miracle will occur, but I'm less optimistic every year. Aren't you?"

"We are indebted to the Katos and will see them again," said Hani confidently.

"I wonder where in Japan Emi is right now," said Leo, picturing her on the Ferris wheel in Vienna, her face so full of worry for him. "In Tokyo I assume. And safe," he added.

The truth was, Leo's lustful thoughts over his years in Shanghai had slowly been transferred from Emi to Agatha. Though nothing had occurred between them beyond Liwei's dance floor, Leo's days were now broken up into the hours before and after he danced with Agatha, and the perfect five minutes that he spent against her body every night. He wanted so badly to hold her outside of the club, to see what was underneath her homemade dresses, but he knew that the last thing she needed was to be involved with a Jewish refugee, even if, in a past life, he was very well-off.

"Mother," said Leo, grabbing his one nice shirt, which Liwei had given him to wear at the club, "the women working in Mr. Zhang's establishment. They're not prostitutes. Just women who men enjoy chatting with," he finished, parroting Liwei's favorite line.

"Fine," said Hani. "I will never again judge a woman for doing what she needs to do to stay alive, especially in a feral city like this one during a war."

"Are you sure you're my mother?" said Leo laughing, letting Hani kiss him on the cheek.

That night, when Leo had finished his shift, a nightclub regular named Hiroyoshi Asai, a wealthy Japanese businessman who had lived in Shanghai since long before the war broke out and still dressed as if he were off to the races instead of a home behind blackout curtains, beckoned to Leo to join him at his center table. Whenever he was sober enough to spot Leo, he would wave him over, as he loved practicing his German, which was very good before he began drinking and nearly perfect after.

Leo came over, prepared to discuss Hiroyoshi's two favorite topics: Shanghai before the war and beautiful women.

"Ah, my favorite Austrian," Hiroyoshi said, gesturing to the waitress to bring Leo a drink. Leo looked out across the crowded room at Liwei, who nodded. Yes, it was fine for him to be entertaining the customers, especially one as rich as Hiroyoshi.

"Sit with me," he said, pushing a small glass of whiskey toward Leo. In Vienna, Leo had had a stocky, athletic frame, but he had grown skinny during his first two years in Shanghai. It wasn't until he started working for Liwei that he started to gain back some weight, his cheeks filling out again.

"Remind me," said Hiroyoshi, "when was it that you arrived in the wicked city of Shanghai."

"January 1939," said Leo, taking a sip of his drink. He had told Hiroyoshi this a dozen times, but he knew that he liked to use it as a segue into reminiscences of old Shanghai.

"Then you missed it all, young man!" said Hiroyoshi, throwing his hands up in the air, his sport jacket creasing perfectly at the elbow. "You missed the miracle city. You should have seen this town in the twenties, in the thirties. The Bund, the women with the blond curls living in the French Concession with their rich, boring husbands. The prostitutes. Those were the girls you turned to after the married French women all went to bed. It was something marvelous. The whole city, it was filthy and full of terrible people, but it sparkled. It was so full of life. What is it full of now?"

"Japanese soldiers," said Leo.

Hiroyoshi shook his head and said, "I don't care for those pompous men walking around here in their brown uniforms with that garish orange rim on their hats. With the swords, always with the swords, like they are going to slice off some poor man's head in the street. I don't like it at all. It's not Japanese to spit on the world as if they own everything. That's not the country or the people I know." He took a long drink and put his glass down in front of Leo. "I'm a practicing Buddhist," he said. He looked at the women around him and added, "Most of the time. This war, the Buddhist monks are against it. I'm against it."

"War doesn't seem in tune with any religion," said Leo, and Hiroyoshi nodded.

"Except it is good for the women, it brings out the best in them," he said, reaching over to Leo to straighten his wrinkled collar.

"Why do you say that?"

"Because their husbands die, and then so many more of them are available." Hiroyoshi broke out laughing and beckoned to Agatha, who was waiting by the dance floor. She came over at once.

"This one is my favorite," he said, patting her curvaceous backside. "Agatha from Germany. She won't marry me. I keep asking, but she just says no."

"Yes, of course I know Agatha," said Leo, removing Hiroyoshi's hand from her body. "Every man in here notices Agatha as soon as they walk in."

"Fine, fine," the businessman said, waving his hand to excuse her. "Go back to doing whatever it is you do. Whatever it is, you do it beautifully. I will come and rediscover you later.

"You like her?" he asked Leo.

"Of course. What's not to like? Though to be honest with you, after nearly three years of watching her, it might be even more than like."

Hiroyoshi drained his glass with one long gulp and squinted at Leo, as if he were trying to keep him in focus.

"Why did you come here? To Shanghai?"

"So that the Nazis wouldn't kill me or my parents."

"A good reason," said Hiroyoshi as a waiter came and replaced his drink. "They truly do hate the Jews. It's strange to hate that much. Tiresome. I didn't come here for any such reason. I came here to make money. For adventure. To escape custom. In Japan, my parents kept threatening me with a wife. All these years later and I still don't have a wife."

"That's . . . depressing," said Leo, laughing.

"The city is depressing now, but I still love it. I should probably stop proposing to Agatha if I don't want a wife. She might say yes one day, and then what?"

"Then you'd have a lovely wife," said Leo. "No, *lovely* isn't strong enough a word. An intoxicating wife. But please don't marry her."

"She's the prettiest one here — a face like a doll and round in all the right places. Though it's the thighs that I'd really like to get my hands on." Hiroyoshi looked around him at the buffed wooden floors and circle of dark green lacquered tables. "I love this place," he declared. "Every day I am thankful that the Kempeitai hasn't shut Liwei down."

"Why would they shut him down?" asked Leo. "Some of them come here, too."

"A surprising turn of events," said Hiroyoshi. "I thought they just raped the women and didn't bother paying them. They'll all be shot when the war is over. Or at least they deserve to be."

Leo nodded and stood up to leave, but Hiroyoshi protested. His hair, worn long and impractical, was falling around his face in two halves, like a theater curtain. His face had grown more chiseled over the years, since, like everyone in Shanghai, he didn't have enough to eat, but his exterior was always polished. He looked to Leo as if he were floating above the war, regarding it as nothing but a small nuisance.

"Stay and sit with me. Tell me about the life of the young and persecuted," he said, tapping his gold ring on the table.

"I can't," said Leo. "If I'm not back in the restricted area in the next hour, I won't eat again until noon tomorrow."

"You picked the wrong time to be a Jew,"

Hiroyoshi said, lighting a cigar. He handed his glass and the last sip of his whiskey to Leo. "For you, because during a war, it's the young men who suffer most of all."

He drank it down and thanked Hiroyoshi, heading to the kitchen to finish off the night. As usual, he took the long way around the room, so he could see Agatha from all angles before he disappeared with the rest of the low-level staff in the back.

Leo was doing a last round of dishes, laughing with Jin about the customers and getting ready to leave, when he heard a collective silence spread through the room. He looked at the front door and plunged his hands back in the hot soapy water to keep from dropping the bowl he was holding. Two men, in German officer's uniforms, had just walked in. He glanced at the back door, prepared to run out, but Jin stopped him from moving.

"Do not say one single word," said Jin, passing behind Leo and greeting them at the door. One stopped to speak to Jin, pointing out the table he wanted, but the other, the more handsome one, went straight to Agatha, kissing her cheek as if he knew her well, or wanted to.

"He does know her," said Jin when he'd returned from seating them and taking their drink orders. Leo looked at him with a worried, searching expression, no longer desperate to leave the room.

"How?" he whispered.

"In 1942," said Jin, turning his face toward the back of the kitchen, "when there were a few German military men in town, that man that just kissed Agatha, Felix Pohl, used to come in regularly. You were working here then. You never saw him?"

Leo shook his head no, afraid to speak.

"Lucky you," said Jin, turning away, but Leo grabbed his shoulder, desperate for more of an explanation.

"You're a glutton for punishment," said Jin, his voice as quiet as Leo's. "Pohl came in many times last year, often with several high-ranking officers. I don't know why they were in Shanghai — maybe meetings with the Japanese — but they stayed a month at least." Jin, who had heard all of Leo's stories about Vienna, tried to calm him then told him to go back to washing dishes. "They are spending the war in Japan. Pohl and the other officer."

"In Japan?" said Leo, thinking of how terrified Emi had been every time she saw an SS officer.

"Yes, Japan. Their ally." Jin placed his finger to his lips and put Leo's hands back in the dishwater. "Just stay calm and quiet. When they're a little drunker and more oblivious, slip out the back. It should only take a few minutes at the rate they're going. You'll make it back before curfew."

Leo focused his energy on the sink and only dared glance out to the main room a few times to see the two officers dancing. The other officer danced with several different women, but Pohl only with Agatha, his hungry hands all over her.

After just a few minutes, Agatha's thin red dress, one of her most low-cut, was wrinkled all over the backside from Pohl reaching for her and Leo saw, out of the corner of his eye, that she was imploring the German to sit back down. "You came in here drunk," she said in German. "You must take a rest. Please."

Pohl, a big man, both tall and wide, his thick brown hair slicked back, leaned into her neck and whispered, too low for Leo to hear.

"Of course, I'm happy to see you," Agatha responded. She was smiling, but Leo could tell that she was anything but happy.

"Aren't you worried about Agatha?" Leo finally said to Jin, abandoning the dishes and forgetting the curfew that was threatening him in Hongkew.

Jin looked out at Agatha, her blond hair messy around her shoulders, her dress wrinkled, and said, "She's dealt with much worse. I've seen him — and many other patrons — much drunker, and so have you. I know you think Agatha is just another one of our innocent girls, pocketing money for survival, but she had an affair with him last year."

"What?" said Leo, too loudly. "She was involved with that Nazi? With Pohl?"

Both Agatha and Pohl looked toward the kitchen.

"Involved because he paid her to be involved," whispered Jin, pulling Leo away from the door out of frustration. "Agatha's parents are dead, you know that. She's lived here alone for years. Don't judge her. She's just trying to stay alive and the German soldiers have money."

"Because they steal it," said Leo. "She shouldn't be with him now. Not this time."

"Why?" said Jin, holding Leo's arm. "She still needs the money. Are you going to give it to her?"

"But he's an SS officer," Leo countered, starting to panic. "Did you see his high-ranking insignia? Do you know the type of things he has certainly done to gain such status? And now he's going to have his hands all over Agatha?"

"They all look the same to me," said Jin, letting Leo go. "Do what you want, but don't cause trouble inside. You know my father will cut your pay if you do."

"Of course I won't," said Leo, rushing out of the hot kitchen to see if Agatha was still in Pohl's arms. He looked around the big room for her, but she was gone, and so was Pohl. The other German officer was in a corner with Svetlana, one of the youngest Russian girls.

Without turning back to tell Jin, Leo ran out the front door, hearing Liwei call out his name as the door closed behind him.

He ran around the most trafficked corner, avoiding rickshaw drivers and drunk young men, and screamed for Agatha, but didn't see her. Turning on his heels, he started running in the other direction. Right away, he spotted them. Pohl, his crisp jacket draped over his arm, was hand in hand with Agatha, the lights of the city encasing their intimacy, though it looked to Leo like she was trying to break free from his grasp.

Leo ran forward and called out her name, letting all sense go. He didn't think about what had happened to his father in front of their apartment, or to his relatives since he'd left Austria. He could only think about beautiful Agatha in bed with a Nazi.

She turned around smiling — her red dress wet at the bottom from the dirty street, her skin even more exposed than it had been inside — but she shook her head when she saw him. "Go away, Leo!" she yelled, breaking free of Pohl. "Go back to Liwei's."

"Who is this boy?" said Pohl, frowning. He was starting to sweat from all the alcohol. "A German? Was he at the dancing club?"

"He's a dishwasher," she said, turning to Pohl and trying to move him along. "Ignore him."

"With pleasure," said Pohl, reaching his hand low on Agatha's waist.

"I'm fine, Leo," she called out, her expression indicating otherwise. "Please don't get involved."

"Yes," said Pohl, pulling her forward, roughly. "She's going to be perfectly fine in my bed all night. I'll return her to taxi dancing tomorrow. Little Agatha, beautiful Agatha, and the exquisite things she will do for money." Pulling her arm out with a jerk, he did a little spin with her in the middle of the busy road, yelling at a rickshaw driver as he ran his lopsided cart close to them.

"Agatha, come back with me!" Leo yelled

out, walking closer to them, his clothes wet with dishwater.

"Get away from us!" said Pohl, turning in Leo's direction. "Listen to the girl. Go back to your washing."

"Agatha, come with me," said Leo again. He was close enough to touch her so he reached out for her hand.

"Is this who is in your bed now?" Pohl asked angrily, his face inches away from Agatha's, shaking her shoulders.

"No," said Agatha, frozen in his grip. "He works with me. You must have seen him at the club, Felix. He's just a dishwasher."

Leo took a step back as someone yelled in Chinese for them to get out of the road, but Felix stayed right where he was, a vise around Agatha's body.

"You don't need money this badly," said Leo, fully realizing how foolish he was being, but he just couldn't stop himself. Agatha would not be climbing in a Nazi's bed, not right in front of him.

"She's not just doing this for the money," said Pohl, still holding on to Agatha, shaking her. "I've known her for many years."

Leo knew he should stay quiet, warn Agatha to be careful and then walk away, but he was fixed to the spot. "Just one year," said Leo, loudly, his heart racing as he thought of Jin's words. "It's only been one year since you met."

Agatha was quietly imploring Leo to leave, but he kept talking over her. "You barely know her. But I know that she will not be with you tonight. She's returning to work with me."

Pohl shoved Agatha aside so he was in front of Leo and she fell to the ground.

"Don't touch her!" Leo screamed, lunging for Agatha, but Pohl stopped him and pushed him so hard that Leo stumbled backward, but managed not to fall. The fact that he'd been drinking most of the night was not helping his judgment, but he knew he was still more sober than Pohl.

"Is this a joke?" the German asked, dropping his coat and smiling as he reached over and knocked Leo to the ground easily. "Some German dishwasher in China is trying to protect your honor?" he asked Agatha, who had righted herself. "Oh, my little beauty," he said when Agatha reached for the side of her dress, which had torn with her fall.

It was the perfect time for Leo to run. Pohl was concerned with Agatha and wasn't looking at him. But Leo's feet felt like lead. He couldn't leave her, and he couldn't let Pohl win. In Vienna, he could never have stood that close to an SS officer without being outnumbered. If a Jew stepped out of line, it meant death. In Shanghai, where Pohl was the first Nazi Leo had seen, he felt protected. And even if the chaos of the city couldn't keep him safe, he was willing to take whatever punishment was bestowed upon him. So instead of running away, he walked over to them and with all his strength, punched Pohl in the side of his jaw. Leo heard the bone crack before Pohl fell to the ground, the most satisfying sound he had ever heard.

Agatha screamed for Leo to run, but it was too late. Pohl was up, despite his broken jaw and bleeding nose, and before Leo could turn around, he had landed a punch clear across his face.

Leo didn't fall to the ground, his lead feet helping to keep him stable. Instead he looked at Pohl and said, "God will punish you for your crimes, you German Nazi filth." Pohl's next punch caused Leo to tilt backward, falling headfirst onto the pavement. He moved his arms up to block his face, but Pohl was too fast, sitting on Leo's chest and landing one punch after the other.

"Stop!" he heard Agatha scream, as his face and body went numb. "Leave him! You're going to kill him!"

No longer able to move, Leo still felt Pohl steal his shoes before going through his pockets and taking his wallet.

"Of course. He's a Jew," Pohl said, looking at Leo's pass for the restricted area. "It's much harder to spot a Jew in China. They can hide easier out of their natural habitat."

Leo's eyes couldn't open, but he heard Pohl start laughing. "And an Austrian Jew! How is he still alive? I can take care of that oversight." Pohl's fists started to attack Leo with rage, hitting his face, his skull, his stomach. Every inch of him that could be beaten was beaten.

Pohl's words were the last Leo heard. He didn't feel Agatha put her head on his heart and start screaming. He didn't feel the hands of the rickshaw driver who put him in the back of his cart and suggested he dump Leo on the side of the road with the other dead. Agatha refused. She insisted on the hospital. Leo Hartmann would not die on the side of a road.

■ ■ ■ ■

PART THREE

■ ■ ■ ■

CHAPTER 25

Christian Lange
November–December 1943

Christian felt that the circumstances of war had forced him to become an adult as quickly as a sunrise. His days and weeks in an orphanage, the family's incarceration in Crystal City; the courtship, physical relationship, and abrupt departure of Emi Kato; the baby's death — all of it had stripped away a distinct layer of his youthful exuberance. Now he felt compelled to abandon one country to serve another. He spent days strangled by guilt, agonizing over how he would tell his parents that he had decided to enlist in the U.S. Army. As expected, his parents were devastated, terrified that they would lose yet another child, their only child. But Christian's conviction was as firm as Lange steel.

Before leaving Crystal City, Christian wrote Jack Walter a letter and addressed it to the Children's Home. Sitting by the swimming pool, anguishing in the void that Emi left, he wrote:

Jack,
You're about to turn 18, and you're going to get the hell out of there. Congratulations, shoe thrower. I wish I were there to throw a steel-toe boot at your head just to show you how much I care. Once you're out, please remember to go to my house in River Hills and steal everything. We've got some good stuff, if my dad's VP hasn't pocketed it all already. Odds are he did, but there might be a few crumbs left for a sad orphan like you.

I know you said you would never enlist, but if you've changed your mind, then you should enlist with me. I've gotten out of going to Germany. My parents are sailing on the repatriation ship sometime in the next year or two, but I'm not going to rot in Crystal City until then. I'm on my way to Camp Fannin in Tyler, Texas, just north of my current hellhole, for seven weeks of infantry basic. Obviously, I had no choice in where I did basic or I wouldn't have chosen to keep frying my ass off in

470

Texas. But from Fannin, I'm heading to Hawaii, joining the 7th Infantry Division currently training at Schofield Barracks on Oahu. It's obviously not the easiest assignment to land — the head of the internment camp in Texas had to make a lot of calls for me to end up there, as Hawaii sure beats the shit out of Texas — but I think society owes you a favor too after orphaning you and giving you that violent streak.

If I'm going to fight, I want to fight in the Pacific, for reasons I'm sure you can guess from my letters. So if you want to watch me make a fool out of myself as I try to become a good soldier, and see a part of the world that's not Wisconsin, you should find a way to get yourself to Hawaii.

If I never see you again — if, as you said, I end up a dead kraut like I deserve — then thanks for helping to save me from myself at the Home. I'm indebted. If I do see you again, I hope it's in Hawaii. Think about it. At the very least, you'll have one new old shoe as a good luck charm when we go fight in the Pacific. I'm bringing it with me.

Kraut

During Christian's first day of basic, his head was shaved — his thick blond hair swept into the garbage by a skinny teenage draftee — his clothes taken, his body put through a prying physical inspection, his name replaced with a number, and his few possessions sent back to Crystal City. At first, he endured it all with easygoing curiosity, thrilled to be out of the internment camp and away from the tight quarters he was forced into with his parents, but he wondered how long it would last. He knew that preparing for war was very different than walking into gunfire. Little by little, as the days went by, he realized that on base, just as in the camp, his world was no longer his. He still belonged to the government — this time to the Army instead of the FBI.

He woke up at 4:45 A.M., marched ten miles a day, ran another ten in the afternoon, learned to dig foxholes with tools that would have been more useful stirring soup, grunted through long hours lying on his stomach at the rifle range, became competent in throwing grenades and engaging in hand-to-hand combat, and, most important, learned along with his fellow enlistees how to care if a comrade died, yet rejoice if the enemy did.

During Christian's second week in the

camp, when he was just getting used to his closest bunkmate, Tom Gibb, snoring solidly from midnight till the drill sergeant routed them all before five, the propaganda machine was cranked up. The men were shown a series of training films seemingly designed to inculcate hate rather than combat skills.

As the projector whirred behind them, a group of stylish, young Japanese women appeared on the screen, peacefully crossing a street in their Western clothes. They fell back as Japanese military vehicles flew through the road, flags waving, the word *Japanazis* appearing on-screen in big flashing letters. Tom leaned over to Christian and said, "I don't think I could shoot those people. Some of those Jap girls are real pretty."

"This sure as shit is some propaganda film," Dave Simon, another of their bunkmates, whispered. He, like Tom, was one of the room's gorilla-like snorers. "They pounded them with endless propaganda during training in the Great War, too. My old man told me all about it. No Japs, but the Germans were described as baby eaters back then. Just munching up their young like ears of corn."

"You're not supposed to shoot the Jap women, you jackass. Just their husbands and fathers," said Frank Tremmel, a black-haired boy from South Texas who drawled so much he sounded as if his tongue were reaching to his Adam's apple.

"The Germans *are* baby killers," said Ray Hagen, another Texan with a ruddy complexion and constantly darting eyes. "Don't you read?"

"Not if I don't have to," said Frank. "Plus, be sensitive. Lange and his parents are baby-killing Germans themselves. He just snuck out of prison down in Crystal City. You don't want to upset him."

Christian regretted ever mentioning the internment camp to Frank.

"Oh yeah!" said Tom. "Of course! We have our own Nazi right here. How did they let you through the gates?" he asked, kicking Christian's chair and doing the Nazi salute.

"At least you're not a Jap," said another soldier named Harvey Chandler, whom Christian had barely spoken to. "That would be a shitty life. To go through it all looking like a Jap."

Christian didn't answer, turning his attention back to the movie as the narrator explained how the Japanese were trying to take over all of Asia, killing women and children in their desperate fight for expansion.

"All this is true," said Harvey. "If we don't stop them, they'll slaughter everyone in Asia — China, the Philippines, everywhere. We better get over there quick and behead them." He made a motion with his hand, as if he were wielding a samurai sword, causing everyone around him to laugh, except for Christian and Dave Simon.

The sergeant in charge came over and screamed at them, and after the movie they spent the evening running ten miles in mud as slippery as cake batter.

When their seven weeks of training was over, Christian was told he'd be transferring to Oahu just before Thanksgiving. The only one from his barracks who would be going over with him was Dave, who Christian learned was a pacifist, as he was raised a Quaker by devout parents in Boston. He'd already been nicknamed the Dove by the other men.

"Sad you're stuck with me on the train, the boat, and God knows what else they shove us on to get there?" Dave said to Christian as they polished their boots next to each other. Dave's big brown eyes, which already had a terrified look about them, turned to Christian and stared at him hopefully.

"Nope," said Christian. "I always wanted

to fight alongside a pacifist."

"Good," said Dave, who had been drafted right before Christian enlisted. "Maybe you can keep me alive when I forget what the captains here taught us. I think I selectively weeded out everything that involves killing my fellow man."

"But the Japanese soldiers are not your fellow man," said Christian, the words feeling strange on his tongue. "I'm not saying we should slaughter civilians — of course not — but the soldiers are going to try to kill us if we don't kill them first."

"That doesn't mean they're not our fellow man," said Dave. "You'll see. You might not think it now because we've been watching those videos that make the Japanese military seem like bloodthirsty pigs, but when you are looking one in the eye, you'll see yourself in him, uniform or not."

"I hope not," said Christian. "Or I'll die pretty fast."

Christian and Dave made it to Hawaii the week before Thanksgiving, and all Dave talked about on their boat over was the wickedness of war and how ready he was for Hawaiian girls after being stuck with Texan boys for the past two months.

"I thought you were so religious," said Christian, laughing at Dave's dreams of girls in grass skirts.

"Just because I don't want to kill people doesn't mean I don't want to sleep with women," said Dave, closing his eyes and smiling. "One is love, the other is death."

"Love?" said Christian laughing. "I don't think we'll be there long enough for you to fall in love." But then he thought of Emi, and how fast he had fallen for her, and patted Dave's shoulder. "Maybe you'll prove me wrong," he said before going on a walk around the boat.

Christian was ready for Hawaii because it was half a world closer to Emi. Missing her was so all-consuming, such a tug on his heart, that it had convinced him to leave his parents, to abandon Germany. He and his father had talked until the sun rose on Christian's last night in Crystal City and had agreed that the war might end before the Langes were sent to Germany.

"It is possible," his father had said harshly, still very angry at his son for leaving his fragile mother.

"You have to understand. It's not my country," said Christian after Franz kept hammering out his disappointment. "I have no ties there. You and Mom are going home, but it's not home to me. I don't want to go there and support a military I don't believe in."

"We aren't going to support the military," Franz had said, his handsome face creased and tired. "We are just going to live there and then return to Wisconsin when they'll have us back."

"I don't have faith that they'll take us back," said Christian. "And I don't want to be gone from here forever. As mad as I am at the American government, for this, for what happened to Mom and the baby, this is still my home."

He had never mentioned Emi to his parents, never explained the source of his real pull to the Pacific. His mother needed him, she told him constantly, but he assured her that he would be there for her again. After he had found Emi. After the war.

The only other person Christian said goodbye to before he left Crystal City was Inge, who leapt into his arms, put her hands behind his neck and whispered that she would be escaping with him.

"Your parents have invited us to Pforzheim with them," said her mother. "Now that you have enlisted, they say there will be more than enough space and everyone claims it's safer than Berlin, where we intended to go. Your mother has really taken a liking to little

Inge. I think she's helping cheer her up."

"Impossible not to be cheered up by Inge," said Christian, shaking her mother's hand.

"I know your parents are angry with you, but I think what you're doing is very brave," she said before Christian went to his parents one last time. "If I could find a way to leave Inge in America, I might. I think it's safer here."

"I will see you again," said Christian, waving to her. He patted Inge on the head, as she cried inconsolably into his shoulder. He gave her a final hug and handed her to her mother before going to his own mother, so she could cry all over him, too.

If Texas had been an abrupt change from River Hills, Hawaii was a slice of an entirely different world. And here he didn't have Franz Lange to help him navigate or his mother to comfort him when he failed. He had a pacifist who was terrified to die and seemed to want to spend the last weeks of his life surrounded by near-naked girls on the beach.

"Black on red. Seven straight and another seven upside down," Christian said to Dave before they arrived in Oahu. He had drawn a picture of the Seventh Infantry's famous insignia and given it to Dave just before their boat docked.

"I thought it was an hourglass," said Dave, holding up the piece of paper.

"It *is* an hourglass. One made from two sevens," said Christian, tracing the sevens on the paper.

"I don't like it," said Dave. "Like we are just waiting for the sand to run out and then poof, we die. I'll probably die walking off this damn boat. I hate boats."

But he did not die. They both survived the first couple of days on base and soon it was Thanksgiving Day and they were ready to celebrate. They took off to Honolulu in military jeeps, down badly paved roads flanked by palm trees. Christian and the others tried to shake off the fear that it could be their last Thanksgiving, while Christian also kept flashing back to one year before, when he and his parents had joyfully celebrated the holiday together, just weeks before the FBI was at their door. It was their last Thanksgiving as the Langes of River Hills. The family they always thought they'd be.

On Thanksgiving Day 1943, Christian had the kind of hangover reserved for inexperienced drinkers. He woke up with a head that felt bruised, squinting in the bright sunlight. His throat was raw and parched and he was desperate for the cool winter air of Wisconsin, which always set his head right. When Christian finally found the strength to leave his barracks, all he got was tropical humidity and the pulsating rays from the sun. He turned on the water in the outdoor sink, letting it run over his face and short hair, and stayed there, bent in half, until he heard someone holler his name.

Christian pulled his head up out of the cold water, half-opened his eyes, and saw Corporal Menkins beside him holding three letters.

"Lange! Mail!" he said, dropping them on the wet sink, his face tan and relaxed. "Came in yesterday. Your mother. Two of them," he added before turning to go off and find the next man.

"What's she say?" Christian yelled to him. Menkins made it a habit to read everyone's mail and he seemed convinced that Christian's was the most interesting since the letter he'd received on arrival contained a picture of Helene Lange. "I'm gonna chop out your pop and pin your mama over my bed," he'd said to Christian when he'd handed him that one. Christian had had to twist his arm back painfully to get the photo from him.

Menkins walked back to Christian, took

the letter, pretending he hadn't opened it, and smiled when they both saw that the envelope flap was unsealed.

"She says Happy Thanksgiving, of course."

"Not the happiest I've ever had, but thanks for this anyway," he said, lifting up the letter.

Menkins grinned and said, "Your pretty mama also begs you to come back to her and says that if you die fighting the Japs that she's throwing herself into the San Antonio River. Oh, she also ends with something about having more proof that Martin did it." He handed the letter back to Christian and said, "Did what?"

"Lied and told the government that we were a bunch of Nazis, which is why we got sent to Crystal City. It's an internment camp in Texas."

"Oh, *that,*" said Menkins. "You're definitely a Nazi. I'm not going anywhere near you when they ship us off, guns in hand. And here I thought only Japs were in those camps." He pointed to Christian's third letter and said, "This one's not from your mother, so I didn't bother to open it. Next time you write her, tell her I love her and ask her to send another picture. This time, with less clothes on. Something cut low in the front, like an open robe. Silk would be a nice touch. They got those in the prison camp?"

That night, when the men were lined up washing their boots, Menkins asked Christian who the third letter was from.

"Jack Walter. A friend," Christian said. "Telling me he enlisted."

"You hear that? Pretty boy's lover enlisted!" Menkins shouted. "Congrats, pretty boy."

"Fuck yourself," said Christian, who, never vulgar at home, had learned the art of cursing since he'd joined the Army. He took the letter from his pocket and walked off to read it again.

Jack had left the Children's Home, he said, and was in basic in Missouri, but in five weeks he would be joining the Seventh in Oahu.

"Rumor has it that everyone in the 7th dies easier than a blind housefly," Jack wrote, "so it doesn't seem too hard to get assigned in, Hawaii or not. They practically cheered when I told them I wanted the 7th. I think those internment camp people lied to your face about doing you a favor because from what I hear, people go in but they don't come out. But what of it, right? Because would you rather be alive in Texas or dead in Hawaii? Never mind, I know your answer to that. Hawaii is closer to Emi, and that's why you're there and not stuck in Camp Kraut. Love in a time of war. That's so poetic of you. I'll see you soon and I'll knock that soft side right out of you. Until then, River Hills."

Christian kept the letter in his pocket as training continued, along with the one from his mother begging him not to die.

At the end of December, just over a month before the Seventh Infantry Division was due to ship out from Pearl Harbor for an offensive on Japanese territory, the base was flooded with new men. Since Christian hadn't heard from Jack in weeks, he thought he might be in the group and during a rare moment of freedom set out to look for him.

In one of the barracks where the arrivals were getting settled amid the piercing commands of a new drill sergeant, Christian asked the man closest to the door where they had come from.

"Jefferson Barracks, out of LeMay, Missouri," the man said quietly, standing at attention, his shirt already sweat-stained around the collar and under the arms.

"Really?" Christian exclaimed. "I've been waiting for the boys from Jefferson all week. Was Jack Walter on your boat? Black hair, about five foot seven. Loves to fight. Probably punched half the men on the ship in the face."

"Sorry," said the boy, motioning to the sergeant and indicating that he didn't want to get in trouble. Christian turned to leave but was hissed at as soon as he was out the door.

"I know Jack Walter," a recruit whispered from the doorway. "He was in my barracks at Jefferson and looks like the fellow you described. Where is your Jack Walter from?"

"Milwaukee. And yours?"

"Milwaukee."

"Know where I can find him?"

"He's supposed to be here, but he's at a bar in Chinatown called the Hula Hula. It's on Hotel Street. You know it?"

" 'Course I do," said Christian of the Honolulu club where every prostitute in town eventually showed up. "Thanks for the tip."

When he could leave the base that day, after the evening mess hall cleanup, he hitched a ride to Chinatown with an officer who dropped Christian at the Hula Hula, saying they had the best girls, and headed off to a place down the street, declaring that he wasn't looking for the best. "Uglier girls are better at making love," he said before

Christian closed the door. "They have to try harder."

"Even prostitutes?" asked Christian. "Aren't they getting paid no matter what?"

"Don't get philosophical, Lange," said the officer, pulling the door shut.

The street was bustling with GIs and young women, some Hawaiian, but many not. He walked straight into the Hula Hula, where he could see at least two dozen girls in the dim room who looked like Emi. They had her straight black hair, and some had her tall, thin build, but none was anything like her. Of that he was sure. It wasn't that some were prostitutes, he thought, only that no one else carried herself quite the way she did.

Christian went up to the bar and looked around, but he didn't see anyone who resembled Jack, either. He ordered a beer and tried to avoid the advances of the girls, bare-shouldered and hovering hopefully about the mainland GIs. As he was getting ready to polish off his drink, he heard Jack's voice, as clear and loud as it had been on a winter day outside the home in Milwaukee. "Kraut!" he yelled.

Christian spun around and saw Jack heading for him, his uniform sloppy, his black hair unwashed, and his face needing a shave.

"Kraut!" he shouted again, his slight body taking up the space of a giant because of the energy he brought into the room.

"Not really the best company to call me kraut in," said Christian as Jack reached him at the bar and slapped him hard on the back. "Want to get me shot before we even get off this island?"

"Nah, I don't want anyone to kill old kraut. Say, what's your real name again?" Jack joked as he sat down next to Christian, smelling like booze.

"Just for that you're not getting your shoe back, you ass," said Christian, signaling for a second beer and one for Jack.

"No way, Christian Lange," Jack said. "You do not have my shoe with you. My old shoe? The best weapon ever wielded in the Milwaukee home for sad abandoned youth?" He took a long drink of his beer and said, "Guess who cried when I left? Streams of big salty tears?"

"Braque."

"Yes, Braque," said Jack. "And every girl over the age of ten." He winked at Christian and started to laugh. "You know I miss it a little. A little," he said, shooting Christian a look before he started to tease him.

"I do have the shoe," said Christian. "You can sleep with it if you want, if you miss it so much. But not the shoelace. Inge has it. She's taking it back with her to Germany. On the train and then in the camp it became our good luck charm. Inge had the lace around her neck on the way to Texas and then I tied it around her wrist before I came here."

"Big kraut and little kraut. What a pair," said Jack, lifting the cold beer to his lips and then holding the wet bottle against his forehead. "Where is she now?" he asked. "Still in that Texas prison?"

"Yeah, still Texas, but she'll repatriate with her family, and mine, in a year, give or take. They're all going to Pforzheim. Unless the war ends first."

"It won't," said Jack, winking at a woman walking in the door. "Jesus Christ. Little kraut in Germany. I don't like that prospect at all. Makes me incredibly nervous. All the bastards here can die, but if little kraut goes, I'm going to have to paddle to Germany to take care of it."

"She'll be fine. She was very happy to be reunited with her mother in Texas."

"The only happy person in Texas," said Jack, trying to get the attention of the Hawaiian woman he'd winked at. They both watched as she walked over, with her pretty little hips swaying in an exaggerated fashion, her floral dress tight over them. She smiled at Jack but sauntered over to an officer instead, his captain insignia shining on his shoulders.

"Tough for you, you enlisted orphan," said Christian laughing. All around him enlisted men, smiling big as children, were thrilled to be surrounded by women and alcohol. The décor in the bar was a garish attempt at tiki, the bar stools made of hardened straw, fake leis draped over everything, including some of the men, but no one seemed to care. Hawaii, they all knew, could be the last welcoming place they ever saw before they moved into hostile territory, where they faced death from every angle.

Christian motioned for another beer for Jack and prayed that he hadn't made the stupidest decision of his life.

"Christ, did you really give that up?" asked Jack. "Your parents, the love of little kraut — all for this?" he said, pointing to a lieutenant with his hand between a woman's thighs.

"Not for that," said Christian, looking away.

"Fine. To go chasing a Japanese girl you only knew for six months? You do know we're not going to Japan? We are going to Kwajalein Atoll and it may be in the hands of the Japanese but it ain't nowhere close to the empire, kraut."

"I'm not chasing her exactly," said Christian, putting down his empty bottle.

"Yes, you are. That's exactly what you're doing. You just don't look as stupid as him."

Christian looked out to where Jack was staring and saw an enlisted man, too tall for his uniform, running after a girl, who had crouched down behind the wooden bar to avoid his advances.

"Fine. I'm chasing her," Christian admitted. "But in my own way."

"I don't blame you," said Jack. "She finally deflowered you. Not in a field of flying monarchs, but the orange trees sounded all right, too."

Jack paused the conversation to let out a loud whistle, his fingers in his mouth like a traffic cop, as a girl walked in wearing not much more than a bathing suit. She was greeted by about a dozen men at the door and escorted to a seat at the other end of the bar.

"Does she know you're out of Crystal City? That you're here and trying real hard to go over there?" asked Jack, his eyes on the peroxide blonde who had caused all the commotion.

"Not yet," Christian admitted. "I have her

address in Tokyo but I haven't written. I will before we sail for Kwajalein. Right now, I just don't know what to say. Besides, Menkin said the letter will never reach her."

"Say you're a pathetic fool who will chase her even with guns pointed at your head. And that you abandoned your parents. I love that part," he said laughing.

Christian rolled his eyes but turned around as he felt bare skin against his neck. A young Asian woman leaned in smiling, more with her cleavage than her mouth, but Christian turned back to Jack before she could say anything. "Emi's not the only reason I didn't want to go to Germany. I want to see her again, but she's also a good excuse not to go. I can't go there. I know I don't belong there."

"Didn't feel like being blown up in the cold? Would rather die under a palm tree?" said Jack, laughing and motioning to the woman that Christian had rebuffed to join him instead.

"In Crystal City we started hearing stories about families who went back to Germany in '42. The men, especially the young ones, the American citizens, were taken as prisoners of war. Suspected of spying. I've been in prison long enough. I don't want to end up in a German prison."

"Plus, no sex under orange trees."

"Another reason," said Christian.

Jack whispered in the ear of the girl he was trying to woo and sent her on her way. "I'll find her later," he said, watching her walk away.

Christian raised his eyebrows and looked at the men in the bar trying their best to seduce the Honolulu prostitutes without having to pay them and suggested to Jack that he not become one of them.

"Don't worry, I've got you and your money now," said Jack smiling.

"Right," said Christian. "So, out of curiosity, how many of the men you came over with hate you?"

"All of them," said Jack. "Except that one." He pointed to a boy twice his size. "He's Samoan and mean as hell, but we got into a fight and I knocked him out. Can you believe it?"

"Yes," said Christian dryly, pointing at his head to remind Jack of the concussion he'd given him.

"Oh, right," said Jack. "How was I to know your skull is about as solid as a paper cup." He looked at the stocky boy and said, "That one was a lot tougher than you. No bullshit infirmary time over a made-up concussion. He just started liking me a lot more when he realized this wiry yet hand-some frame hid the strength of a madman."

"You're definitely a madman," said Christian as he stood up. It was time for both of them to go back to base, but Jack shook his head no and clutched the bar. "I'll take the punishment," he said. "I'm not leaving here yet."

"Never mind madman. You're still an idiot," said Christian. He had to get outside quickly or he would not be in time to hitch a ride back to base with the other soldiers in the bar.

"Idiot! That's not what these girls have been saying. They love me. You're right, Hawaii's sure as shit better than Wisconsin. If we die here, we die here!" said Jack, standing up and throwing his hands in the air.

"I'll see you back on base," Christian said, leaving money on the bar for both of them. "Don't get syphilis."

CHAPTER 26

Emi Kato
December 1943–January 1944

While Claire Ohkawa had gone on about how much food the Germans in Karuizawa had compared to the Japanese and other foreigners, Emi still felt an enormous amount of guilt about accepting to play at Standartenführer Drexel's party. But between Claire's insistence and the Moris' obviously hollow state, she felt she had a moral obligation to play and return home with food. She could not let her revulsion of the German military keep her away.

"You play, you eat, keep to yourself, and if possible, you bring some food with you when you leave," Jiro Mori had suggested when Emi had returned to his home on her first full day in Karuizawa. While the Moris had insisted that they were thrilled to have her with them, she understood very quickly that they lacked the energy to play host. The

494

war had already taken a toll on their aged bodies, and all they had the strength for was staying warm and getting enough to eat. As they had given her a tour of their house, their bodies moving slowly through the quaint summer cottage, which felt as warm as a tent in December, they had made it clear that life in Karuizawa, especially in winter, was not easy. Despite their physical limitations, they looked every day in the forest for watercress, chestnuts, acorns, and matsutake mushrooms. There was sometimes wild boar and pheasants to hunt, but they weren't able to do that themselves, both of them nearing their mid-eighties. They had friends who would sometimes bring them those delicacies, if they were lucky enough to find them, but mostly they lived on their meager government rations. Emi promised she would help, that she would learn to navigate Karuizawa and bring home what she could. She thought of writing to her parents and asking how aware they were of the Moris' state, if they knew she was going to have to spend winter frozen and eating hand to mouth, but decided against it. They were already terrified for her safety; she didn't want to worry them further.

"You played for the Nazis just now,"

Claire pointed out when Emi expressed her hesitation as they left the Mampei Hotel. "That officer, Hans Drexel, he was listening to you. That's why he approached you. So what's the difference if you play in the hotel or if you play at a party?"

"The difference," Emi said, "is that at Drexel's I can eat and bring home food for you and the Moris, yes?"

"I hope so," said Claire.

"So I will go."

The morning of their first encounter, Claire took Emi on a brisk walk around the small town, down country roads, pointing out the places where watercress grew in streams, which kind of mushrooms were edible and which were poisonous, and the fields where strawberries would grow in the spring.

"There used to be ducks in this pond," said Claire, "but as you can guess, they've all been eaten."

"It's still quite beautiful," said Emi, unused to such dense greenery, trees tall as buildings.

"It is," said Claire. "That's why so many people come here, but mostly in the summer because it stays so cool. Before the war it was packed with American missionaries, but they're all gone now. More space for us,

I suppose. We're one thousand meters up, and it makes all the difference in temperature. Celebrities used to visit, too. I was here — had just married Kiyoshi — when Charles Lindbergh was celebrated at a banquet in town after he flew into Japan. The American ambassador had a large summer home in Karuizawa in the early thirties. And Douglas Fairbanks — do you know him? The American actor?"

Emi nodded her head yes.

"He came here in thirty-three. Played golf with the ambassador. That was all before the ski resort was built in '35. That's when the Germans started coming. Do all Germans ski? It seems like it here."

"I think the rich ones do," said Emi, pointing to a few squat mushrooms growing on a log nestled in the light green moss beneath a dense grove of bamboo grass.

"If you see anything edible, take it," Claire advised, reassuring Emi that the mushrooms were shiitake and not poisonous. "Do the Moris have any animals? A cow or a goat?" she asked as Emi dug in the ground with her bare hands, the only sound that of bush warblers flying overhead.

"No, I don't think so," said Emi, putting the dirty mushrooms in the pocket of her coat. "They don't seem in a state to be tending animals. They are much more elderly than I was made to believe."

"That's too bad," said Claire. "We have a milking goat and it's kept us from melting away. We drink the milk and when I leave it on the stove, it curdles and turns to cottage cheese. You're already very thin; you'll have to be careful. Perhaps you can trade some of your possessions for one — though it won't be easy. I'll try to help," she said, pointing out a fox on the road.

"Do you eat those, too?" Emi asked, watching the red animal dart between two small trees.

"No," said Claire. "Not yet. We still consider them sacred. But ask me again next year."

"I wasn't aware that there was such a food shortage here," said Emi, putting her hand against her mushrooms.

"But it must be the same in Tokyo," said Claire, stopping Emi and pointing out a large hole in the ground. "Worse, with such a large population. You can't find mushrooms in the middle of the city, can you?"

"I'd be surprised," said Emi. "Perhaps my parents were just hiding the truth from me, or they are being treated better than most, for now. I couldn't say."

"This hole," said Claire, "all this." She ran

her hands against a large wall of dirt. "It's pumice from a terrible volcanic eruption, about a hundred and fifty years ago. It killed thousands, tens of thousands, the eruption itself and then the famine it caused."

"Mount Asama?" asked Emi, of the large active volcano that loomed over the town.

"That's the one."

Claire put her finger to her lips as they heard the step of a deer that had just come through the brush. "A Sika doe. Those we do eat," she whispered. "Do you have a gun with you?"

"Of course not," Emi whispered back. The animal, startled by the women, turned around and bounded off.

"Too bad," said Claire, motioning for Emi to follow her to the main street. "Maybe you'll get to eat venison with the German officers."

Emi hadn't had meat since the *Gripsholm,* and the cuts of beef on the ship were mostly browned fat remolded to look like steak. She'd had venison in Germany and Austria before and though she found the taste too rich, she was coming to understand that in Karuizawa, as Claire said, if it was edible, you ate it.

Perhaps it was luck that Emi wasn't feeling hunger pains yet, or it was that her body had adapted to surviving on much less after her boat journey. She said as much to Claire, who pointed out that Emi's pants were almost slipping off her frame. Emi looked down, unbuttoned her coat, and pulled them up, rolling the waistband twice.

"Start with trying to get some sustenance at Drexel's party," said Claire. "My advice is play late into the night, and then when they are drunk — and they will be wildly drunk — you pack up all the remaining food and bring it home. Don't pick and choose, just take anything. Take their half-eaten chicken legs, crumbs from the floor. Steal it all. Even if it's soup, find a way to transport it. If you have enough, bring some to me the next day. But feed the Moris first, of course. What a way to live out their twilight years," said Claire as the town's main street, the *ginza,* came into view. "With more war."

A wet snow had begun to fall the afternoon of the party, starting and stopping like bursts of tears throughout the day, but Emi rode Mrs. Mori's old bicycle, the spokes stiff with rust, to Hans Drexel's house at the other end of Karuizawa anyway. She felt like she deserved some sort of physical punishment before entertaining men like Drexel. The Moris had warned her that if anything untoward were to happen, that she was to leave at once, food or not, and had pleaded with her to take their old car. Emi admitted to them that she was a poor driver, always having been ferried by others, or hopping on and off public transport all over the world.

"I understand we need food but I don't like you going," Jiro had said, watching Emi take the bicycle out of the Moris' garden shed. "Especially not on that old contraption."

"I'll be all right," said Emi, after she had finished putting air in the tires, but she was as nervous as Jiro Mori. What had happened to the girl in Austria who held hands with Leo? Now she was going to a Nazi officer's party.

In her best dress, tucked into wool pants and under a winter coat, she tried not to fall in the slush, walking the bicycle up the small hills until she reached the wooded corner that hid Drexel's house. The large home, a former American missionary's, was set well back, like most of the summer places were. Emi only saw three cars parked out front and guessed that Drexel was having her, one of the help, arrive before the guests.

There were no Christmas decorations on

the porch or façade, like Emi was used to seeing in Europe; instead there was the only adornment that the Nazis had cared about since 1920: the swastika. The party flag hung above the front door, attached to a line of cedar bark that edged the roof. The first time she had seen that flag hanging vertically was when Adolf Hitler spoke at the Heldenplatz in Vienna. Now she was walking into a house that displayed it, and in her own country. She pulled her eyes down, sickened to think what she was prepared to do for something to eat.

She stepped onto the porch, past a line of handcarved rockers, and knocked softly on the door. A young Caucasian woman in a perfectly steamed evening dress opened the door and looked with disdain at Emi in her thick, muddy clothes.

"Incorrect house," she said in accented Japanese, her face cold and dismissive. She moved to close the door but Emi was able to catch it with her shoe before it slammed shut in her face.

"I'm here to play the piano," Emi said in German, assuming it was her mother tongue. She pressed the door open a few more inches with her toe and looked down at the done-up woman, who was, despite her heels, several inches shorter than her. "I was invited by Standartenführer Hans Drexel."

She looked at Emi's wet coat and the black bicycle against the tree behind her, raised her pencil-drawn eyebrows, and said, "Wait."

When Hans Drexel appeared, several minutes later, he was not wearing the heavy, gray-green Nazi uniform that he had on at the hotel, but a tuxedo-styled dress uniform covered in SS insignia. It showed off his firm build and handsome appearance, made more striking by his dark hair and light eyes. Like Leo, Emi thought.

"You have come to entertain us. And you brought winter with you." Drexel took in her shabby appearance with evident disapproval, his green eyes moving slowly over her shapeless, wool-covered body.

"I'm sorry," she said, her apology turning her stomach. "I don't intend to play in these clothes. If you let me change, I will return looking better."

"Thank goodness," he said, and let her move farther inside the house. "My bedroom is just upstairs." He put his hand on her back and rubbed it hard along her vertebrae, all the way past her tailbone. "Let me escort you up. We have some time before you need to start playing."

"A bathroom will suffice," Emi said, stepping away, the feel of his fingers hot and lingering.

Drexel laughed, his wide pink mouth turned up, amused, and held his hands up. "They all start off like this, but they change quickly," he whispered. He pointed across the living room to a bathroom and Emi hurried over.

As she took off her layer of wet clothes, pushing them into the bag she'd brought to hide food in, she looked in the mirror and shook her head at her reflection. His hand on her back, the uninvited touch — she couldn't help but think of the day behind Leo's house, Kirsten and her Hitlerjugend pin, the boys who had stripped her of her dignity between bouts of untroubled laughter. Emi had spent the years since pushing away any thoughts that might remind her of that day, that would set off the memory. She had succeeded in turning it into a distant nightmare, one that she refused to let occupy her mind or body, but Drexel's hand on her had allowed the winter of 1938 to march right back in.

Abruptly, she wiped off the red lipstick she had applied with precision at the Moris'. She should not have said yes to an offer like Drexel's until she or her hosts were on the brink of starvation.

"Fool," she muttered as she splashed water on her face. "Stupid, ignorant fool."

When Emi emerged from the bathroom, she was in her figure-hugging wool dress and heeled shoes. Drexel eyed her, but she moved aside before he could touch her again.

His hand hovering near her slender hips, encased in the red fabric, he led her to the Mampei Hotel's piano and said, "Sit now and play. Keep playing until I tell you to stop."

He stayed close to her as she sat on the bench, adjusting it, then reached down and placed her hands on the keys, pushing them down forcefully.

"Play," he said loudly, breathing in her ear. "Play now."

She nodded yes, and when he finally left her, she let out a deep breath and started Debussy's "Clair de Lune." She had played just a few bars when Drexel rushed back and slammed his fist on top of the piano, causing heads to turn.

"Nothing French!" he bellowed, his other fist pushing down on her fingers again. "Beethoven! Brahms! Bach! Schumann! I think Germany has produced enough composers to keep you busy. And don't even consider the *jude* Mendelssohn."

Emi apologized and switched to Brahms, her arms shaking.

When Drexel had moved across the room, she dared to look about, noticing that there were still very few guests, but those in her line of sight were grouped about drinking. Alcohol was hard to come by across the country, because of the scarcity of rice, but the Germans had surmounted the problem. The smell of sake being heated in the kitchen — floral but with a distinct dryness — was wafting through the house like a forgotten perfume.

As she inhaled, she noticed that more Japanese guests arrived, and almost missed a note when she realized that many of the men coming in were Kempeitai. They were a branch of the army police who sought out spies and kept Japan under draconian order, but Emi hadn't glimpsed any in Tokyo when she'd arrived. She'd seen them back in the thirties as they'd been active in the occupation of Manchuria, and knew they were deployed all over the country now, especially where there were large foreign populations, but seeing them uniformed and en masse stopped her breath.

Our very own SS, thought Emi as she watched the Kempeitai in the room, in their

506

olive green uniforms with tight black collars, armbands with *Ken* and *Hei* kanji — law and soldier — and polished knee-high boots. Though they were stone-faced, their body language betrayed their expressions, as they seemed happy to be attending a party rather than hunting out those deemed "undesirables."

"They are staying at the Mikasa Hotel, a pretty structure in the shadow of Mount Asama. But they're in town, and here in the forest, all the time. They came and questioned us once," Jiro had said when he was telling Emi about Karuizawa — and who she should avoid — on the day she arrived. "Because I spent so much time in America as a diplomat," he'd explained before she could ask why. "Mostly they just spy on the foreigners, but they have deemed me, and a few other Japanese, worthy of their time as well. If they knock on the door and you are home alone, slip out the back and hide in the woods. But sometimes," he said, clearing his throat, "they don't bother to knock."

When the room had filled up with warm, hungry bodies, the food was brought out from the kitchen and set on a large, Western-style table. Emi tried not to turn her head as Japanese women brought out serving trays, but she knew she wouldn't see such a feast for a long time.

After the guests had helped themselves to a first and second serving, Emi was allowed to follow. She filled a plate with ham and potatoes — real potatoes, with salt — cooked vegetables, and thick slices of brown German bread with soft, flour-dusted crusts. She slathered a slice with butter and held it up to her nose — it smelled like warm salt and fat — before taking large bites of it, biting again before she'd swallowed any, the butter melting on the corners of her mouth. She wasn't suffering from starvation or malnutrition yet, but having well-cooked, fattening food in her mouth made her realize how hungry, how desperate for flavors, she was.

"The ham is exceptional," she heard the girl who opened the front door say to Drexel as the guests all did the round of the table again, never moving very far away from the food. She was allowing him to have his hands on her back and elsewhere. "I thought it was only tuna fish in tin cans that came on the last boat."

"It was," said Drexel. "A disgrace. But you know we have our ways. The German military has been in this town long enough to know how to enjoy life here. We are not going to let our women starve, are we?"

"No," said the girl, helping herself to even more ham. "But there aren't many German women here now. We will see how generous you are when hundreds more come this year."

"We will be as generous as always," said Drexel, putting his arm around her. Noticing Emi watching them, he motioned for her to go back to the piano, but before she did, she helped herself to one more plate of food — ham, chicken, different kinds of cheeses, fried bread dipped in cream sauce, carrot soup, and mashed potatoes.

When she was finished, she brought her plate to the kitchen, which was staffed with a half-dozen Japanese girls.

She handed her plate to one of them, and then looking to see that Drexel was still occupied, asked about the food. "How do they have this much to eat?" she asked, very curious about Drexel and the girl's conversation. "I heard about the bread, but this is so much more."

"I don't know," said the girl, not looking at Emi. "But they always seem to have this much. When I work for them, they let me eat some if there's a lot of fat on a slice of ham or if the bread falls in the oven."

Emi nodded politely and went back to the piano, where she stayed until well past midnight, when there were only ten guests left at the party, all so drunk that they looked near falling over or falling asleep.

Drexel motioned to her with a flick of his hand that she could stop playing, and Emi stood up and looked out at the table, still covered in trays of food.

"Give me your watch and I'll tell you where the food comes from," one of the kitchen girls whispered to her when she got close enough. Emi looked down at her, her apron tied around her waist twice, she was so thin. And young. She barely looked like a teenager.

"My watch?" said Emi, quietly, looking down at her timepiece, which was one of her mother's old ones. She had not been permitted to take her good watch with her to Karuizawa, since her parents wanted her to blend in. "Why would you want it?"

"Who cares why I want it, I want it," she whispered back in coarse Japanese. "Give it to me and I'll tell you where they hide the ham."

"Hide the ham . . ." Emi replied, walking to the bathroom as Drexel had made it clear that her work was done. She just needed to change and put as much food in her bag as she could without making a commotion.

The kitchen girl followed her in and held

out her hand. Seeing that Emi had other clothes with her, she said, "Give me that dress, too. I want it."

Too curious to say no, Emi removed her dress in front of the girl and took off her watch.

The girl looked at Emi's other clothes and seeming satisfied, said, "They have a farm. The Germans. It's a long walk from town, north of the Mampei Hotel, past the Kumanokōtai Shrine."

"How do you know about it?" Emi asked skeptically.

"I worked there once," she said defensively.

"In what capacity?"

"What's it matter to you?" She paused and looked at Emi. "Give me those shoes, too. The heeled ones."

"They won't fit you. I'm half a meter taller than you," said Emi, not stepping out of them.

"I don't care," said the girl. "You have the other ugly pair in that bag. I saw you when you came in."

Emi looked at the girl's feet, pressed into a pair of worn heels, the shoe leather nearly porous, and gave them to her.

"You telling me about a farm is worth all this?" she asked, slipping on her pants and coat over her silk slip.

"They have food," she said shrugging. "That officer seems to like you. Maybe he will let you eat some. You need it. You look like a twig."

"You're not fat yourself," said Emi.

"Which is why I've been to the farm." She slipped out of the bathroom door, leaving Emi to collect herself before she left.

When Emi opened the door a few minutes later, Drexel was standing next to it.

"This is what you want, yes?" He didn't ask about the kitchen girl, instead handing her a heavy paper bag. Already, the bottom was soaked in oil from the food.

"Yes," said Emi, reaching out for it.

"I will look for you in town," said Drexel. "You'll play for me at the hotel when I'm there. Whatever song I want."

"Of course," said Emi, "if I know it."

When she left she didn't thank him, instead opening the door quickly and leaving him to close it behind her. She stood on the porch and let the cold air, colder than even a winter in Vienna, spiral into her lungs. She was surprised and she didn't know what to do with her surprise. The men at the party, other than Drexel when she'd arrived, had not acted like beasts. It was almost worse, she thought, to see traces of their humanity married with the barbarity of their uniforms.

Emi got onto her bicycle, the seat wet with snow and rain, and started to pedal away from the house. She had only gone a few yards when she heard her name, and then saw Claire, stepping out from the woods behind the house.

Emi nearly fell, the bicycle tipping, the food managing to stay in the basket.

"Did you get any food?" asked Claire, rushing over to her.

"You scared me," said Emi, trying to steady herself. "I did and I would have brought you some tomorrow. How long have you been hiding?"

"Tonight it will taste so much better than tomorrow," said Claire, eyeing the bag.

Emi started to untie it, as Claire asked her about the party. Consumed in what they were doing, they did not hear the footsteps until the people were next to them. Emi looked up and saw the pretty German woman who had opened the door standing next to her, one arm linked with a member of the Kempeitai.

The woman smiled at Emi and then knocked the bag of food to the ground with her gloved hand. "No English," she declared as her Kempeitai escort laughed.

"No English," he repeated, stepping on the large loaf of bread that had rolled out. He looked at the ham, too, which had also fallen out, but it was already submerged in a puddle.

Emi and Claire stood still, watching the two walk to their car, parked by the side of the road, and didn't move until they had driven off.

"Quick!" yelled Claire, pouncing on the bag. "Get that ham out of the water. We can rinse it off." Emi got on her knees and reached for it as Claire pulled the flattened bread up, trying to pull dirt and twigs off it.

"Take half of this," said Emi, ripping the chunk of the wet ham apart with her hands, wishing Claire had just waited until the following day.

"Do you know where the Germans get all this food?" she asked, watching her wrap it in a paper sack that she had brought.

"They make most of it," said Claire, tying the bag closed. "They have their own farm, north of the Mampei Hotel. And unlike everyone else in the prefecture, they have healthy animals — pigs, cows, chickens, goats — vegetables and grain."

"You know about the farm?" asked Emi, caught unaware.

"Of course," said Claire, holding the bread

up to her nose and inhaling deeply. "A lot of people do."

"Of course," said Emi, regretting how vulnerable she had been just moments before.

"Don't tell the Moris that the food fell in the mud," said Claire, taking a large bite out of the bread, despite its layer of filth.

Emi nodded and pushed her bike up the hill away from Claire. She was sure that it was the start of her telling the Moris very little.

CHAPTER 27

Leo Hartmann
January–April 1944

Leo's green eyes did not open for thirty days. The Chinese doctors at the mission hospital, where Agatha had taken him in a rickshaw, his near-lifeless body bouncing on the wooden seat like a corpse, said that his left lung had collapsed and that his right eye had been so badly damaged that he'd probably lost his vision on that side. It was also possible, they warned her, that he might never wake up.

Agatha — wearing a white doctor's coat given to her by one of the religious nurses who had nearly fainted when she'd seen her exposed cleavage — cried for hours over Leo's broken body the first night. She was scared of everything, she told the medical staff, who came into the bleak room constantly — the hospital, the darkness outside, Leo's slack, torpid face.

She'd last been in that particular hospital when her mother died in 1933, she'd explained, hysteria finding her once again.

"From what?" a doctor asked gently.

"From misery!" she had shouted. "From this awful city!"

When she started screaming as blood began leaking out of Leo's nose like a harbinger of death, the same nurse who had ensured Agatha's ample assets were covered gave her a pill to make her sleep, which she did, on the floor beside Leo until noon the following day.

It was not until eighteen hours after the assault by Pohl's hand that Hani and Max were notified by Agatha — still in her revealing dress and doctor's coat, makeup smeared across her face like watercolor — that their only son was in the hospital on Zhizaoju Road, barely holding on to life. The grief-stricken Hartmanns stayed by Leo's side as much as possible, but because their money in Vienna was still frozen, or had disappeared, they had no choice but to depart for their jobs every day. And when they left, Agatha discreetly appeared.

It was on the thirtieth day in his hospital bed that Leo finally opened his one good eye. He tried to move up in bed, to lift his hands to his face, but his body felt shattered, no longer one continuous line of oxygen and carbon, but thousands of pieces held precariously together by bandages and gauze.

"Agatha," he said, but no sound came out of his mouth.

He stayed still, closing his eye again for several minutes. When he opened it, he saw a nurse was in his room, and deciphered that he was in a hospital.

"You are in the Bethel Hospital," she said to him, her face full of relief. "Can you see me?"

"Yes," Leo whispered when she removed a tube from his mouth, this time hearing his weak voice.

"Good. You've given us quite a scare, especially with your eyes," she said, coming closer to him. "You've been here a month, you know." She put her small hand on his bandaged one. "Your friend, she is still here watching over you," the kindly nurse said motioning to the hallway, but Leo couldn't turn his head to follow. "She is a German, but her Chinese is very good. She can even scream in our language."

"What happened to my other eye?" said Leo, when the nurse started to inspect his face again. He was sure she meant Agatha, but feeling so much physical pain, and so suddenly, he could only think of himself.

"We'll have to find out," she replied. "Right now it's bandaged. I'll call in a doctor who can take the dressing off. Perhaps."

The senior doctor tending to Leo did take off his bandages, wanting to run a series of tests to see if Leo had any vision left on his right side.

"May I have a mirror?" Leo asked him when his face was uncovered.

"First tell me if you can see anything at all," said the Chinese doctor, Dr. Zhou, in accented British English. "Open your eye, very slowly."

"Is it open?" Leo asked, skeptically, feeling as if his skin was breaking apart.

"It is," the doctor said, leaning in and looking closely. "Can you see anything?"

"Nothing," said Leo, his throat constricting over the word. "Some dim gray light."

"And the other eye?" asked the doctor, with a strong headlight focused on Leo's face.

"I can see . . . my left eye seems fine." Leo moved his hand up slowly, only making it to his neck, but the doctor stopped him.

"We've been without you for a month. Don't try to stretch too much, not just yet. Take it very easy but let's not give up hope yet about your right eye," he said. "Your vision may get better over time. The rest of you certainly will. But, to be very honest," he said, motioning to Leo's face, "it isn't very pretty to look at now. And then we must talk about your worst-case scenario, which is that your sight may be compromised."

"Blind," said Leo, the word sticking dryly in his throat.

"Yes, you may be blind in your right eye for the rest of your life," said Dr. Zhou. "But luckily we have two eyes, and you will learn to see with just one."

"Could I see my face now?" asked Leo, not feeling like he could believe what the doctor said until he saw his reflection. Dr. Zhou first ran a series of tests, but when he deemed Leo strong enough, he had a nurse bring a mirror.

"Why should it be today?" she asked him, holding the mirror behind her back. "You just woke up. Maybe tomorrow is the better day."

"Today is the right day," said Leo, motioning to her. She positioned the glass for him and looked away as he looked into it.

He wanted to ask her if it was really him, but of course it was. His other eye was still green as springtime, but the rest of his face was unrecognizable. His cheeks were thicker from the bruising, he had a long scab on the side of his mouth, crusted as thick as pie, and a stitched-up wound along his jaw-line, the black thread looking like it could barely keep his skin together. Leo turned his head slightly and saw that his right ear was bent and the skin just below his neck was covered in fading bruises. Leo had been told about his lung, but he was sure that even without the collapse, he wouldn't be able to breathe at the sight of himself.

"It will all heal," said the nurse, trying to comfort him. "Your face, your body. Dr. Zhou says that your eyesight could improve, and even if it doesn't, at least it's still in its socket, where it should be. You must focus on the fact that you are alive. We were very worried that there was irreparable brain trauma and that you'd never wake up."

Leo nodded, trying to be thankful for the outcome. "I hit a German SS officer," he said, still looking at his eye, which refused to look back at him. "Unfortunately, he hit me harder."

"Next time," said the Chinese nurse, "hit a Japanese."

For the first two weeks after he was dismissed from the hospital, Hani didn't allow anyone in the apartment other than Max and the medical staff. Liwei had given them money to have a nurse help during the day, but he'd also relayed the fact that Agatha was desperate to care for Leo.

"I don't think so," Hani had said firmly, assuring Agatha that she would be able to see Leo again in time. And she was, when Leo prevailed on his mother that it could be no other way.

"She is the reason that this happened to you," said Hani, crying in their apartment on a February morning. "That my beautiful Froschi is . . . is what? Blind?"

"I'm not blind," said Leo, comforting his mother, who still looked so out of place in her cheap dresses, pacing the cramped, frigid apartment. "I'm partially blind." Though he was as anxious as his mother was about his state, he tried not to show his unease to his rattled parents, and tried to focus on healing and placating them.

"That's still blind," said Hani, leaning her head on his shoulder and holding him as if he might float away. "I hate the way your eye just sits there still, like a marble. Oh Froschi," she said, starting to cry, a daily activity for her since Leo was injured. "All this way and then you are attacked by an SS officer. Here. In China!"

"For the last time," said Leo, sitting up

slowly, his ribs still feeling bent backward, "I attacked him. Felix Pohl. I left Liwei's on my own accord and chased him and Agatha through the streets. She is not to blame; she even tried to stop me. But I wanted to hit him, so desperately. From the moment I saw him in Liwei's, his hands on Agatha, wearing *that* uniform in *this* city, something just took off in me. I was not going to let the night turn to day without attacking Pohl. It was something bigger than being rational or irrational; it was me finally doing something about what happened in Vienna."

"But why?" asked Hani incredulously. "We fled Vienna, only for you to chase after danger here?"

"Aren't you hearing me?" asked Leo, starting to wheeze.

The Hartmanns had urgently wanted to take Leo somewhere other than their apartment to convalesce in, as winter had only exacerbated their leaking ceiling with mold. Their neighborhood was so crowded that there seemed to be residents falling out the windows.

"I hit him for you, for me, for our abducted factory manager, for what they did to Father in Vienna, for what they are doing to our relatives, our friends. That is why I attacked him. It wasn't just for Agatha."

"Oh, Leo. I didn't raise a foolish boy, a brute carrying the weight of the world on his shoulders. We don't even know what they are doing in Europe," said Hani, frustrated. "We are so isolated from the news here."

"The Nazis? Come, Mother," said Leo, motioning for her to sit with him. "We have a pretty good idea, don't we?" He knew Hani read the *Shanghai Jewish Chronicle,* which was printed in German and distributed to the community.

"I still blame the girl," said Hani, her arms around her son again.

"You must stop," said Leo, peeling her away from his torso. "Pohl would not have hit me if I hadn't followed them. I'm to blame, only me. Don't you understand, after all our years away from Vienna? I had to win at something. Just one thing."

"Is this how you won?" she asked, looking like she didn't know what to do with her arms if they weren't around Leo. "By going blind?"

"I'm alive, am I not?" he said, exhaustion starting to get the better of him. "I wouldn't be if I had done the same thing in Austria."

"No, you would not be," said Hani sighing. She threw her hands up in frustration and turned to leave for her piano lessons but stopped at the door.

"I only say this for you, Leo," she said, pausing.

"Say what?" he replied.

"Agatha can start taking care of you instead of Meifen," she said of the nurse who had been tending to Leo during the day. "We've accepted enough of Liwei's money."

With Hani's reluctant permission, the days went from Leo being fussed over by a caring nurse, to Leo being warmly embraced — flesh-to-flesh when he had grown strong enough — by Agatha Huber.

The return of his health — and of his lust for Agatha, finally played out on his makeshift bed — moved in with the spring. Shanghai was coming alive again, with the death toll from the cold and starvation beginning to decline. News of the Red Army pushing the Germans out of Crimea was bringing a ray of hope to the Jewish residents of Shanghai.

Leo and Agatha, who themselves were restricted to making love during daylight hours, spoke of the war, but more often, spoke of each other, and eventually, of them together.

"The night you first came to work at Liwei's, I thought you were the funniest thing," said Agatha. It was the first hot day of April and she was stretching her bare legs out in the apartment that she'd become a fixture in. As Leo's bruises had gone from blue to yellow, and his eye had stopped aching, Agatha's guilt — which Leo assured her was misplaced — started to wane. Joy, and an appreciation of their time together, firmly took root. "I remember the expression on your face," she continued, "like a ten-year-old boy who had no idea that such things went on. The dancing, the sex. Liwei and Jin were oblivious to your shock, but we, all the girls, noticed. It was a welcome change," she said, smiling and showing off her pretty teeth. "Innocence and Shanghai seldom go together."

"I didn't look that surprised, did I?" said Leo. He wanted to blurt out that he had lost his innocence long ago, many times over with Emi, but compared to the men Agatha was used to, he was exceptionally green.

"You definitely did," said Agatha laughing, her body wrapped in Leo's worn-out bedsheet and nothing else. "The girls all used to call you *luchik*. It means sunbeam in Russian — but we say it to mean sweetheart, or baby."

"I'm offended," said Leo, laughing. He grasped for his chest, which was still strained by sudden movements.

"Don't, *luchik,*" said Agatha, trying to get him to lie down. "Your poor lungs."

"You're making me laugh," said Leo, taking her arm and pulling her next to him. "But I bet that SS officer never laughs again. Not after being punched by a Jew and losing you."

"He never had me," said Agatha, reaching for Leo's bare torso, as thin as it was during his first year in Shanghai. "Not in that way."

"But in the other way," said Leo jealously.

"Yes, in this way," she said, touching his body. "You've known that since the day Pohl walked in. Jin told you. He's a bigger gossip than any of the girls at Liwei's."

"Is he?" asked Leo, who never noticed any of Jin's faults. "He told me because he knew how much I would care."

"Because you're Jewish?" Agatha asked, her hand moving to Leo's face. "And Pohl . . . is not," she added.

"Is not!" said Leo, pulling away from her. "Felix Pohl is an SS officer. That makes him not only *not* Jewish, but actively trying to eradicate an entire race of people."

"He never spoke about it to me," said Agatha, apologizing. "I left Germany many years ago. I was a child. I didn't pay attention to any of the political talk."

527

"And you don't pay attention to it now, either?" asked Leo, surprised by Agatha's ignorance.

"A little bit," she said. "Of course. But I don't care that you're a Jew. I care that you are being persecuted, that you had to leave Austria, but your religion doesn't bother me. I haven't believed in God in a very long time. It makes my job easier."

"I doubt your job is ever easy," said Leo, trying to understand what it would be like to be so far removed from Nazi Germany. Agatha had spent most of her life in China. Perhaps that's why she went so easily with Pohl, he mused. Or perhaps it was just different if you weren't a Jew.

"What I do at Liwei's — and after — it's shameful. I know it is," said Agatha quietly. "But it pays, and I've been on my own for eleven years now. I've told you before — I first came to Shanghai when I was ten years old, after my father died. My mother followed a British missionary here. It was a terrible idea, but she was a woman who was always enticed by terrible ideas. When she died in '33, and I was a teenager alone in Shanghai, I lived with the help of the church for a few years, but they could only do so much."

"So, Liwei," said Leo, who understood

well the choices for women like Agatha in their city.

She nodded and he watched her rub the edge of the dirty sheet with her painted fingernails, like a security blanket. "I never went to high school. Instead I just learned English working in the church that the British ran. As for Chinese, I guess I learned that in the street. Speaking both languages helped me at Liwei's, far more than a high school diploma would have."

"Shanghai is an education in itself," said Leo.

"To say the least." Agatha closed her eyes and put her hand over Leo's bad one, as had become a habit for her. "I turned twenty-five this year, but this city makes you feel much older."

Perhaps a romance of some sort was inevitable, thought Leo, his fingers running down Agatha's bare leg. He hadn't been with another woman since Emi and night after night Agatha had been there, right in front of him, in her low-cut dresses, embodying male desire. But in the privacy of the Hartmanns' dark, charmless apartment, without her hair done or her lips painted, Leo liked her even more. He liked the control she had on her life, how hardship of any kind didn't seem to diminish her. By

April, he realized, she had become a whole person for him — and, he hoped, he had become more than the boy who ran after her.

"I have to go to work," Agatha said sadly, standing up and putting on her clothes.

"Don't dance with anyone," Leo protested, propping himself up on his elbows to watch her. His field of vision was cut off, but no one needed two eyes to see how beautiful Agatha was in a state of undress.

"I could lie and tell you I won't, but what choice do I have?" said Agatha, stepping into her pants.

"None," said Leo, remembering Jin's words to not judge Agatha too harshly. "But I have to say it."

"Fine. Let's pretend that I won't," she said, bending to kiss his forehead. "And in two weeks, you'll be back," she added, as Leo had announced that he would return to Liwei's on the first day of May.

Agatha walked to the door and turned to look at Leo one more time before she left. She leaned her head against the door frame, nicked and worm eaten, and said, "*Luchik,* do you think I'm in love with you?"

Leo sat up quickly, his head light, and asked, "Should I think that?"

"I think you should," Agatha replied, pulling the door closed behind her.

CHAPTER 28

Christian Lange
January–February 1944

Christian moved his feet through the mire, weighed down by anxiety and illness. His lungs felt blackened and his skin irritated and burning, his thick Army uniform abrasive in the heat. But somehow, he was walking fast, low branches full of long thorns tearing at his arms as he protected his face.

In training in Texas and Hawaii, his commanders had said that combat skills would all become second nature. That a soldier's instincts to kill or be killed was honed in the Army training grounds. "You'll learn everything you need to know during your training," Christian's sergeant had said. "It will all become mechanical. Then, when you are fighting on the ground against the enemy, your adrenaline will just push go and you'll find yourself brawling like the devil."

But as far as Christian was concerned, those assurances failed to address two problems: he had no real desire to kill anyone, for freedom or country, and he was in love with Emi Kato, an enemy citizen.

The Seventh Infantry Division had gone through amphibious assault training on Maui for weeks and then been assigned to V Amphibious Corps under the Marines. Christian had gone to Maui only near the end of the training, and Jack Walter even later. But at the end of January, because of the size of the force needed for an offensive on Japanese territory, the two found themselves on one of the massive ships heading deep into the Pacific toward Kwajalein Atoll for the U.S. military's long-planned Operation Flintlock.

The soldiers spent eight days on the boat, the ship moving swiftly into the South Pacific. The enlisted men were made to go over their operation with their superiors, from beginning to end, day after day, making sure they were as prepared as could be. Sitting on that boat, smoking and cursing with the others, Christian was ready. He wasn't exactly what the Army wanted, but he felt he could do his job and survive. Even Jack had slapped him on the back — then, as was more his style, on the side of the head — and said, "You're tough enough to do this, kraut — believe!"

But what he was about to engage in had not become clear to Christian until they reached Carlson Island, one of the smaller islands in the Kwajalein Atoll, part of the Pacific's Marshall Islands under Japanese rule.

The landing went smoothly, but as soon as Christian's boots were in the water, then on land on Carlson — the humid, soggy, foreign land — he knew something was wrong. He wasn't driven by anger and adrenaline, as the boys around him seemed to be, but instead with a terrible sense of wrong-doing.

With his feet on enemy territory, the reality of war hit him like a fist to the jaw. He'd been dropped into the wrong place and given the wrong job — worse, it was one he'd willingly signed up for.

As the soldiers ahead of him gunned down the few enemy troops they came upon, Christian and his unit were tasked with hauling ammunition and weapons onto land. Setting out to cross the island in the dark, Christian tried to keep his eyes and his thoughts fixed on the man ahead of him, but all he could think was that he should have gone to Germany. He shouldn't have been so quick to abandon his family. "I might have died, but I wouldn't have had to kill anyone else," he said to Jack as he carried artillery across the wet soil. "Now I'll die here, with blood on my hands. Why did I think I could do this?"

"Shut up with the introspective crap," said Jack, grunting under the weight of the machinery he was shouldering. "You'd better shoot any bastard who is about to shoot me, kraut. If you can't be trusted, I'm leaving you to be speared by the Japanese. You like them so much now, but I bet you'll sing a different tune when you're in their POW camps. You'll see what mean bastards they can be."

"Most of the Japanese I met were American citizens," Christian pointed out, but of course, Emi wasn't.

"Listen. Stop overthinking things and just shoot them," Jack said, his gun strapped to him, ready to do just that at all times. "Forget about souls and mothers and fathers and all those details and just fire away. If you don't, you're not going to leave here alive, and because I feel some strange kinship to you after being your babysitter in Wisconsin, I probably won't, either."

"And I won't, either," said Dave, who still hadn't shaken off his nickname. "Because none of these assholes will try to save a pacifist. My best shot is the both of you."

"It is pretty funny," said Jack, trying to step on the Dove's foot, which was tapping like a heartbeat. "How'd they let you in here anyway?"

"It's called a draft," said Dave. "Just shoot someone if they're trying to shoot me, Lange," he said, looking at Christian. "You know Jack won't."

Jack started to argue, but then he said, "You're right. I need to cover someone who'll actually cover me back. Kraut, you'll have to save the Dove. Though it's not very pacifist to ask someone to take someone else's life just to save yours," Jack scolded.

Christian hoped that he would be able to. That he'd be fearless enough to pull the trigger, if it came to that. When he'd been training in Texas, he hadn't doubted his ability to fire at the enemy. They weren't Emi. They were men trained to kill. But now, with bullets in his gun meant for someone else's temple, he wasn't so sure of himself.

On Carlson Island, they were tasked, like most of the unit's other grunts, with setting up the artillery they had just carried. A February 1 assault on the larger Kwajalein Island was about to begin. When Carlson looked as if it had enough explosive power to take out the entire island chains all the way to Japan, they retired to their assigned camp, swarms of mosquitoes feasting on them as they waited for their orders to begin.

In their section, Dave had set up a wooden cross, little more than two sticks held together with a paper tie. Because he was sure it was the right thing to do when one's life was on shaky ground, Christian knelt in front of it next to Dave and clasped his hands. He prayed for himself and for his parents and Inge at the camp. His mother had written to say that they were being repatriated to Germany in February along with Inge and her family. She sounded relieved that they were finally leaving Crystal City, and wrote that if they didn't survive the voyage, she forgave Christian for enlisting. She confessed that she was scared of the boat ride and that she didn't want to die angry at her only child. Christian had quickly written back saying that of course she wouldn't die and that he was sorry and would see her very soon. But he was much sorrier now, praying in the middle of the Pacific, that he'd made the decision he did.

Seeing that Dave still had his eyes tight shut, Christian also prayed for Emi's safety in Tokyo, and that one of the letters he had sent would reach her somehow and compel her to write back. And because the Dove looked like he was going to utter devotions all night, Christian threw Jack and Kurt from Crystal City into his prayers, too.

Jack came up to them after a few minutes and said, "Just about everyone in the world is praying for someone to stay alive. You can't expect your prayers to be answered first, gentlemen. And with the look of that crappy cross, they'll probably be answered last. If I were God, I'd be offended by that craftsmanship." He bent down and broke off part of it, carving a toothpick from the wood.

"I can pray for as many unrealistic outcomes as I want," said Christian, leaning back on his boot heels. "You have to be blindly optimistic during war, right, Dave? If not, every enlisted man would end up deserting. If you let the fear and pessimism win, you're not going to stick around to see if a bullet gets you or not."

Dave nodded.

"Good, because I already feel extremely pessimistic. I need some sort of divine intervention."

"What you need is some fight in you,

River Hills," said Jack. "You're too emotional."

"Kneel down and pray," Dave said to Jack, moving over for him.

Jack shook his head and kicked the cross over with finality. "I did enough praying for my parents after they disappeared, and they never came back, did they? They died instead. Haven't bothered praying since."

They all slept badly that night and by the time the sun was visible in the sky, the Seventh was already on the move toward Kwajalein.

"How many Japs are gonna be on this thing?" Christian heard one of the soldiers in their unit ask Dave on the boat.

"I don't know," Dave said, so nervous he had his head between his legs. "But it only takes one to kill you."

"Shut your mouths!" their sergeant yelled. "There's a huge air and Navy fleet to back up your asses. Look around you! We heavily outnumber the Japs. They should be the ones crying, not you. But they'll fight till they die — remember that. And Simon, if you throw up on this boat, I will tie a rock to your foot and tip you overboard!"

The men knew that American air and naval bombardments had targeted the island chain for the last two months, but the

Seventh would put the first Allied boots on the ground.

"Are you ready for this?" Dave asked Christian, his head still on his knee.

"Absolutely not," said Christian, as stoic as Dave was panicked. "But we have no choice. We have to jump into the fire."

"That's right," said Jack gleefully. "I was meant for fire." He looked down at Christian and said, "Chin up, River Hills. It's just life or death. Yours or theirs. Why be so serious?"

"Silly of me," said Christian, feeling a lot more like Dave Simon than Jack.

"Hey, you know what I never told you about?" said Jack, suddenly smiling. "Calling you by your formal name, River Hills, reminded me."

"What's that?" asked Christian, trying to look at the horizon line to steady himself.

"I went to your house. I went to River Hills, kraut!"

Christian looked back at Jack. "Really?"

Jack gave him a brilliant smile and said, "What a house, kraut. You're a lucky bastard. Even if you get your brains shot out here, today, you're still luckier than I'll ever be."

"I know," said Christian, who hadn't felt lucky since Emi left him. "So what happened to the house? Did you get inside?"

"I didn't get very far," Jack admitted. "I was going to dress up all in black and sneak in a window, but before I did, I saw that there was someone living there."

"What? Who?" said Christian, sitting up.

"The one you said would be there," said Jack. "The one who reported your dad. Martin something."

"Martin Macht. I knew it," said Christian, too nervous to be angry. "Did you speak to him?"

Jack took a long drink of his water and said, "Only a bit. I knocked on the door and he opened it. I asked if you were there, which must have thrown him off, because that's when he told me who he was." Jack dropped his gun in Christian's lap and said. "So if you're wondering if that's who fucked you, that's who fucked you."

"You didn't call the police? Write to me?" he asked.

"Nah," said Jack smiling. "I was about to ship out and see you. Thought it would be more fun to tell you myself."

"But you didn't," said Christian. "Tell me."

"That's right. I didn't. Know why? Because there isn't shit you or your parents can do about it. You're about to die in the

Pacific," said Jack, waving his hand at their surroundings, "and your parents are in an internment camp. So I said to myself, why bother the krauts?"

"You're right," said Christian, taking Jack's canteen and pouring the water over his head. "I sure as shit am going to die here."

Just before eleven in the morning, they had Kwajalein's shore in sight and were ready to run up the sand. Christian and the other troops looked out at the black smoke billowing up from the already heavily bombed island and after the order from their sergeant, let out a collective yell.

"It's fucking doomsday!" Jack screamed as they jumped from the boat.

Christian let out his breath, holding his rifle in front of him, and prayed one last time, hoping that somehow his parents, or some higher power, could hear him. Then he jumped into the ocean behind Jack. Between the warm, translucent water and the white sand beaches, the Kwajalein Atoll looked like a brochure for a vacation, not a place for young men to die.

Behind them, American battleships and destroyers were bobbing in the water, and above them, shells were screaming in from the artillery they had set up on Carlson

Island the night before. Just a year ago, Christian had been asleep in his pajamas, his parents mere feet away, all comfortably swaddled in happiness and comfort. Now he was walking into gunfire. How could his world have turned on him so quickly?

Jack led Christian and Dave up the beach and into the trees, moving steadily until they heard the gunfire from a Japanese sniper. Christian instinctively pulled Dave down with him into the brush, but Jack was still standing twenty yards ahead of them. Finally, after another round of gunfire erupted, they saw Jack throw himself on the ground and crawl into the brush below the palm trees, their tops seared from the ammunition being dropped by the planes.

The pungent smells of gun shells and burned flesh were knit into the jungle heat, choking the three men as they continued to inch forward with their unit. Christian flinched as a light tank from the Seventh rolled past them, clearing the ground ahead, and Jack hissed at him to stop acting like an abused dog.

Several hundred feet on, they knelt down in foxholes and took turns manning the mortar at that position. When Christian was told to run from his foxhole to one farther on, he stared blankly at his ranking officer,

Sergeant Perko.

"We've got forty-eight howitzers set up on Carlson, remember, Lange? You have so much cover you might as well be wearing armor!" he shouted. "Now move your ass. We need to move thousands of yards north, not five." Christian took off, and spent the rest of the day keeping up that pace, as he was tasked with clearing the brush for the other men. It was a job for a disposable soldier, one who wasn't particularly brave or a good shot, but Christian was glad to have it, especially since he was nowhere ready to fire his gun. He thought of John Sasaki at the camp telling him to enlist. Did he see in Christian the same bravery that his son in the 442nd had? Christian doubted it. It was a recommendation based on love, more than war. Love, it turned out, he was far better at.

Their first day on Kwajalein, the Americans only lost seventeen men, but while they slept under their tarps that night, the Seventh was blindsided by a late Japanese offensive.

The relentless enemy fire continued into morning, and as soon as the sky was streaked with blue, Christian was back in a foxhole, with new orders. No more ripping out bushes on hands and knees; today he would be shooting at Japanese soldiers.

For the first hour, it was nothing but the sound of the jungle coupled with the thrum of his own heartbeat and whispers from Jack about the afterlife. "You'll be fine if you die, kraut," he assured Christian. "You're used to something as boring as heaven. You're from the suburbs."

Perko kicked Jack in the knee and they all stayed quiet until they heard movement in the brush.

On signal, Christian rested his elbows on the dirt and tried to get his trigger finger to stop shaking. He held it in his mouth and listened as Perko hissed, "Lange. Pull your fucking trigger. Right now, Lange." When they both saw that the Japanese soldiers were no longer just sounds, but men in front of them, he screamed, "Shoot!" and Christian stared ahead, still unable to pull.

For the first time, he saw enemy faces. They were distant, but he saw bodies, eyes, skin. He saw men. He looked at them advancing toward them and his hands remained still. Dave was right. When it came down to it, everyone was the same, just blood vessels and heart. All of a sudden, every one of the Japanese men in their drab khaki uniforms felt like him. He shot a desperate glance at Jack, who was reloading his gun, having already fired dozens of rounds.

"Shoot, kraut!" he heard Jack's voice shouting. "You're going to get us killed. Shoot!"

Christian turned back to look at the Japanese soldiers and curled his finger around the trigger. He felt the metal against his sweaty skin and thought about all the rounds he had fired in training. Those rounds, despite his sergeant's assurances, had not prepared him enough. His mind was in a fog, and the buzz of his panic drowned out even Jack's urgent voice. Finally, he closed his eyes for a split second and pulled.

At first, he only fired straight ahead, aiming at random. But then he spotted a Japanese soldier exposed behind a grove of trees, running toward them, and he fired directly at him. As soon as he pulled, his body tensed and Christian was sure he could see the bullet fly from his gun straight into the man's heart. He dropped his gun and looked out as the man fell to the ground. He started to stand up, instinctually wanting to run to him, but a hand shoved him roughly down.

"Lange? What in hell are you doing? Get down! You're going to get killed!" This time it was Dave who was screaming at him.

He'd killed a man. He felt that for the rest of his life, everything would coil around that moment — before he'd stopped someone's heartbeat, and after. Could you really fight for the Americans? Emi had asked. No, it turned out. He could barely fight at all.

That night, after they had advanced halfway across the island and taken hundreds of enemy lives, Sergeant Perko sat down near Christian and grabbed one of Jack's hand-rolled cigarettes.

"Finally! Dead Japs," he said. "I've been waiting a lifetime for today." Perko pretended his hands were a gun and emptied an imaginary round into Christian's face.

"What's wrong with you, Lange?" he said as Christian grabbed his hand and pushed it down. "You got at least one kill. I saw that bastard go down. Let's celebrate. Tomorrow we do it again," he said, handing him a canteen. "Have some water. Pretend it's beer."

"I'm going to sleep," said Christian, standing up and heading to his soggy sleeping bag, feeling that sleep would never come easily to him again.

As he lay awake, the only man in his tent, he pictured the Japanese soldier's face. He could see it perfectly — young and terrified.

Did he think about his parents before he'd died? About a girl? Or had he just prayed that Christian might miss? Did he feel any pain when the bullet entered his body? Christian started sweating under his regulation blanket and kicked it off. Trying to calm down, he reached inside his bag for his paper and wrote a letter to Inge, as he'd done many times since leaving Crystal City.

"Tell me only good things, little kraut," he wrote. "I am feeling unwell." He folded the letter, put it in an envelope, and addressed it to Texas. He didn't know when he'd be able to send it, or if it would make it before the ship left for Germany, but it made him feel better to have written her name. Somewhere in the world, he told himself, there were children, alive and well.

He slid his left wrist under his pillow to hide the time and tried again to fall asleep. He wondered about Inge, about his parents, and where Emi was at that moment. Maybe she was working as a nurse for the Japanese after her training in Crystal City. He pictured her in a white uniform, like the one she wore in Texas, easing the suffering of others, just as she had done for him. But that made him jealous, the idea of her tending to wounded young men. Or maybe she was taking shelter from American bombardment, hiding in a basement with her mother. He hoped she had somewhere safe to go, where American bombs dropped by men like him couldn't touch her. He hoped Emi thought about him, too. Just sometimes. He hoped she missed him and, despite what she was living through, that she was happy. He put his arms under his head, looked up at the peak of his tent, and lay awake for the rest of the night.

CHAPTER 29

Emi Kato
February–March 1944

It was at the end of February, when Karuizawa was enveloped in a bitter cold — negative 15 degrees Celsius in the hills near Mount Asama — that Emi began to notice that Jiro Mori's already fragile health was declining rapidly.

In the late afternoon, leading into dinner, Emi often sat with him in the small wood-paneled kitchen and they spoke about the war and the world. The world before the war was what Emi preferred to discuss, but inevitably, they would move on to the present war. She was intrigued by Jiro's unwavering affection for America, a sentiment she had never quite developed.

"The Americans didn't have such hate for us in the 1920s; there was intrigue, perhaps on par with what you experienced in your beloved Vienna," Jiro explained on a particularly cold afternoon in early March. Though his body was frail, and his clothes closer to blankets than garments, he still had an elegance about him — a head of thick gray hair, expensive metal eyeglasses, and a refined way of speaking — that reminded Emi of the men currently in the diplomatic corps. "This country was devastated by the Kanto earthquake when I was there. But America — it was a country on fire," he said, his limbs crossed for warmth. "Everyone was still rejoicing the end of the Great War and there was a film of happiness over everything. The Roaring Twenties they called it. And I loved driving those great big American cars. I found an illegal track south of Washington and would race the Italian embassy staff on Sundays — and beat them flat." He and Emi were sitting in the kitchen, enjoying the coal in the iron stove that they had received in their monthly ration, but they only dared burn it by the handful.

"That sounds better than Catholic school and a series of internment camps," said Emi.

They listened to the rhythmic tap of a Japanese green woodpecker that hovered around the Moris' trees while eating their meager dinners as slowly as possible. Yuka Mori had forgone dinner, instead going into town with a neighbor to see if she couldn't barter carrots for meat, a very unlikely prospect unless someone took pity on her. The Moris had just run out of the ham that Emi had brought from the German party — rationed to just a few bites a day — and it had whet a craving for sustenance that they were all trying to extinguish.

"I don't know how you can say nice things about America now," said Emi. "Now that they're attacking us."

"I don't know that I'm saying nice things. I think I'm just expressing fond memories. A country can change. This country certainly has, don't you think?" asked Jiro, coughing into his hand, unable to get the food down very easily.

"I suppose," said Emi, offering Jiro water and taking a small bite of brown rice with an unidentifiable dried river fish cut on top. She had learned to eat slowly, to put fewer than ten grains of rice on her chopsticks and in her mouth at a time, all to make her food last. Perhaps it was having the rich German food and then going back to scraps, but Emi had started to feel real, painful hunger for the first time that month.

She had thought often about what Chiyo and Naoko Kuriyama had said to her on the boat to Japan. That the Katos' money, their position, would make no difference in a country at war. In many ways they were right. Emi still wasn't receiving mail from either Christian or Leo, and from what Claire Ohkawa had told her, they were likely not receiving her attempts at communication, either. When she mentioned that her father had been able to write to her in Texas, she suggested Emi send her letters from the foreign ministry in Tokyo, or through an embassy, where they'd have a better chance of making it onto foreign shores. Not wanting her father to read her letters, or know a thing about Christian, Emi instead asked Evgeni's friend at the Soviet Embassy, housed in the Mampei Hotel, to help. Two letters were mailed to Christian and Leo, both devoid of any sentiment or words of war, but still, after almost two months, she had no response. That silence was as physically painful to her as a lack of food.

She reached down for another bite of fish and checked to make sure that Jiro was finishing his meal. He had been complaining about sharp stomach pains and she was worried that they might prevent him from eating even their scant portions.

"Japan has changed dramatically," said Jiro, who still had fish on his plate. "I will speak frankly with you because Yuka is out of the house and your father told me that he always tells you the truth." He put down his bowl of rice, his hands unsteady, and said, "Japan is going to lose this war. I'm sure of it, your father is sure, and I think the leaders of the Japanese Navy are, too. It's just the Imperial Army that keeps the propaganda machine running. They were the ones so desperate to enter the war and now they refuse to end it."

"Lose the war?" Emi said, shocked that Jiro would dare voice such an opinion.

Her pulse picked up. Her country, the country she was in, was going to lose the war. What would it take for that to occur? How much devastation? And what would happen after? "But why can't rational men — men like you — use their influence?" asked Emi. She suddenly felt like her nervous system was under attack, her body begging her to escape her dire circumstances. She knew her father had his doubts about the war but it was the first time she had ever heard anyone declare so assuredly that Japan would lose. Emi always thought that despite it being a terrible conflict, and her disagreeing wholeheartedly with her country's alliance with Nazi Germany, that somehow Japan would prevail. Because that was what Japan taught her to believe.

"Not this time," said Jiro, asking Emi to

put another three briquettes of coal in the fire. "Any government or military man who has spent significant time in America knows that we shouldn't have entered to begin with. But now that we have both feet in the conflict, both feet are going to be shot off."

"My father is frank with me," said Emi, the conversation and her hunger unsettling her greatly. "But never like this."

"I apologize," said Jiro. "Perhaps it's my age, that I have been out of the service for so long, or that I am just very frustrated with Japan. The way they are forcing the citizens to be grateful that we are at war, convincing them that they should give their lives, their sons' lives — it's an indoctrination from the highest level. The newspapers only report on battles won, never lost, and we are all expected to believe them."

"But like you said," Emi replied, wiping her charcoal-stained hands on her thick pants, "if there are men against it — who know we will lose — men who still hold important government positions, can't they exercise some influence and end the war now?"

"Men have been trying since the beginning," said Jiro, his voice laced with frustration. "Admiral Yamamoto, the commander of the navy, whom I admired very much, he tried. He was against it from the start, before Japan entered the conflict, but Yamamoto died last year, shot down by the Americans over Bougainville. They were desperate for his head."

"Isoroku Yamamoto?" Emi asked, saying his famous name slowly. She'd heard many stories about him from her father. "But wasn't he integral in the bombing of Pearl Harbor?" she asked. "I remember my father saying so when we were still interned in America. He used to tell me quite a lot then, in the confines of the hotel — though I'm sure he wasn't supposed to. I think he just liked that I was interested in the diplomacy behind the tragedies."

"Yes, Yamamoto was," said Jiro, moving his chair closer to the stove, which was already emitting the last of its heat. "But only because his superiors had already decided on war. He said that a prolonged war would mean defeat for Japan, and he was right. I don't know when this war will end, but I know that when it does, we will have been defeated. The army has blinders on, and they have ensured that most citizens do, too. I suppose they had to, to keep the country from rebellion and chaos, but it's unfair. America is too big a country, with unlimited resources, and too powerful a

556

military. We are outmatched."

"Still," said Emi, loathing the fear that was taking her over, "I don't see how you can admire the mastermind behind Pearl Harbor. Especially liking America as you do."

"Emiko, you're not understanding," said Jiro patiently. "He was very much against war, but once he had no choice, then he did his job. In 1940, Yamamoto was adamantly opposed to the Tripartite Pact. That should earn your respect, no?"

"Yes," said Emi. "I may have some disdain for the Americans after being locked up, but I — as my parents seem to have told you — hate Nazi Germany much more."

It was then when Emi noticed that Jiro's usually spare face looked swollen, and by mid-March it was so swollen that Yuka insisted he stay in the living room, never moving far from his thick futon.

"If you don't mind," said Emi, stopping Yuka as she came into the hallway after checking on her husband, "I think Jiro-san is suffering from malnutrition." Yuka, a stoic woman, didn't change her expression as Emi continued. "I worked as a nurse's aide when we were interned in America and it was something we treated. A swollen face," said Emi. "It's not a good sign. It means the malnutrition is advanced. Rest is good," she said assuring Yuka, whose body had grown rigid, "but he needs food. Real, nutritious food. Rice is not enough."

"I will give him mine," whispered Yuka, her frail body, like her husband's, wrapped in homespun wool. "Whatever I can give. I'll be the one to subsist on rice."

"No," said Emi, knowing how weak Yuka herself had become. "That's not the solution."

The following morning, with Jiro's health and their need for sustenance on her mind, Emi went into town looking for either Claire Ohkawa or Evgeni and Ayumi. They had, in just two months' time, become her lifeline in Karuizawa.

Walking to the *machi* at 9 A.M., Emi wasn't surprised when she saw Evgeni by the road. He had taken to sitting outside his shop, even in the still dangerously cold weather.

"Outside again?" asked Emi when she'd reached him.

"I have a theory that perhaps if people see me, they might remember that my shop is here," said Evgeni in his fluent Japanese. "That they might want to buy something." The town's housewives milled around the main street, not coming anywhere near the shop as Evgeni tried to make eye contact

558

with them.

"What are you selling today?" asked Emi, who knew that the inventory of Evgeni's shop changed according to what was available for him to sell.

"I have metal buckets, men's shoes, *hibachi*, and *monpe*, of course," he said. "Kazuko Takahashi makes the *monpe* for me. She lives alone in the hills, near Mount Asama, so you wouldn't have met her yet. Her husband is in the Philippines and her two sons also in the fight. I make the journey up the hills every few weeks to pick up what I can. It's hard to live here, but it's harder to live up there alone."

"I could certainly use another pair of *monpe*," said Emi cheerfully, knowing that she did not have any use for new clothes. What she needed was food, but with two children and Ayumi, Evgeni didn't have any more than she did, and none to sell.

"You have no use for them," said Evgeni, who had already sold Emi five pairs since she'd arrived in Karuizawa. "But I can't say no to your generosity." He motioned for her to follow him into the nearly empty store.

"Am I your first customer today?" asked Emi as Evgeni turned on a light.

"My second," he said, pulling a pair of pants down from the wall for Emi. "Tom

Tóth was here just after I opened."

"Tóth?" asked Emi, shaking her head and handing her money to Evgeni. Sugar cost six hundred yen on the black market, if it could be found, but handmade pants were nearly free. "Too many *gaijin* to get to know in a few months," she said of the foreign name.

"He's a Hungarian . . . Jewish," Evgeni explained as he went to package the pants. Emi stopped him and took them unwrapped and folded them under her arm. "He's a photographer, a very talented one. Too bad he's not allowed to photograph anything right now. All his cameras were taken away by the Kempaitai. I wonder what they are doing with them. Taking pictures of each other's disagreeable faces."

Emi laughed, but stopped short as she noticed that a group of German soldiers and officers — some of whom she recognized from the party — were walking on the *ginza*. She moved back from the large front window, out of sight.

"Avoiding the Germans? Not after you played at their New Year's party. You need to get used to seeing them, as there will be many more coming this year," said Evgeni.

"Why aren't they fighting their own war at home?" asked Emi incredulously.

"Not soldiers, but citizens," Evgeni clarified. "The government is rounding them up. They are no longer allowed to live freely in Japan but must either go to Hakone or come here."

"It's not the citizens I want to avoid," said Emi, relieved, watching as one of the officers spit on the ground. "This photographer you mentioned," she said. "Do they know he's Jewish?" she asked, motioning with a tilt of her head to the men outside.

"Of course they do," said Evgeni. "They know who every Jew is, even if they aren't forcing them to wear a Star of David. It's quite obvious, and besides, the Kempeitai keeps watch on all foreigners, Jew or not."

"They don't care? They never harass the Jews, more than the others? The Germans or the Kempaitai?" Emi had been told many times that it was the case in Karuizawa, but she still had trouble believing such behavior was possible.

"The Jews here live in peace," said Evgeni with finality.

"I doubt that will last." Emi looked longingly at the *hibachi,* wishing she had something to cook on them.

"Then no more piano playing for Hans Drexel?" asked Evgeni, appearing happy to give Emi a difficult time for her indiscretion.

"Never again," said Emi, though she knew how much Jiro would have been helped by a fattening German meal in his state. Hesitating before she left Evgeni's shop, Emi asked, "Do you know about the farm? That the German military has its own farm?"

"I know something about that," said Evgeni after a pause. "Claire Ohkawa mentioned it before. It's out that way," he gestured, his voice uneasy. "North of the hotel. It's not far from Kazuko Takahashi's house. I saw it before, the fence, when I was helping her outside. But best not go anywhere near it," said Evgeni, in a warning tone. "If that's what you're thinking."

Emi's face gave away that it was exactly what she was thinking.

"They may be different here toward the Jews, but they're not entirely different from the men you encountered in Austria," he warned.

"Jiro Mori is ill," said Emi, her hand on the doorknob. "In the past few weeks, I think his hunger has developed from an annoyance to malnutrition. Where else is there to get food besides the Germans? Our rations are getting scanter. Even if you line up

562

before the sun is out, the food they are providing is nearly spoiled. There is almost nothing to buy on the black market. I bought butter for an exorbitant price and it was extremely bitter. Nearly inedible. We had to cook it down until we could only use it for browning mushrooms and potatoes."

"More goods might be available soon," said Evgeni, not one to lose hope. "Until then we have hunting, a barter with friends, making do with rations like we're supposed to. Ice fishing," he added. "You might learn to ice fish."

"I don't think that will be good enough," said Emi, thanking Evgeni for the pants and leaving the store.

Emi had complained many times to Christian about the food in Crystal City, but what she would have done for it now. She had written to her parents, finally explaining the food shortage in Karuizawa, but still not mentioning the Moris' ill health. They had written back to say it was the same in Tokyo. They had given her what they could when she was home, but the situation had become dire in the capital city. They insisted that she was still better off in the countryside, where she could forage for food.

Emi walked slowly back to the Moris. Ahead of her she saw two young foxes scampering across the dirt road and she sped up to see them better. They were hidden in a thick grove of Japanese larch and white birch trees before she could catch up to them. Of course catching a fox with her bare hands was not an option, and she wondered if she should learn how to shoot a gun, if that was something that could help save Jiro Mori from declining. Like most of the able-bodied Japanese women in Karuizawa, she was working for the women's volunteer labor corps, as was encouraged by the government, but they certainly hadn't armed her or shown her how to shoot.

Feeling like she was made of nothing but worry, Emi reversed her route, deciding to walk out of town, past the Mampei Hotel, in what she surmised was the direction of the German farm. She knew Evgeni was right to warn her against it. The German military may have been keeping to themselves in Karuizawa, but they certainly wouldn't if their food was stolen, and the Kempeitai was always there to punish with very harsh methods. She had heard stories about their torturing Japanese as well as foreigners.

As she walked, and the hours passed, Emi tried to remember what she had eaten that month. What the Moris had eaten. It was enough for a week, not four, she decided, thinking of the small pickled plums, the leathery squirrel meat, dried fish, and homemade cheese that Claire had brought them.

When Emi had been walking uphill for nearly four hours, she passed by a shrine with stone foxes guarding the entrance. About a half mile later, she saw only farm-houses in the distance. Her body feeling frozen solid, she waved down a truck on the road, which pulled over. She asked the elderly man driving it for a ride to Kazuko Takahashi's house, the only landmark she knew of in the area. To her relief, the driver, who lived on a farm nearby, knew the house.

He dropped her in front of it, the rusted door of his truck creaking as Emi jumped out. She looked at the small wooden house — the roof covered in a snow that hadn't made it down the mountain to town, thick blankets draped over the windows from the inside. She considered knocking but thought, the fewer people who had seen her near the German's farm, the better.

Evgeni had said that the fence was visible from the Takahashi house. Looking around, Emi could see nothing but wild grass, frozen on the ends, and farmland, still retaining the square shapes it had been bundled and tamed into. She moved around the house until it was several yards behind her, and looked again, toward the dying daylight. She thought she saw something metal glinting in the orange sun and ran in its direction until she was out of breath.

A hundred yards, then two hundred, five hundred, before suddenly she saw it. Barbed wire, coiled like it had been above the fences in Crystal City. It looked like it went on for a couple of miles, at the top of a meticulously built fence. It wasn't the style of low wooden fence that was used to pen animals in Karuizawa, made from long split logs. These were made with horizontal wires, attached to heavy wooden posts. The wires were taut and about four inches apart. It looked to Emi, even from a fair distance, impenetrable.

Moving closer to a line of trees, Emi thought of Drexel's hand on her back at the party, of Leo being taunted in the chemistry room, of the destruction of Vienna during Kristallnacht, and of Jiro Mori, so weak that he could barely find his words, and she kept walking toward the farm. A hundred yards away she spotted dozens of chickens, and goats, and though she couldn't see them, she could hear the grunting of pigs. When she noticed a guard making his way around a corner, near the large barn, she rushed back behind the trees. She waited until he was close enough to her so that she could see his face and confirm that he was German. Then she stayed hidden until he was around the other side of the building, as she tried to muster the courage to get closer. The chickens were moving to the edge of the fence, and she thought that maybe, she might be able to reach her hand in and take one. But if it clucked loudly, she would certainly be caught.

She was about to try to run to the fence when she saw a boy rush out from east of her and crouch down close to where a chicken was. The sun had almost completely set but she was sure it was a young boy. Without thinking, she ran up and grabbed him by the coat.

"Hey!" the boy hissed, trying to squirm out of her grip. When he realized that she was a young Japanese woman, he stopped moving and stared at her. She was about to say something when he leaned down and bit her hard on the hand, the only part of her body that was exposed. He scampered to his feet as Emi looked at his childish face — she was sure he wasn't older than nine or ten — and tried to keep from screaming out in pain. "Who are you?" he hissed, his body and most of his face hidden under the puff of black winter clothing.

"You're stealing food," she said, looking at both him and the barn to see if the guard had come around again.

"I'm going to get that chicken," the boy said pointing, no longer seeming to view Emi as a threat. "See how it keeps coming to the fence, away from the others?"

"But you'll be punished if you're caught," Emi said, watching the boy. "Won't you?"

"Punished? I'll be killed," he said, not taking his eyes off the bird. "Everyone knows that. Why do you think there are still chickens to steal here?"

"Then leave," Emi whispered into his ear. "You think one chicken is worth dying for?"

"You think starving is better?" he said, pushing Emi to the side. "You're stupid for coming here. Especially if you don't want food."

"Who says I don't want food?" she said, listening to the snort of the pigs. It sounded like there were a hundred of them.

"You don't look like you know what you're doing so you must not," the boy said, his voice muffled from his coat.

"I don't," said Emi. "Know what I'm doing."

Suddenly, Emi felt someone touch her shoulder and then slam her body to the ground. Her breath knocked out, she looked up to see the face of a Caucasian teenager. As she was on the ground, she saw the Japanese boy slip to the side of the fence, put his arms in between the wires, grab the chicken, which had just waddled close enough, cut its throat, and pull it through, all in a few seconds.

"Who are you?" the boy on top of her asked in Japanese, pinning her down. He was older than the Japanese boy, but still a teenager.

"I'm Emi Kato, I live in Karuizawa, and I came here to steal food, just like you," said Emi, trying to push him off her.

"If they see you here, they'll kill you," the teenager said, moving off her. "Get back, away from the fence," he said, motioning to the dense trees. "You're as tall as a telephone pole; they've probably seen you already."

Even though Emi was not used to being insulted and ordered around by some *gaijin* teenager, she was happy to step out of the line of sight.

With the Japanese boy back next to them, his hands covered in the chicken's blood, the teenager motioned for them all to follow him, and they ran to where there was a car hidden half a mile away in the trees.

"You want a ride back or what?" the boy asked as Emi stared at his car, pretty sure he wasn't old enough to drive. "You can sleep out here if you want. Why don't you give a nice firm knock on the farm door."

"I'll take a ride," said Emi, opening the passenger door to the car.

"Thought so."

"Won't they see that a chicken is missing?" Emi asked as she shut the car door. "They aren't going to think it flew away."

"They might," said the teenager. "But they won't know who took it. Like I said, stick around, maybe they'll blame you."

The boy started the car and when they were a safe distance away from the farm, Emi asked how long they had been stealing from the Germans.

"Not long enough," said the *gaijin* expertly handling the dark, frozen roads.

"I'll come back with you tomorrow," said Emi as they wove down the hills.

The boy started to laugh. "Why would we want you?" he asked in his accented Japanese.

"Because unlike you, and him," she said motioning to the backseat, "I speak German. He's Japanese and you're . . . ?"

"Polish."

"Right. I don't think the German guards speak Polish, nor much Japanese or English. I'll come back with you and find out when they're doing their rounds, when is a safe time to take more than just a chicken."

"Say something," said the Polish boy, swerving to miss a deer. "Say something in German."

Emi started to tell her story with Leo, going on about how proud he would be of her right then.

"Fine," the teenager said, interrupting her. "We won't come back for a month. When we do, you can come, too," he said, putting his hand on Emi's thigh and sliding it down. She rolled her eyes and placed it back on the steering wheel.

"Don't even think about it, Polish. I'm twenty-three years old," she said, eyeing him.

"Oh, really?" he said smiling. "My favorite age."

CHAPTER 30

Christian Lange
August–December 1944

When Jack rolled over and looked at Christian on a hot Hawaii morning, he mumbled, "You look sick, kraut," and threw him his metal canteen.

Christian opened it, as he was sure his was dry from his night of nursing it, desperate for hydration to counter his alcohol intake and the August heat.

"I'm worse than sick. I'm green," said Christian, doubling over and putting his feet on the ground of their concrete bunk. "And I'm never going to that slum again," he said, trying to block out the images of their long night at the Hula Hula. He took a swig from Jack's canteen and immediately spit the contents on the floor.

"What is this?" he said, smelling the bottle. "Vomit?"

"Whiskey!" said Jack, laughing at Christian's contorted, pale face. "Or actually," he said, sitting up, "maybe I did puke in it. I can't remember. What a night, kraut, what a spectacular night we had at the splendid Hula Hula," he said with a hip shake. "That place is heaven on earth."

"Because you slept with a prostitute in a car?" asked Christian, getting up to spit outside.

"Did I?" asked Jack. "That sounds divine, too. I wasn't thinking of that, kraut. I was referring to our walk on the beach, brother-to-brother, man-to-man. How far we've come since the infirmary in Wisconsin." He laughed and ripped off the white shirt he was wearing. August in Hawaii had inspired Jack to wear as few clothes as he was allowed, his wiry body having gone from Wisconsin white to bronzed or red, depending on the week. "I never thought I'd take a shine to you when you came into the home like a dejected family pet, but you've grown on me, kraut."

Christian had a vague recollection of walking on the beach with Jack in the dark while he sang some sort of schmaltz by Bing Crosby at the top of his lungs and tried to get every girl in their sight line to join them.

"I'm sure it changed my life for the better," said Christian, the content of Jack's canteen lingering painfully on his tongue.

" 'Course it did!" said Jack. "I should charge you for our conversations. I've added a lot to your life, kraut. Even if you can't see it."

"Was the car better than the monarchs?" Christian asked, feeling an ache of longing for the simplicity of their days in Milwaukee. Everything there, in one way or the other, was about childhood. Everything in Hawaii was about being a man before your time.

"Nothing will ever be better than the monarchs," said Jack.

"Poetic," said Christian, spitting and telling Jack to get him some water before he fainted.

"You are one of the weakest bastards I have ever known," Jack said, kicking Christian's foot on his way out the door. "What did your parents do? Let you sleep on a bed of roses in River Hills?"

"Pretty much," said Christian. He watched Jack as he headed off, his pants rolled up at the ankles, and knew that it would somehow take him an hour to fetch water. En route, he would find a dozen people he had to speak to, and then take a few cigarette breaks before showing up back at the bunk not remembering why he had left in the first place. Christian spent a lot of time waiting for Jack, or being dragged into something he was reluctant to do, like a liquor-fueled night with prostitutes at the Hula Hula. But he knew that without Jack, the nightmares of war would be winning over his sanity, which he'd pulled a little closer in during his R&R months back in Hawaii.

To Christian's surprise, Jack returned to the bunk after only thirty minutes, his arms full with a large jug of water.

"Is this from the toilet?" Christian asked, pressing his face against the cool glass before knocking it back.

"No, kraut!" said Jack gleefully. "It's from beautiful waterfalls. The best we have on base. I wouldn't poison you twice in one day," he said, reclining on Christian's bed. "Especially after all your dramatics last night. I really did feel sorry for you when you nearly cried talking about how you still haven't received a letter from Emi. The intriguing enemy, so pretty, yet so far away."

"I should cry," said Christian, not able to eradicate the fear that Emi had never made it to Tokyo, or that if she had, she hadn't lasted long. "But I'm trying to blame the war. An American's letters to the enemy nation, the odds aren't good, right?"

"Kraut, your odds haven't been good since you got dragged by the ear out of

River Hills. But yes," said Jack, pointing to his watch. They had to be across base in ten minutes and Christian wasn't dressed yet. "I doubt the Japanese post office is prioritizing mail from lovesick American boys. They're probably using it as kindling, laughing as your lust goes up in flames."

"I hope so," said Christian. "Because if she made it back to Japan only to —"

"Don't think that way," said Jack, interrupting him sternly. "Worry about staying alive in the Philippines. You've started to break out of your gutless state of terror since we've been back on American territory, but I worry about you on Leyte," he said of the Pacific island they were heading to in two months. "You could snap again." He threw Christian's shoes at him and said, "You scared the soul right out of me on Kwajalein. Don't think about doing it again." Helping him up, he said, "Come on. Let's go pretend to pay attention in training drills today. It might keep you alive in October."

By the time the Seventh was ready to ship out that fall, Christian had gone from thinking the Japanese mail service didn't deliver letters from boys like him, to believing either that Emi had died, or he had died for her. Not in flesh, but in her memory.

"It doesn't sound like invented, unrequited mumbo-jumbo to me," said Jack, a week before they were to leave Hawaii again. "Everything she said to you naked in those orange trees. Plus that letter? She's not blind to you, kraut," said Jack. "It's just the mail service that's against you. That's pretty obvious. But you've got to get your mind off it — off her — now. This isn't poetry camp we're going to."

"I wish it was," said Christian, pushing away a plate of pineapple that they were eating at dinner. Pineapple, he had learned, was the Army's version of meat and potatoes for the boys in the tropics.

"Don't fall down the rabbit hole yet," said Jack, looking at Christian's somber face. "The first campaign is the hardest. Now you're already a murderer, so the Philippines will be different. You'll find your backbone. Maybe a little patriotism."

"Patriotism isn't the problem," said Christian, watching Jack eat pineapple hungrily, like he hadn't just had it for breakfast and lunch. "I love this country, and I would give my life for it. Obviously I would. I'm still here. But this war: killing strangers because some men we've never met decided we should. It just doesn't lay right with me anymore."

"Even if those strangers are trying to

destroy the world?" said Jack, reaching his arm out like a Nazi soldier.

"Even if," said Christian. "There should be another way. They shouldn't just send out boys with weapons."

"I'm going to start calling you the Dove, too," said Jack, and true to his word, that's what he yelled at Christian two months later as they landed in the small coastal town of Dulag on October 20. They began moving inland as soon as Dulag was secure, heading for Japanese airfields after they'd already been attacked by American planes.

On the twenty-eighth of October, Christian, Jack, and Dave were lined up with the rest of their unit outside a Japanese pillbox captured the night before, Christian's moral compass still spinning.

"It's snipers and bunkers today, boys!" Perko shouted. "Remember, tend to the wounded but get them to the water fast. There are hospital boats right offshore. You know the drill. Don't sit there wondering if someone is going to die. Move him out of this cesspool to guarantee that he won't."

It was on that day that Christian and his unit saw kamikaze pilots for the first time, crashing their Zero fighter planes into the giant U.S. ships floating in Leyte Gulf.

"Jesus Christ," said Jack, looking up at the

Japanese planes falling out of the sky. "It's like they're crashing on purpose. Killing themselves."

"That's exactly what they're doing," said Perko, looking up, too. "We're going to take a major hit on the water."

But it wasn't just from the sky that the Japanese came at them with apparent disregard for their own lives. It was on land, where Christian's unit was, too.

"I could never be that brave," Christian said to Jack, wiping the sweat out of his face as they squatted down in a bunker. "I've already gotten sick just thinking about grounding the nose of a plane like that."

"That's not bravery, what the Japanese are doing, kraut. That's stupidity."

They heard gunfire immediately above them and Jack yelled for them all to hit the dirt, but Dave wasn't fast enough. Christian and Jack could hear him scream even over the din of the shooting.

Christian reached Dave first and saw bleeding from his chest.

"Jesus Christ!" Christian cried out, turning him over. Blood was also trickling from his mouth.

"Gunshot! I need a medic!" Christian screamed while Jack kept firing at the enemy line.

No one was coming to their aid, so Christian picked up his gun, crouched down, reloaded, and felt Jack slide down next to him. "What the fuck are you doing still down here, kraut?" he screamed. "Get back up and kill the assholes who shot Dave!"

Christian shook his head, pointing at Dave curled up on the ground, clutching his bleeding stomach. "Someone needs to help him!"

"Get the hell back up, kraut!" Jack shouted, pulling Christian by the arm. "Do your job!"

Jack repositioned himself and started firing again, even as he continued to berate Christian. "The Japanese shouldn't have gotten their hands all over the Philippines. That was a stupid move and now they're dying like insects!"

He fired round after round before throwing himself to the ground, grabbing for Dave's gun. "Kraut, take over! I can't feel my arms."

Christian glanced at Jack, then at Dave, who looked just a few breaths from death, stood up, and fired off every bullet they had left between them.

Between rounds, he could hear Jack talking softly to Dave.

"How about you don't die here in this

hellhole so you can impregnate a whole bunch of women after the war?" said Jack, wiping Dave's mouth with his sleeve.

"Thanks for shooting him," said Dave, his eyes closed. "Thanks for shooting the fucker who shot me."

"Of course," said Jack, resting his hand on Dave's forehead. "You would have done the same for me."

"No, I wouldn't have," said Dave. "I didn't fire my gun. Not even once."

Christian turned to look at them just as Jack was turning Dave over on the ground. He was dead.

"Write to the Dove's parents and lie like crazy," Jack told Christian when they finally had time to grieve that night. "Say he killed all sorts of men and ran into the onslaught of armed commanders. Don't say he never fired a single shot."

"Why not?" asked Christian. "I think there's something pretty honorable in that."

"Yeah, at a kid's birthday party, kraut! Not in the middle of a war. It just means you're a coward who won't defend the cause or your fellow man. I'll write the goddamn letter. Everything will be spelled wrong, but at least the lies will be the right ones."

By December, the American hold on Leyte was solid. The Seventh helped capture

Ormoc City on the western coast and the body count on the Japanese side was over a thousand from the push to Ormoc alone.

Walking through the dead with his superiors, Christian left Jack and ripped off his shirt, throwing it over a particularly maimed Japanese body. He walked on the scorched earth in nothing but his sleeveless white undershirt, his torn pants, and his boots. So many corpses littered the ground that he almost couldn't get to his sergeant without stepping on their hands and feet.

"They all get cremated anyway," said Perko. "Good enough to leave them here half-charred. The job is almost done. And for free."

"You've got a heart of gold," said Christian, bending down and closing the eyes of one who looked as if he wasn't a day over fourteen.

"You going to go around and do that to all of them?" Perko asked, laughing. "You're going to be mighty busy."

Christian thought about Lora's tiny body and how sick it had made him to see it. Now, with hundreds of bodies around him, he was steady.

Christian took Perko's water and splashed it on his face, then followed his sergeant around to the back of a building, which was nothing more than a shell. It provided a slip of shade for the injured Americans waiting to be transferred to the hospital boat.

Beyond them he could see a group of Japanese prisoners, sitting in a tight row in the scorching sun, their hands tied behind their backs.

"Who are those men over there?" Christian asked Perko, pointing to a small group farther away. "Why aren't they with the others?" He watched as an American guard stripped a young prisoner naked and dragged him across the grass to the group of men.

"Them?" said Perko. He was smoking the very end of a cigarette and took a long inhale. He managed one more before he dropped the butt in the pile he had between his legs. "We just got that group. They tied themselves to the trees, if you can believe that. We've been shooting and shooting, up and up, waiting for those bastards to fall out like buzzards. But even the dead ones stayed up there. Tied to the branches. Sampson's dealing with them now. He speaks some Jap," he said pointing.

"How come Sampson speaks Japanese?" Christian asked, watching him scream at the men.

"He's from San Francisco," said Perko.

"Grew up with Japs. He can't really speak it all that well; he just knows a mighty fine amount of curse words. Want to know how to say 'go fuck your mother' in Japanese?"

"Not especially," said Christian, handing him one of his expertly rolled cigarettes. He left Perko and headed toward the group of men beyond the line of leafless palm trees. By the time he reached them, Sampson had walked off. Christian forced himself not to make eye contact. He went a few yards farther and stood in a small grove of trees that somehow had escaped the bombing. He turned to sit down, but scrambled backward when he spotted another prisoner, this one alone.

Christian stared at him. He was stark naked and blindfolded. The cloth covering his eyes was a ripped piece of an American military uniform. Christian walked slowly over to where he was huddled next to a large palm tree. His chest was moving up and down quickly, and he was trying to feel around with his bound hands. Christian knelt down and put his hand in the man's. He glanced around to make sure he was still alone, then pulled off the blindfold. Startled, the man looked at Christian, and Christian looked back squarely into his dark, terrified eyes. As fast as he could, he took the knife out of his pocket and cut the rope tying the man's hands together and his body to the tree. He picked up the rope and placed it in the prisoner's hands. No point leaving evidence of how he'd been cut free. The man stared at him, as if in shock, and Christian helped him stand up. They looked at each other a moment longer, then Christian said one of the ten Japanese words that Emi had taught him. *Hashitte.* Run.

CHAPTER 31

Emi Kato
May–December 1944

By the end of May, Emi, Ernst Abrus — the Polish teenager, who Emi soon learned was a Jewish refugee, in Japan since 1937 — and his accomplice Kenji Magara, the young boy thin enough to get through the fence, had made two trips to the German farm and had taken chickens and, quite by accident, a baby goat. It had wandered near the fence, away from its mother, and Kenji had been able to slit its throat without climbing through. They all knew the smart thing to do was to take it alive and use it as a milking goat, but they couldn't risk removing a live animal. Kenji, whose father worked as a butcher before he was sent to war, could slit an animal's throat silently. It was why Ernst had recruited him.

With the group's learned patience, waiting in the woods until an animal came close enough to them, they had stolen enough meat to improve the health of all their families. Kenji had taught Emi how to use every single part of the animal, down to the feet and bone marrow, and she had been able to make a single chicken last nearly a month.

After the second trip, Yuka questioned where Emi was getting the food. "From the Germans," she'd said, not specifying by what means. Because, in the two months that Emi had taken over the cooking, Jiro's face began to look normal again, Yuka did not press her.

When the three went back to the German farm in June, sure to always avoid each other in town until a trip needed to be planned, Ernst said he thought there were others stealing food.

"We have to be more careful this time," he said as the truck rattled up the familiar path. They had decided to go much later in the day and it was nearly midnight when they approached the farm. "I heard a woman in town, a Japanese woman, talking about a miracle goat that her son had brought home. That he had found it lost in the woods."

"Who was the woman?" asked Emi. She had gotten to know the townspeople very well in her six months there.

"I don't know. A thin, hungry woman, just like the rest of them," he said, turning on another road when he saw the headlights of a car traveling in their direction.

"Everyone is starving now," said Emi. "It's much worse than last year. I'm not surprised that we're not the only ones."

"We just can't be the ones to get caught," said Ernst. "Wouldn't that be a pity? Because then we could never get married." He put his arm around Emi, who plucked it off, though she let it rest a few seconds longer than she had the month before. She cursed in Polish, something Ernst had been teaching her on their long nights standing in the woods, and pointed at the little road that took them near the farm. Behind them, Kenji was asleep, his face young and peaceful. How unfair, thought Emi, to be putting a nine-year-old child like him through such tests of war.

Emi got out of the car first, walking to the front of the farm where the German guards kept watch. Their numbers changed — the first time there was only one, the next time three — but their conversations barely differed. They talked about what they were going to do when they got home — what they would eat, the women they would have, the places they would go. And arbitrarily, they would patrol the farm. When one took off on foot, Emi would motion to Ernst, who would then make sure Kenji wasn't near the fence, but on that late night in May, Emi stopped short before she got close enough to the guards to hear them. For the first time since they'd been going up into the hills, the pigs were out.

Making their way slowly around the grass in the dark were about a dozen fat pink pigs. She looked at them shocked, trying to determine if they would be able to fit them through the fence or not. Instead of moving to the guards like she was supposed to, she ran back to Ernst and told him.

"We need one," he said excitedly, motioning for Kenji to follow him. "I don't think we can carry more than one, but we should take it out alive."

When the three of them were close enough to the fence to see the animals, Kenji shook his head. "They won't fit through the wires. Maybe we can get a smaller one."

"We have time," said Ernst, refusing to give up on the several-months supply of food grunting in front of him.

"Have you ever slaughtered a pig?" asked Kenji, getting down on the ground to assess them further.

"No," said Ernst. "I'm from Warsaw." He followed Kenji's lead and said, "Just don't do a good job. Cut the suckers lengthwise and slip them through."

"If he says he can't, he can't," said Emi, putting her hand on Kenji's slight shoulder. "It's not worth the risk."

"Really?" said Ernst. "Is your mother nearly dead?"

"I can try," said Kenji, interrupting them. "But you," he said, motioning to Emi, "have to make sure I have time."

Emi nodded reluctantly and moved quietly through the thick larch trees to the perch she'd discovered in April. Behind a large grouping of rocks, slick with moss, she was totally covered but still able to hear the Germans' conversation. There were unfortunately three guards out that night, as it was one of the warmest nights they'd had all year.

Emi waited for one of the guards to finish walking the periphery of the property, which he did quickly, then returned to the other men to continue a conversation about the Soviet troops, who, Emi knew from Evgeni and his diplomatic connections, were winning the war against Germany.

The conversation quickly became heated and Emi motioned to Ernst that it was time to send Kenji to the fence.

She watched as the little boy came out from the cover of the trees, dropped to his stomach, and slithered to the metal wires. He put his hand out between the lowest rung, food on his palm, and waited for the pigs to come.

None of the stubborn animals moved close enough to Kenji before one of the German guards started to do his rounds. Emi motioned to Ernst to get him back and he ran and picked up Kenji from the ground, getting them both behind the tree line in time.

An hour passed before they were able to try again. This time Kenji put his head and arms all the way through the fence, Ernst watching him and Emi watching the guards. None of the pigs were coming close and Emi was sure she would have to signal to Ernst to pull him back again. She was about to, as the German guards' conversation had hit a lull, when she saw Kenji crawl under the fence and into the farm, running several yards. He grabbed one of the smaller pigs and it let out a loud squeal. Despite the noise, he dragged it to the fence, where Ernst had run up to meet him.

Not knowing if she should stay by the guards or help them, Emi went back to the trees and ran to where the boys were. She saw that Kenji had made his way back through the fence but was struggling to get the animal between the wires, the little pig much fatter than a half-starved Japanese boy.

Ernst leaned in and pulled the pig by the tail. "Both of you get to the trees," he hissed at them as he worked. "When I have it through the fence, come back."

"It's too loud," said Kenji, worriedly. "Look at him!" he hissed. He moved to the edge of the trees, and was about to go to Ernst when they heard a shout, so strong that it sounded like a foghorn piercing the silence of the mountain town.

A light went on and Emi saw that it was a flashlight in the hand of a German guard who had run out of the barn. Suddenly, with his shout, the three in the front of the barn ran toward them, too.

"Leave!" Ernst yelled in Japanese, dropping the pig but not moving back or turning around to face the woods where Emi and Kenji were hiding. "Leave right now, take the car, and don't talk to anyone!"

Emi started to move toward Ernst, but Kenji pulled her back, his little hand in hers. "No," he said firmly. "We need to leave. We need to take the car and leave. Right now. If the guards don't understand Japanese, then we could be all right."

"But Ernst!" said Emi, pulling her hand away, terrified for him.

"They have him now. And he's a *gaijin,*" said Kenji, anxiously. "Even if he ran now, they would find him."

Emi thought for a second, hearing the men with their lights coming closer, turned, and ran away with Kenji, driving the truck back toward town at dangerous speeds. Not knowing what to do with it when they got close, they left it, with the keys in the ignition, by the side of the road near the shrine just north of the Mampei Hotel.

Emi no longer had a watch, but she could tell from the sky that dawn was only an hour out.

"What do we do?" asked Kenji, once they were past the shrine.

"I don't know," said Emi. "Do as Ernst said, I suppose. Don't talk to anyone. I'll see what I can do on my end and I'll find you when I have any semblance of a plan. Until then, stay quiet."

She patted him on the head, feeling his fear, and watched as he ran toward his house, one she knew was filled with his newly widowed mother and four siblings, all trying to stay alive.

Instead of going home, where the Moris did very little to keep tabs on her, she went to the main street and sat in front of Evgeni's store, waiting for him. She agreed with Ernst that Kenji shouldn't talk to anybody, but she had to. She held her knees to her chest as she thought of the soldiers running at Ernst. Had it been her fault? Had the soldiers ever mentioned another man inside? She shook her head hard, trying not to think about it. She had to focus on keeping Ernst alive, not the moments that had just passed.

Three hours later, the sun was up and it was nearly nine, the hour when the shops opened. She looked down the road for Evgeni, sure he would be one of the first in town.

When she saw a foreigner coming her way, after a smattering of older Japanese women, she stood up, sure it was Evgeni, and had to stop herself from screaming when she saw it was Ernst. His hands were clean and he was in different clothes.

"They took me home," he said in passing, not slowing down. He was heading toward the path that ended at the Christian church hidden deep in the woods. "Then they took my father. They wanted him instead of me." He didn't wait for Emi to reply; he just kept walking and soon was out of sight.

Word got around town very quickly that Oskar Abrus had been removed from his home by German soldiers, but it was said just a few weeks later that they had handed him over to the Kempeitai.

When he hadn't returned for a month, Ernst passed by Emi near the Mampei Hotel one afternoon and said, "See what you can do," before continuing on toward the boys' Catholic school.

To free a *gaijin* from the Kempeitai? What could she do?

After school, she stopped Kenji and told him what Ernst had said.

"Are you going to give us up?" said Kenji after they'd walked silently together. Hidden away near the Shiraito waterfall north of the *machi,* he started to cry. "It's not going to save Ernst's father if you do. They will just kill us, too. Or they will kill my mother. She can't die. My father already died!" he said, growing hysterical. "They can kill anyone they want. Don't you know that?"

Emi walked through the woods with Kenji until he was calm, assuring him that she was not going to turn herself or him in. When they were back on the street, she took him with her to Evgeni's store.

"I need to tell my father," said Emi to Evgeni, whom she had confided in weeks ago. "Don't you think? He could do something."

"It's not a good idea," said Evgeni. "They'll just punish him, too. A man in the government whose daughter is a thief at best, a traitor at worst? You'll kill your father by telling him." He shook his head. "Emi, why didn't you listen? I told you not to go."

"I know," said Emi, embarrassed. "But I couldn't just let Jiro Mori die in front of me. I didn't know what else to do."

"There are much younger men starving," said Evgeni. "Boys like Kenji," he said, looking at him. "It is worse to see the youth die."

When another month had passed with no word and even Ernst had stopped asking Emi for help, she tried to get Evgeni to help her approach an embassy. The Swiss Embassy was now in Karuizawa, and she knew they often acted as go-betweens for government affairs.

"For a Jewish refugee? They're not going to want to touch it," said Evgeni. "Do you know how many foreigners the Kempeitai have tortured and killed already? The Swiss are not going to get involved with them."

"The Polish Embassy?" asked Emi, her guilt and desperation building like a disease.

"Not here. It was in Tokyo but was forced to shut down in '41," said Evgeni. "Emi," he sighed, "Ernst was there before you, yes? You did not force him to steal the food. He would have been caught with you there or without you there. Don't put your life at risk to help his father."

"But I should have been caught, too," said Emi. "I should have been the one at the fence."

"You weren't," said Evgeni firmly. "Stop trying to get yourself killed now."

For the next six months, Emi, Kenji, and Ernst shared the streets of the town, but never a conversation. All were focused on finding enough food for their families, but it was becoming so scarce that people in town were dying by the dozens from malnutrition. Evgeni and Ayumi's youngest daughter had become very ill, not strong enough to even stand, and Jiro's swelling had come back. He was bedridden again, and like everyone else in town, this time Emi did not know what to do to help. The forest had been pillaged of all things edible, so much so that Emi never saw deer or even fox in the woods anymore. There were no mushrooms, no watercress, daikon, or carrots, and even the milking goats were being slaughtered out of desperation for meat. The government rations had practically stopped and the black market was wiped clean.

Just before the new year, Emi was headed to the shrine on the way to the German farm, to pray for a different outcome for 1945, when Evgeni stopped her with a shout.

"Is it your daughter?" she asked, when he was close and she saw the grief on his face. She knew they were afraid that Kiko would not last the winter.

"No," he said, his hands on his thighs, resting and trying to find his breath. "The Kempeitai brought Oskar Abrus home this morning. They marched him through the street, holding him up like a marionette. He was so beaten, Emi," he said, looking at the ground. "I didn't even know it was him until someone screamed out his name."

"But he's home!" said Emi, relief overwhelming her.

Evgeni shook his head. "He died just hours after coming home. He told his family that they'd tortured him every day for the last six months. They put a water hose down his throat then kicked his stomach. They burned him all over his body with hot irons. They even hung him by a rope before cutting it down moments before he suffocated."

"And then he died? Right after they released him? How do you know all this?"

she said, wanting to run to the Abruses' house.

"Ernst told me. He came to the store. He's looking for you."

"For me?" said Emi, taking a step back. "His father just died. Why is he looking for me?"

"He didn't say," said Evgeni.

"Do you think Oscar said anything about me? About Kenji?" said Emi, whispering.

"I don't know," said Evgeni, his frustration with Emi still apparent. "But if you're being tortured by the Kempeitai, anything is possible."

CHAPTER 32

Christian Lange
February–June 1945

"I'll eat it," said Christian as Jack eyed him suspiciously during a particularly animated dinner in the Philippines at the end of February. Leyte had been secured by the Americans at the beginning of the month and the Seventh was staying on the island, training for their next Pacific campaign. No longer being riddled with gunfire, and eating food cooked by Filipino families, the men were high on the fact that they'd made it through two Pacific campaigns without dying. Before they'd shipped out, there had been a nervous silence all over base, a shared frisson of fear. That was now replaced by a shared relief and occasional pulsating joy.

"Damn it's hot here but I love this weather," said Jack, slipping on a pair of sunglasses, even though they were inside.

600

"Do you remember Wisconsin in February, kraut? Cold. Painfully, freezing cold. But how 'bout it here? Beautiful . . . where are we?"

"Leyte," said Christian. "Still Leyte."

"Right, Leyte. Beautiful island. Warmer than a virgin's —"

"Stop!" said Christian, cutting him off.

"Still so innocent," said Jack, laughing. "I love it. I'm glad you forced me to enlist, kraut. Because it turns out, I may have nine lives after all."

"Fine, it's decent here," said Christian laughing. He'd never minded the weather in Wisconsin, but Southeast Asia in February, for boys who had escaped death yet again, was a much-needed opiate.

"I even appreciate this disgusting pineapple," Christian said, putting several slices on his plate. "We're in an entirely different country and they're still giving us pineapple." He smiled at the Filipino woman who was serving them lunch and held out his plate for more.

Jack and Christian bounced off their joy for the next week, constantly buoying each other up. There was news that the Red Army had pushed into Germany, gaining unstoppable momentum. And though their unit was training much farther south than Manila, they were told that the units stationed in the north had almost liberated the Philippine capital from the Japanese military. But on a day when their elation felt as if it would go on forever, the realities of war brought it crashing down.

On the morning of February 24, Perko appeared in their bunk before they had left to hit the showers, which were little more than a bucket with a string. He looked right at Christian and said, "Lange, Jesus Christ. I have terrible news."

"My parents are dead," said Christian, sure that there was no other reason that Perko would approach him that way. "My mother," he said, his voice cracking at the thought of Helene Lange as dead as her baby girl.

"No," said Perko as he gestured for Christian to follow him outside. He stopped Jack from following them out the door and walked with Christian a hundred feet away from the bunk. "Your parents . . . they might be dead," he said clearing his throat. "I've never given news this way. It's always the reverse. Sending the dispatch to the parents that their son has died, not telling the son that the parents have died. *Could* have died," he said, correcting himself. He looked to Christian for an emotional reaction, but

Christian stood there stoically, listening, holding tightly to the word *could*.

"We got news over the wire this morning that the British bombed Pforzheim late last night," said Perko. "Similar to the campaign on Dresden." That aerial assault had taken place just weeks before. "They won't talk of casualties in the papers, and besides, we don't get papers out here anyways. But I remembered your parents are in Pforzheim and I got some specifics over the wire. They're saying a quarter, maybe half the population of the city was killed. Are your parents right in Pforzheim?" he asked, his usual gruffness gone.

"Not in the inner city," said Christian, trying to picture his grandparents' house, which he'd only been to once. "But not far."

"That could make the difference," said Perko, clearing his throat.

"When will we know who died?" asked Christian. "Will they release a list of names?"

"Since it's Germans who died, we won't be getting a list of names at all. Meaning the Army, America, anyone. I'm afraid you'll most likely have to wait until the war is over to find out about your parents, unless there is someone in Germany who can write and tell you. But even if there is someone, a relative, the chance of them getting a letter through is low. Especially with you being out here. It will be tough."

"Thanks for your honesty, sir," said Christian, saluting his officer and walking away.

"I'm real sorry, Lange!" Perko called after him.

As soon as Christian turned toward the barracks, he saw Jack running toward him.

"They bombed Pforzheim last night," said Christian as Jack grabbed his arm. "The Royal Air Force. Perko said maybe half the town was killed, maybe less, though. They're not sure, and they're not going to be sure for a long time."

"Jesus, kraut," said Jack. "Your whole goddamned family is holed up there." He paused and then let go of Christian's arm, backing away. "Kraut," he said again, stunned. "Inge is there, too." His stoic face fell and he started screaming and punching the side of their makeshift bunk until every knuckle was bleeding.

Christian watched him, wishing he could do the same thing, feeling the terror building up in him, but he just stood there, stockstill, just as he had when he was fired upon, or when the FBI had walked into his house.

"Am I an orphan at nineteen?" he asked Jack flatly, once he'd stopped assaulting the wall. "Or am I just some sad bastard whose parents died."

"You don't know that they died," said Jack, wiping his hands against his pants. "But you can always feel like an orphan. Just because I'm over eighteen now doesn't mean I went from being an orphan to being an adult man whose parents happen to be dead. I still feel like the world wronged me too early." He fell silent and closed his eyes in exhaustion. Christian had never heard him speak with so little bravado.

"I'd be angrier than you are," said Christian, looking out at the spot where Perko had just given him the news.

"You don't think I'm angry?" said Jack, lifting his bleeding hands, his eyes still shut.

"I don't," said Christian. "I think in every way, you're above us all."

A month after the bombing of Pforzheim, a cousin in Berlin managed to get a letter to him in the Philippines with the help of the INS, who had kept tabs on Christian's whereabouts. Helene and Franz Lange, along with his grandparents, had died.

Three days after Perko gave Christian the telegram, he was on a boat from Leyte to Okinawa, Jack trying to hold him together, the American flag cracking in the wind behind them.

■ ■ ■ ■

Meat and potatoes. Good meat — a thick, bloody steak — and mashed potatoes with butter. That's what Christian and Jack ate on the boat the night before they landed on the main island of Okinawa in April.

This time, Christian was not scared of the fight. After a week on the island, tired from pulling a trigger so many times, he looked down at his hands and realized he had become numb to killing Japanese soldiers. It would come back to haunt him later, he was sure — the stunned faces, the rows of black eyes staring at him, peering at death. But for now, he felt as lifeless as the bodies he'd leveled.

On May 8 came the news that Germany had surrendered. On Okinawa, and everywhere the American and Allied soldiers were stationed, victory was celebrated. Now, Perko reminded them, pausing their revelry, they just had to defeat Japan.

By the beginning of June, the Seventh had been fighting in Okinawa for more than two months. Somehow, Christian was still alive, Jack was next to him, and they were both still fighting in the intense heat, through a weight of despair.

On their seventieth day of fighting, Christian and his unit were hit by yet another onshore assault.

"You want to stay alive?" said Jack, as Christian crouched down in his foxhole. "Stop bobbing your head out of the bunkers like a dolphin doing tricks. My hand is gonna get blown off because I have to shove you down every single day."

"For someone who didn't plan on enlisting, you sure have taken a liking to this soldiering crap," said Christian.

"I know," said Jack, shaking his head, soaked in sweat. They'd all agreed that the hellish heat in Okinawa was the worst they'd ever experienced. The pounding sun of Leyte felt like winter compared to the jungles of southern Japan. "It's disturbing. Maybe I just need people telling me what to do, like in the Children's Home. Over ten years in that dump, and I can't think for myself anymore."

"You're a much better soldier than I'll ever be," he said, remembering what he'd done in the Philippines.

"That is definitely true," said Jack. "Because you're awful. But right now, I won't hold it against you. Losing your parents, not knowing about Inge. It's total shit. So I'll keep pushing your head down, and you just keep on going."

Christian nodded and felt for the piece of wood in his pocket — the toothpick that Jack had made from the cross that Dave put up on Kwajalein. Jack's shoe had become too big a good luck charm. In battle, he traded it for a crudely whittled toothpick.

"But if you're like this wherever we end up next," Jack warned, "I'm just going to let you die."

"Where we end up next?" said Christian. "How long have we been in this shithole? Over seventy days? The war is ending soon. It has to."

"That's what we said after Leyte," said Jack. "So is this the end?"

"The end of us, probably," said Christian, starting to fire, the first in his hole to pull his trigger.

When 3 A.M. rolled in that morning, the tenth of June, Christian and Jack were still awake. Christian, as he'd done every night in Okinawa, spent the quiet hours thinking about his parents. His little family had been flattened by the hell of war. And why? Because the FBI thought his aunt was a Nazi and his father's colleague turned out to be a power-starved liar. Meanwhile, the people of Okinawa were dying simply because they lived in the wrong place at the wrong time. Christian wrestled with his thoughts, wishing he had Emi to confide in, even by pen and paper. He let the hard ground provide a few moments of cool until he felt Jack's kick.

"Kraut," Jack said, as he had every morning since they reached Okinawa. "It's time."

The tenth marked the seventy-first day in Okinawa for Christian, Jack, and the rest of the Seventh. Shellfire had become their soundtrack and they'd seen men in their unit start to go mad from it, shutting down, no longer speaking, barely able to pick up their guns and return to the trenches. Other men were weak with malaria; more still were dead, their lifeless limbs propped up in waist-high mud. But by June, the Americans' position was very strong and so were their numbers. Hundreds of ships had kept up their amphibious assault on the island while Christian and Jack and thousands of others pushed overland toward Okinawa's southern end.

On June 10, the division, facing severely weakened Japanese troops, was closing in on Yuza in the south. Knowing that the Japanese had lost far more men than the Seventh had, the division's commanders didn't expect the barrage of firepower that came suddenly from behind Yuza-Dake peak. Perko screamed for his men to get behind the rocks as the tanks plowed forward. As they scrambled for cover, Christian heard Jack's voice behind him.

"Watch out to your left, kraut!" Jack yelled. "They're in the caves! To the left! Get down!"

Christian felt a bullet nick his helmet, but they all made it behind the rocks, the air around them already reeking of dead flesh.

As they reloaded their guns, with Perko bent over his map but still hollering orders, they heard someone howling behind them. Christian looked back to see one of their men, his face turning white. A bullet had gone through his hand. He looked at it, at the place where his fingers had been, and collapsed, but there were not enough men to tend to him. Jack and Christian stared for a few seconds, then resumed firing.

As soon as they were ordered to move again, they ran for a dense cluster of palm trees, hoping to escape the offensive fire raining down from the peak. When the whistle of shells finally slowed, Christian moved to another tree, and Jack waved to indicate that he should run past him a few more feet. He did, but with the sound of gunfire starting up again, he pivoted to his right and began firing back at random. In the next instant, he saw that in his haste, he wasn't firing at soldiers. He had fired into a group of terrified women. One fell to the ground, a child on top of her, his legs moving, still alive.

"No!" Christian screamed, falling to his knees. He crawled out from behind his cover, making for the women, but Jack grabbed him and pulled him back. Christian turned and rested his head against the palm tree, Jack's hands still on him. "I didn't see her. Jesus Christ. I just killed that woman. Did you see? Did you see her child?"

Jack grabbed his arms from behind his back and said, "How many women have we already killed? Get over it and keep going!"

Christian had never imagined anything like Okinawa. It had been a year and a half since he enlisted. He had fought in the Marshall Islands and spent five months in the Philippines. But until Okinawa, he hadn't known such horror could exist in the world. And in such a tiny corner of it. Since they'd come ashore on Easter Sunday, he'd seen families running into shelters for safety only to burn alive seconds later; civilians who had been living in trenches gunned down, their insides spilling out of their kimonos; mothers clutching their babies and drowning themselves, throwing their bodies from cliffs without a look back; children blown up as they ran toward their parents for help. He'd held his fellow soldiers as they died and seen dozens of young women limping from rape. But this was the first time he'd fired a bullet into a woman's body at such close range. A civilian. Someone's mother. He lifted his hand to his mouth and tasted the blood.

"I don't want to do this anymore," he said, shaking his arms free and stepping back from Jack and his gun.

Jack picked it up and thrust it into his chest, ramming him back until he was pinned against a tree. "Just because you're the only fool on this planet who joined the Army for love doesn't mean you can give up now," he said through gritted teeth. "Or maybe you can," he said, pointing to Yuza-Dake peak. "Walk into the open right now and take the bullets. Then Emi can marry some Japanese soldier and this whole mission of yours will be for nothing."

"It wasn't just for Emi," said Christian, finally wiping his hands on what was left of his shirt. "I didn't want to die in Germany."

"What was that?" asked Jack.

"I didn't want to die in Germany!" Christian screamed in his face.

"And you were right!" Jack yelled back. "Everyone in your family has died but you! So don't fucking die here instead."

Christian ran to a foxhole, fell belly down on the ground, then rolled himself up to sit against a mud wall. He thought about his last letter from Inge. He'd received it just before she sailed for Germany.

In her small childish hand, she'd written, "Please don't die, because you never finished telling me the story on the train and you promised you would. You promised."

Instead it was Inge who had likely died.

Christian picked up his gun, aimed toward the distance, put his finger on the trigger, and let the bullets fly.

CHAPTER 33

Emi Kato
January–March 1945

"Act as normally as you can," Evgeni had advised her after two weeks had gone by following Oskar's death. "No one has come looking for you, so don't go looking for them."

She had relayed the message to Kenji, who'd seemed thrilled to avoid her, returning to his life as an elementary school student instead of a for-hire butcher, even if it did mean much less to eat.

Emi didn't know what normal meant for her anymore. She had never developed a routine in Karuizawa; her days were entirely centered on survival. There was no leisure, no moments of real joy. Everything was clouded by a fear of starving and the terror of death. But this time she would listen to Evgeni; she would try to find normal again.

Since the most habitual thing for Emi was

to play the piano, she asked Claire if she might play at the Mampei Hotel in the afternoons.

Claire's husband was thrilled to have someone who could lift community spirits, so Emi was invited to play every Wednesday and Friday evening. At first, no one stopped much to listen, but by February, as the extreme cold settled on the town, coupled with an even greater food shortage, she started to see familiar faces in the lobby. She even saw Ernst and his mother late one night, although he didn't make eye contact with her and Emi turned her face away in shame.

By the beginning of March, feeling that luck had found her instead of the Germans, Emi had attained some calm again. So it shook her to the core when she heard a familiar voice behind her as she was finishing Saint-Saëns's *The Swan* one snowy Friday evening.

"It's you. The prudish piano girl," said Hans Drexel, the German consul, whispering behind her. "I see you in town sometimes and you never say hello. Did we scare you that much at our party so many months ago? You aren't friendly anymore?"

"You didn't scare me at all," said Emi, absolutely terrified. Drexel had never been at the farm when they'd been there — she knew he was far too high up for surveillance rounds — but it was very possible that he'd been told about the theft.

Emi kept playing, her fingers moving without much thought behind them, as he sat down next to her. "Still playing French songs, too," he said. "Now that's a disappointment."

"It's hard to play with company," said Emi, sure she wouldn't be able to keep her composure with his elbow touching her. "Even simple French songs."

"I'll move if you play Handel for me," said Drexel, his uniform wet on the cuffs from the weather outside. He put his hand on her arm and said, "It reminds me of home and it's been a difficult month."

"I'm comfortable with Handel," said Emi, ignoring his hand and starting to play one of Handel's sonatinas, desperate for him to stand up.

"You people don't know anything here," said Drexel, not moving. "I wonder if they keep the German citizens as cloistered from information as they do you Japanese?"

"They — your government — probably do," said Emi. "Isn't that part of the propaganda of war?"

"It's for morale, not propaganda," said

616

Drexel sighing. "Which I could use. A heavy dose of morale is needed around here. Germany has been cut off at the throat this month. Berlin, bombed twice in February. Dresden, decimated. Even little Pforzheim. What is there in Dresden or Pforzheim that the Allies want to destroy? Nothing. They're just operating under a campaign of terror."

Emi wanted to tell Drexel that if there was anyone operating a campaign of terror it was Germany. That she had seen it with her own eyes in Vienna, before war was even declared. But all she could hold on to was the word *Pforzheim*.

"Pforzheim was bombed?" she said, stunned. "When?"

"Pforzheim?" he said looking at her. "Weren't you in Berlin?" she nodded her head yes, but pressed on about Pforzheim.

"A week ago. February twenty-third, at night, of course. Like I said, the Allies are driven only by cruelty." He motioned for Emi to keep playing.

"I have a friend there," she explained, looking at Drexel as she found her place in the song. "An important one. How would I find out if he survived the bombing?" Emi couldn't let herself frame the question any other way. Of course Christian had made it, just like she would and just like Leo would.

She stumbled on a note, her nerves taking over, and stared at Drexel.

"You will never find out. Or perhaps when the war ends, but certainly not before then."

That weekend, Emi left the Moris and went to search the newspapers sold by a frail woman at a stand in town. She read them cover-to-cover, but as usual, they reported only Japanese victories, saying very little about Europe.

She rushed home, noticing a trail of smoke coming out of sloping Mount Asama, one of her favorite sights in Karuizawa. She took it as a good omen. Christian could not be dead. She wouldn't make it until the end of the war if she thought that way. His being alive, it was one of the things that kept the fight in her. She worried endlessly about Leo's safety, but Christian, his life, was something she counted on. He had to be invincible in the face of war.

She pushed the wooden front door open with her gloved hand, seeing that Jiro was awake in the living room. She sat by him and relayed what Drexel had said.

"The government hides everything from us," she said. "But he must be right. Why would he lie?"

"About bombings by the Allies in Germany? In cities as important as Berlin?" said

Jiro, his eyes closed, as they always seemed to be. "He wouldn't."

CHAPTER 34

Leo Hartmann
July–September 1945

"What are you going to do?"

"Hmm?" said Leo, looking out at the expanse of summer blue sky over the cramped neighborhood. Now that he had only one good eye, it seemed to have gotten stronger, even though his field of vision had been severely truncated.

"About Agatha," said Jin, waving down a rickshaw. Jin's father had given them money for a ride back to the ghetto since Leo had forgotten his work shirt and Liwei wouldn't let him inside in his dirty day clothes. Two rickshaw drivers saw Jin at the same time and the younger one pushed the other into the gutter full of night soil and trash to guarantee his fare. Leo took a step, to go help the man who had fallen, but Jin put out his hand and stopped him. "I'll pay for one ride, not two," he said as Leo climbed on after him.

"I am sure I wouldn't be alive without her," said Leo, putting his hand over the scar on his face and his bad eye. "She took me straight to the hospital, stayed with me there for a month."

"But you wouldn't have been almost dead if it weren't for her. If you had listened to me and stayed inside instead of being so foolish."

"That was my choice," said Leo. "You know that. Nursing me back to health was hers."

"Is that what you call it these days? I didn't know you could get pregnant by nursing someone back to health," said Jin grinning.

"It worked, didn't it?" said Leo, not letting Jin rattle him. "Look how healthy I am."

"The healthiest blind man in Shanghai," said Jin, putting his hands behind his head. "Partially blind," he corrected himself before Leo could. "I'm very happy for you. For her, too. She deserves something good in her life."

"She does," said Leo, calming down.

"Does she know how rich you were? Back in Vienna? Does she know about the money?" asked Jin, without looking at his friend.

"I don't think so," said Leo, agitated by Jin's questioning. "Besides, we might not ever see it again."

"Then she loves you for wonderful you," Jin said. "As it should be." After a few minutes he turned to Leo again. "But what if the baby is Pohl's? Or another customer's. Have you ever asked her?"

"She was never with Pohl," said Leo, sitting up straighter and looking angrily at Jin. "I stopped that from happening by offering up my skull instead. Besides, he's been gone from Shanghai since last January."

"If you believe her, then I believe her," said Jin, saying something in Chinese to the driver, who took an abrupt left on Jin's command.

"You've known her much longer than I have," said Leo. "Do I have reason not to believe her? She's only five months pregnant. Pohl has been gone for over a year."

"I'd believe her," said Jin. "But I'd also make sure that baby has dark curly hair," he said, pointing to Leo's head.

"Really?" said Leo, who hadn't dared question Agatha about such an indiscreet thing. When Agatha had told him in April that she was a month pregnant, he had felt a fighting combination of panic and joy. He cared for — perhaps even loved — Agatha, did not want their nights — and especially their days — to end, but the voice from childhood whispering Emi Kato's name had never gone silent. With the news of the baby, Leo had to silence it for good.

"Do you love her?" asked Jin, smiling until his dimples showed. "Because I love her. So does every man who has ever patronized Li-wei's. Want me to marry her instead?"

"No," said Leo. "I'm marrying her."

"Despite the Japanese girl."

"Emi Kato," said Leo, as they got to the bridge. He waited as Leo and the driver bowed to the Japanese guard, and then said, "She's not just any Japanese girl."

"You can't be dreaming of her still," said Jin, scowling at the back of the Japanese guard and then leaning in the old rickshaw like he was the king of Shanghai. "It's not a male trait. We aren't faithful."

"That just goes to show that you don't know Emi," said Leo, trying to mimic his pose. "She inspires a lot more than faith."

"And Agatha?"

"She inspires something else all together."

"Don't I know it," said Jin, letting out a low whistle.

Leo closed his eyes and let the whir of the city buzz through his ears, appreciative that Jin was paying for their rickshaw, which he'd realized was making turns all over the city so they could avoid work a little longer. It was funny what felt like luxury to Leo now — not a chauffeured Mercedes, but a splintered wooden cart.

They went over the bumps and holes of Shanghai, then called out to a group of young Chinese girls on a street corner playing catch with a half-dead fish.

"That's truly disgusting," said Leo, looking at them.

Jin yelled out in Chinese and one of the girls ran over and gave him the fish and he gave her the money to buy a live one. He threw the dead one at Leo's feet and they both laughed and twisted away from it, until Leo kicked it into the gutter.

As they made their way to the edge of Hongkew, Leo's ears started to buzz, and he turned around to see if there was a truck behind him. All he could see were children in the street and Chinese women doing their washing. "The city gets louder every day!" he shouted to Jin.

Jin looked behind them, too, and then stood up to see farther in front of them, holding Leo's shoulder for balance. "But it shouldn't be," he said. "We're almost out of Hongkew."

"What?" screamed Leo, barely able to

hear him.

Instead of repeating himself, Jin shook his head and yelled something to a man in an alley, but he couldn't understand him, either.

Leo looked at Jin worried, and before either could speak, they heard an even louder noise and both turned their eyes to the sky.

"Is that noise not coming from the street?" Leo asked Jin.

Jin yelled at the rickshaw puller to stop. "I'm not sure!" he shouted back. After a moment of peering around them again, he stopped and pointed to the sky. "Planes."

They saw the American planes at the same time. The heavy silver aircraft had been flying above the city for months, but always low and fast. This time they were coming in high but noticeably slower, which could mean only one thing.

The rickshaw puller looked up too, dropped the handles of the cart, and started to run. Just as Leo and Jin slid to the ground, the siren went off. The planes were carrying bombs, and they were about to drop them on the city.

Such a raid had been anticipated for months, and the Japanese had built trenches and foxholes around Shanghai, but there was no plan for the restricted area and there were no bomb shelters in Hongkew.

"Where should we go?" Leo shouted at Jin, following the rickshaw puller out of instinct.

"We don't have time to get back to your house," said Jin, looking around him as they ran. "And it's no safer than where we are now." He looked at Leo, who was frozen in the street, and screamed, "Just run! Start running! We can't be uncovered like this."

They were near a crowded market and Leo pointed to it, but Jin shook his head.

"Too many people!" he yelled, trying to be heard over the whine of planes' engines. "They'll all be trying to hide under the same tables. There won't be enough room."

Leo saw children running from the market and took a step back. Jin spotted a concrete building where a restaurant was being built near the market and motioned for Leo to follow. They sprinted over, kicked in a back window, and crawled inside, the jagged glass cutting up their legs. The floor hadn't been finished yet and they slipped on the dust and concrete fragments, trying to find something to hide under.

As soon as they had righted themselves, they heard the first blast. Jin screamed, while Leo covered his ears and crouched down on the ground. "We have to get undercover!" Leo yelled.

"The ground is soft enough for us to dig!" Jin shouted back, getting down.

"We don't have time," said Leo, running over to a big wooden table and crawling under it. Jin joined him and they started digging with their hands and fragments of concrete blocks. When the bombs got louder, falling closer, the ground shook heavily at each explosion, and Jin yelled for them to stop.

"Forget it! Get down! Lie down flat on your stomach. Cover your good eye with your hands!" he said, grabbing Leo and pushing him to the ground.

Elbow to elbow, faces in the dirt, they waited in silence as the American bombs rained down.

Leo started to pray under his breath, for his parents, for Jin's family, for Agatha and the baby, until the explosions were so loud he couldn't even think straight enough to pray. All he could do was pinch his eyes shut and wait to see if he was meant to die that day.

He heard Jin breathing fast next to him and realized that suddenly it was quiet. The siren had stopped, along with the deafening blasts. The planes had passed over.

Leo looked at Jin and they both moved their faces out of the dirt and listened. The city was eerily still. Leo finally heard someone crying softly and turned to see that they were not alone in the restaurant. A Chinese family had come in, too, and they all looked at each other, the young men under the table staring at the parents and children.

"Is it over?" Jin asked Leo. "Are we alive?"

Leo crept out and leaned against the table. "I don't know if it's over," he said, "but we are definitely alive."

Jin spoke to the family in Chinese, his voice snapping them out of their terror, and all three of the children — shoeless and covered in dust — started to wail. That was the end of their quiet. At the same moment, they became aware of ambulance sirens and screams outside.

Jin and Leo climbed out the window they had come in through. Jin was out first and he stopped short. The stalls, the people in the open-air market, they saw, had been decimated. The air was full of dust, as the chaos of the downed buildings hadn't settled yet. The people who were running around were covered in layers of debris, looking like they'd rolled in a fireplace.

Leo grabbed Jin's arm and they both ran toward what was left of the market, battling their way through piles of rubble. They tried to heave aside the pieces of broken concrete, but they were too heavy. Jin called out to the swarm of men gathering on the street to come help them. With their aid, they were able to shift several jagged slabs from atop the mound. As the largest slab fell to the side, they saw two crumpled bodies. Chinese bodies. Leo climbed up to another section, moved heavy rubble with the help of more men, and saw another dead face.

"No one here has survived this!" he cried. He shoved aside another piece of concrete and the sight of a severed arm knocked the breath out of him. As the work proceeded, they uncovered more bodies, piled on top of others.

"How do you know they're all dead?" Jin said. "We have to lift every piece. What if there is someone alive at the bottom?"

"But the person on the top is dead!" Leo yelled. "How can the others underneath be alive?"

"Go inside and get more help. I'm not leaving!" Jin screamed, desperately trying to move the heavy rubble with his bleeding hands.

Fire trucks and ambulances approached, their sirens blaring, and men were already starting to haul the dust-covered bodies of the dead out of the market in rickshaws. A team of medics arrived and ran inside, and Jin called out to them to help. Two broke off and came to dig through the rubble with them, but as Leo had thought, every body they found had had the life knocked out of them by the American bombs.

"I can't see one more dead child," said Jin as the Chinese medics took more bodies away. There had been only two foreigners in the rubble; every other one, more than a hundred so far, were Chinese.

"We can't help anymore," Jin said after four hours had passed. "I can barely hold my hands open."

Leo wiped the dust from his eyes and said, "We can't leave now," even though he was desperate to go find Agatha and his family.

"Of course we can," said Jin. "The dead are dead and neither of us knows how to save the ones who are barely still alive. I'm going to check on my father. You go home and make sure your parents are alive. Make sure Agatha is alive. I know that's all you're thinking about anyway."

Leo nodded and said, "Then I'll come to work. Because if they are alive, we'll need the money."

As he moved through the torn-apart city, he barely looked at the bodies in the street, the devastation. Like Jin said, all he could think about was his family and the girl who was becoming family.

Back on Yuhang Road, he ran up the flights of stairs to the apartment, which was unharmed, but also empty. He sprinted back down, taking two steps at a time, and flew into the street. Noticing a commotion the next block over, he moved toward it, but before he reached the crowd, he heard someone scream out his name. He turned around to see his mother, who was crying from the sight of her son. Leo ran to her and threw his arms around her, as he had done so many times in childhood.

"Froschi," Hani said through her tears. "You survived. You're alive."

"Of course I am," he said, still holding his mother. "I already escaped death once. Why not twice?"

"And Jin is alive?" she said, crying. "You were together?"

"He is alive," said Leo, wiping his mother's face with his shirtsleeve. "Where is father?" asked Leo, looking around them. He saw that the commotion at the end of the street was people trying to move a dead body out of the road. He could hear a woman wailing as the crowd started to dissipate.

"Your father is with Agatha, in Chongan's

shop," she said pointing. "When we heard the planes we all ran down to the store, to hide under his tables." The dumpling shop had long wooden tables inside and out, and though the dumplings were mostly a sticky starch coating with no filling, if someone in Hongkew had money, they ate at Chongan's.

Hand in hand, they rushed over, pushing through a crowd, calling Max's name, but it wasn't Max who came out of the store first, it was Agatha. She looked at Leo, burst into tears, too, and waited for him to reach her before she collapsed in his arms.

Leo held her tightly, before letting go and examining her to make sure she wasn't harmed. It was the first time he noticed that she looked pregnant, visibly pregnant, with his child. He put his hand on her stomach. The month before, she had stopped working at Liwei's, as a pregnant taxi dancer was not part of the customers' fantasy. Instead, she spent her nights with Hani and Max, who, after realizing that their son had offered to do the honorable thing and marry Agatha, had taken her in. She wasn't Jewish, she wasn't Emi Kato, but as Max had said to Hani many times, their son was alive, and happy, and in 1945, that was what mattered.

"I knew you were alive," said Hani, sniffing back tears. "We made it. Somehow, we all made it."

Leo reached out for Agatha and kissed her long and hard. "I can't wait to be your one-eyed husband," he whispered.

"You have two eyes," said Agatha. "One is just decoration."

Three weeks after the American assault on Shanghai, the family read about the enormous bombs that had been dropped on Hiroshima and Nagasaki. Then, one day in August, when the sun was low in the sky and the ghetto was as loud and chaotic as ever, they walked out into the street and the Japanese military presence was gone. Ghoya was not there acting out his dream role as king of the Jews; there was no one to check if they had a pass to leave the restricted area. It was just the Jews and the Chinese. For forty-eight hours, no one knew what to make of it, but Liwei brought out his best liquor anyway, and the only Japanese man there to share in it was Hiroyoshi.

Liwei poured all his workers a drink and said, "If the Japanese military are gone, it means the war is over." They all got very drunk, and the next day they learned Liwei was right. Japan had surrendered.

The Americans arrived, and with them came food. A few weeks later, on September 3, the ghetto was liberated.

"Now that the war is over and mail may go through again, we must write to Norio Kato and tell him we made it," said Max. "Thank him."

"Yes," said Leo, feeling a tug on his heart. "We must." Emi, the Katos, had kept his family from perishing in Europe, and Emi with her unwavering youthful love had saved Leo from the hell that was 1938. He prayed that she had survived the war, that her whole family had, and that she would understand what his life had become.

His mother's joyous expression changed to wistfulness as Max mentioned the Katos, and Leo felt the pain of a missed opportunity. What if the war hadn't pushed them around the world? Could things have ended differently? He looked at Agatha's stomach and knew it wasn't fair for him to wonder.

Agatha and Leo decided to marry in a civil ceremony attended only by his parents, Liwei and Jin. After the wedding, they watched as Chiang Kai-shek's army marched like toy soldiers through the newly unrestricted streets and avenues.

"The Americans should be marching,

too," said Max, watching the precise movements of the Chinese.

"I think they're more interested in wandering about the city," said Agatha. "They'll
probably all end up at Liwei's."

"The ones who I spoke to have been on
boats for four years, constantly at sea," said
Max.

"There is a lot of talk of boats in Hongkew," said Leo, not turning his head away
from the parade, his hand firmly in Agatha's. "Not the American ships, but boats
that will take the Jews to America. To
Israel," said Leo.

As soon as the Japanese military had fled
the city, the talk among the Jewish community had centered on leaving. Where
would they go and how would they get
there? Many wanted to go to Israel, though
most knew they would end up in the United
States. The old Jewish community in Shanghai wanted to stay, as their lives had roots
there, but there was already talk that the
foreign concessions would be abandoned
and the Jews would no longer be able to
stay, even those who had been there for
more than a generation.

"Let's not be hopeful yet," said Max.
"They say it could take years to leave
Shanghai. For the boats to start making the

trip to Israel or America. Right now, the Americans have brought food and the invisible walls around Hongkew have been knocked down. The war is over. You two are married and in two months, there will be a baby. We don't need to think about the next step."

"America is the next step," said Hani. "Even if it does take years. Have you written to your family in Germany yet, Agatha?" said Hani, taking her hand from Leo. "Your extended family?"

"I will now," said Agatha. "Now that the war is over, maybe the mail will travel with regularity again."

From a room above them, they heard a record turning on a phonograph, and Leo wondered who had found such a luxury in Hongkew. They looked up, but all they could see was the open window, a white curtain fluttering out of it like a flag of surrender.

Agatha took a step forward to see more of the parade and Leo leaned over to his father. "You'll have to write to Emi for me. Tell her about Agatha, the baby, the wedding," he said softly. "I won't be able to write the words."

CHAPTER 35

Emi Kato
May 1945

"Hitler is dead!" screamed Claire Ohkawa, rushing into the Moris' house, not bothering to even knock on the door. "Dead!" she screamed again, hysterical.

"What?" said Emi running out of the kitchen. "How do you know? Are you sure?"

"I just saw Philippe Bussinger of the Swiss delegation in the hotel. He was rejoicing," said Claire, motioning with her hands. "He confirmed it. Hitler shot himself in the head at the end of April but they found him yesterday. Dead! It's not in the papers or on the radio here yet, but it will be soon," she said, rushing to Emi and throwing her arms around her. "Can you believe it?"

"I can because you're saying it," said Emi, hugging Claire back. "And the Swiss delegation knows everything first."

"Yes, we're lucky to live in Karuizawa,"

said Claire. "Citizens of the world at our doorsteps. At least we aren't kept totally in the dark like the others." She looked at Yuka Mori, who was standing stunned, and said, "Quick! Mrs. Mori. Turn on the radio!"

As Claire had said, there was still nothing on the radio about Hitler's death, so Emi and Claire biked into town. The last two months had been terrible for Japan. In early March, the Americans had firebombed Tokyo, far worse than they had before, decimating the city in two days and killing thousands, more than a hundred thousand perhaps, her father had written to say. There were charred bodies all over the city, and most of the people he saw alive were homeless, living under tarpaulins, shacks made of burned wood, pieces of corrugated metal — anything that could serve as a roof. The malnutrition had been bad before the bombing, he stressed, but now the majority of the capital's citizens were on the brink of starvation. He and her mother had hidden in a bomb shelter in the ministry, he'd assured her, as safe as the emperor, he'd said, but their house had been flattened, all of their possessions turned to ash.

Her father stressed that he'd repeatedly begged Emi's mother to join her in Karuizawa, but she would not go. A stubborn woman from the old generation, he'd called her.

She was wrong, thought Emi, as she looked out at the town after she and Claire had arrived on the *ginza.* Her mother, she was sure, would have loved to see what was in front of her.

The street was full of people, *gaijin* and Japanese, as word about Hitler had traveled from both the Swiss and Swedish embassies. There was diplomatic staff everywhere — Russians, Swiss, Swedes, and Turks — and no Germans at all. No citizens or soldiers.

"Germany will have to surrender now," said Ayumi, when she saw Emi. She was near tears herself. "And after Germany surrenders, what choice will Japan have? We will surrender. Then the war will be over. Finally," she said, one of her daughters behind her, holding the waist of her pants. "We will have peace again."

A man from the Swiss delegation whom Evgeni was friendly with was behind them as well. He came around and smiled at them, his elation apparent. "Germany will surrender this week," he said. "I'm sure of it."

Emi looked around at the *ginza* and thought about the day she spent with Leo in the Heldenplatz in Vienna. The Austrians were crying tears of joy to see Hitler, and now the foreigners in Japan, and even some Japanese, were crying tears of joy because he was dead. Leo must know, she thought to herself. He had to.

The Swiss diplomat was right. Germany surrendered to the Allies on May 7, and in Karuizawa, all the talk turned to what Japan was going to do next. The German soldiers in town had started to disappear, though the citizens were permitted to stay. Of the soldiers, it was said by the diplomats that they were going into hiding, headed to Gora in Hakone. With them went Emi's fears of getting arrested for theft from their farm. Japan had not yet found peace, but she could put one of her fears to rest.

The hopes that Japan's surrender was imminent were shot down by firm statements issued by the government soon after Hitler's death and Germany's surrender. The prime minister had implored the people of Japan to keep fighting like kamikaze pilots. Shigenori Tōgō, the minister of foreign affairs, made it clear that Germany's defeat would make no difference in Japan's fight against America and Britain. Japan was not dropping their weapons.

"Not yet," said Ayumi to Emi and her

children, who were gathered in the store to listen to the radio announcements. "Not quite yet."

CHAPTER 36

Emi Kato
August 1945–January 1946
At precisely twelve noon on August 15, the radio crackled in the lobby of the Mampei Hotel. First, there was nothing but static, then the voice of Emperor Hirohito, which most of the Japanese people had never heard, came over the airwaves. For the first time in Japan's history, the emperor was addressing the entire nation.

"To our good and loyal subjects," he said, barely audible, even on the hotel's expensive radio. "After pondering deeply the general trends of the world and the actual conditions obtaining in Our Empire today, we have decided to effect a settlement of the present situation by resorting to an extraordinary measure. We have ordered Our Government to communicate to the Governments of the United States, Great Britain, China, and the Soviet Union that Our

Empire accepts the provisions of their Joint Declaration."

The emperor kept speaking, in his formal way, so formal that even Emi and Ayumi could barely understand a word. The little that Emi could understand was being drowned out by the bad connection, but the foreign diplomats in the room assured the crowd that what the emperor had announced was Japan's surrender.

"Finally," said Emi to Ayumi, who was holding her children tight against her legs. "It's finally over." She soon felt the embrace of Claire Ohkawa, the only person in the room who ignored every cultural norm.

"All those poor dead boys," said Claire crying. "Hiroshima, Nagasaki, Tokyo. Why didn't we surrender sooner?"

"I don't know," said Emi, hugging her back. "But it's over now."

She needed to talk to her parents, to finally see them after so long. And maybe now she could find out about Christian and put to rest the fear she'd been carrying that he was dead. Maybe she could confirm that the Hartmanns were safe in Shanghai. She could write a letter that might get delivered. Her life, the one she had put on hold, felt nearly within reach.

"Mr. Mori survived," said Ayumi, looking

at him. He was sick, but still with them. "My daughter survived. There were too many dead," she said. "But look how many are still here."

After the Moris were home safe, Emi walked to the shrine behind the hotel, the one on the hill leading to the Germans' farm, which had been raided down to the grass seeds after they left town, and said a prayer for her parents, thanking them for sending her away from Tokyo, for helping her survive the war and allowing her to discover the strange, charming enclave of Karuizawa.

Two weeks after the emperor's broadcast, their town was in the hands of the Americans. Emi stood by the side of the *ginza* with Claire as the Americans flooded the town, driving slowly through the streets, hanging out of their military jeeps. One car stopped in front of Claire and its occupants honked and howled. When Claire yelled a profanity at them, a young soldier climbed out and asked her whether she spoke English or just cursed in it.

"Of course I speak English," Claire said, as the soldiers whooped at her Aussie accent. "So does she," Claire said, nodding at Emi. "And German."

"And Japanese," said Emi. "But so does

she," she said, pointing at Claire. The boy talking to her was tall and blond, far more confident than Christian, but reminded her so much of him that she could almost smell the oranges in Crystal City. She had sent a letter to the address Christian had given her in Pforzheim, hoping that now the letter might make it overseas, and that if it did, that there would be a house left standing to receive it and people inside. She knew now that the Americans had bombed Shanghai. The Swiss delegation had again produced that information, but they'd informed her that it had been almost all Chinese who'd died. But about Christian, she struggled not to think the worst. She was sure the war would not feel over until she knew he was alive.

The baby-faced soldier who was flirting with Claire said, "I don't even want to know why you girls speak all those languages. Hell, I don't even care if you're spies at this point." He turned to the other men in the jeep and told them to make room for the two women. " 'Cause we could use your help. Come on. Jump in," he said, reaching for Emi's hand. "Help us out, will you?"

"I will not," said Emi, pulling her hands behind her back. She wasn't ready to start working for the Americans, who had come close to charring her parents while their allies had possibly killed Christian Lange. "Why should we help you?"

"Because we're going to open the German warehouse," he said. "And you speak German. I doubt there are any German soldiers left in hiding here, but you never know. Now, if you don't care what's inside, then don't come."

Claire grabbed Emi's hand and dragged her toward the car. "She's coming," she said. "Lift us into this thing."

"Fine," said Emi, allowing herself to be pulled up. "But if there is food there, I'm taking some. I'm taking a lot."

"We're all taking a lot," said the soldier, slamming the car into gear. "We're cleaning them out and handing it over to you all. This town looks hungry."

The German warehouse, in the countryside in the opposite direction of the Mampei Hotel, and which neither Emi nor Claire had known about, was stocked with canned food, every inch of every shelf covered. Emi and Claire gasped when the door was opened, and Emi thought how much easier it would have been to take a can of beans than to try to steal a pig. Along with the canned goods, there were barrels of lard, sacks of potatoes and rice, jars of pickled radishes and plums, buckets of root vegetables, and even dried meat.

"Jesus Christ," said Claire. "The town has been eating grass while the Germans had all this?"

"The German Navy captured freighters full of supplies for the Allied troops. More than once we were told. And a lot of it ended up here," said the blond soldier, putting the cans in bags.

"I take back every nice thing I ever said about them," Claire whispered to Emi. "But I guess grass tastes better than gunpowder."

The American troops started removing the food by the truckload. Claire and Emi were about to leave since they saw there was no translation needed. Theft seemed to be understood in every language.

"Wait!" one of the American soldiers called to Emi when she was a few yards away. He brought her a bag, heavy with provisions, and told her they'd be looking for her again. "A Jap . . . a Japanese girl who speaks English and German. You should work for us," he said, helping her steady the cloth bag on her thin arms.

I'll never work for you, she thought, holding the food tight to her chest and thanking him.

Emi and her parents had spoken by phone in September, with the help of the Swiss delegation, and they had decided that it would be best for Emi to stay in Karuizawa until there was a home for her to come back to. They were living in a very small government-provided apartment that survived the bombing and fire. Because there wasn't much of Tokyo left, they decided Emi would be happier with the Moris.

They promised to write, to call if they could, and Emi smiled at the prospect of letters. The small pieces of paper that had held her together for so many years — finally, they would be hers again.

She received a thick envelope from her father in November, when the leaves of Karuizawa turned to blazing colors. She supposed they had looked like that every year, but she didn't notice such things in 1944. Now she could finally look up.

When she reached the lake, she sat on a rock, surprised to see the silver tail of a fish right below the surface of the clear water. How strange, she thought, to not have to dive in to get it. Jiro was getting much stronger with the help of the Americans and their food, no longer confined to his futon, and even Ayumi's daughter had started school again, having missed an entire year. And somehow, Emi had become a person who enjoyed the countryside.

She pulled out the letter. She expected to see her father's large handwriting, but instead, the letter was in English, and it wasn't addressed to her, but to her father, Norio Kato.

Dear Mr. Kato,

I am holding my breath that this letter arrives to you safely as I have addressed it to the Japanese Ministry of Foreign Affairs rather than your home address. In March, we heard about the terrible bombing of Tokyo, one of many it seems, and have prayed daily for your and your family's safety. I am hoping that no news is good news and that you have all survived the war, as we have, thanks to your incredible kindness. For the rest of our lives, we will be so very thankful for your aid in helping us flee Vienna.

I know from Leo's attempts to communicate with Emi that the mail system hasn't been kind to them, but I'm hoping, now that the war is over, that our letters will reach each other.

Though we are ready to leave China, we will be remaining in Shanghai until we have passage on a boat to the United States. We don't plan on staying forever — Leo is adamant about eventually returning to Austria — but for now, it is the safest option, we've been told.

Of all of us, I never would have thought that Leo would be the one to almost lose his life during these difficult times, but such was the case. In 1943, he engaged in a fight with a German officer and was hospitalized for a month. He still has limited lung capacity and has lost sight entirely in his right eye. I know that compared to other families, our loss is insignificant, but it was a very trying time for us.

A woman he had become acquainted with through his work in Shanghai, a German girl named Agatha Huber, nursed Leo back to health. Much to our surprise (and I think to his, too), they became romantically involved. They were married recently and are expecting a baby in November. I hope Emi will forgive Leo for not writing to tell her himself, but I think writing that letter would have broken him. I don't doubt that he still very much loves your daughter, but he does love Agatha, too, and I believe they will be happy together.

The war turned the world upside down for Leo, but I know Emi's guiding hand, as his first love, his best friend in Vienna, will always be with him. Please give her our best and send us your news when you are able to. I have enclosed the address of an establishment called Liwei's. It is best to send letters there, as there is at least a chance over zero that we will receive them.

May God be with you,
Max Hartmann

Emi held the letter so tightly that she ripped the edge of the paper. Leo was alive. He was alive, but he had been severely injured. Emi thought of his beautiful green eyes and closed her own. She wanted to dwell on the pain he'd endured, about how he'd fought a German officer to the point of being hospitalized for a month. He, who was so skilled at letting the hate, the abuse, not affect him. But instead, all she could focus on was that Leo was marrying someone else, and having a baby with her that very month. She had lost Leo years ago, she knew that. But she never thought it would end this way, with him married, a father.

She folded the piece of paper, put it back in the envelope, and walked toward town. The letter from Leo that she'd been so desperate for, for so many years, had just put out the remaining lights of her childhood, extinguishing the Emi Kato that had existed before the war. Somehow, it was time for her to discover someone new.

By 1946, Emi had been to Tokyo and back, had seen the ash and debris that had once been her house, and had returned to Karuizawa to make herself as useful as she could be, without working for the Americans. They had approached her again, but she had agreed to volunteer in the medical clinic instead, returning to her white uniform, just as she had worn daily in Crystal City.

She still thought of Leo often. He hadn't waited for "what might have been" but had just forged on with his life instead. She didn't know if she was angry with him or angry at herself, but she knew that she needed that anger to diminish and that keeping busy helped.

When she was in America, she had gone on. She had found Christian. But now, even he, lost somewhere in the world, felt very long ago.

So instead of love, memories, or the past to keep her company, Emi threw herself into her present. Japan didn't need scared girls playing the piano or stealing food anymore; it needed to be pieced back together. So that's what Emi did, everything she'd been taught in Texas, by the underpaid doctors, coming back to her in time.

"I told you this town is better when there's no war," said Claire one evening when she was picking up Emi after work. "It's starting to feel like it used to," she said. "You should think about staying, even after your parents' house is rebuilt. You're what, twenty-four now? Maybe it's time you didn't share a roof with Kato-san. Or the Moris," she added.

"You may have a point," said Emi, linking her arm with Claire's.

When they got to the Mampei Hotel, which had slowly become a regular hotel again, instead of a makeshift group embassy, Ayumi was waiting out front. She waved excitedly to them both, a piece of paper in her hand.

"There is an American soldier looking for you," she said to Emi.

"An American soldier?" said Emi with a frown. "I've said so many times already that I have no interest working for them."

"I don't think it's one of them," said Ayumi, who was finally, like all the women, wearing something other than *monpe.* "This one, I haven't seen him here before." She put the letter she was holding in Emi's hand and said, "He gave me this to give to you. I insisted that I knew you, that I would get it to you."

Emi looked down at the letter. It had been sent by her father, but addressed to her in Crystal City.

"What was his name?" she said, her heart sprinting ahead of her tongue. "Ayumi," she said grabbing her arm. "Did he tell you?"

"Christian Lange," Ayumi said smiling, as Emi's expression changed to elation. "Does that mean something to you?"

"To say the least," said Emi, not able to hold back her tears.

"If he means that much to you," said Ayumi, "then I might as well tell you that he said he'd wait for you — for the next year if he had to. I don't know where he went exactly, but I suggested he head to Hatsue Saga's tea shop. Now that they have tea again."

Emi dried her face and ran off, stopping halfway to the *ginza* when she realized that she hadn't even read the letter. It had certainly never reached her in Crystal City.

She turned the envelope around to remove the paper and noticed that something had been written on the back of the envelope in English:

You sounded very much in love in your last letter, Emiko-chan. And I will never be the one to criticize you falling for an American. I am, after all, the one who brought you there. Despite the geography of Japan, the world is not an island.

Since you asked in your last letter, I'm still doing just fine, though the house is silent without you. It misses you very much, just like I do. I will write more soon, but I just wanted you to know that even the architecture is longing to see you.

She pulled out the actual letter, sure that she had never uttered a word about Christian to her father, and saw that it was much shorter. All it said was:

I'm still doing just fine, though the house is silent without you. It misses you very much, just like I do. I will write more soon, but I just wanted you to know that even the architecture is longing to see you.

Emi didn't understand the discrepancy in translation, but she sensed that somehow, it had gotten Christian to Karuizawa. And looking at the return address, which was her father's office, Norio Kato had now lent a hand.

She closed her eyes, clutching the letter tightly, completely overwhelmed by the fact that Christian was here. She had desperately wanted to see him alive, to see him two years older. Had his face changed? Had he been injured? How had he escaped Germany?

When Emi reached the *ginza,* she began to run in her nurse's uniform, but she didn't see him anywhere. She walked into Hatsue Saga's tea shop, hoping he would be there, but it was almost empty. She was afraid that if she kept moving, she would miss him completely, so she took a seat at the window. She ordered a cup of tea and took her hair down so it looked the way it had in Crystal City.

After her tea was drained to just the torn leaves, a food delivery truck, which had been partially blocking her view since she sat down, drove off. She put her cup on the table and stared out the window, her body and face moving toward the cold glass.

There stood Christian Lange. Still arrestingly handsome, and alive.

He was standing across the road in an

American military uniform, watching a group of older Japanese women sitting on the stairs of Evgeni's shop, talking and laughing, as if the memories of war were already far behind them. Christian took a few steps forward, as if he intended to approach them, but stopped when he was still several feet back and kept observing them instead.

His blond hair was short, and he had an Army cap and a heavy black wool overcoat on, but he still looked like Christian Lange from Crystal City, the boy from the orchard. Emi savored watching him, knowing that in a few seconds, her life would transform again, this time into something much better. She would know why he was in an American military uniform, not a German one, and how he had gotten from Crystal City, Texas, to Karuizawa, Japan.

She stood, put her hand against the glass window, leaving a smudge, and thought of what she had said to him in Crystal City. "Please come and find me." Somehow, the world had aligned itself just right — if only for a fleeting moment — and he had.

Maybe they would talk all afternoon and then part ways forever. Perhaps they would see one another each day that he was in Japan. Or maybe, years from now, they would still be seeing each other, in very different circumstances. Happier circumstances.

The future. Their future, together or apart, it existed. They'd survived when the world had tried so hard to keep them from living. Now, tomorrow, the days ahead; they were wonderful things to dream about. She ran her hands over her hair, took his letter from her pocket, and stepped out the door, a silver bell clanging auspiciously against the glass as she called his name.

ACKNOWLEDGMENTS

An enormous thank you to my editor, Sarah Cantin, whose patience and gift with the red pen shaped this book. I'm so lucky to have her and her dazzling brain on my side. Also at Atria, a huge thank you to president and publisher Judith Curr, Tory Lowy, Haley Weaver, Tom Pitoniak, Donna Cheng, and Mark LaFlaur.

Bridget Matzie, my brilliant agent, knew early on that this book idea was a perfect fit for me. Bridget, thank you for constantly being two steps ahead and always championing the right idea.

Elizabeth Ward served as my first-draft editor, and her polishing prowess was critical to getting this book from very rough to ready for print.

Many thanks to my PR gurus Gilda Squire, Simone Cooper, and Rockelle Henderson.

I am forever indebted to Kari-Lynn

Rockefeller, who read each draft and quelled my numerous panic attacks with her mastery of research.

Sarah Hager championed this story every step of the way. Sarah, you are always on the right side of history and the world is lucky to have you in it.

My parents and brother continue to support me through love, food, and sage advice, while my ever-patient husband, Craig Fischer, gives me life with his unwavering love and encouragement.

I could not have written about Karuizawa, Japan, in an authentic way without the help and generosity of our family friend Jean Mayer. Jean lived in Japan with her parents, Dr. Paul S. Mayer and Frances Mayer, and gave me access to a wonderful memoir written by her mother. The book beautifully chronicled the missionary family's years in Japan, including their life in Karuizawa, and their repatriation trip back to the United States during the war.

Tom Haar, my father's schoolmate at St. Joseph College in Yokohama, was also kind enough to share details about his fascinating life. Tom spent his war years in Karuizawa with his parents, Irene and Francis (like Tom, a celebrated photographer), and their accounts of the food shortages that crippled the town were essential to my research. Just before the Nazis arrived, his Hungarian parents fled Paris and emigrated to Japan. Their brave and unique experience was a tremendous inspiration.

My research was aided immensely by the following books: *The Train to Crystal City* by Jan Jarboe Russell, *Somehow, We'll Survive* by George Sidline, *Undue Process* by Arnold Krammer, *Shanghai Refuge* by Ernest G. Heppner, *An Uncommon Journey* by Deborah Strobin and Ilie Wacs, and *Bridge to the Sun* by Gwen Terasaki. The musical *Allegiance,* the brainchild of actor and activist George Takei, helped spark the idea for the book and I'm grateful for all George does to remind Americans of the injustices of internment.

Lastly, I'd like to thank those who are no longer with us, but whose shared memories over several decades made *The Diplomat's Daughter* come alive: Yeiichi "Kelly" Kuwayama, who served as a highly decorated medic in the 442nd Infantry Regiment and whom Senator Daniel Inouye credited for saving his life, and Mr. Kuwayama's ever-elegant wife, Fumiko, who was a victim of internment. Also, Walter Minao Nishimura, grandfather to my dear friend Keisha Nishimura and father to Francis Nishimura, who was interned at Minidoka Relocation Center in Jerome, Idaho, and also served honorably in the 442nd. Let us hope that those difficult times in our history are never repeated.

ABOUT THE AUTHOR

Karin Tanabe is the author of *The Gilded Years*, *The Price of Inheritance*, and *The List*. A former Politico reporter, her writing has also appeared in the *Miami Herald*, *Chicago Tribune*, *Newsday*, and *The Washington Post*. She has made frequent appearances as a celebrity and politics expert on *Entertainment Tonight*, CNN, and **The CBS Early Show**. A graduate of Vassar College, Karin lives in Washington, DC. To learn more visit KarinTanabe.com.